INSURGENCY

Tales of the Empire, book 4

by S.J.A. Turney

1st Edition

For Gemma and Graeme. May 2016 live on for you both in happy memories. Congratulations.

I would like to thank everyone who made this book possible, and those who helped to bring this second edition into the world. Jenny and Tracey for their help in initial editing, my agent Sallyanne for her vision and encouragement, Mike and Simon and all the guys at Canelo for being the most proactive and insightful publishers imaginable.

Published in this format 2016 by Victrix Books

First Edition

Also by S. J. A. Turney:

Continuing the Tales of the Empire
Interregnum (2009)
Ironroot (2010)
Dark Empress (2011)

The Marius' Mules Series
Marius' Mules I: The Invasion of Gaul (2009)
Marius' Mules II: The Belgae (2010)
Marius' Mules III: Gallia Invicta (2011)
Marius' Mules IV: Conspiracy of Eagles (2012)
Marius' Mules V: Hades Gate (2013)
Marius' Mules VI: Caesar's Vow (2014)
Marius' Mules VII: The Great Revolt (2014)
Marius' Mules VIII: Sons of Taranis (2015)
Marius' Mules IX: Pax Gallica (2016)

The Ottoman Cycle
The Thief's Tale (2013)
The Priest's Tale (2013)
The Assassin's Tale (2014)
The Pasha's Tale (2015)

The Praetorian Series
Praetorian – The Great Game (2015)
Praetorian – The Price of Treason (2015)

The Legion Series (Childrens' books)
Crocodile Legion (2016)

Short story compilations & contributions:
Tales of Ancient Rome vol. 1 - S.J.A. Turney (2011)
Tortured Hearts Vol 2 - Various (2012)
Tortured Hearts Vol 3 - Various (2012)
Temporal Tales - Various (2013)
Historical Tales - Various (2013)
A Year of Ravens (2015)
A Song of War (2016)

For more information visit http://www.sjaturney.co.uk/
or http://www.facebook.com/SJATurney
or follow Simon on Twitter @SJATurney

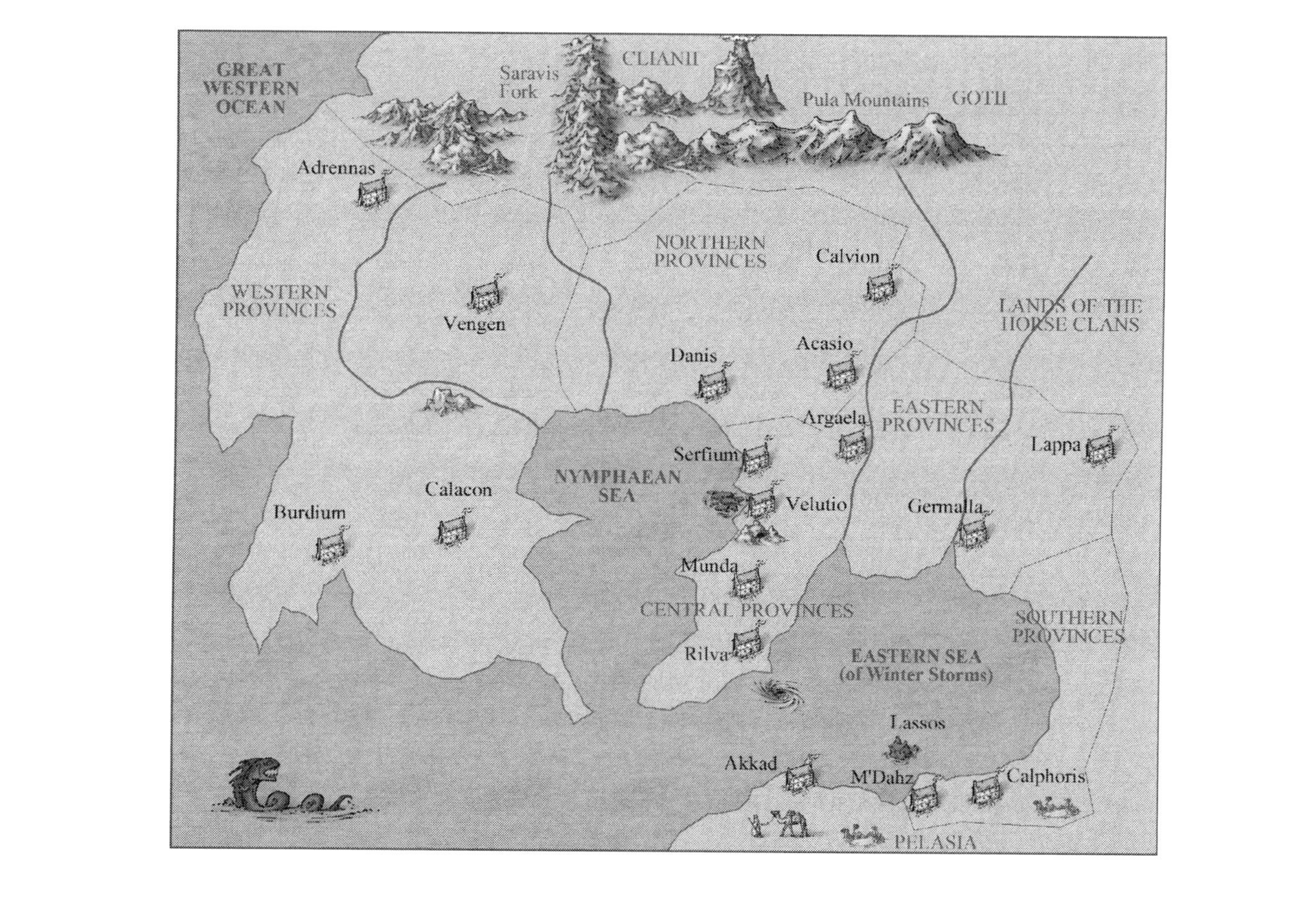

GREAT WESTERN OCEAN
Saravis Fork
CLIANII
Pula Mountains
GOTII
Adrennas
NORTHERN PROVINCES
Calvion
WESTERN PROVINCES
Vengen
LANDS OF THE HORSE CLANS
Danis
Acasio
EASTERN PROVINCES
Argaela
Lappa
Serfium
NYMPHAEAN SEA
Velutio
Calacon
Burdium
Germalla
Munda
CENTRAL PROVINCES
SOUTHERN PROVINCES
Rilva
EASTERN SEA (of Winter Storms)
Lassos
Akkad
M'Dahz
Calphoris
PELASIA

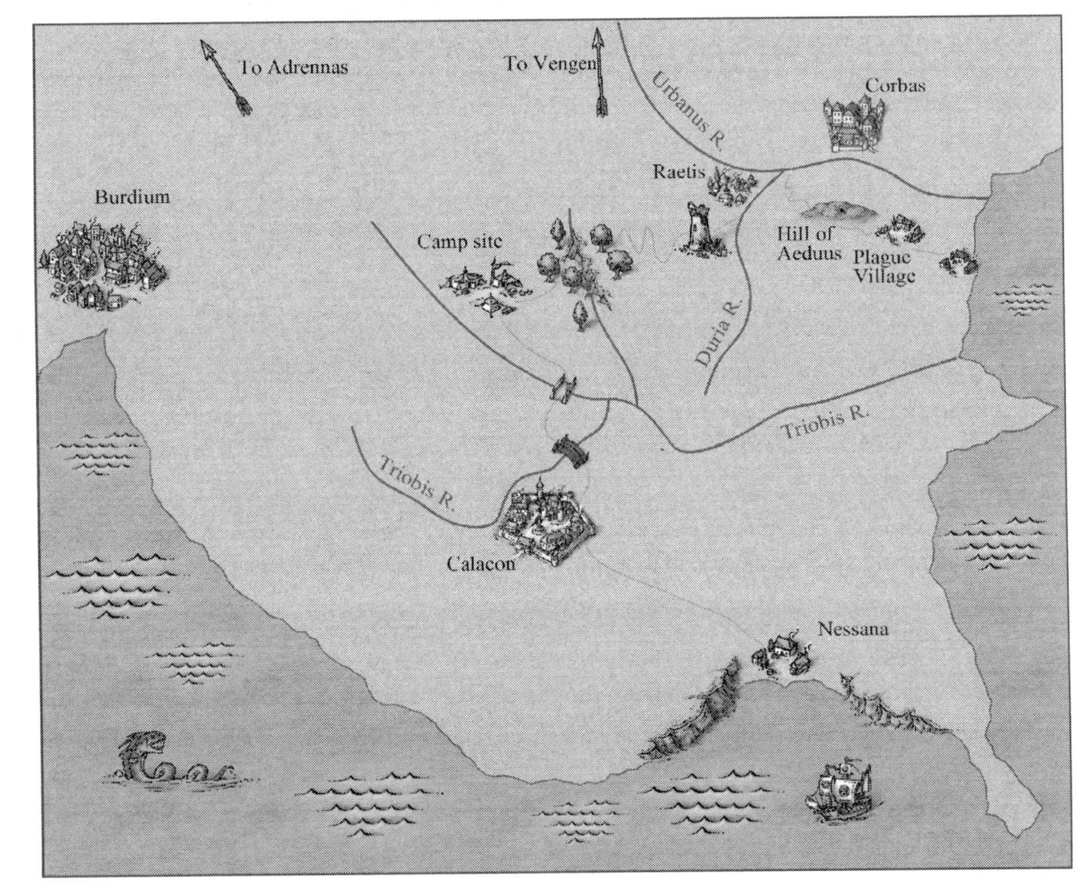
To Adrennas
To Vengen
Urbanus R.
Corbas
Raetis
Burdium
Camp site
Hill of
Aeduus
Plague
Village
Duria R.
Triobis R.
Triobis R.
Calacon
Nessana

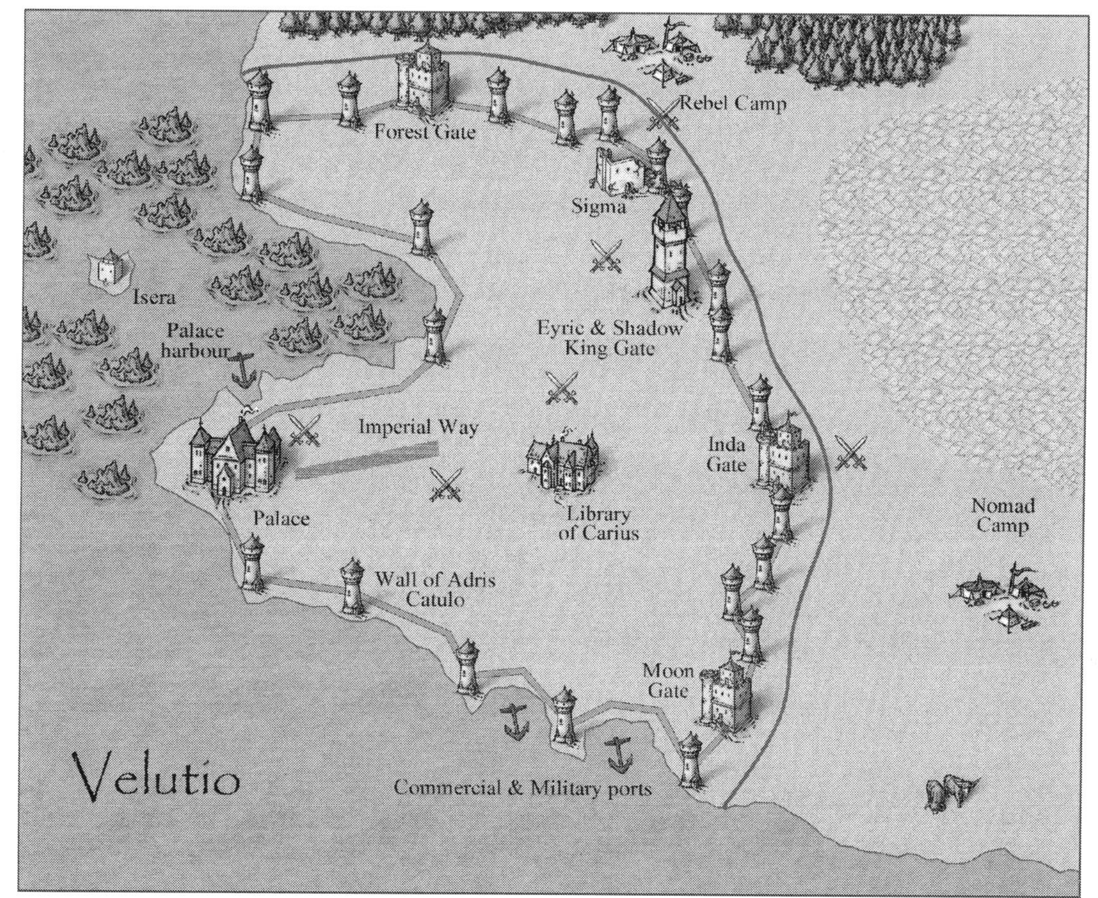
Forest Gate
Rebel Camp
Sigma
Isera
Palace
harbour
Eyric & Shadow
King Gate
Imperial Way
Inda
Gate
Palace
Library
of Carius
Nomad
Camp
Wall of Adris
Catulo
Moon
Gate
Velutio
Commercial & Military ports

PROLOGUE

There is a strange saying among the northern folk:
'A tripod may stand solid, but a ladder can be climbed.'

The Emperor Kiva moved about his court like a gilded moth, flittering from flame to flame, moving on briskly before his wings were singed. A tall, willowy figure with slim build and slender fingers, a wise contemplative face and his father's eyes, Kiva played the role of ruler of the civilized world with aplomb. He was a master of tact and tactics, playing down the argumentative, suppressing the sycophantic, embracing the distant and fending off the o'er-close. Even now, as he was cornered by some brash western lord with rosy cheeks and an even rosier nose, Kiva laughed off some accidental slight, deftly swiping a crystal goblet of wine from a passing tray, slipping it smoothly into the drunken lord's hand and removing the empty with barely a glance. As the lord realized he had a full glass once more, he reached down and took a deep swig. When he looked up, the emperor was gone, swirling in the dance of sociability, quick-stepping with an ambassador from Pelasia.

Quintillian watched from the sidelines.

Not for him the pageantry of the imperial celebrations. He danced with the best of men, but only when his hand held a blade and the end of the dance meant the end of a life. Instead, the younger brother of the emperor, senior marshal of the armies and lord of Vengen, stood on a narrow, balustraded balcony overlooking the grand events of the evening, half hidden in the shadows above the hall. Here, in the old days, musicians would sit by lamplight playing their hearts out. In these times it was more common for such entertainment to be placed among the guests for better captivation of their melody.

The balcony was dark and Quintillian smiled as he took a sip of his wine and watched his brother at work. They had always been close, he and Kiva, closer than most brothers. But their father had brought them up like that – to believe that family was all and that nothing in the world had the right, nor the power, to stand between two brothers who loved each other. Their father, of course, had suffered in his life, losing the friend who had been as close as a brother – Quintillian's namesake, in fact – during the great interregnum. And he had lost a father – a *great* father – before he had even found out who he was. And so the Emperor Darius had instilled in his sons the need for that bond and for a closeness with no secrets.

No secrets…

Some secrets were kept out of love, though. Hadn't their father ever considered that?

It had been a hard time, five years ago, when their father had died. Darius had been an active emperor and a good one, long-reigning. After the 20 years of civil war and anarchy, he had put the empire back together, healed the wounds of the land and its people, and initiated a golden age that had lasted longer than anyone could have hoped. When he had finally passed on, in his chambers on the island of Isera, it had been after a full life and with a reign fulfilled. And he had followed all his friends to the grave, knowing that they were all waiting for him in the afterlife, for he was not a man to believe in the divinity of rulers, just like his sons.

Kiva had taken the purple cloak and the obsidian sceptre, the orb of the heavens in his other hand, the very next day. There had, of course, been no dissent over the natural succession of the eldest son, though there *had* been a few voices that had expressed the quiet, careful opinion that the younger brother might have been stronger in the role. Not that they would have pushed for a change, and most certainly Quintillian would have refused. Not that he couldn't have done the job, not that he would be unwilling to, but his brother was natural heir and that was all there was to it.

And Kiva was good at it. There was no denying that.

Five years to the day since the accession and the blessings, that purple cloak almost gleaming in the sun, so well brushed was the velvet. Five years of growth for the empire and of peace within its borders. Five years of strong economies and excellent external relations. It had seemed wholly appropriate to celebrate such a milestone in this manner, with everyone of any rank both within and without the empire all gathered at the palace in Velutio. And among the tanned visages of the imperial lords, governors, officers and administrators, there were different faces – *interesting* faces. The King of the Gotii beyond the Pula mountains with his retinue, for instance. It was the first time those violent raiders had visited the capital – the first time in the empire's history when relations between the two peoples had been good enough. The Gota king sat with his three wives and his close companions not far from the emperor's seat. He was a tall and broad man with a flat face, strong jaw, flaxen hair and ice blue eyes. His wives were… well, Quintillian had oft heard it said that the Gota prized strength and ability to bear children above simple looks. It had taken Quintillian some time to distinguish the wives from the bodyguards, of whom there were five, including relations of the king himself. They had been denied the right to carry weapons this close to the emperor, but there was no doubt in Quintillian's mind that each of them could kill in the blink of an eye with just their bare hands. And there was the king's seer: an old man with hair down to his backside, who wore dirty rags and the pelts of a number of unfortunate small animals, their bones clattering in his hair as he moved. He gave Quintillian the shivers, not least since he seemed to be the only person aware that the younger brother was here, having looked up into the shadows directly at him.

There were other northern chieftains who were in the process of buying into the imperial model in Kiva's new world, too, though they all looked a little like the Gota king would have, had he tried to assimilate into imperial culture.

There were two kings from the dark-skinned lands south of Pelasia. *They* were interesting, but required a translator to pass even the slightest time of day, and Quintillian's brief introduction to them at the start of the celebration had been hard work. Their world was so alien, and most of Quintillian's hungry questions had been lost on them with no mutual frame of reference. Invitations had even been sent to the lords of that peculiar eastern world beyond the steppes from whence silk came, though they had not come. Very likely the messengers never reached those lands. Few did, for the route to the silk lands crossed the most dangerous territories in the world. That had been a shame, though. Quintillian liked the feel of silk and it was said that the sharper a blade was, the more likely the miraculous material was to turn it aside. The idea of a light fabric that could stop a blade was simply too fascinating to him. One day, if they did not come here, he would have to go to them.

And, of course, there were the Pelasians. Three of their highest nobles were present, including a prince of the realm. Young Ashar Parishid, though – son of Ashar the great, and God-King of Pelasia – sadly could not be here. A riding accident had left him with a badly broken leg a week earlier, and he had been advised by the best physicians in the world that he would recover fully, but there was simply no way he could leave his chambers for several weeks. It must have been a terrible blow for Ashar, for while he and the emperor – and Quintillian too, for that matter – were as close friends as it was possible for neighbouring rulers to be, Ashar would be particularly missing the opportunity to visit his beloved sister.

Jala.

The empress.

Jala, unlike her husband, sat upon her comfortable divan at the heart of proceedings, smiling and doling out compliments. Each of her honeyed words was as sought after as a lordship or a chest of gold, and each was prized and tightly-held once received. Her soft skin, the light brown of the deep desert, was more on show than was traditional among imperial ladies. But then Jala was no ordinary imperial lady. She was a Princess of Pelasia, sister to the god-king, and now, for five years, wife of the Emperor Kiva. And she was exquisite.

Yes, some secrets had to be kept for the good of all concerned.

For two years now, Kiva had been pushing him to marry – to take a wife from among the many beauties of the imperial court. His brother simply could not understand why Quintillian remained alone. But how could he marry a woman knowing that his heart was already in the care of another. It beat silently, deep in his chest, only for Jala. And it would beat silently for her until the end of his days, for even the hint of such a thing carried the scent of tragedy, and neither Kiva nor Jala deserved such a thing. So Quintillian would remain alone. What need had he of a wife, anyway? True soldiers should not take wives, for a warrior took a promising girl and turned her into a hollow widow. It was the way of things. And while there was no true need for an officer of such high command to involve himself directly in combat, there was something in the song of steel and the dance of blades that called to Quintillian. He could no more refuse to fight than he could refuse to breathe… than he could open his heart…

Something was happening now, down in the hall. Quintillian squinted into the thick, cloying atmosphere of oil lamps, braziers and incense.

An argument had broken out between two guests. Ordinarily such things would be unthinkable in the imperial presence, but the variety of uncivilized figures present had made such things almost an inevitability. That was why his favourite marshal, Titus, son of Tythias, had positioned burly, competent imperial guards in strategic positions around the hall, subtly armed.

Quintillian contemplated descending from the balcony to deal with the problem, but Titus's men were already moving to contain the trouble, so the younger brother relaxed a little and leaned on the balustrade, watching.

'Trouble,' muttered a familiar voice behind him. Quintillian didn't rise or turn, simply smiling as he continued to lean on the balcony.

'Titus. How did you know where I was?'

'I am your brother's best officer and commander of his guard. I know where *everyone* is. It's part of my job.' Titus Tythianus slipped in next to Quintillian, leaning his scarred forearms on the stone rail, waggling his nine remaining fingers.

'Yes, it seems there's a spot of trouble,' Quintillian noted. 'Shall we intervene?'

Titus snorted. 'Not unless they threaten *imperial* guests. In some of these cultures they murder each other for entertainment. If it gets out of hand my men will deal with it. It's unseemly anyway for a member of the imperial family to involve himself in a brawl.'

Quintillian chuckled and watched as the two arguing groups moved closer.

'I recognize the Gota one, but I can't place the white-haired one,' Quintillian said conversationally.

Below, the crowd was beginning to pull apart, leaving a circle at the centre where one of the Gotii – a strapping young man… not a woman? No, not one of the wives. A big strong warrior with a face like an abused turnip was stamping his feet like a petulant child, roaring imprecations in a tongue that sounded like someone gargling with broken glass. The crowd was fascinated, though not enough to involve themselves any closer than at the level of interested spectator.

At the far side of the expanding circle, one of the northern lords was sneering and waving a deprecating finger at the Gota warrior. But it was not that lord who was stepping forward. It was a strange pale figure. Both northerners – lord and servant – looked in build and physical make-up to have far more in common with the king of the Gotii than their imperial hosts, yet they wore breeches and tunic in the imperial style, if of an outdated northern cut and in semi-barbaric colours.

Borderlanders.

It was a recent process, begun by the Emperor Darius, but continued by Kiva in the same vein. You took the barbarian tribes who lived around the borders and you brought them to the empire. You introduced them to the benefits of imperial culture, engineering and science, and you dazzled them with what they could have. Then you offered to send them men to help build aqueducts and temples, bridges and mills. You often built their chiefs palaces to house their egos. And all you asked in return was that they pay lip service to the emperor and protect the borders from the less civilized barbarians beyond. As a system it made sense. And it had proven to work, too, for already, a decade on, some of those barbarian nobles had brought their lands into the empire entire, becoming lords in their own right and expanding the borders through gentle, subtle assimilation, as the same process then began on the tribes beyond.

But they were decades away from being true imperial subjects, even if that were *ever* to happen.

Certainly, looking at the behaviour unfolding in the hall below, this particular northern border lord seemed to be far from cultured.

'The noble is Aldegund, Lord of Adrennas,' Titus said quietly. 'He's one of the ones your father first settled. He's been a lord now for over five years, and two more semi-barbarian border tribes owe him fealty already. He's all right, I suppose. A bit brash and still far from courtier material, but he's loyal and he knows he's onto a good thing. His ghost I don't know, but he's a reedy fellow. Don't much fancy his chances against the Gota.'

'Will you have your men stop it?'

Titus shook his head. 'Aldegund should know better, and his man is about to learn a horrible lesson. But once he's seen this, he won't do the same again. The Gotii take insults very personally, and they cleanse their spirit of insult with the blood of the offender. That pale, ghostly fellow is about to die. Unless he's very lucky. Maybe the Gota warrior's feeling generous and he'll just rip off an arm. They are celebrating and having a drink after all.'

The Gota warrior had removed his leather vest and was stretching his arms, moving like a dancer. Quintillian appreciated his form. He was a warrior bred to the art. The white-haired, pale northerner opposite him just sneered and took another drink from his cup.

'He really doesn't know what he's in for,' Titus snorted.

Quintillian frowned. 'A gold corona on the pale one.'

Titus' eyebrow ratcheted upward. 'Are you mad?'

'He's not afraid.'

'Maybe that's because he's stupid? Aldegund certainly seems to be. And that half-naked warrior is the third bastard son of the Gota king. He'll have been trained with the best of the Gotii.'

'There's something about the white one. I think you're underestimating him. Is it a wager?'

'Damn right it's a wager,' Titus retorted. 'And make it five.'

'Five it is.'

Down below, the crowd was now in a wide circle around the two combatants, Titus's guardsmen in plain evidence, making sure the duel was contained. The Gota was snarling again in his horrible language. The icy white opponent was examining his nails.

'Make it ten,' Quintillian said quietly.

'Done.'

At a command from the king, the two men moved towards one another. On the balcony, Quintillian glanced to the side. Titus looked hungry, like a spectator at the pit fights, and the sight of him leering down at the two men made the prince smile.

The Gota warrior struck the first blow, which had seemed inevitable. Stepping the last pace into the fight, the hairy north-easterner with the naked torso and the leather kirtle delivered a powerful punch to the ghost's upper left arm at a point that would surely deaden the muscle for some time. Barely had the white-haired northerner had a breath to recover before the second blow took him in the gut, followed by a head-butt that sent him staggering back a pace. The Gota threw his arms out and roared as his father and the other Gotii cheered him on. The crowd thrummed with inappropriate interest.

'Easiest money I'll ever make,' snorted Titus.

'I'm still not so sure.'

The white man was stepping slowly back, regaining his senses as he went, while the Gota played to the crowd, roaring and beating his chest.

'He's not really got going yet,' Titus hissed. 'I've fought Gotii. This is just warming up. I kid you not – he'll rip off the man's arm. I've seen it done and by smaller Gotii than him!'

'He's predictable. The ghost isn't.'

'*I* predict he's going to die,' said Titus. 'He never even raised a fist to block that flurry!'

'Precisely. He never even tried. He was seeing what the man could do. Testing him.'

'If he's very lucky he'll test him to death.'

The pale figure had stopped now and was pacing forward again. He still didn't appear prepared for the fight. He was sauntering as though he wandered quiet gardens. The Gota warrior snarled and came on once more, smacking his fists against his hips and then bringing up his hands into a fighting stance. As they closed to three or four paces the Gota leapt, swinging his punch, aiming for the pale man's other arm to deaden a second muscle and leave him largely helpless.

It all happened in such a blur that the pair on the balcony almost missed it. A moment later, the ghost was standing behind his opponent and the Gota was dead.

Titus blinked.

As the burly warrior had swung and stepped into the strike, the white-haired man had simply bent like a stalk of grass in the wind, slipped beneath the lunging arm, and delivered his own blows – three in such quick succession that they were almost invisible to the naked eye. But Quintillian had seen the angle of the moves and could see the results clearly enough to identify the strikes. The numb arm he'd been unable to raise but he had instead used it to grab hold of the pronounced hamstring behind his opponent's knee, wrenching it agonizingly. And even in the blink of an eye that his opponent had begun to collapse, white-hair's other hand had jabbed twice. The first blow had struck at the point where shoulder meets neck, paralysing the muscle there and thus – along with the hamstring – rendering the Gota's entire left side useless. But as quick as the thumb had left the flesh, it struck again, a jagged thumbnail tearing a small nick in the neck. It was a minute hole. But it was well placed. The vein beneath was an important one, and the dark blood was jetting from it with impressive strength.

The white man straightened, examined his nails again, and now chewed off the jagged point he'd deliberately left as he strolled around the stricken man and back to his lord.

'Shit on a fat stick!' breathed Titus, slapping the balustrade. 'How the hell did he do that?'

'Planning,' Quintillian smiled. 'He was willing to take a couple of blows to size up his chances.'

'I'm glad he's on our side. At least I won't worry so much about the northern borders any more!'

Quintillian chuckled as Titus slipped the coins grudgingly into his palm. Down below, Lord Aldegund was congratulating his man in a quiet, steady tone – the white man's name, it transpired, was Halfdan. No one seemed to be paying any attention to the dying Gota at the centre of the circle, who had collapsed to the floor, entirely useless and paralysed on one side, desperately trying to hold his vein shut with his other arm as he slipped and slid in the growing pool of his own blood. But the pressure was too much and he was already becoming weak. The warrior looked up imploringly at his father, the Gota king, but all he found there was contempt as the king turned his face from the bastard son who had so clearly disappointed him.

The Gota champion died unsung and alone on the floor, and such was the speed and efficiency of the palace staff and the guard that within a matter of minutes all that remained to mark the passing of these events was a clean, damp section of marble.

Quintillian gave an odd half smile as Titus disappeared back to the stairs, muttering to himself. The younger brother could see the emperor moving among them now, absolving Aldegund and his man of any blame in what had happened and giving reassurance, then passing on to the Gota king – not commiserating, since clearly the king cared little – but *empathizing* and discussing the qualities of warriors. Kiva may not have the makings of a fighter himself, but he knew what made one, and he was a consummate politician.

Perhaps Titus was right and men like this Halfdan were the future of border defences. It certainly freed up the military from dull garrison life on the edge of empire and made them useful for such things as construction of roads and aqueducts, keeping banditry down and clearing the seas of pirates. The north, then, was protected, and with Pelasia tied to them by marriage, the south was settled. To the west: the open ocean. Only the lands to the east were still troublesome, but they would ever be so.

For a moment, Quintillian wondered whether the nomad horse clans of the steppe would be amenable to a similar arrangement as the barbarians in the north. No… they had no concept of home or ownership. They were nomadic. How could a people who never stopped moving guard a border? Besides, trying to get the thousand disparate horse clans to agree on anything together would be like trying to nail fog to a tree. The east would always be a fluid border with the risk of banditry and raids, and the imperial military would need to keep men around that edge of the world for safety.

Lost in thought about the strange eastern land of silk-makers, the ephemeral nature of the horse clans and the solidity of imperial frontiers, Quintillian had no idea he had company until there was a faint rustle behind him. He turned, startled.

Jala stood silhouetted in the faint light of the stairwell, the back-glow making her robe surprisingly gauzy and throwing her shape into sharp relief most inappropriately. Quintillian swallowed down his panic and his desire somewhat noisily and threw a fraternal smile across his face.

'Dearest sister.'

'Quintillian, why will you not join the festivities? Must you lurk here in the shadows like some monster in a poor play?'

She reached out and grasped his upper arms in her warm, sensuous fingers, and Quintillian gave an involuntary shudder.

'I... I don't like parties. I don't socialize well.'

'Nonsense.' Jala smiled. 'I have seen you do just that many times.'

'I'm not in the mood, Jala.'

Her lip stuck out slightly in a barely discernible pout, and Quintillian almost laughed despite himself.

'Come on, dear Quintillian.'

'I really cannot. I should be doing many other things. And you should be with your husband down there.'

Without warning, Jala leaned close and planted a kiss upon his lips before leaning back with a strange smile. 'Your brother is too busy with affairs of state to keep me company, and I tire of all these rough northerners. I need company, Quintillian. *Good* company.'

Quintillian stared in abject panic.

'You look like a hare caught in the hunter's gaze.' She chuckled. 'Will you come join me, then?'

Quintillian's voice seemed to have vanished. It was there somewhere, though, deep inside, and it took a great deal of coaxing to draw it up into his throat where it still wavered and croaked.

'I'll be down shortly.'

'Don't keep me waiting.' Jala smiled, and swayed off back into the stairwell.

Quintillian stared at her retreating form and continued to gaze at the empty archway long after she had gone. His mind was churning like a winter sea, his heart hammering out like a cavalry horse at the charge. Had that been innocent? Was he reading something into what just happened that wasn't truly there?

But Quintillian prided himself on his ability to read people. Had not his instincts just won him ten gold corona? And he had seen Jala's eyes as she'd lunged forth and kissed him. It had been as deliberate a blow as any he'd ever struck with a sword. It had been no kiss of brother and sister, for all its seeming innocent from the outside. He had seen *through* her eyes. He had seen into her soul. And there it had been: the reflection of himself. The longing. The desire. Suppressed beneath a veneer of civilization and correctness. She had wanted him as he wanted her!

The realization almost floored him.

He turned back to the room, suddenly aware he was trembling and sweating coldly. Down below, he saw Jala emerge once more into the hall, barely noticed amid the rich and the powerful. Kiva spotted her through the crowd and gave her a warm smile, which she returned easily, but he was trapped in conversation by a pair of stocky, swarthy lords and as soon as smiles had been exchanged he was back again, drawn into their talk. Jala took her seat at the room's centre once more, where she became an island amid a sea of busy socializing.

Quintillian stared at her.

What should he do? What *could* he do?

A line had been crossed, a barrier broken. And no hand in the world could repair that barrier. No digit could redraw the line. Why were human hearts such fragile things? As fragile as an empire, perhaps? An empire could not ruin a heart, but for certain a heart could shatter an empire if misused.

The panic was gone, but it had left a desolate, hollow uncertainty in its place.

He had to do something, but what?

He made the mistake – *or was it a mistake?* – of looking down at Jala just as she looked up at him from her divan, and his gaze swept in through her eyes and deep into her heart once more, leaving him in absolutely no doubt now that Jala shared his feelings. Oh, he did not doubt that she loved Kiva. And so did he. And therein lay the worst of the problem, for he could no more hurt his brother than he could strike off his own head.

Fragile. Hearts and empires.

Whatever he did, it would have to take him away from Jala, he realized, for if they remained in the same place, no matter how hard they might fight it, trouble would be inevitable. One man could live with impossible, unrequited love, no matter how painful. But to have that love shared could bring down the whole empire.

No, he had to find a way out somehow.

And soon.

PART ONE

THE EAST

'No matter how far a man runs from his troubles, they are never more than a few steps behind him.'

Pelasian proverb

CHAPTER I

Of Lies and Most Necessary Escapes

'What's your name again?'

'Quintus,' Quintillian lied quickly. Using the mad old emperor's name no longer bore the stigma it had two generations ago. The burnings and the insanity that had triggered the civil war were history now, and distant history to most.

The man in the dusty leathers, weighted down with business-like weapons and travelling kit, eyed him suspiciously. Under other circumstances Quintillian would have baulked and sweated nervously. He was not a liar by nature, despite the one great untruth with which he had lived since Jala came to Velutio, though it seemed now that every passing week brought a new barrage of fabrications and deceptions for him to uphold. This latest – a shift in name for the sake of anonymity – was not the tallest lie he'd had to tell, just the latest.

The rough soldier looked him up and down as though appraising his abilities from his shell alone.

'Can you swing that thing?' he asked, gesturing to the blade belted at Quintillian's side.

'As well as most, better than some.'

The man grunted, apparently still unsure for some reason. Quintillian was itching to point out that men like this fellow were hardly in a position to be too choosy about who they took on. Or perhaps he was wrong?

'Go in. The master will be here in a few minutes.'

Quintillian nodded as the soldier turned his attention to something else, instantly dismissing all thought of the newcomer, and the emperor's brother strode into the doorway. He paused at the threshold and turned to look up. The walls of Velutio rose impregnable and imposing behind him, banners fluttering atop in the spring breeze. The day was already promising unseasonal warmth and the soldiers atop the battlements would be sweating in their mail, praying to gods of comfort that soon their shift would be over and they could visit the baths.

The walls of Velutio… The tower of angels, the Moon Gate, the wall of Adris Catulo. He knew every stone, had walked every pace of them in his life in the city. And when he'd been away on campaign, those great bastions had welcomed him home like old friends.

His city.

His home.

And behind them, far across the busy throng and the noise and the life: the palace.

Kiva would be at his morning ablutions now, preparing for the day. Jala would be lounging in their bed…

He turned his glistening eyes away from the walls. This was no time for weakness. He had made the decision and it had been a necessary one. Two months had passed since that awful celebration where the depth of his peril had been laid open before him. He had tried again and again to come up with a solution that involved anything but this, but the Fates kept dashing all other hopes and returning him to the inevitable.

Two more weeks in the palace had strengthened his belief that the situation had become untenable. As though that kiss on the balcony had been a fracture in the wall of a dam, the pressure had begun to mount, and other cracks had begun to appear in relationships at court. Sooner or later, they both knew, a tryst would occur. It was inevitable. Alone, Quintillian had had the strength to deny it and hold it back, but with Jala in the same position, it was inescapable.

Quintillian had wracked his brain for a happier solution.

He had asked for a military posting. When his brother had laughed and asked if he really smelled *that* bad, Quintillian had tried to make light of it, simply citing the fact that he was getting bored with the lack of action, and practice was important to any warrior. Kiva had chuckled and told him to hire a sparring partner. He was staying in Velutio. He was too important to lose to some pointless provincial posting.

Gradually, Quintillian had increased his pleas, possibly to the point of beginning to sound desperate, for Kiva had started to show concern over his brother's health and state of mind.

'Could I take an ambassadorial position in Pelasia?'

'Don't be ridiculous. We have politicians to do that, not soldiers and princes.'

'But princes do nothing useful and you won't *let* me be a soldier!'

'You are a marshal of the army. Can I help it if there's peace and you're not needed.'

'Vengen needs to be brought under control. I hear things are becoming slovenly in the provinces.'

'I hear no such thing. And there is a marshal already in Vengen. You're not needed there.'

'There have been incursions in the northern mountains. Let me gather a force…'

'There are *always* incursions there. And now we have our borderland lords to do such jobs for us. Why send imperial soldiers when we pay the old tribes up there to keep us safe?'

And so it had gone on. An almost constant begging to be sent away, and each time a rebuffal. It was obvious to Quintillian why, of course. Apart from brief campaigns and missions the brothers had never been apart, and even Quintillian, strong and independent as he was, felt a nagging emptiness in his being when he was away from his brother. Kiva was worse. He *hated* being apart, and Quintillian knew it. But there was no choice, now.

A week ago the peril in which they floundered had become a little more panic-inducing. Jala had met Quintillian on a narrow staircase in the north tower of the palace and there had been the usual chuckling and joking as they each dodged this way and that to try and let the other pass. And then somehow, with no apparent intention on either side, they had kissed. The gaiety and humour of the situation had evaporated in a heartbeat, leaving a cold realization and a fresh level of hell for them to inhabit.

Even Jala had been shocked, and had scurried away with Kiva's name on breathless lips.

That was when Quintillian had decided that it was no longer viable to plead endlessly with his brother for a new posting. Even if the emperor ever reached the point where he would grant a leave of absence, with the worrying progression of matters in the palace it would be too late by then. Either Quintillian would have surrendered to his heart, or Jala would, and everything would come crashing down like a badly-built siege tower.

And so he had taken the last option: flight.

Last evening, Quintillian had made sure his horse was in the farthest stable, that his saddle, bridle and saddlebags were all easily accessible, and that the stable hands responsible would be off-shift before morning. He had packed everything he considered truly important, and was rather disappointed to realize in what a small pack he could fit his entire world. He had gathered up his sword – which had been his grandfather's and was a blade made for a soldier, not a courtier – and donned his riding leathers rather than the usual fine clothes of palace wear.

This morning, before the sun rose, he had gathered everything, saddled Phyteia and ridden with no ceremony out of the Forest Gate at the northern edge of the city. The guards would never stop a member of the imperial family, of course, but it was not just a matter of stopping him. He had to buy enough time to disappear. Only when he was safely away from Jala and Kiva would he be able to let up. But he habitually rose for early rides on days when his conscience was bothering him, so the guards would have thought nothing of his exit from the city.

He'd had to go.

There was no other way. Jala would hurt, and Kiva would be broken by it, he knew. And once the initial thrill of daring was over, he would begin to feel the familiar tearing void caused by his brother's absence. For Kiva, with the separation so unexpected and unexplained, it would be far worse. But what was the alternative? Ruin not only his brother's marriage, but the stability of the empire, their collective reputations, and all hope of a lasting peace with Pelasia? That was unthinkable.

They would all heal in time, and while Jala might yearn for Quintillian, he knew that she did really also love Kiva. As long as both brothers were there, she would have an impossible choice and in the end the strain would tear them all apart. Separate they would feel wounded, but they could heal.

With a deep indrawn breath, Quintillian turned and made his way through the doorway.

After leaving the city, he had circled around the outskirts to the mercantile camps, a semi-permanent canvas city below the eastern walls. He had found this place easily, given that he had subtly enquired about it over the past week, and his horse was now corralled with the others, happily munching soft, verdant grass while she waited. And he was here.

The enclosure was ringed with canvas walls but open to the warm, buzzing spring air. Opposite the wooden-framed door through which he'd entered was a separate opening that led to a huge, dim tent interior. Two more of the dusty, clearly very competent, guards stood to the sides barring admittance to the common folk.

Quintillian looked around the open ring. He was not the only applicant. Six others stood in the circle waiting patiently, and Quintillian took a moment to size them up. Two of the men were clearly twins, so alike were they. Each was swarthy with black, floppy hair held back by a narrow, soft leather band. Each wore a sword with a slight curve to it, mimicking an old Pelasian design. They looked enthusiastic, excited even. He dismissed them in his mind. Interesting they might be, but they were inexperienced and probably rather rash. Their excitement and apparent bravado was covering a lack of practice and capability. Unless the master of this camp was foolish – and foolish people didn't last long in this trade – those two would be staying right here.

A woman? Now *that* was a surprise. It was not unknown for women to take on the role of warriors in the eastern provinces, and in the ancient days it was said there were whole tribes of them. But still, a woman with a sword was a rarity, even in the fighting pits. This woman might well have come from those very contests, looking at the ugly scar that began below her left ear and carried on down over her collar bone and beneath the neckline of her tunic. Her blade was a cheap one, though functional and obviously well used. She was a possibility. If Quintillian had been master here, he'd have considered her, at least. She was broke, obviously. Her clothes and blade were clearly the last things she owned, and she had that look of someone who has been going hungry recently, though her body-muscle disguised any approach of malnutrition. Was she still strong enough to fight properly, or was she already weakened? It was hard to tell without putting her through her paces. She would certainly be a gamble, even if she performed for them. But a gamble that might pay dividends.

The boy he easily brushed aside. He was disconsolate. A tearful runaway. Ha! *There* was irony. A beaten servant or abused or homeless child fled here for a new start only to find himself on a level field with a prince of the realm. Only he couldn't *know* that, of course. And it wasn't really a level field, as the lad would soon find out when he drew that toothpick. No, the boy was a no-go.

The northerner was another gamble. He was clearly at home with his blade, and the way he stood suggested he was equally comfortable in the saddle. But there was something about his eyes that spoke of unpredictability. Possibly even defiance. Could he be trusted to do as he was told? Because obedience would be as important as ability here. Perhaps…

The last man, though, he could see would most definitely be joining them. He stood with a hunter's poise, a bow over his shoulder and quiver at his side. But that was not what made him stand out for Quintillian. Nor even was it the soldier's sword at his side that so clearly marked him as a military veteran. What *marked* him was that he was weighing up his companions in the same manner as the prince. His eyes met Quintillian's and something passed between them in a single glance. An approval of a kindred spirit, perhaps? A recognition of an equal…

They were drawn back to the tent by a clapping of hands as a large man emerged. He was not a young man, his age perhaps just past 50 summers, and his middle had run to a paunch, but there was a hardness about him despite it all. His face was etched with lines of care and hard work, his hands were big and calloused, and his arms had that peculiar jutting out that spoke of bicep muscles just a little too large to sit comfortably alongside his barrel chest. He wore a loose-fitting robe of light cotton, not black like the Pelasians, but dazzling white like the nomads who lived in the deep desert on their periphery. His curly black locks were held back by a gilded cord. His boots were expensive but solid and well-worn. His appearance overall spoke of wealth and influence, but tempered with common sense and practicality. Quintillian instantly approved of the man.

'You, you and you,' the man said, gesturing at the boy and the twins, 'I'm afraid I have no work for you at this time. My apologies and I hope you secure gainful employment this day elsewhere. Take a single corona for your time from my guard as you leave.'

Disconsolately the three trooped out. The woman, the northerner, the soldier and Quintillian shared glances.

'On this particular trip my overheads are necessarily tight,' the merchant went on in a matter-of-fact tone, 'and I can manage only three more guards at the sort of wage you will be willing to accept. You all seem eminently capable to me. I have no intention of setting you to fighting to prove your worth. I am sure you are all more than competent with your blades, and we are not barbarians here. Tell me in one sentence why I should hire you. You first.' He gestured to the former soldier.

'Because I know the terrain and can help feed you.'

The rich man nodded approvingly. 'You, woman?'

'Because even now you are underestimating me.'

The man chuckled and nodded. 'What about you, northerner?'

The fair-haired mountain man shrugged. 'Because you'll find no better today.'

'Resolve and confidence. I approve. What of you, mister riding leathers?'

Quintillian pursed his lips. 'Because I require no payment.'

The other three frowned at him, and the rich man narrowed his eyes. 'That makes me nervous, mister horseman. If you're not in it for the money, then you're either doing it for excitement and adventure, which are the most appallingly dangerous reasons, or you're desperate to get away from something, which makes me even more troubled. Would you care to enlighten me?'

Quintillian shrugged. Some lies had to be kept but others did not. Some truths might help glue together the shield of fiction that surrounded him

'I have to admit to a burning curiosity about the lands to the east. But that is not the reason for my presence, which owes more to my rather pressing need to leave something behind. So, in essence, I'm everything you fear. But the main reason I do not seek *payment* is because I need no money. Feed me and house me and I am content. And I am not a man given to precipitous action, either, so worry not on that count. Given what you intend, unless you have another reason to turn me away you cannot afford to leave guards behind. If I seek no payment, you can afford all four of us.'

The man frowned for a while, then looked around at the others. 'Are you all comfortable with this?'

'So long as he doesn't get in my way,' the northerner grunted.

'Me too,' purred the warrior woman.

The soldier looked him up and down. 'Whatever he's running from it's not going to touch you,' he said quietly. 'It's personal, not legal or brutal. I've seen that look in men who fled bad situations to join the army.'

After a considerable pause, the rich merchant stretched and nodded. 'Very well, then. All four of you. I already have thirteen men in my permanent employ, but I lost three on the last trip to a fever contracted around some flea-bitten lake in the east. Be assured that you will work on this journey, and you will work hard. And the dangers are almost uncountable. From raiders to illness to weather disasters to bad-tempered toll-collectors to madmen to mountain sickness to parasites to prowling predators as big as a man and bigger... you have never taken a trip in your life as fraught with peril as this. Be under no illusion. You will *earn* your money. Or your food, in one case. This is not a journey for the faint of heart. If you are going to endanger the entire caravan better you turn back now. Anyone wish to step out?'

Predictably, silence met his words.

'Very well. We will be leaving a little after the second morning bell. By noon I intend to be out of sight of Velutio entirely, and we strike east as far and as fast as we can today. I have a dedicated regular campsite by the Tyras River, near Argaela. That is a lot of leagues from here, and it will be dark before we arrive, but I intend to push hard for several days. Once we pass outside imperial borders towards the lands of the Inda, we will by necessity move slower and with a great deal more care, so we make up what speed we can upon the safe metalled roads of the empire early on.'

Nods all round.

'You,' he gestured to the soldier. 'You said you know the terrain? How so?'

The man shrugged. 'I was posted out there with the Third Army on the eastern border for almost a decade. I was a scout, both mounted and foot at different times, and in the line of duty I have forayed more than a hundred miles beyond the borders both into Inda lands and into the steppes of the horse clans. I'm familiar with what territory we'll meet at least until we hit the high mountains.'

The man rumbled his approval once more. 'Good. In eight days we will cross the border, if all goes as planned. From there we skirt the steppes, as they are too dangerous to cross. The Inda are content to let caravans pass through their lands in return for what they consider extortionate taxes due to their lack of understanding of western coinage, but are in truth a pittance. Inda lands are an endless repeat of swamp and sweltering jungle until we reach the foothills of the mountains. There we turn north, neatly skirting the edge of the horse lords' lands and moving through the realm of the mountain nomads. They are herders and will trade with us. Our main dangers up there will be from nature and the gods. Then we will descend to the Kan-Chalad basin, where there is a great city built long ago by some forgotten king, but which serves as a central market for thousands of miles of grassland. There we can make a huge profit and still resupply. Then we are down into the lands of the eastern kingdoms of the Jade Emperor, where we will be endlessly harassed by officials, soldiers and tax collectors until we finally reach distant Jiong-Xhu by the sea, where we will unload the last of our western wares and acquire silk for the return journey. The entire trip will take nine months if we are *very* lucky. I have known more than a year to pass on a single trip. Right, get yourselves ready.'

Behind the man, two of his servants had begun to unfurl a huge, hand-drawn map of the route. The other three moved across and began to pore over it, examining what they were to face. As the merchant disappeared inside once more, leaving the new guards to gather their belongings and prepare to move off, Quintillian stepped to the far side of the circle and looked back and up.

Above the canvas surround, beyond the impressive city walls, he could just see the towers of the imperial palace on the crest of the hill in the distance. Nothing there would appear untoward at the moment. Then, as noon passed and Kiva began to wonder why he'd not seen his brother, questions would be asked. It would transpire that he went out for a ride, and all would then be well again until nightfall, when he still had not reappeared. Worry would then creep into the palace. More questions, and then a search of Quintillian's rooms. Kiva would see what he'd taken and know that he went on purpose and with no intention of returning in the foreseeable future, so they would all be spared the worry that he had been injured or kidnapped. No, he had left of his own accord. And Kiva would trawl back through all those pleas to be sent away and decide that it was all purposeful and connected.

Which was good…

…as long as he never worked out why.

Behind Kiva, two camels on the far side of the canvas snorted, reminding him now what lay ahead.

CHAPTER II

Of the Ephemeral Nature of Fortune

The days seemed to pass in a blur of spring green, cloying brown and hazy golden sunshine, endless clouds of dust thrown up by the pack horses and camels, cart beasts and escort steeds, constant shouts, calls, herding of support animals, interminable unscheduled stops to repack, check, rearrange and secure things. Quintillian hadn't been sure what to expect from a trade caravan, but the sense of urgency and the importance of speed that the merchant had imparted during the hiring had certainly created a much different picture to this slow, irksome slog.

Still, he was heading east. No matter how slow and interrupted his steps might be, each one took him further from the capital and closer to the strange and exotic world of the silk lands. And at least the weather had been kind thus far, the sun a pleasant warmth rather than a blistering heat, with no hint of rain or fog, though Quintillian could only be grateful that he was atop his horse rather than walking alongside the pack animals like some of the handlers. Any man with experience of military command knew how awful very dry weather could be for a column of men and animals on the move. Even on the horse he had to keep his scarf wrapped around the lower half of his face to ward off the stifling dust. Those on foot moved amid a constant thick cloud of it, and every other footstep was planted in the fresh dung of one animal or another.

Fourteen days they had travelled so far, passing outside the central provinces after the first seven and moving from dusty highway to dusty highway among the sparser, less organized eastern provinces. Out here the cities were older, belonging to a civilization long gone, said to be the progenitor of the Western Empire, and every town or village they passed held the carved and constructed memories of that disappeared world, from graceful arches supporting nothing to great crumbling auditoria now used to contain herds of animals.

Though he would have to admit that the majority of the reason for it was his avoidance of pondering his problems, the anonymous prince had found a certain fascination in the journey, even thus far, inside his own lands. He had travelled in the east, of course, but only ever at speed on imperial business or at the head of an army. Neither situation had afforded him the time to pause and look about on his journey, and now he was relishing the fact that he could examine and take in this strange, decayed glory that surrounded them.

Ahead, he could see the barbarian northerner – Gisalric his name was, apparently – deep in conversation with the woman – Danu – who was busy polishing a nick from the edge of her belt knife as they rode. The pair were… friendly wasn't the word. They were accommodating. They allowed him his privacy and his secrets, since he made no attempt to draw from them their stories beyond the few facts they revealed on a daily basis. The four new arrivals were billeted together and travelled close by, assigned to one of the rear sections of wagons where the strings of support animals were also led. It was clearly not that they were not trusted, for in this position, heading into the unknown as they were, *everyone* had to be trusted – there was no real alternative. It was more that they had not yet earned their place in the hierarchy of the caravan, and until they were accepted they felt more comfortable keeping their own company.

Quintillian – *Quintus* as he was known to these people – had formed an odd bond early on with the ex-soldier in their group. Asander shared more in common with him than did the others, and they both knew it. Asander had addressed the group during the evening meal on their first day and commented that everyone had their secrets, but comrades had to know something of one another else they could not hope to work well together. He would answer one question about himself each day, and suggested the others follow suit. In those first few days it had become clear which questions were not going to be answered, but less revealing and less harmful ones *were*, and slowly the group came to know one another a little better. And the more they learned, the easier it was to share. Quintillian had even given a somewhat glossed-over and vague version of his true reason for being there, a hopeless love shared by his brother's wife, but that he had to leave lest their family and holdings collapse through romantic disaster. It was true, just not quite what 'holdings' were at stake.

Ahead there was a shout – a familiar one by now, and the column rumbled slowly to a halt so that some unknown mercantile personnel could attend to the latest impediment. Quintillian, pulled from his reverie, peered on down the valley. The dust here was worse than usual, for a seasonal stream had dried up after the winter and left the valley floor grimy and powdered, the grass a stubby brown variety that had little life to it. To the right, the slope was steep and covered in a scree that only added to the choking air, stacks of oddly-shaped rock above them looking like petrified monsters dotted along the crest of the hill. *Trolls*, Gisalric had told them in earnest tones the night before, when they'd first seen them. To the left, the valley side was much more gentle, sloping up with a covering of that same brown grass, giving way here and there to patches of bare rock.

'You served out here?'

Quintillian turned in surprise to see Asander reining in alongside him.

'I did. Not specifically *here*, of course. My unit was active south of here near Lappa. I was with the cavalry of the Third Army, not the settled border forces.'

'You know how close we are to the border right now, Quintus?'

Quintillian frowned. His eyes drifted up that gentle brown slope to the stone tower that jutted up like a fang into the cerulean sky. That was one of the border outpost towers. Of course, they weren't due to pass out of eastern lands for another 12 days, but for a while before that they would run parallel with the border where it took an east-west angle. He blinked. On the other side of that hill was t*erra incognita.* Except to Asander, of course, who had worked this border during his service.

'I'd not realized. When did we get so close?'

'About three hours ago. That's when I saw the first tower. There's been one every mile since then.'

'Must be like home to you.'

Asander shook his head. He wasn't smiling. 'I do not like this, Quintus.'

'What?'

The scout gestured up to the hilltop with an arm. 'What do you see?'

'A watchtower.'

'Details, man. Details.'

Frowning, Quintillian peered into the bright light, squinting. 'I see the tower itself. I see the compound alongside for stabling and storage. I see a thin trail of smoke coming from the hearth outlet. Must have been cold up there last night.'

'And the flag?' prompted Asander.

Quintillian peered. No. No flag. 'Why no flag?'

'Precisely. All the previous towers have had them, even if they were tattered. This one does not. It makes me nervous.'

The prince opened his mouth to play down the minor discrepancy, but a shiver ran up his spine and settled on the nape of his neck, and suddenly he didn't feel quite so much like playing it down.

'Where are the birds?' he noted quietly, his hand going to the hilt of his sword.

'Indeed. Come on.'

Asander kicked his horse's flanks and drove the beast forward. Ahead, the rich master merchant, Nikos, was deep in discussion with one of his men who was pointing at a broken cartwheel and gesticulating wildly as his men tried to prop the cart up to mend it. Quintillian rode in his friend's wake and reined in near the merchant.

'Why are you out of position?' the captain of the guards grunted from his position next to the merchant. Asander ignored him and gestured to Nikos, who held up a quieting hand to his assistant and turned his attention to the horsemen.

'What is it?'

'You've two choices, sir,' Asander said quietly. 'Either abandon this ruined cart and move on *really, really* fast, or have your guard officers pull everything into a defensive formation right now and hope like shit the gods are smiling on you today.'

The merchant's brow folded and he sucked his lower lip. 'Casta?' The captain who had challenged them shrugged. 'I have no idea what he's on about.'

'We're in severe danger, sir,' Asander hissed.

Quintillian nodded emphatically. 'Something's about to happen. We need to be prepared or gone, one or the other.'

'The overactive imagination of fresh meat,' Captain Casta grunted. 'When you've been out here more than once you learn to stop jumping at shadows.'

'I'm telling you, sir,' Asander said, his voice little more than a whisper, 'there's a storm about to break. A shitstorm.'

'Get back to your places,' Casta snapped, gesturing angrily back towards the rear of the column.

'Listen to the man,' Quintillian hissed. 'He spent years out here. He knows what he's talking about.'

To his credit, the merchant dithered for a moment, undecided. He glanced at the two recent recruits, then at Casta for reassurance. The captain gave him a firm nod. 'Back to your places,' the merchant confirmed, though not in unkind tones.

'At least send someone up to check out the tower,' Quintillian said quickly, Asander nodding at his side.

'What?'

'If all is well there will be four soldiers up there with two horses in the stable, but I don't think you'll find any of those. I think we've trundled into someone's snare.'

Casta snorted and rolled his shoulders. 'If you're thinking it's horse nomads from across the border, they don't *do* things like that. They just come in screaming blue murder and hit you hard and fast. This is just your imagination.'

'Then prove me wrong,' Quintillian snapped. 'What else will you do, other than stand around watching the wheel get fixed?'

Casta glared at him for a moment, then grabbed a lance from one of his men and pointed it threateningly at Quintillian and Asander. 'I'll check it out myself. You two get back to your places. We'll be ready to move again soon enough.'

As the captain urged his horse up the gentle, brown scrub grass incline, Nikos the merchant nodded at them and gestured for them to return to their places. The two men wheeled their horses and rode back along the line, Asander drawing his blade as he rode.

'You're sure?' Quintillian murmured.

'Absolutely. And this lot are in trouble.'

As they passed Gisalric and Danu, Asander shouted for them to get ready for trouble, and the two other friends looked around sharply, drawing their own blades. Arriving at their position, Quintillian drew his own sword and swung it experimentally a few times. In the wagon nearby, the three women who cooked for every meal and kept the stores and cooking equipment in order looked up in sharp panic.

'What is it?' one of them whispered.

'Stay down beneath the wagon cover and don't come out until you know it's safe.'

The three women did just that, as did the teamster who drove the wagon, a fat man with a ruddy face and nervous eyes. Asander and Quintillian held their blades ready and turned to look back along the valley.

The lone figure of Casta was two thirds of the way up the valley side, making for the tower. His horse skittered this way and that as it found a patch of rock, but quickly gained turf again and was then closing on the crest. Quintillian held his breath. Somehow he knew something awful was about to happen. Casta neared the top, and from their angle the two friends could see the captain on his steed silhouetted against the blue sky as he crested.

And suddenly he was not alone.

A spear burst through Casta's middle, and the captain toppled backward off his horse, rolling down the slope, the shaft that had claimed his life snapping and splintering as he barrelled through the scrub grass. All along the ridge, horsemen appeared in a seemingly endless line, black forbidding shapes against the blue.

'Fuck, that's a lot.'

Quintillian couldn't find words to express his own thoughts, but Asander had nailed the nub of it, certainly.

Without Casta 16 professional, talented guards now protected the caravan, which consisted of 15 vehicles and perhaps 60 beasts of burden. In all his days of commanding men, Quintillian had learned time and again that a well-trained, well-motivated force with high morale could hope to take on and defeat an enemy three times their number as long as the ground was not unfavourable and the conditions roughly equal. Even a cursory glance up at the ridge told him that they were facing more than a hundred riders, who had the advantage of terrain. No commander would commit to such an action. Still, what was the alternative? Flight and abandoning the wagons and the civilians? His father had brought him up better than that. A nobleman of the empire – *especially* a prince – needed to be prepared to make sacrifices for the people.

'We're in trouble,' Asander muttered.

'Take as many as you can, keep your back to the wagons, don't let them get to the civilians and make every strike count,' Quintillian said with purpose, flexing his shoulders.

'You were an officer,' the scout grinned. 'An *important* one, weren't you?'

'Do they have bows?'

Asander nodded. 'And they're very good with them. They can loose arrows accurately even at a gallop.'

'Then make sure you face them head on, else your horse makes a huge target.'

They looked up. The force of horsemen was now on the move, flowing down the gentle slope like a tidal wave of black and brown death, oddly silent, but for the thunder of countless hooves.

'Casta said they came in screaming,' Asander murmured, 'and that's my experience of them too.'

'Something's clearly changed.'

The two men hefted their weapons and watched as the nomad horsemen swarmed down to the level ground and flooded across the valley. This was no army such as the empire fielded, or the Pelasians. Nor even like the tribes of the northern mountains. Quintillian was impressed despite himself. He had fought on the eastern border and dealt with minor vassal revolts near the Pelasian border, but he'd never had cause to fight the nomad riders. They rarely crossed the border, even in the hungrier raiding seasons and, from a grand strategic point of view, the damage they caused was too insignificant to merit full-scale military intervention. Somehow it seemed more significant from this angle.

Each rider was attired and equipped differently. They wore a dazzling array of colours, from mustard yellow to deep blue to blood red, with a thousand different browns. Some wore leather armour, boiled to hardness like steel, others lacquered wood. Some wore no armour at all, and some had full coats of leather covered with small fish-scale plates. Some even wore stolen or captured imperial armour. Many had bows either in hand or at their shoulder or in a case attached to the saddle. Some held long, straight swords, some axes with a straight blade and a heavy hammer point to the rear. Others lunged with spears, their blades variously leaf-shaped, long and tapering, or even the shape of two joined diamonds. Their hair was braided or tied at the back, or covered with hoods of fur or leather. There were just two things uniform about the force that rode down the merchant column. They were full of purpose to a man. And fear was not in evidence anywhere along the line.

'See you on the other side, brother,' Asander said as he braced.

'Spears,' shouted one the merchant teamsters nearby, and five of the lads and old men who tended the vehicles and animals were suddenly with them, facing the enemy with long spears held ready. With practised precision the servants braced themselves, stamping the spear butts into the ground as best they could and slamming their boots down atop them. Clearly there were men in this caravan who had faced horsemen before and were prepared. Indeed, all along the line, civilians stepped out and braced spears taken from unseen places among the wagons. It still wouldn't be enough, of course. Not even close.

The arrows began to thrum and hiss through the air from the oncoming horsemen. Quintillian braced himself. Without a shield all he could really do against arrows was hope and pray. But the riders were clever, and their arrows were not aimed at the waiting guards on their horses, but at those same poor civilians with their spears. All along the valley there were agonized screams as men and children fell to the dust peppered with shafts, their spears collapsing harmlessly to the dirt. The pole-arms had represented a sparse but effective anti-cavalry measure, and in one barrage of arrows they were neutralized. Next to Quintillian the last of them fell, a boy of perhaps nine, with an arrow lodged in the notch at the base of his throat, one in his bicep and another deeply embedded in his eye. Blood sprayed from him and he barely had a chance to hiss in pain before he fell dead to the ground, the spear clattering uselessly from his hands.

Quintillian took a deep breath. A nomad with a coat of blue padded material and a skirt of interlocking metal plates was bearing down on him. His black, shining hair streamed in three tails behind him, and a strange pointed beard and moustache framed bared white teeth that shone like his eyes. His left hand held the reins of his steed and his right held a long spear in an overhand grip. Quintillian saw the man tense and shift and reacted instantly, jerking his reins to the right and neatly side-stepping his horse as the spear arced through the air, passed through the empty space where he'd been a moment earlier, and then thudded into the side of a wagon and thrummed there as it vibrated. Even as Quintillian righted himself and prepared, the man was coming again, drawing his long, straight blade and angling for the attack.

The prince's sword met the nomad's resulting in the spine-chilling shriek of steel scraping along steel. The rider was quick and the sword was pulled back and coming around for a second strike even as the man manoeuvred the horse expertly a pace to the left to give him better room to fight, though his companions were now coming in close behind and making it difficult. Quintillian's sword caught the nomad's and turned it aside once more. Again, the man was quick, bringing his blade around for a third strike. As Quintillian mirrored the manoeuvre, his left hand dipped to his belt and drew his heavy, broad dagger. This was no time for the nobility of the duel. This was a fight to the death and everything counted.

Both swords came round again and met once more. This time the nomad had the better of the angle and it was Quintillian's blade that skittered away, but *this time* it was not the sword that counted. As the steel kissed and separated, his left hand came up and the dagger scored a heavy rent across the man's sword arm. Even as the nomad brought the blade back for his next strike he realized that he had been properly injured, and his arm lost some of its strength and feeling, his sword wobbling in his grip. By the time the sword was coming around for the blow, it was barely held at all, the cut having neatly sliced through the forearm tendons. Quintillian ignored the sword coming for him, since it now held barely enough strength to pass through the air, let alone flesh and bone. His own blade lanced out in a jab this time, rather than a swing, punching deep into the surprised nomad's chest.

The prince turned his attention to the next opponent, counting the last a dead man already. An axe swung at him and only lurching in his saddle prevented a blow that would have taken a neat slice from the top of his head. Taking advantage of the nomad's exposed position with the heavy axe leading his arm, he arced up with his sharp blade, his sword catching the swinging arm just below the elbow. There was a thud and a moment of resistance, the crack of bone and the shearing of muscle and the axe continued in its arc, hurtling off to the turf, half an arm still connected to it. Blood pumped from the stump as the startled axeman stared at his injury in disbelief.

Quintillian's dagger slammed into his ribs as the prince stepped his horse a pace forward and leaned in for the killing blow, his sword even now coming up to block a swing from another assailant.

Then his world fell out from under him.

Or at least, his steed did.

A spear, whether thrown or thrust in the melee, he couldn't tell, struck the poor beast in the throat. One moment, the prince was in control, cutting and parrying, holding off the enemy, the next he had a brief vision of the spear slamming into the animal beneath him, then his vision was filled with blue sky as the horse reared in agony. And then he was in the dust, choking and scrambling, desperate to be out of the way when the horse fell. He'd seen enough cavalrymen in combat trapped under their animals to know that it was often a death sentence. He felt something slam against his back and reached around with his dagger hand. It was the wheel of the wagon. All he could see was roiling dust and countless conflicting shadows. A tremendous thud nearby signalled the landing of his dying horse and while he felt for the poor beast, he was also filled with gratitude that at least he wasn't underneath it.

Desperate, choking and with his eyes stinging from the dust, Quintillian struggled upright, his back against the wheel, forcing himself to the world of the living. Miraculously, somehow, he had kept hold of both weapons through his fall and shuffling. As he came up from the worst of the dust cloud, he stared in horror at another nomad's sword coming down at him, his own blade rising only just in time to turn it aside. Desperately he fought, parrying blow after blow, but two nomads were on him now. In a tiny moment of respite, he managed to lunge out with his knife hand and stab one of the riders' horses. It was only a light flesh wound with no real damage, but it panicked the beast and sent the rider out of the fight as he fought to control his steed. Even the best horsemen in the world struggle for dominance over a wounded mount.

This bought him enough time to gain a better position against the remaining nomad. It was hopeless, though. He could see three more behind the man, and suddenly another figure thumped against him. Risking a glance, he recognized Asander, now also unhorsed, beside him, fighting for his life.

Swords danced and rang and meat was cleaved, the tearing of muscle and the shattering of bone filling his world. Quintillian roared with the desperation of the man fighting a battle that was already lost, and felt the first wound, then the second, then the third. Suddenly, as though the battle had been halted by some unheard signal, the assailants backed off. Quintillian and Asander shared a surprised and suspicious look. The dust began slowly to settle and the two men took in their surroundings with heavy hearts. The column was lost, utterly. They may well be the last two guards still fighting. For sure he could see the blue-eyed, flaxen-haired head of Gisalric bouncing along further down the caravan on the tip of a spear. Of Danu there was no sign. They seemed to be the last, he and Asander. And a semi-circle of perhaps a dozen nomads surrounded them, spears levelled.

One of them raised a bow and nocked an arrow, but one of his companions shouted at him. An argument ensued in their strange, garbled tongue. Quintillian stared in incomprehension.

'They can't decide whether we're more valuable as slaves or corpses,' Asander whispered.

'You know their language?'

'A bit. Don't forget I served out here for years. I'm not sure whether I wouldn't rather be a corpse than a slave, though. They work their slaves to death anyway.'

Quintillian nodded. 'We go out like soldiers then, eh? For the emperor, blood and steel, eh?'

'Blood and steel, brother,' Asander huffed. 'For the emperor.'

Quintillian knew it wouldn't be much of a fight. He'd taken a small gash to his right thigh, which was gradually weakening his leg, and a cut to his left arm had left it quite numb, making his dagger largely useless now. The shoulder wound was nothing. But the next blow would probably be lethal – he was in no position to block it properly.

All along the line nomads were ransacking the wagons, throwing out anything that was of no interest and whooping with delight when they found goods they wanted. Quintillian and Asander braced themselves and raised their blades defiantly. There was another heated discussion between three or four of the nomads, and then one nodded and pointed at the two of them, garbling something at them.

'He wants us to put down our swords.'

'Fat fucking chance,' Quintillian sniffed, wiping blood from his face with his numb left arm.

Several of the horsemen raised bows nocking arrows, and Quintillian was about to yell his defiance at them when he realized the missiles were not aimed at him, but had lifted to a point above his head. He turned, frowning, to look up. The carter had risen from beneath the wagon cover, his hands held up in surrender.

'Ah, shit.'

Moments later the three cooker women were standing too, their hands held high. Quintillian felt his heart sink. The arrows were aimed for the four figures on the wagon. The spokesman growled something else out in his native tongue, and Asander sighed. 'He says…'

'Yes. I can guess.' Quintillian squeezed his eyes shut for a moment. In many ways a quick death by arrow might be better for all of them, but that was not his decision to make. Not now. A true imperial noblemen, and an officer no less, had a duty to the empire and its citizens that surpassed his own needs and wishes. With a sigh of defeat, he threw his sword to the dusty ground and raised his right arm, his left one not passing shoulder level with the aching numbness of his wound.

Asander cast down his own sword and coughed. 'We probably only bought them periodic rape and permanent servitude instead of a quick death, you realize?'

'Not our decision. The military can't presume to make choices for the population,' Quintillian hissed. 'That's how despots begin.'

'You sound like a politician now,' Asander whispered. 'Who *are* you, Quintus?'

'A slave,' the prince replied with a sigh and dropped to his knees at a gesture from the nomads. As three nomads came and searched him, removing his belt and his scabbards, his eating knife and his pouch of coins, and wrapping a thick leather cord around his wrists so tight it bit into the flesh, all along the caravan whooping riders celebrated their victory and displayed their prizes. The incongruous sight of a nomad warrior the size of a bear with a huge braided beard trying to don a noblewoman's delicate cotton cloak was just one in a sea of images that Quintillian caught in passing as he was bound and gagged.

Asander and he were tied to a rope which in turn was attached to a saddle, and others were slowly brought to join them, bound and gagged in the same manner, mostly good-looking women or well-built men. Quintillian cursed himself as behind them the three cooker women were brought down to the ground and made to pleasure the riders in rotation, while two more nomads entertained themselves beating the carter to insensibility. The nightmare scene was only brought to an end when what appeared to be the chieftain came trotting along the line. Quintillian couldn't help but note that four disembodied heads swung from his saddle horns, clonking against each other with heavy bony sounds in time with the horse's steps. Nikos the merchant and Captain Casta were among them. Judging by the open mouth of horror on Nikos's face he had been taken alive and made to watch the blade coming to decapitate him.

The chieftain made a short barked announcement and gestured to the three poor, abused women on the floor. One of the nomads moved among the weeping women, slitting their throats, then they quickly dispatched the barely-conscious carter and remounted.

Animals!

Quintillian chewed on his lip as he looked up along the slave line. Fourteen of them. Of a column that had begun with 17 guards and perhaps a hundred civilians, just 14 now remained, and most of them were suffering minor wounds. It was clear what the handsome women had been taken for, and if Asander was right, the menfolk had little to look forward to but being slowly worked into the grave.

Quintillian turned back to his friend. 'I'm going to make them pay for this.'

Asander rolled his eyes. 'Don't be so dramatic. We've lost. That's all there is to it.'

'For you, maybe. Not for me. Not by a long way. My father would turn in his grave if he thought I just lay down and accepted this.'

'Who *are* you?' Asander hissed again.

'If we survive long enough to end up somewhere private, I'll tell you. It'll probably make you laugh.'

'I doubt it.'

A discordant horn blast signalled some decision and the last of the wagons were picked over for items of use. Nomads began leading the strings of captured animals away, and the riders prepared to depart imperial lands once more. No. This was not over…

CHAPTER III

Of Journeys Most Foul

The first hour was the worst.

It seemed that the nomads were less concerned with slaves than with mobility, for the clan travelled at a light trot alternated with a fast walk, regardless of the poor, ruined, exhausted prisoners roped in a line from the back of a horse. In fact, Quintillian's trained general's mind suggested, the clan was travelling at the fastest comfortable pace for the pack beasts and meat animals they had taken from the caravan. It suggested a bleak future for the imperial captives that the captured animals were clearly more valuable than the humans.

Quintillian was lucky, as were Asander and a few of the captives, in that they were fit and hearty enough that the run was not too difficult, even with the wounds. Two of them, though, a beefy carter and a pretty young woman, were in trouble fairly early on. The girl was not fit, despite being a pleasing shape. She was puffing and panting and groaning by the time they crossed the second valley, and the big carter roped just in front of her had suffered a wound to his left thigh, with which he was clearly struggling despite being in excellent shape otherwise.

That first hour, the 14 captives had to adjust to their situation, find their pace and try and maintain it. It was not easy, given the terrain. The grassy steppe, with its wide, shallow valleys and low, rolling hills – a sea of grass with gentle green waves – might look like easy terrain, and for a rider it was just that, but for a human, running at pace, it was treacherous. The grass was rough and tall, growing in tufts and concealing dangerous dips and rabbit holes. It was, to Quintillian's mind, a miracle that they made it through the first hour without a broken ankle.

He estimated the clan to number around 250, with almost half that number being male warriors of good age. The rest were the children, old folk and women of the clan, yet each and every one old enough to walk and speak rode their own horse and did it with a level of skill that would make an imperial cavalry trainer proud. The clan took with them perhaps 60 extra steeds, each of which doubled as a pack beast with the entire tribe's belongings on their backs. They were a truly nomadic people, able to settle wherever they wished with little difficulty.

Quintillian watched carefully throughout the run, taking in everything he could. There was no chance to catch any of their speech, of course. Not a single one spoke the imperial tongue and there was no hope of Quintillian being able to pick up even the basics of their guttural language. Asander, roped in front of him, *could* understand them, of course, but with the run, he needed to save all his breath and could not afford to chatter and pass on scraps of information.

The warrior who rode the horse to which they were roped was clearly important. He seemed to be in perhaps his 40th year – though these nomads were so weathered and etched and sun-blazoned it was hard to tell their age even to the decade – which put him around the same age as the chieftain. Given the way the two men spoke to one another, missing the deference offered by the younger warriors and the women, and the number of gold and bronze accoutrements about his person, Quintillian surmised that the rider was probably the chieftain's brother, or a close cousin at least. He was certainly respected. And he was hard.

He would be a difficult proposition when the time came for Quintillian to turn the tables on their captors. He would need to free himself, and Asander too. And any of the others who might help. It would be a suicide mission, of course. Even if all 14 of them could be freed, armed and turn on their captors, 14 against 200 or more was insane. But instead of slowly fading as slaves, they could at least make a good account of themselves. At the very least, the chieftain and this brother had to die, along with the warriors who had raped the cooker women at the caravan. He'd memorized *their* faces. They would pay. But it would have to be carefully and slowly planned. It was no good being precipitous and leaping at their first opportunity. That way abject failure lay.

He was contemplating the man on the horse ahead of them and wondering whether the big knife at his belt was loose enough to draw without it being noticed when he suddenly felt a jerk on the rope and almost lost his footing. Turning, he peered past the thickset blacksmith roped directly behind him, who was also craning his neck.

The girl at the rear – the one Quintillian had already had his doubts about – had lost her footing altogether and was now on the ground, being dragged through the scratchy grass and across the humps and bumps by her wrists. She was screaming in pain and her legs were flailing and kicking and bouncing behind her. Even as Quintillian closed his eyes for a moment, saddened by her predicament, he heard the snapping of a leg bone. That did it. If there had been any hope that the nomad might stop and let her travel easier, it was lost now. Human captives were treated worse than the animals. What use was a slave girl who couldn't walk?

Regardless, the rider did not seem inclined to slow. The girl continued to shriek and bellow and cry as she bounced and thumped along the ground at the back, bones snapping and cracking, legs floundering at unnatural angles as she died in the most excruciating pain. Quintillian was about to turn away and wish her a swift passing when he saw her jerking arms catch the bad leg of the carter in front of her. The man gave a cry of shock and was suddenly down just like her, bouncing and caroming through the tufts. His cries were deeper and more surprised than hers, but no less heart-rending. Quintillian watched as the man desperately tried to haul himself upright on the rope, but his leg was now far too bad and he slipped again and fell, bouncing once more and cracking his head on a rock.

The new lurching on the rope threatened to bring the rest of them down, and along with the other 11 captives, Quintillian found himself desperately trying to keep his feet. Still, the nomad leading them failed to even slacken the pace, despite the fact that now the rear two figures on the rope were prone and ruined, either dead or so nearly they would be better off that way.

Even as the prince cleared his throat to try and suggest Asander speak to the rider, a boy of perhaps seven came alongside on a bay mare with a white patch over one eye. The lad had dropped back from the bulk of the clan. Even at his tender age, he was clearly being trained as a warrior, for he had a bow and quiver at his saddle and a spear on his back. The boy pulled level with the fallen slaves and, in a manoeuvre that would have imperial cavalry officers impressed and blowing through their teeth, leaned out over the side of his steed, holding the saddle with his left hand, a knife in his right. Expertly, the boy edged the horse closer to the fallen captives, and with only two attempts, he neatly snicked the rope, before sliding back up into the saddle as though gravity had no hold on him.

The two broken, battered figures – the girl and the carter – bounced slowly to a halt in a heap. Quintillian, finding the going suddenly easier again without the pressure on the rope, watched as the boy put away his knife, drew his spear and circled the bodies, thrusting the long shaft down into each figure to make sure they were dead before urging his horse on once more and rejoining his clan.

The day passed in misery and hardship. With the example of the fallen pair, even exhausted and in agony, every captive made sure to keep to their feet. It was almost impossible to tell the time, but Quintillian estimated that they had run for five solid hours by the time the clan stopped.

The sun was beginning to sink slowly into the west, and the descent told Quintillian that they had been travelling northeast almost all day. He estimated that they had covered 25 or 30 miles. His legs told him it had been more like 300.

It was quite likely that the first time they stopped would be their best chance at unexpected escape, but even with the best will in the world, Quintillian could no more have overcome a guard at the end of the day's run than attempt to leap up to the moon. The fact that they were simply dropped, roped still, to the grass to sit felt like an incredible blessing. One of the nomads hammered an enormous iron ring into the ground and the rope was fastened to it at both ends, the remaining 12 prisoners on the loop. Three of the young trainee warriors were set to watch them by the fading light of the sun while the clan set up their camp for the night. As the last of the light faded, torches coated with pig fat were ignited, sending up greasy black smoke and filling the lifeless air with a thick stench of cooked pork. The three youths were eagle-eyed, Quintillian noted, though he had no intention of testing them tonight anyway.

He must have dozed off almost instantly, for when he awoke suddenly it was true dark and the temperature had dropped considerably. The three boys with their spears were now paying only scant attention to the roped slaves, talking among themselves instead. Quintillian tried to work out what had disturbed him, then he felt it again. The blacksmith beside him was nudging his ribs. He frowned and looked around.

'Shhh,' the smith whispered, and held up a hand for a moment, to demonstrate that he had freed it from the leather binding that had held him to the rope.

'How did you do that?'

'I've had a flake of flint in my hand for the last few hours. Been working on the leather. If I can get my other hand out, you can have the flint. With two of us we might make it away?' He caught the look on Quintillian's face and shrugged. 'Your friend too if he can get free fast enough. But we have to go quick.'

Quintillian felt an unintentional surge of hope, but bit down on his lip and forced that false confidence back down deep into his gut where it belonged. Now was not the time.

'You can't go now. Don't be a fool.'

'They've set children to guard us, man. *Children.*'

'Don't be fooled,' Quintillian whispered carefully. 'Those children are stronger and quicker than most of the guards on the caravan were. These clans teach their young to fight as soon as they can sit in a saddle, and they learn to do *that* once they walk. Be careful and sensible. Take things slow. Loop the leather around your wrist as though it were still intact. We can each get a hand free over the next night or two if you share that flint around. Then we can weaken the other one. That way, when we're better prepared, we can all go at once. All 12 of us. Those who want to can run for the hills. The rest of us can bring the fight back to the nomads.'

The blacksmith blinked. '*Fight?* Are you mad.' His hand pulled back, drawing the flint from sight.

'We wouldn't stop you going, but these bastards have to pay for what they've done.'

'Screw you, soldier boy,' the blacksmith whispered heavily. 'I'm not freeing you to draw attention. We have to go quietly, and if you won't, then you can stay here.'

There was a snicking noise, and the blacksmith suddenly had both hands free. Pursing his lips, he cast the flake of flint some three paces away across the grass. 'There it is. You'll be able to get it when you move in the morning. But I'll be long gone by then.'

Quintillian shook his head. 'Don't be a fool, man. They're more alert than you think, and better warriors at eight summers than you'll ever make. Stay with us and wait for the right time.'

But the smith was up into a crouch now. 'Gods go with you,' the man muttered, 'Because I won't.'

Taking advantage of the fact that just for a moment the three youths were examining a spear tip intently, the smith was suddenly up and running. Asander, disturbed from sleep, blinked and opened his mouth. Before he could make a noise, Quintillian clapped a hand over his lower face, causing the whole rope to jerk, and pointed as best he could. Asander squinted into the darkness and his eyes widened as he picked out the smith running in a crouch, making for the side of one of the huge, low, drum-shaped tents the clan had erected.

'Go, man,' urged Quintillian in the quietest of whispers.

It looked for just a moment as though he'd make it, but then the three boys were on their feet, yelling at one another, two began to sprint after the fleeing slave, but the third, a disdainful sneer on his lips, simply lifted his bow, nocked an arrow, and let it fly so quickly he hardly seemed to have had time to aim.

Quintillian felt his momentary elation sink as the silhouette of the smith against the indigo sky vanished downward with a squawk. The other two youths were on him then, and even at a hundred paces, Quintillian could hear the sounds of butchery as he saw the boys' arms rising and falling and tried not to listen to the blood-curdling screams of the man.

'Careless,' Asander whispered.

'I tried to tell him.'

'Our time will come,' the scout agreed and sagged back.

The youths, spattered with the smith's blood, came back to the slaves and quickly checked all their leather bindings. Satisfied that the remaining 11 were intact, they returned to their conversation. Perhaps an hour later a woman with skin like a saddlebag brought around a pot of something steaming. She put a wooden bowl in each pair of hands and ladled something watery and greasy that smelled like smoked meat into each bowl, before dropping in chunks of flatbread with the consistency of leather. Ravenous, Quintillian and Asander attacked their meals like animals, cramming the hard, dry bread into their mouths and washing it down with the thick, pungent stew. Another half hour later the woman returned with water for them all, which was consumed just as eagerly.

Quintillian was sitting peacefully, sighing with relief at the food in his belly and the alleviation of his parched mouth, when the next fuss began. Somewhere off to his right, past Asander, a girl was shouting. His brow furrowed as he listened. She was arguing... fighting someone off. Asander was paying attention too, now, and Quintillian leaned next to his friend. One of the carters was busy trying to force himself with some difficulty on the young woman roped next to him.

'Come on, girl. What else have we got to look forward to. Let me in.'

The girl was spitting at him and fighting back, kicking and writhing. Neither of them had the use of their hands, and the scene was ridiculous, or would have been had it not proved to what level of barbarity a desperate man could sink.

'Leave her,' grunted Asander.

The carter snorted. 'Mind your business. If you lot had been worth your money we wouldn't be in this mess.'

Asander turned to glance at Quintillian, and the prince was surprised at the look of intense hatred in the scout's eyes. Asander flicked back to the scene before them.

'Last warning, man. Leave her alone.'

'Piss off.'

The bulky carter had succeeded in getting his breeches down to his knees and was pinning the girl's legs to the ground.

'Give me some slack,' whispered Asander. Quintillian pulled the rope towards him and his friend, there being a little extra give now the blacksmith was absent. With sudden freedom of movement, Asander leapt on the carter who gave a shout of alarm as the scout's hands closed on his head. The would-be rapist managed to get out half a syllable before Asander twisted his head sharply to the left with a jerk. There was a crack of bones and the carter's word became a gurgling noise as he shook and shuddered and fell to the grass, jerking and dying. The girl pulled herself back in horror.

'Rest easy, lass.' Asander smiled at her, then sat back and sighed. 'This is not the sort of vacation I had in mind.'

The night passed quietly after that, the remaining ten captives cold and huddled tight in the dark. The three youths eventually went to their rest, to be replaced by two older warriors. Quintillian and Asander were woken with the rest by the rough kicks of the nomads as the first faint glow of dawn threatened behind the distant eastern mountains. There was a brief argument among the warriors about the body of the carter with the broken neck, but in the end he was simply cut free and thrown into a ditch for carrion eaters. After a brief snack of hard cheese, flatbread and yogurt, they were hauled to their feet, fastened to the saddle of that same warrior, and off again across the seemingly endless sea of grass.

The second day was, if anything, worse than the first. Despite his level of fitness, Quintillian was not used to the strenuous and constant activity, and the night of sitting on the cold ground, motionless, had caused his muscles to seize up. Only as the sun approached its apex had his muscles all loosened up and his running eased into a mile-eating pace. The others achieved the same state with varying levels of difficulty. Quintillian marked a tall man with a hooked nose as the next to go, and sure enough, sometime during the afternoon, the man's legs gave way and he fell with a cry. He was separated from the others with a swipe of the knife and dispatched with a spear like the two fallen the day before. The remaining nine captives, Quintillian decided, would likely make it the next few days unless they suffered some sort of accident. All the remaining slaves had found an easy pace. Five burly men and four athletic-looking girls ran on.

As they jogged, Quintillian wondered what use they could be as slaves. If this was the nomad life the clan lived, travelling during the day and camping at night, when would slaves be used for work? It seemed inconceivable. The clan must move from site to site and set up camp for extended periods, depending on the terrain and the season. Likely they were just moving fast at the moment to be far from the imperial border and the likelihood of reprisals.

The second night there was a shower of rain and against all expectations, the nomad who led them during the day had the nine captives moved inside one of the huge, heavy tents along with a dozen warriors who would keep watch on them. If Quintillian had hoped for a chance at freedom that night, he was disappointed. With the death of the carter the first night, a closer watch was now kept on them, and their bonds were checked every three or four hours.

The third day the captives had settled into more of a routine. The running became easier, their muscles becoming accustomed to the constant strain. With no further incidents, their captors seemed to treat them a little better, allowing them a pause for food at noon. And with the more troublesome among them now gone, the remaining nine were more comfortable in each other's company. The third evening they began to talk quietly, to learn each other's names and discover something about one another. The fourth and fifth day the routine was set and the run seemed much easier.

Then, as the sun slid slowly towards the horizon on the sixth day, shouting rose from the front of the clan somewhere. As the riders crested a rise and began the descent of the long, low slope, the captives found themselves with a view of something new. After days of endless green grass with the mountains framing the steppe at a great distance, this was a sight to behold. Quintillian's eyes widened in surprise.

Here, the swathes of undulating grassland gave way to an enormous, shallow basin. The far side of the depression was pock-marked with craggy stones not unlike Gisalric's 'trolls' on the hillside the day of the attack. In fact, the odd stone formations reached around like a horseshoe, covering perhaps two-thirds of the circumference. But it was not the basin itself or the surroundings that caused Quintillian's sharp intake of breath.

The floor of the basin was of neat, short turf and at its centre stood a massive palisade of trunks probably 50 feet tall. The great wooden wall formed a circle over a mile across with a single gate at the northern edge, and fighting platforms seemed to have been constructed periodically around the circumference, for nomads stood at the parapet as if on guard. Inside the great fence, just visible from this angle, were more of the great circular tents than Quintillian could ever imagine being assembled in one place. He had counted 13 tents among the clan as they had travelled. There were *hundreds* in that great ring. How many clans were gathered here? Certainly there were millions of stock animals in pens around the depression, and enough horses to mount half the imperial army.

'I thought the nomads had no permanent settlements?'

Asander shrugged with difficulty. 'That's what I thought too. In years of dealing with them I never heard of one. Maybe it's just a seasonal meeting place? Like a market?'

But Quintillian didn't think so. At the far side of the huge circle, opposite the gate, stood a great wooden house, two storeys tall, with a veranda and furs and carpets hanging from the windows. The sun glinted from glazed tiles on the roof. That structure was no seasonal market.

'This is not a temporary camp, Asander. That looks more like a palace or a castle of timber. This place is their idea of a city, I reckon, but they're not supposed to think like that. They don't gather in groups often, according to our sources, because the clans are almost permanently at war. They certainly shouldn't be congregating in that sort of number.'

Asander nodded. 'Something odd is definitely going on. Well, at least we're going to get a nice close look.'

The clan rode down the hill, their pace picking up slightly as they neared the enormous palisade gate. The prisoners, stumbling along exhausted on their rope, relished the moment of pause as they were stopped at the great portal while the nomads in charge of the gate questioned the new arrivals. The captives were too far back for Asander to hear what was said, but after a few minutes they were led on inside. The newly arrived clan were led to an area of open ground where they could pitch their own tents, lost amid the sea of similar homes. While the clan set about the usual evening routine of preparing camp, some of the warriors from the gate joined those from the raiders and led off the captured animals to find a place for them, and the chief's brother dismounted and handed the rope of slaves to one of the others, who jerked the rope and led them off.

Even had Quintillian considered the possibility of escape, which would clearly be insane right here and now, half a dozen new warriors joined the column, escorting them through the strange nomad settlement. The prince could see the grand wooden structure as they approached and for a moment wondered why they were being taken there. Then, at the last minute, as they emerged from the sea of tents into an open space that surrounded the great house, the warrior jerked the rope again and led them to the side. Another palisade, smaller but still powerful in its own right, stood within the open ground. Torches burned around it and nomads sat by them, chatting and playing games with stones on grids carved in the earth. A door was dragged open in the palisade as they approached and were thrust roughly inside.

As a warrior cut the leather bindings and freed them from the rope, Quintillian took in their new surroundings. This palisade was perhaps 50 feet across. One side had been turned into a rudimentary latrine with a stinking pit dug in the earth surrounded by a cloud of buzzing insects. The stench rolled over them even near the door, which boded badly for the possibility of any breathable air in the foreseeable future. The only shelter was afforded by a canvas roof held up by four poles at the far side, beneath which perhaps a hundred emaciated, broken humans cowered. Quintillian noted a distinct absence of females.

Slave quarters for the men.

'You... talk... empire,' said a heavyset man with a fish-like mouth beneath a curtain of black moustaches. 'I talk empire. You slave. Man here. All man. You think?'

'We think, all right,' Asander grunted.

'You sleep from ride. Sleep one dark. Then work. You think?'

'We think perfectly,' Quintillian nodded. One day.

A shriek made him turn to see that the warriors were busy tearing the clothes from the women. One of the men made to stop them, but Asander held him fast. 'Nothing you can do. You interfere and they'll just beat you.'

Once the women were naked, they were trooped off out of the gate once more. A nomad with a sour face picked up the piles of clothing and, carrying them over, flung them into the latrine trench. Once he had returned to the entrance and left, just fish-mouth remained with a couple of lackeys.

'Sleep. One dark.'

Then they too retreated and the door crashed shut, the sound of a heavy bar sliding into place on the far side their last sign of the outside world. The five men staggered over towards the huddled crowd.

'Welcome to hell,' grunted an old man with straggly grey hair.

CHAPTER IV

Of the Lives of Slaves

Quintillian felt muscles straining and screaming at him – muscles he was unused to exercising. He'd always assumed that between his daily exercise routine, weapon training and riding, he used more or less every muscle available. He'd been wrong. It was impressive, in fact, how such a simple task as forestry helped him discover new and untested muscles. The first day had nearly killed him. Now, on the fourth, he was starting to get used to it, but was in that unpleasant lull phase when the muscles are still torn and painful but have not yet begun to harden and acclimatize.

Gritting his teeth and trying hard to ignore the constant, insistent pains in his back, arms and shoulders, Quintillian swung the axe back and chopped again, biting deep into the hard timber, feeling the reverberation all the way up the axe's shaft, through his arms and into his spine. Wrenching it out with some difficulty, he took that tiny moment for a breather as Asander swung and tore another chunk from the iron-hard wood, deepening the V-shaped hole.

Did they breed some kind of special tree out here? Surely wood wasn't usually this hard? If this was normal, he was going to have to plan some recruitment drive one day to draw woodcutters into the military…

Asander stepped back and Quintillian sighed, spat on his hands and pulled the axe up and behind his head, swinging hard once more.

Swing. Wrench. Pause. Clench. Swing. Wrench. Pause. Clench.

The numbing routine had become natural, like breathing. As soon as the sun put in an appearance above the distant eastern mountains each morning, they were roped and marched off to the sparse wood that dotted the slope around the stone stacks on the northern crest of the basin. There they would cut timber until the sun was perhaps a half hour from the horizon, when they would pack up and return to their enclosure to lick their wounds. It seemed that somewhere along the line the felled, trimmed, and adzed tree trunks were taken away by nomads, presumably dragged behind horses just like slaves. Where they went, Quintillian couldn't guess. They certainly didn't seem to be put anywhere in the great circle. It was something of a mystery why a nomad clan, or collection thereof, might need so much timber. Maybe they were planning to expand this place, whose name, it transpired, was Ual-Aahbor, which Asander believed meant Place of Bones and Grass.

It had occurred to the pair of them that during timber felling would be an excellent time to attempt an escape, but the old grey-hair had warned them off it. The woods would be watched from every angle, and nomads on horseback could ride you down in heartbeats. Many had tried it. None had even managed to get out of sight of the trees. And attempted flight brought about appalling punishments. So Quintillian resigned himself to waiting. His father had been a believer in patience. Had not patience delivered him an empire, while o'er-hasty action had got his childhood friend killed? Sooner or later an opportunity would present itself, he was sure.

'Have you noticed the increase in the clans?'

Quintillian quickly flashed his gaze this way and that. It was forbidden for the slaves to speak, and he had seen other new arrivals being beaten harshly for just exchanging a few words.

'Be quiet,' he hissed at Asander.

'Oh, come on, Arse-hat has been gone half an hour. He's sheltering somewhere cool.'

The nomad they had affectionately named Arse-hat for the strangely dual-buttock-shaped headgear he wore had been gone for some time, and he often disappeared for well over an hour. Probably for a snooze.

'Well, at least stick to a whisper,' he said quietly, and took another swing at the tree, grunting with the effort.

'But have you noticed?' Asander prompted again.

'There does seem to have been something of an influx,' Quintillian conceded, waiting for his friend's swing and then preparing for his own.

'The clans are still gathering. I reckon there's thirty thousand people at Ual-Aahbor now.'

'Maybe it's a festival? Or a market? Maybe there's a wedding on or something, and the bride's father has offered a dowry of a thousand tree trunks?'

Asander snorted and swung again. There was an ominous creaking noise. 'She's going to go with the next swing or two.'

Quintillian nodded. 'An hour or so and we'll be herded back. I wonder what slop's on the table tonight? Horse or horse or horse?'

The former scout laughed. 'It may all be made of horse, but it tastes more like horse*shit*. Sometimes the meals smell worse than the latrines.'

'You could always stop eating.'

They both fell silent, thinking about Domenicus, the old priest who had been captured a week or two before them and had already been worked close to death. In the end, he had decided to make an end of it on his own rather than going on hoping that there would be a light at the end of this dark passageway of life. He had stopped eating two days ago and already the effects were dreadful. He had lost the ability to stand and simply soiled himself in the corner of the covered area. His ribs stood out like a scroll rack and his face was stretched and taut. He had a day or two left, at most. Perhaps he was lucky? Despite their forced levity, both Quintillian and Asander knew that when they looked at Domenicus, they were seeing their own future, for one way or another they would die here, emaciated and broken. At least two slaves a day expired, to be replaced by fresh meat brought in by the latest arrivals.

Quintillian broke the mood with another swing, and as his blade thunked into the wood, there was another heavy groan.

'It's going.'

The two men stepped away to one side and watched as the monstrous bole began to lean and groan more and more. Then there was a snap and the whole thing came down with a sound like the sea crashing against a cliff. The woods seemed oddly silent in the aftermath, but gradually bird life returned and the two men paused for a few moments, waiting for Arse-hat to return and check on them. When nothing happened, they turned their attention to stripping the branches from the great tree with the long, two-man saw.

'You were going to tell me who you were when we had some privacy. I think this is the most privacy we're going to get this side of the grave.'

Quintillian looked around again, but they were practically alone. If he concentrated he could hear the sound of other pairs working on other trees, but with whispered conversation, they were more or less secluded.

'You won't believe me.'

'Try me.'

Quintillian let go of the saw and straightened. 'You are aware, I presume, of the emperor.'

'Well.' Asander chuckled. 'I am alive and awake, so yes.'

'He's my brother.'

'You're a lying sack of horse vomit.'

'Told you you wouldn't believe me.'

'You're not Quintillian. I've seen him on coins. He's got a big nose and a stronger chin than you. And I saw him in person once. During the campaign down near Margdis, when some lord thought he could secede and take a whole chunk of border territory with him. Marshal Quintillian gave a rousing speech. He was taller than you.'

'I was standing on a dais, you fool. And it wasn't much of a rousing speech. I'd got blind drunk with Titus the night before and I could hardly see during that address. I kept getting my words wrong.'

Asander frowned at him.

'One of the captains shouted something. I didn't hear what, but it made the marshal laugh.'

'Now *you're* lying, Asander. *Everyone* in the army heard him. He joked that we were only moving on Lord Vaelis's lands because he had the best vintage wines in the east and we couldn't afford to lose his vineyards. Given how much of it Titus and I drank the night before, he was probably quite justified in his comment!'

Asander whistled gently through his teeth. 'I don't suppose you're going to tell me what brings you into this stupid situation then, Prince Quintillian? 'Cause it's damn sure no unrequited love thing.'

Quintillian stood silent for a moment, his eyes downcast.

'*It is?* This is over the *empress*? Seven sacred shits in a wooden cup! And you ran away? Like a boy who falls out with his parents? I mean, begging your pardon, Highness, for a lack of appropriate etiquette, but what kind of arsehole are you?'

Quintillian floundered, feeling the colour rising in his cheeks. No one since his mother had been able to provoke that reaction.

'I had to get out. She… she felt the same. It's dangerous. You can't have that sort of thing happen in the court. It could be damaging for the empire.'

'Arsehole,' snapped Asander again. 'Instead you get yourself lost in the wilds. And no one in the capital knows where you are? The army's effectively lost its leader. The emperor will be going out of his mind with worry. And for what? So you don't disturb the harmony of the court? You're an idiot, Your Highness.'

'You don't understand.'

'Bollocks. I'm here because I killed a good man. It was an accident, but the authorities don't know that. I had to get away or I'd be dancing the jig in a tree by now. I had to hide. You? You ran away from making kissy faces? Empires are more robust than that! The empire survived a twenty-year civil war because of men like your father and your grandfather. It can survive a bit of misplaced rumpy.'

Quintillian stared at the man in silence for a long moment, and then began to laugh. He laughed so hard, in fact, that he found difficulty in breathing. Asander simply stood with his arms folded, one eyebrow raised disapprovingly, and catching sight of him like that just made the laughter worse.

'*Bleta alak ulda ghursig!*' bellowed a guttural voice.

'Shit!' Asander quickly grabbed the end of the saw and tried to heave it through the thick branch, with little success since Quintillian was out of breath, recovering from his howling laughter. The prince held up a hand to try and mollify the approaching nomad, whose face was a picture of rage beneath his curious rectal headgear. Arse-hat stepped across two of the fallen branches and shoved Quintillian roughly. The prince staggered a few paces backward but managed to retain his footing.

Asander, giving up on the branch on his own, watched the irate nomad closing on his friend again, and saw the hilarity slide from Quintillian's face, leaving a bleak visage of utter hatred. The scout felt a knot of fear rise into his throat and started to shake his head. Arse-hat was now ranting at the prince in his garbled tongue, too fast and with too unusual words for Asander to be able to follow much. The man shoved Quintillian again, hard, with the palms of his hands, sending the prince tripping back over the next branch. Quintillian recovered himself and rose once more, and Asander felt his spirits sink as he saw his friend's face.

'Don't do it.'

But Quintillian's eyes were flashing angrily.

'Quintus, don't do it!'

Arse-hat gestured towards the deeper forest as he ranted, waving his other arm in the air.

Quintillian hit him.

Asander stared in horror. The blow shouldn't have been a particularly powerful one. There hadn't been a swing, after all, just a short jab, and there wasn't much room for a good thump, but he couldn't deny the evidence of his eyes. The prince's blow had spread the nomad's already wide nose across his face. Blood sheeted down his lips and chin and as Arse-hat staggered back, his mouth opened in shock, and he was now missing both top incisors. His remaining yellow-brown teeth were swimming in blood, which continued to pour from his face as Quintillian lowered his hand, his ire sated for a moment.

'Tell him if he wants to kill me he can, but I will always be better than him.'

Asander shook his head. 'If you do that…'

'*Tell him!*' barked Quintillian, and in that moment he was as imperial as he'd ever been. Asander could see the blood of Darius the Just in him. He turned to the nomad and cleared his throat. Slowly, with some searching for words, he paraphrased Quintillian carefully. The nomad's eyes widened in surprise, then narrowed in anger. Then he began to speak, slowly, so that Asander could follow him. The scout coughed nervously.

'He says he will definitely kill you. But not here. You have insulted him and he wants to kill you in public. We're to go to the nomads' campsite on the edge of the woods and there he will rip you in two.'

'I'll still be better than him.'

Asander scurried over as the nomad probed his nose, hissing, 'Quintus...*Quintillian*...apologize to him. Try and make amends. You're my best hope of getting out of this. I can't afford to let you die in a fight just because you're too proud to bow to him.'

'What makes you think *I'll* die?'

'Will you apologize, you bloody idiot?'

Quintillian stood silent, and as the nomad began shouting to his friends, Asander snorted and folded his arms. 'I wish I didn't know who you are. As a guard you were excellent. As a prince, you're a moron.'

'Call it a test,' Quintillian murmured. 'If we just go on cutting down trees and festering in that disease pit back at Ual-Aahbor, we'll be dead within the month. We have to do something to change the situation. Maybe this is it?'

'And maybe you'll be dead within the hour instead.'

Two more nomads appeared through the woods and after a brief exchange with the wounded Arse-hat they grabbed Quintillian's shoulders and began to manhandle him through the forest. The bloodied nomad drew his straight, razor-edged blade and gestured at Asander to follow.

As they passed through the forest, it became clear that all work had halted. The other worker pairs were being herded to the grassland at the edge of the woods, where they were arranged in a wide circle. The nomads, each with naked blades in their hands, took position around the edge on partial tree trunks or the occasional rocks jutting from the turf.

'I'm guessing this'll be to the death,' Quintillian hissed to his friend as they were herded towards the circle.

'I presume so. Yours, of course.'

With little preamble, Quintillian was shoved roughly through the slaves into the open circle of grass. The wounded nomad took a moment to carefully blot his face, removing the worst of the blood, then he gestured to his face and made some harsh comment that brought a guttural laugh from his friends.

'So how does this work?' Quintillian asked loudly of no one in particular. In answer, Arse-hat drew his sword again and gave it three experimental slashes through the open air, narrowly missing taking the face off one of the circle of slaves. Another of the nomads cast a blade into the ring. It fell to the turf in front of Quintillian and he looked at it with a raised eyebrow.

'Pick it up,' Asander said. 'You have to be armed. It's a matter of pride for him. He has to kill you while you're theoretically able to stop him, else he just looks even worse.'

Quintillian bent and collected the sword, weighing it for a moment, testing the balance and the length. It was a little longer than the sort he was used to, and a little heavier in the blade, but close enough to an imperial cavalry sword that he should be able to handle it reasonably well.

'You were a general,' Asander called, 'but you're also a good fighter. I remember you at the caravan. Hold onto that, and try and survive.'

Quintillian nodded. 'It was high on my list of priorities already, as it happens.'

'Could have fooled me.'

There was a single barked word from one of the nomads and Arse-hat closed on him, swinging his blade back and forth, moving from side to side. It was well done, keeping Quintillian watching every move, unable to commit his balance. The nomad knew enough not to allow his opponent to anticipate an attack too easily. With a sudden side-step to his right, Arse-hat brought his sword up in a diagonal, backhand, aiming for Quintillian's armpit. The prince's blade met the nomad's just in time, knocking it aside but close enough that the sword scored a long, narrow gash across Quintillian's chest, his tunic flapping open and blood suffusing the material in an instant.

The nomads roared their approval as Arse-hat pivoted, spinning back out of reach before the prince could manage a thrust.

'Come on, Quintillian. He's dancing around you.'

The old grey-hair turned to Asander. 'I thought he was called Quintus?'

'Long story. Stupid one, too.'

Arse-hat was coming in again, leaping from foot to foot bow-legged, tossing his sword from right to left, left to right. Quintillian watched as carefully as he could. Where would the next strike come from?

A lunge almost punctured his shoulder, and the leap back out of the way was awkward. Quintillian fell backward and tumbled to the grass, rolling out of harm's way and coming up again close to the edge of the circle, only to discover that the nomad had retreated once more anyway.

'He's playing with you,' Asander shouted.

'I know.'

'You're going to have to put him down.'

'I know.'

The nomad was coming in for a third time, dancing this way and that, grinning bloodily around his missing teeth.

'Do you remember the tale of the Battle of Samada?' Quintillian said quietly. Asander frowned. Of course he did. It was one of the stock battles of antiquity that all soldiers knew about. The first great marshal of the early empire had fought the Pelasian War, and Samada was one of the key strategic locations on the border. Twice, in two successive years, Marshal Crispus had taken the city and held it, only to have it ripped from his grasp by a vastly superior Pelasian force. Then, in the third year of the war, he took it and held it again. This time, when the Pelasian satrap came to rip Samada from his grasp, the aggressor found the city empty. As the Pelasians stalked through the city looking for their suddenly absent foe, the entire place collapsed into the earth, taking a sizeable Pelasian force with it. Crispus had spent six months undermining the place in preparation.

Quintillian had taken two strikes with hardly any attempt at resistance…

Asander straightened, grinning, and looked over the heads of the assembled slaves.

'Go, Marshal. Undermine the bastard!'

As Arse-hat danced closer and closer, he was as unpredictable as ever. Quintillian remained perfectly still, unable to anticipate where the attack would come from. But he knew one thing. He knew where the ground was.

Arse-hat reached the edge of sword-range and began to lurch more, preparing for his blow.

Quintillian dropped to the turf, his blade swinging out wide. The sharp steel smashed into the man's shins as he lurched, rending the flesh and cracking bones. Even as the nomad howled in pain, Quintillian was rolling to the side, a second swing taking the nomad in the back of the legs. There was an unpleasant snapping noise as the metal edge snicked through the tendon at the rear of the man's ankle.

Arse-hat fell, shrieking.

'Undermined,' Quintillian said, as he rolled away from the howling nomad's flailing blade and sprang to his feet with surprising dexterity.

'You have to kill him,' Asander said flatly.

'He can still ride with a ruined ankle.'

'It's nothing to do with that. You've humiliated him twice now. If you don't kill him this afternoon, he will kill you soon, be under no illusion about it.'

Quintillian shrugged. 'Maybe. But one thing I've learned in my time is that a man can surprise you. A corpse can't. Magnanimity is usually rewarded by the gods.'

'Stupidity and lack of foresight aren't,' Asander grunted. 'This isn't court. There's no nobility here. Just brutality and survival.'

But Quintillian had cast the sword back to the turf. Arse-hat was in no state to fight back now, as he rolled around on the grass, screaming and clutching his ruined ankle. Quintillian pushed his way into the circle of slaves and none of the nomads seemed inclined to stop him. Most of them were staring in surprise at the man on the floor, as though they couldn't possibly believe that a slave had bested him. The prince staggered across to Asander and slumped onto a stone next to him, reaching up and running a finger along the fine cut across his chest with a hiss of pain.

'It won't need stitches,' Asander noted. 'With any luck you'll get a day off the logging while it heals, 'cause that'll keep opening up if you work with it unhealed.'

'I'm tiring of this place,' Quintillian whispered. 'I'm starting to think it's time we begin to put together the bare bones of a plan.'

'To escape? I thought you wanted to free yourself and then kill a few of the worst of them?'

'Things have changed,' Quintillian hissed. 'I don't even know where the clan that attacked the caravan are now. There are too many of them, and more by the day and it heralds trouble back home. I think word of this needs to reach an imperial garrison. There's more at stake now than vengeance. We start thinking about feasible ways out. Just you and me. Too many people and we'll fail. Has to be just a couple of us to even stand a chance of success. And while we think and we plan, keep your eyes and your ears open. When we do get out of here, I want to be able to tell our people as much as possible.'

'You really think we'll get out?' Asander muttered.

'I know it. There's too much at stake not to. This isn't a gathering of clans any more, Asander.'

'No?'

'No. It's an army at muster.'

'The clans don't band together to fight. It's not what they do.'

'Evidence suggests things have changed a little.'

Asander frowned, and Quintillian raised a finger and pointed past the gathered crowds. The scout followed his gesture and squinted off over the gentle rise. It took a moment to spot what Quintillian was pointing at, then his eyes widened.

'Shit. *That's* what we're logging for?'

Just visible across the top of the rise were the unmistakable tips of siege engines and artillery. Catapults, bolt-throwers, siege towers, mobile shelters.

'Who taught them that? They're nomads. They don't *do* artillery!'

'Again, evidence suggests that they do now. A people who don't work together are gathering and arming. And there can only really be one target.'

CHAPTER V

Of Powerful Men

The enslaved prince's mercy was repaid, though not in the manner he'd anticipated.

Arse-hat spent the following week glaring furiously at Quintillian. The prince was fairly sure that the nomad would have dismembered him had it not been for his new-found and most unexpected protectors. The situation had required no translation by Asander – it had been easy enough to grasp with just a little observation. Arse-hat, it seemed, had already been not the *most* popular warrior among the clans assigned to slave duties. It appeared that he had done something in the past that both haunted him and tainted his reputation with his own people – perhaps that something had been what had turned him into such a sour specimen in the first place.

Then, being bested by a slave had plunged the man deep into a personal hell. It had made him the laughing stock of his clan. His ignominious defeat and subsequent survival at the whim of Quintillian had left in tatters any reputation the man might still have had.

And so Arse-hat had spent a week scowling at Quintillian, yet unable to do anything about it. While he undoubtedly harboured brutal images of revenge in his heart, he was impotent. Those riders who had taken strongly against Arse-hat had begun to treat Quintillian as some kind of pet. He received extra food rations, had a nice new thick blanket to sleep under, was given first cup of the water at each break, and so on.

Arse-hat openly resented it, and the first opportunity he found to be alone with Quintillian, one of them would surely die. Perhaps he *had* been short-sighted to let the man live, after all. And yet, in a world of hardship and starvation, he was suddenly winning. Well fed, he'd been given a comb and had even been permitted to shave after the imperial fashion. There was a word the nomad womenfolk used around him – *Ba'atu* – which he suspected meant lord or sir, or some such honorific.

Yet despite his odd change in perceived status, nothing had altered fundamentally. He was still a slave. He still cut trees and slept in the compound. And although he still needed to escape, first he had to know more of what they were dealing with. Patience, he kept reminding himself. Precipitous action would only result in failure in some way. And so, over days, Quintillian, with the help of Asander's translation and the freedom of his new-found celebrity, began to ask subtle questions of the few nomads – mostly womenfolk – who would talk to him. Few of them even knew what the empire was, and could name no famous emperor or imperial city. When subtly probed about war, most seemed to consider the Jade Emperor in the east to be the most virulent enemy of the horse clans. He had begun a wall 'as high as the heavens that reached an embrace around his world' to keep the clans out, according to one unusually loquacious source. And the longer Quintillian watched the siege engines growing in size and number, the more he pondered whether they might actually be meant for this strange eastern warlord and not for the empire at all. Perhaps he had leapt to the wrong conclusion initially? But then the slaves cutting the timber were all imperial, he noted, and not one of this eastern monarch's people were in evidence. He had to know more.

Standing in the line behind Asander, Quintillian probed his eye. Two days after the fight, he had been cornered at the latrine trench. Someone – one of his fellow slaves – had thrown a punch that blacked the prince's eye, but before he'd fallen in the latrine and drowned in shit, three nomads had miraculously appeared and helped him out, killing the poor slave who Quintillian assumed had been suborned by Arse-hat simply with the bribe of an extra chunk of bread.

'What's the hold up, I wonder?' Asander murmured, risking a beating just for opening his mouth in the work detail.

Quintillian chewed his lip. 'Something's definitely happening. Have you noticed the walls? The number of guards up there has more than doubled and they're all the best men, I reckon. Lots of shiny armour in evidence. If it weren't for the fact that the gate's open and the foragers are out, I'd think an attack was imminent.'

His friend nodded and the pair fell silent again as a nomad began to stroll along the line, eyeing them all carefully and smacking a few with his stick through simple maliciousness. As he reached Quintillian, he gave the prince a gap-toothed grin, patted him rather hard on the head, and then moved on to abuse some other poor bastard. Once he had disappeared again and the line stood waiting to move, Asander turned his head.

'Look.'

Quintillian glanced past to where his friend nodded, and was interested to see that several of the huge tents were being moved. Not packed for a journey, but repositioned so that a wide path was left from the gate into the heart of the settlement.

'Fascinating.'

Silence reigned in the column, though not in Ual-Aahbor as a whole, where the sounds of nomad life went on unabated. No, not so much *went on* as *increased*. There was a new energy about the place. An expectancy that translated itself into the very noise of the settlement. Time passed, and Quintillian began to hop from one foot to the other and back to keep his legs from seizing up through lack of activity. No one in the queue moved. Despite the fact that the nomads watching them were mostly concentrated in a small group at the front and only occasionally wandered along to check on them, everyone knew better than to move out of line. They were still inside the settlement and punishment would be harsh, if not fatal, for anyone presumptuous enough to step away.

Quintillian frowned. He was sure he'd heard something then amid the general din, but as he concentrated there was nothing to be heard. He sighed and relaxed once more, but then there it was again, insistent and nagging at the edge of his mind.

This time, he could hear it continuing as a tiny thread in the aural tapestry of Ual-Aahbor.

Drums!

A rhythmic beat was being maintained somewhere in the distance, but even as he tried to concentrate on that sound alone, he realized it was getting louder. Whoever it was, they were coming to the settlement. Quintillian perked up with interest. None of the other clans had come or gone with such ceremony.

'Can you hear that?' Asander muttered.

'Yes. Getting closer, too.'

The noise suddenly increased to become the dominant sound in the general hubbub. Despite their view of the outside world being obscured by the high palisade, Quintillian surmised that the drummers – for they were clearly numerous – had just crested the hill and begun the descent into the basin.

Suddenly, the nomad work escort were moving the line. Quintillian and Asander fell into step as the column of slaves were shuffled forward and to the side, further clearing space at the centre. By chance of positioning, they would be among the first to witness the new arrivals, whoever they were.

The drumming, heavy and rhythmic, continued to increase in volume and was soon joined by the slow step of many horses and men and the creak of wooden wheels. Quintillian found himself almost twitching with anticipation.

It seemed ages, though couldn't in truth have been much more than a quarter of an hour, before the nomads near the gate were urged back out of the way and the source of the sounds put in their appearance.

With pomp that would not have been out of place at an imperial procession, the drummers moved through the great, heavy timber gate. Each rode a horse with a red-tasselled caparison, and each wore identical clothing, something Quintillian had not seen thus far among the nomads. The musicians each had a large, heavy drum to their left side, anchored to the saddle, and beat it in time with their horses' steps. Of course, few humans could rival the nomads for their equestrian skills, so not a single hoof was out of step. Quintillian decided to count them too late, and had lost track of how many had entered the settlement before the last put in an appearance, but he'd have put it at around 50, riding in pairs.

There was a gap of perhaps three horse-lengths after the drummers, then came warriors – presumably the best and the bravest, for they rode with the gait and poise of heroes who know their worth. Each of them wore different armour and clothing, but all were a cut above the average nomad's gear, the armour being of the quality and style that an imperial officer would be happy to own. Each had a short, strangely recurved bow over their shoulder. They rode in pairs through the gate and this time, Quintillian counted 32.

The next figure was truly impressive. A lone horseman, he wore silk in blues and browns, with a single engraved steel breastplate his only concession to armour. His face was broad and flat like all the nomads, but with a slightly different look. His eyes were a little more angular, and his hair a glossy black, shaved back from the forehead to behind the ears, where the rest was gathered in a top knot.

He was big. Quintillian hadn't noticed at first, but now he realized that was because of a lack of comparison. His horse was also large, and the man must have stood at almost 7 feet tall when dismounted. The bow over his saddle horn was black and yellow and of clearly unsurpassed quality, and the sword slung at his side was quite simply the longest blade Quintillian had ever seen. He doubted anyone smaller than the rider could manage to handle it.

Asander whistled quietly through his teeth, unable to speak without landing himself in trouble. He'd clearly formed the same opinions as Quintillian.

Here was a truly powerful man, the prince noted. He'd wondered what could ever bring the clans together, and here was a ready answer: the strength of one man. It boded ill for the west, or perhaps for this Jade Emperor in the east. Or possibly both. The horse clans were said to be numberless, roaming the endless steppe right to the roof of the world. And yet despite their skill with bows and horses, their belligerent nature and the sheer number of them, they had never been considered more than a vague threat to border settlements or merchants because they never worked together. Any conflict with a clan of nomads was just that: *a* clan. It was not in their nature to work together. On that all the historians had agreed, and everything Quintillian had observed about their nature in the time he had been here had reinforced that opinion. They may currently be gathered together, but getting them to do anything more complex than simply exist in the same place should be impossible.

Yet somehow they were gathering like an army. The fractious, internecine-warring clans who were incapable of concerted action were breaking the mould. It was a shudder-inducing thought. Suddenly the threat the northern barbarian tribes posed to the empire seemed a paltry thing. This new development presented a very real and very dangerous possibility.

The next horseman, following close behind, he immediately assumed to be some sort of advisor or counsellor. He was older, perhaps nearing 50 summers, and his black hair was shot through with grey. His moustaches and beard were approaching white in colour, and his eyes were also more angular than seemed the norm. He wore no armour and bore no weapons, and his silk robe was a dark red with little ornament.

Then the old man's head turned and his eyes played across the scene, including the slaves, and Quintillian found himself instantly reassessing the situation. The huge warrior was clearly important, but his eyes were hard and stony – a warrior's gaze. *This* man's eyes were like deep wells, reaching into a subterranean sea of dark wisdom. His scrutiny, even in the brief moment it passed Quintillian, was horrifyingly shrewd. While the prince would hate to find himself in a ring of watchers facing off against that huge warrior, the possibility seemed a blessing when compared to the chance of pitting his wits against this old man.

Here was the power in Ual-Aahbor, not the muscle and steel of the man in front. Here was a mind and a will that could take a thousand arguing clans and forge them into an army.

Here was a man who could conquer the world.

Quintillian shivered.

'Shit.'

He hadn't realized he'd said it out loud until the nomad who'd earlier patted him on the head hurried over to him and smacked him painfully on the shoulder with his stick, hissing something at him, and referring to him as *Ba'atu.*

The column of new arrivals stopped at a raised hand from the old man. Behind him came a wagon full of even older men in rich clothes and then another group of mounted warriors, but they all stopped dead. The slave guard realized he'd attracted the attention of the most important people in Ual-Aahbor and turned, ashen-faced, bowing deeply to the old man. The huge warrior turned to look at the guard, one eyebrow lifting curiously.

The older man pursed his lips and regarded both the guard with the stick and Quintillian. Then he opened his mouth and spoke. The prince wasn't sure what he'd expected from the master of Ual-Aahbor – possibly a reedy or hoarse tone – but he certainly wasn't anticipating the smooth, urbane voice that emerged, like silk flowing over a blade. He spoke the guttural tongue of the horse lords, but his velvety tone cancelled out the harshness Quintillian associated with the language. He was fascinated by this man, and it occurred to him that the fact might be mutual, for the old man was questioning the guard and using that same title: *Ba'atu.*

Quintillian stood silent, listening to the exchange. Asander could hopefully translate later on.

Then, suddenly, in that silky voice, the old man addressed Quintillian directly.

'This man tells me that you are a nobleman. Possibly even a prince. What do you have to say for yourself?'

Quintillian blinked. The man spoke the imperial tongue with absolute precision and a very slight accent of the eastern provinces. For a moment he floundered. If he told the truth, then he could be placing himself in grave peril – worse than simply being worked to death. A prince of the imperial family would be a valuable hostage, after all. But then Asander had already revealed damning information during the duel at the forest, which had led to this *Ba'atu* title being associated with him. He'd used his real name and referred to him as a marshal. The empire only had four marshals and anyone who was remotely familiar with the west in the current generation would put marshal and Quintillian together and come up with just one inescapable conclusion. Plus, he was fairly certain that this man was clever enough to piece almost anything together given even the most rudimentary facts. Honesty, it seemed, was the only feasible option.

'I have the honour of being Marshal Quintillian, commander of the Third Army, prince and brother of the emperor, Lord of Munda. In rather reduced circumstances currently, due to a twist of fate.'

There was a heavy silence for a moment, then the huge warrior muttered something in his own tongue, to which the old man replied with a smile. Then he turned back to Quintillian.

'An imperial marshal. I am impressed. And rather saddened to find you in such a situation, despite the clear advantage at which it places me. I would speak with you when I am settled in my palace.' He gestured at the guard, and spoke once more in their indecipherable tongue. The man bowed again and the old man smiled and kicked his steed into action, urging the procession onward.

'That was dangerous,' Asander whispered, once the column was moving. The guard glared at him for speaking, but clearly felt nervous about disciplining him after the previous incident.

'Drawing attention to myself or giving my real identity?'

'Both. You'll be the centre of attention now.'

'That might be good, Asander. I've been wracking my brains trying to think of a way to break out, but leaving that slave compound seems impossible. Perhaps this change in circumstances will give me the opportunity I'm looking for.'

'Not me, though,' sighed Asander.

'I'll make sure to bring you with me. This monkey with his stick might not be amenable to persuasion, but I suspect I can convince the old man that I need you.'

'I hope so.'

The guard finally decided that enough was enough and jammed his stick between the two of them, pushing Asander away. Another of the slave detail gave the command to march and the column began to file towards the gate, but the man with the stick held Quintillian back and gestured to the compound. It appeared there would be no log-cutting for the prince today.

He had an appointment to keep.

CHAPTER VI

Of Clans and Overlords

The palace wasn't what Quintillian had expected. Of course, with no frame of reference, he wasn't at all sure what he expected, but this definitely wasn't it. He had seen enough of the inside of the nomads' great circular tents now to form an opinion of their decor. It involved a lot of rugs, both on the ground and hanging on walls. Everything seemed to be made of horse. Even the rugs, he suspected, were woven by hand from horse tails. The horse clans were a people who had virtually nothing, so they wasted no part of what they did have. Their only concessions to outside goods seemed to be armour and weapons and the silk that came from the east. It was all dyed with basic hues acquired from plants, and yet somehow contrived to be drab even with a mix of colours.

Not so the palace.

In the large lobby where he'd been escorted by the guard with the stick and made to wait, he'd been surprised to see a painting some 20 feet long stretching along a wall. Strolling over, assuming he would be allowed, he examined it. It had been painted by a master on a single long sheet of quality paper. Impressive. No manufacturer in the empire could make paper that fine, and certainly not in long continuous strips. Most writing was still done on vellum. The painting seemed to be a story and told of a battle between two nations that looked very similar – similar to the old man and the huge warrior in particular. Neither were horse clans. Both armies were huge and involved a number of infantry.

The battle raged across a walled city that, if it were real, would probably rival Velutio for its impressive defences. It seemed the besieging army were the heroes of the piece, and yet the tale told of a defeat and the ignominious destruction of the army.

Quintillian rocked back on his heels, feeling the plushness of the fine blue carpet beneath.

'It is my grandfather.'

He turned in surprise. The huge, powerful warrior had entered the lobby with impressive stealth for one so large, and was standing with his arms folded not far from Quintillian.

'Which one?'

'The one having his head removed before the walls of the city he failed to take.'

Quintillian nodded and cleared his throat. 'Isn't it unusual to commemorate a failure in such a manner?'

The big man stepped across and stood next to Quintillian, which he found to be rather disturbing, since his head was not quite at the man's shoulder. 'My father had the painting commissioned as a reminder. A warning to push him ever onward, for to pause is to fail and to fail is to die.'

'The... lord... of Ual-Aahbor is your father?'

The big man nodded. 'He is the Khan. The overlord of the clans. And he wishes to see you. Come.'

The warrior turned and strode off through the palace. As Quintillian fell in alongside him, the huge man glanced sidelong at him.

'You are clever. And dangerous. Your eyes remind me of my father's.'

'I shall try to take that as a compliment.'

'You should know that I have already made my feelings known. That you should be executed immediately. The council of elders believe that you are too important to waste, and my father's ideas are an enigma as always, but I? I see only trouble from you. I would kill you myself, were it not for my father staying my hand... for now.'

'But then how would we have such delightful conversations?' Quintillian smiled.

The warrior grunted, and moments later they emerged into a wide corridor lined with coloured paper lamps that glowed with fascinating images of dragons and monsters. At the end of the vestibule were twin doors with gold handles, they were covered with red leather picked out in gold patterns. Two guards stood at the door, well-armed and clearly very competent. At a gesture from the big warrior, the doors were swung open and Quintillian entered the Khan's throne room.

This large chamber was lit with similar paper lanterns and heated by braziers that contained some heady spice that gave the entire room a pleasant aroma. The old man sat on a carved wooden chair, draped with colourful materials. In the corner, a young man with sightless, staring white eyes picked out a beautiful melody on some sort of strange harp. The old men who had arrived in the cart were seated on low cushions around a firepit.

'Ah, good,' the Khan spoke. 'The prince.'

Quintillian bowed his head. This Khan was the equivalent of his brother, or the God-King of Pelasia, and the rules of etiquette were clear.

'My advisors will not be taking part in this meeting, though they will remain in the room. None of them speak your tongue. In fact, only my son and I have a good grasp of it, barring a few clansmen who have spent time in your borderlands. Translation will be difficult for them and it is not appropriate for the great Khan or the champion warrior of the clans to demean themselves and sink to the level of interpreter.'

Quintillian paused for a moment to make sure the old man was not about to continue, then smiled. 'I have a friend in the slave camp who is competent in both tongues. Perhaps he could fill in the role?'

The Khan chewed his lip for a moment. 'Yes. The next time we speak – if there *is* a next time – you may bring him. I wish to ask you a few questions.'

Quintillian smiled cautiously. 'You will be aware that I am not willing to give out information that would imperil my people.'

The Khan laughed. 'I do not seek military information, young prince. Be assured that anything I wish to know of the empire's defences I will find out readily enough in due course. No, I wish to know about your world.'

The prince remained silent and the Khan leaned forward, his chin resting on his palm. 'I am very familiar with the lands of the Jade Emperor, and with the steppe of my nomad brothers, but I have never seen your empire. In the libraries of Jiong-Xhu are texts written by eastern travellers who have made contact with the empire in the export of silk. They say that the empire's lands are universally fertile. That any crop will grow there and grow well.

They say your emperors have built palaces of silver and gold. They are almost certainly exaggerated, fantastical tales. But most tales begin with a grain of truth. I wish to know what the empire is like. To live in, I mean.'

Quintillian stretched and folded his arms. 'I will tell you of my empire, but first tell me why you wish to know.'

'Is it not obvious?' the old man frowned. 'I intend to own it.'

And there it was. The confirmation that Quintillian needed. This Khan had no designs on the Jade Emperor's lands. In fact, it seemed likely that he was *from* there, originally. He felt a jolt of dread as there could now be no doubt that the weight of the innumerable horse clans and that growing collection of siege engines were meant for the west. He had to warn his brother… unless, perhaps, the Khan could be persuaded away from such a course of action? He was a superbly intelligent man, after all.

'I have brought the clans together with a dream,' the Khan said in a dream-like voice. 'A dream of conquest. The riders know your empire to be easy pickings, for they have raided across your borders for centuries. But now they will come in force, and will take your empire for their own.'

Quintillian shook his head. 'The clans do not *need* our lands. I have seen how they live. They would never adjust to such a life.'

'I see things differently. I am descended from a people to the north of the Jade Emperor's lands, who were nomadic in just the same manner as these clans. And they became a settled culture in time. All it requires is the will to impose change, and I have that will. Where my father failed and lost a world, I shall succeed and create a new one. I have achieved the impossible and turned the warring clans into a unified people. Now we will seek out more agreeable lands for them.'

'All so you can have a new painting made where it is my brother dying in disgrace while your flag flies over the walls of Velutio? That seems at odds with the wisdom so evident in your manner.'

'Do not presume to speak of things you do not understand, Prince Quintillian.'

'You do not need to invade,' Quintillian said quietly. 'Our palaces are built of stone, not gold or silver. There are places in our empire where the sun sears the land and little will grow, and other places where the snow never departs and crops are but a dream. We have as many problems as any other nation. If you seek in the empire a new idyll for your people, then you are mistaken. And the empire has a large, professional army. We have fought wars for a thousand years, honing our skills. To achieve this fantasy paradise, the conquest would be a hard fight and with uncertain outcome – would you wish to have your son instead commit a new painting showing your own death before the walls of Velutio?'

The Khan's eyes hardened for a moment. 'Be careful, young prince. I do not anger easily, but when I do, my rage unchecked can kill kingdoms.'

'All I wish is to avoid a conflict that will ruin two peoples. If you seek the advantages that the empire has to offer, they can easily and readily be obtained through trade and negotiation, and I am the perfect broker for that work.'

The Khan shook his head. 'You do not understand the fundamental nature of the clans. They understand trade and negotiation and will practise such when there is no alternative. But their very culture is based upon taking what they want and using everything up. The dream I have given them is of conquest. I gave them a vision of the future and in return they give me their strength and loyalty. If I take away that dream and offer them only negotiation, this alliance will fall apart in a heartbeat. Be grateful, young prince, that I have impressed upon them the importance and value of conquest and occupation. There are many that do not understand the need to occupy and would be happier ravaging the empire, firing its cities, stealing its valuables and raping and slaughtering its inhabitants. They are a simple people, Prince Quintillian. They see compromise as weakness and negotiation as failure. To them there is only the raid. You may think that I am the only thing focusing them on your empire, but now, I am rather the only thing keeping them focused on occupation rather than devastation.'

'You bring siege engines and cavalry to take the empire, though? A mismatched force, surely? Your people are not besiegers. They are raiders. They are not suited to attacking cities and fortresses. I would hate to meet their like on the plains in open battle, but behind walls? They will be to Velutio as gnat bites to a horse. Faced by the full imperial might of the four armies, you cannot hope to achieve your goal. Abandon this folly now, Khan, before half the world is strewn with corpses.'

'I am growing tired of the direction of this conversation, Prince Quintillian. I brought you here to ask you about your empire and instead I find myself justifying my actions to you instead. Quit your bargaining, young lord. The campaign is already begun and nothing can turn the clans from their course. Soon we will cross the border. We will make for your capital and we will break it, for unlike the clans, the empire is like a serpent: when the head is removed, the body will shudder and die. And I fear not your military. I am no fool. I have had agents in the west for over a year paving the way for me. You would be surprised – horrified too, I might suggest – at the lack of resistance we will meet when we come. The best future for the empire now is to lay down their arms and accept us when we come, for I would have your people intact, not festering in the burial pits. I have no wish to rule a land of bones and dead flesh.'

'I find that I also have entirely lost my appetite for this discussion,' Quintillian said in a quiet, acidic tone.

The Khan simply waved him away, and Quintillian turned, the huge warrior falling in next to him. As they passed back out into the corridor and the doors closed behind them, the big man grinned. 'You did well.'

'I did?'

'Yes. My father is very hard to anger. Keep going like this and he will acquiesce to my demand to tear you limb from limb.'

'Wonderful.'

'When he has calmed down and considered matters he will send for you again. But you smell of the latrine. It is not fitting that you stand in my father's hall looking and smelling like this. I will have a room made ready for you in the palace and clean clothes sent to you.'

Quintillian frowned. 'Solicitude now, on the back of death threats? You are every bit as enigmatic as your father, you know that?'

'Oh, no, Prince soldier, I am not a complicated man. I am a warrior and a Khan's son. I wish to make my father proud, and so I will look after you as long as he sees a need for you. But as soon as he has no further use for you, I shall gut you and leave you for a sky burial.'

Quintillian frowned again as he realized they were not making their way to the main entrance again, but had instead turned into a new area of the palace. The warrior threw open a door and the prince stared. In the centre of the wooden room stood a huge bronze bath tub, its fittings moulded into the shape of a dragon, so that it stood upon four clawed feet.

'A bath?'

'So that you do not smell of shit when you are next called. The clansmen care not whether they smell of horses or blood, or dirt or faeces, but my father has refined tastes. Slaves will come with hot water and appropriate lotions for you.' He gave Quintillian a hard glance from hooded, inscrutable eyes. 'Try not to drown. I am looking forward to your death in so many inventive ways.'

And then the big man was gone, closing the doors, and Quintillian was alone in the bathroom. Well, even though his worst fears for the empire had been realized, one good thing had come out of this: he was in the palace and no longer trapped in that slave compound. And if Asander could be brought here too, then their chances of flight had just increased dramatically.

And so had the necessity for it.

CHAPTER VII

Of the Invisibility of Slaves

Four days passed with a strange sense of strangled civility. The perfectly refined and cultured situation in the palace could easily have been an echo of Quintillian's previous life in Velutio, were it not for the constant overhanging sense of threat. Each day, Quintillian had been sent for by the Khan at around the time ofthe noon meal, and the two would sit in an edgy courteousness, discussing the most odd and mundane of topics. It had quickly become clear that the Khan had been entirely truthful in that he had no interest in learning of military matters.

The subjects had flowed quick and fast, but with the smoothness of interested conversation, from the architecture of the great bathhouses and the triumphal arches of long-gone emperors to the paintings of the eastern masters to the best methods of growing cabbages – though on subjects like the latter, Quintillian could be of little help. They discussed the sources of the best dyes, the nature of both red and black pottery and its aesthetic value. What were the various dialectical differences between regions? Was market day observed on the same day throughout the empire? Were markets small individual civic affairs or were they more like the nomads' version where clans would travel for many days to attend a giant central market?

It went on.

The one thing they learned to avoid was any hint of the coming conflict. After the first day's meeting, the Khan had refused to be drawn on the matter. The second day had almost ended in violence when Quintillian pushed the subject of conciliation just a little too hard and drove the Khan to anger. Now, the threat of war hung over them like a bad smell, but just like a smell, could not become the subject of polite conversation.

Asander had joined them on the third day and had proved invaluable, being brought into the palace and given a room next to Quintillian. With the former scout acting as a high-speed translator, it was possible for the council of elders to become involved, and they had almost as many questions as their master.

Apart from the hour or two each day when their presence was required to inform the Khan more and more about the world of which he intended to become master, the two men were left largely to their own devices. They were subtly checked upon periodically when slaves came to sort their bedding or bring them food or extra clothes and the like. But there was no doubt that for all the pleasantness of their current life compared with their compatriots in the outer compound, they were still very definitely slaves. When they strayed too close to the vestibule, which seemed to be the only way in or out of the palace, the guards rather forcefully turned them back, making it clear that they were to stay where they were told. Similarly, their rooms had no windows and were illuminated only by the small oil lamps that the slaves kept fuelled. They were not permitted into the Khan's personal area of the palace, and the guards there were even more forthright about the two slaves' lack of freedom.

And yet they were well fed, and their privileged status was easily seen reflected in the envious eyes of the other slaves who attended them, who themselves had to return to the outside compound at night and defecate in a ditch. Asander and Quintillian were allowed to use the latrine in the bathroom, which consisted of a wooden seat over a drop into a quagmire outside the palace, which had been sown with the most powerfully-scented plants that grew on the steppe in an attempt to lessen the stink. It largely failed. That first day, Quintillian had examined the seats with a view to squeezing through the latrines and swimming the cesspool for escape. Ignoring entirely the clearly unpleasant aspects of the plan, it was clear that no human being, no matter how diminutive, was going to fit through the hole. The Khan's men weren't that stupid.

But there *would* be a way out. Quintillian was sure of it.

Here, now, on the fifth day since the Khan's arrival at Ual-Aahbor, Quintillian stood in the corner of the bathroom, busily fastening the strange eastern clothes he had been given, then flattening his damp hair with the palms of his hands. They were required by the Khan within the hour, and it had become customary to bathe and dress in fresh clothes for the meetings – both he and Asander.

The scout busily towelled himself off. Both men had served on campaign and, despite Quintillian's lofty rank, he had made it his business to share the hardships of his soldiers. One thing his father had always impressed on him was the value of being seen as one of the men. It was, to a politician or a general, worth more than gold. And so both men had shared bathing facilities with others. Of course, Quintillian had also bathed in public in the great bathhouses of Velutio, though it seemed that Asander had visited the capital only once, the day of the hiring, and was otherwise used only to smaller provincial bathing establishments.

The two men tidied themselves for the coming meeting in silence as the slave scooped a bucket of used water from the bath and took it away for disposal. Once he was gone and they were alone, Asander closed the door.

'I spoke to one of the more talkative slaves this morning.'

'Oh?'

'The slave compound is unusually full today. It seems that the logging party has not been out over the last two days. You know what that means?'

Quintillian nodded sombrely. 'That they've stopped. They've finished the siege engines. I've also noted that the newly-arrived clan chiefs generally present themselves to the Khan, and there have been between five and ten a day until yesterday. Since yesterday morning there have been two. I think the full strength of the clans has finally gathered. Their army is almost ready to move.'

'You know that if we're going to go, we have to go soon, then.'

Quintillian smiled. 'It is foremost in my mind, Asander.'

'And yet we're no closer to finding a way.'

'Ah,' the prince said with a sly grin, 'I think I might have an idea there.'

Asander finished drying himself and threw on his nomad-style leather trousers and loose-fitting tunic. 'Well?'

'Slaves might as well be invisible, you agree?'

'To the masters, slaves are little more than furniture, especially here.'

'I've been watching the slaves in this place, and they keep taking away our used plates and cups, our bathwater, the pisspot from the rooms and so on.'

'Yes?'

'Well, where do they take them?'

Asander frowned. 'I have no idea. Why hadn't that occurred to me?'

'I know they don't take them out through the vestibule, 'cause I've seen slaves being turned back by the guards there, just like we are. And wherever they take all the waste, they can't be keeping it inside the palace. The Khan is too civilized for that. Which means that they are leaving the palace somehow, or at the very least there is an aperture…'

'A what?'

'An aperture. A window, then. Big enough to empty a bucket through. And if that's the case, there is always the possibility that a person can get through it.'

'What do you suggest, then?'

Quintillian shrugged. 'Only way we're going to learn more is to follow them. How about now, since we've more than half an hour still to waste?'

They peered at the bath. There were probably still three buckets' worth of used water to get rid of. Sure enough, as they fell silent and waited, Asander fastening his belt and pulling on the strange leather slippers he had been left, they could hear the slave approaching once more with his clunking bucket.

'We'll have to be really careful,' Asander hissed. 'You know what these slaves are like. They've been pushed to the edge of their humanity. If they think we're causing trouble, they'll sell us out to the Khan's men in a heartbeat. They'll see it as a chance to improve their own lot.'

Quintillian nodded. 'And I don't want to give them any more fuel to prod the Khan into giving me to his son.'

The Khan's offspring, whose name they had discovered was Ganbaatar, had settled into a habit of constant threat to both men, making it quite clear that the moment his father lost interest in them, he would personally supervise their execution, and would make it sublimely painful. He had already taken to carrying his favourite flaying knives in his belt against the very chance his father tired of the new pets.

The huge warrior made Quintillian shudder. Not because of his strength and power, or even because of the clear streak of vicious cruelty that ran through his veins, but because that cruelty was so neatly and expertly bound up in civility. It was like speaking to a demon in the shape of a priest. You could talk to Ganbaatar and find yourself enjoying the pleasant banter right up to the point where he mentioned feeding you your own testicles.

It seemed that Ganbaatar was the Khan's son by the daughter of a horse clan chieftain, so while the Khan maintained a tenuous control over the assembled fractious army by pure wit and strength of mind, the nomads saw the son as one of their own. He was revered partially for his skills with sword, bow and horse, and partially for his fanatical loyalty to the clans and hatred of their neighbour states.

The prince's musings halted suddenly as the slave with the bucket bumbled into the room and scooped up another load of bathwater, turning and carrying it from the room once more. The two men waited until he was gone and then started to move quietly out into the corridor, following him at a discreet distance. It took only a few steps to realize that the leather slippers were too creaky and heavy to allow for a stealthy pursuit, and both men quickly slipped them off and tucked them into their belts before moving off again.

The slave seemed entirely oblivious to the two men behind him as he carried his sloshing bucket, his burden and his own footfalls largely masking the sounds of pursuit. After a few turns, the slave moved through one of the larger main sections of the palace where two nomad guards were busy chattering. Neither even glanced at the small, stooped figure with the bucket. Quintillian and Asander, still in the shadows a small way back, shared a look and shrugged. Brazen seemed the most sensible option, so the pair waited until the slave had moved into the next corridor, slipped their leather shoes back on, and strolled out into the open area, muttering meaningless nothings to each other, certain that the guards couldn't follow their language anyway.

Sure enough, despite their mode of dress, the guards managed a quick glance in their direction, wrote them off as meaningless, and went on with their conversation. Quintillian and Asander moved into the next corridor and, ten steps into the shadows, slipped off the shoes once more, padding fast in their bare feet to catch up. They reached a junction, and with no sight of the bucket slave, paused for a moment. The palace hummed with life, but it took only a moment to pick out the sound of something wooden being opened somewhere in the distance to their left. Presuming this to be the work of the slave, the pair scurried along in that direction.

They rounded another corner, the sound of pouring liquid now confirming their path, and then another as they heard the wooden portal shut.

Quintillian's heart thumped as they rounded yet another corner and came face to face with the bucket slave. The man yelped and raised his bucket threateningly.

'What are you doing here?' he snapped in a northern imperial accent. His eyes narrowed suspiciously.

'We got lost,' Asander said quietly, his voice cracking with tension at the surprise encounter.

'Barefoot?' the man hissed. 'It ain't *that* warm. What are you *really* up to?'

'Listen,' Quintillian began, but the slave took a step back. 'I think we should talk to the guards, eh?'

'There's no need for that,' Quintillian murmured placatingly. The slave opened his mouth to reply, his expression hard, but nothing emerged as Asander's arm shot out and grabbed the man by the throat, choking off sound. The smaller, older man struggled furiously, and tried to smash the bucket down on Asander's head, but the blow failed, painfully trapping his own wrist in the handle instead.

'Don't kill him,' hissed Quintillian.

'What?'

'He's one of us. An imperial citizen. Don't kill him.'

'Bollocks, my prince.'

'And he might be missed.'

'While that's true, he's less likely to rat us out to the guards for an extra meal if he's cold and grey.'

Quintillian gave his friend a hard look, but Asander met his gaze with steely indifference as he squeezed until there was a crunch from the slave's neck and his head lolled to one side, the life fading from his eyes.

'There was no need for that,' accused Quintillian.

'I disagree. Princes can afford fancy morals and principles, but slaves can't. It was him or us, whether you believe that or not. Come on.'

Asander moved off along the shadowed corridor, the lamps burning only at very sparse intervals against the danger of fire in a wooden palace. There had been a moment when Quintillian had contemplated the potential of firing the entire palace in order to create the chaos required to effect a convincing escape. But the sad truth was that the most likely outcome of such a course of action would be the pair of them burning to death rather than escaping. The treated timber would go up just a little *too* easily.

As the former scout carried the old man's body with relative ease, Quintillian stooped and scooped up the bucket, following on. One more turn, and they entered a small timber room. Quintillian breathed a sigh of relief. Here was a barrel of water, a table with a stone slab, presumably used for preparing meat, and a wooden door, heavy and basic, held shut with a single bar that slid into sockets on either side.

'That looks promising.'

Placing the bucket on the slab, Quintillian crossed to the door and as quietly and carefully as he could, lifted the bar from its place, standing it to one side. Asander joined him as, very slowly, he inched the door open, enough to apply an eye to the gap.

It took a moment after the dingy corridors to adjust to the bright daylight of late morning.

Outside, he could see the high palisade wall of Ual-Aahbor, with one of the watch platforms almost directly opposite, the guard atop it and a ladder reaching from there to the grass below. There were perhaps 40 paces of open ground between the palace wall and the palisade. At this time of day there would be little hope of crossing from the one to the other without drawing deadly attention.

At night, though?

And then there was the pit.

The palace's small door was, after all, here for a reason. Immediately outside the door stood another pit, not unlike the one that lurked below the latrines. This one didn't smell quite so bad, since it seemed that no one defecated in it. But waste had been poured into it continually for months, and very likely urine had gone into the mix. And the pit was large, stretching some 10-feet-by-10-feet and at least 3 feet down to the crusted surface, which now swam with recently added bath water.

They *might* be able to get round it…

'I wonder how solid that surface is?' Quintillian murmured, pulling the door open wider so that Asander could also assess the situation.

'I'll find out,' the scout replied casually, and dropped the body of the bucket slave into the pit. The corpse hit the unpleasant surface with a squelch and a crack, and then, with revolted fascination, the two men watched the crust open up like a wound and give vent to the most godawful stink. The body slid with disgusting finality into the mire below the surface, vanishing with a gloopy noise that Quintillian suspected would revisit him in his dreams for the rest of his life.

'Then we'll have to get round it. Shouldn't be too much trouble, though we'll have to do it at night, obviously.'

'Do we go tonight?' Asander asked.

'I don't think so. We can't really afford to delay, but then we also can't afford to go without adequate preparation. How do we get up the ladder without simply being picked off by the man at the top? How do we get down the other side? That's almost a 50-foot drop. I don't know about you, but I've never jumped that far in my life. Sounds like a broken leg waiting to happen.'

Asander shrugged. 'We bring our blankets from our rooms. Tie them together, anchor them at the top of the palisade and use them to get most of the way down the outside. That should make it safer.'

'Good. Though each platform is within sight of the next, so we'll have to figure out how to do it without being seen by the guards to either side. And still we need to actually get up there and deal with the man at the top first. He's unlikely to let two slaves climb his ladder unchallenged.'

'True.'

The two men paused for one last look out of the door, then closed it and slid the bar back into place. The slave might be missed but given his resting place it seemed highly unlikely he would ever be found. Slowly, they padded back to the bathroom, bringing the bucket with them to reduce suspicion that anything had happened in that small chamber. Fortunately, as they passed the more open area, the two guards had now gone, and the pair reached the bath suite unobserved. There they finished dressing and slipped their footwear back on.

'We don't smell of that pit, do we?'

'I don't think so.'

'Time to head off to our meeting with his noble majesty, then,' Asander muttered.

The two men slipped from the bathroom and made their way through the more familiar ways of the palace. As they passed into the large hallway which contained the doors to the Khan's throne room, Quintillian suddenly grabbed hold of Asander's shoulder, arresting his movement.

'What is it?'

'What is it?' Quintillian grinned. 'It's the answer. Look.'

The two weary guards at the Khan's door were busy shouldering their weapons and then strode off out toward the outer vestibule as two fresh, energetic men took their place, readying their own pole-arms.

'Guard change,' the two men said in unison.

'They swap four times a day on the walls,' Asander muttered quietly. 'I remember seeing them from the slave compound. Noon, dusk, midnight and dawn, or near enough.'

'Midnight's our time, then,' Quintillian nodded. We can take the place of the relief guard, who can climb the ladder without arousing suspicion. We'll have to be ready and in position at least an hour before, in case we miss him. I'm thinking now that we might be better going tonight.'

'Agreed.'

With speeding hearts and a sense of palpable expectation, the two men crossed the room to the guards, who nodded to them and swung open the door. They were expected.

The following hour represented a new height of strangeness for the two slaves as they answered banal questions on the nature of life in the empire. As they discussed various crafts and factories that dealt with goods entirely unheard of by the nomads, Quintillian maintained as blank and plain an expression as he could manage, though all the time, his brain threw questions and images at him.

How would they bring down the relief guard and take his place unnoticed?

Could they guarantee moving through the palace to the slave door without being seen?

How would they deal with the makeshift blanket rope from the platform without being noticed by others?

Once they were down the other side, how would they get away without being caught by riders?

And, periodically, his mind would furnish him with unsought images. The slave in Asander's grip, his head tilting unnaturally with a crack. The body sinking into the oozy surface of the refuse pit. Ganbaatar's expression of barely suppressed lust at the thought of their execution as he fingered his flaying knives.

From the look on Asander's face, he also was struggling with similar images and ponderances. Quintillian hoped he was managing to look less troubled and distracted than his friend, though he was less than sure he had managed.

This time, the Khan was a little more forthcoming with his own thoughts, though not of the intended invasion itself. Conversation had drifted to the subject of fishing. The Khan was familiar with fishing fleets from his time in the Jade Emperor's lands, but the nomads, including his council of elders, were entirely uncomprehending of the subject. The closest the clans had ever come to the subject of fishing fleets was dropping a net or a baited line into one of the high mountain rivers and catching occasional freshwater fish. The Khan even chuckled as he described how the nomads had reacted when he'd first explained the sea and ships to them.

'They could not comprehend the very idea of an ocean. I had to describe it as being like the endless grass of the steppe, but made instead of water. I used the analogy of horses and carts as ships and the clans as fleets. The conversation went on for many days, and even now I do not think they believe what I told them. When they see your Eastern Sea and Nymphaean Sea, they will be collectively baffled. I have to admit to looking forward to that.'

He went on to explain that just as the craftsmen who worked in things with which the nomads were unfamiliar would be exalted among the conquered and would have a special place in the new world, so also would the empire's sailors. Because there would be none among the conquerors who could even understand a boat, let alone handle one, the sailors would be greatly treasured by their new overlords.

By the time the session had been completed, Quintillian had answered only one of his own questions:

Once they were over from the wall, the main danger would be from archers on the platforms. On the assumption that by the time they hit the ground running, their escape would be noticed, they would need to zig and zag across the grass to reduce the risk of taking an arrow, and hope that the gods were looking favourably upon them, given the acknowledged high level of archery skill among the nomads. It would take precious moments for the unprepared riders to grab their horses and open the great gate in the wall, which was kept sealed at night. Then they would need to circumnavigate the outside of Ual-Aahbor to get to the point of the escape which, fortunately due to the rear position of the palace, would be diametrically opposite the gate. That would take time. They could ride fast, but Quintillian had been in battle more than once and knew the turn of speed of which a human was capable when desperation nipped at his heels.

It would be touch and go, but he believed the two of them could make it to the lip of the great depression before the riders were in the right area and ascending to pursue. Once at the top they would lose themselves among those twisted rock formations, and gradually circle round to the southeast. Quintillian had been thinking long and hard on their estimated location. He had estimated the distance they had come and the direction since their capture, and he was fairly sure that a south by southeast route would bring them into the edge of the eastern provinces not far from the border with the Inda. There, they could find an imperial outpost, acquire horses, and move fast along good metalled roads to the heart of the empire. With luck, two things would happen. The Khan and his men would believe that Quintillian had gone directly west, that being the shortest route to the capital. And the Khan's army would move slowly, rather than with the traditional swiftness of the nomads, due to the need to protect the slow siege engines. If all worked out the way he hoped, he would have time to take the safest, most circuitous, route home, and yet could still get there in time to warn his brother of what was coming.

Finally, the interview was over, and the two men were escorted out, as usual, by Ganbaatar. As the doors swung to behind them and the two guards moved to block the entrance once more, the big warrior fell in behind them as they walked.

'My father believes there is something troubling you. He thinks you are distracted. He tasks me with discovering what weighs upon your mind. In myself I think you are sly and untrustworthy and are planning something. My father is too trusting and womanly sometimes. He cannot see the darkness in you, because he seeks only the light. Give me your lie, that I might take it to him and tell him what it truly is.'

Quintillian shrugged as naturally as he could manage, his heart racing.

'I am nervous. You are ready to move against the empire. We have seen that the engines are complete and the clans are almost fully assembled. I am looking at the end of my world gathering around me. I would challenge you to feel any different.'

Next to him, Asander nodded and tried to convey a similar fear through his expression.

Ganbaatar sneered. 'I think you are made stronger than that, prince liar. I think you are planning something. But I will take this lie to my father. It is as good as any other. Know that my eyes will be upon you and when you prove me right I will first strip the flesh from your bodies and salt the raw pink, and *then* explain myself to my father.'

With a last glare of hatred, the warrior turned and made his way back to the throne room.

'That settles it,' Quintillian muttered, as they turned the corner into the slave quarters. 'Now we *have* to go tonight.'

CHAPTER VIII

Of Plans and Their Execution

The palace still thrummed with faint sounds of activity even now that many of the occupants were abed. The Khan himself and some of his cronies would likely be awake, since it had come to Quintillian's attention that the overlord of the clans slept little and late, planning or conversing with those of like mind far into the night. Fortunately, the route from their rooms to the slave door skirted around the noble areas of the palace and would at no point come into proximity with the Khan.

'How does it look?'

Quintillian peered out from the corridor left and right and then pulled his head back in sharply.

'Shit. There are people in the main hall.'

'No chance of getting past them, I suppose?'

The prince rearranged the blanket rope that hung across his shoulder and peeked out again. In the brighter-lit area, where the vestibule was wider and higher and contained more lamps, four figures were in conversation with a fifth, who he couldn't quite see, out of sight around a corner.

'Five of them at least. Too chancy. I suppose we could be slaves carrying fresh blankets, but it's not worth risking everything now. I say we wait for them to go first.'

Asander nodded and the pair lurked in the corridor, casting up prayers to the gods that no slave came along the shadowy passage and happened upon them in such a suspicious position. Quintillian focused on the conversation in the room. He'd picked up at most four or five basic words of the nomad tongue, but it was often interesting how easy it was to determine the nature of a conversation just from the tone of voice of the participants.

His blood chilled. 'I know that voice.'

Asander squeezed his eyes shut as he listened. 'Ganbaatar,' he muttered. 'He's rearranging the guard. Why?'

'Could be to do with the fact that they're preparing to move in the next few days? The clans are probably already being readied. Could be just a freak thing, maybe. Or it could be the bastard's suspicious mind. For a big, lumbering man, he's not as daft as I expected.'

Asander listened some more. 'He's distributing men around the palace. That can't be a coincidence. We should have gone yesterday.'

'Very helpful.'

They stood in nervous silence for a moment, and then the conversation broke up. The unseen figure of Ganbaatar moved off, taking three of the four others with him and leaving one guard in the vestibule.

'That tears it. If we commit now, we have to be really fast,' Quintillian sighed.

'I guess there'll be no bare-facing our way past him.'

The prince shook his head. 'If Ganbaatar is setting extra guards because he's sure something's up, then those men are going to question every unexpected move. We'll never get past him by stealth. We'll have to take him out on the way past, quickly and quietly.'

Asander fixed him with a calculating look. 'You realize what that means? They're bound to check on him every now and then. As soon as they find him gone, the alarm will go up and the whole palace will be looking for us.'

'So we go now and we go quickly. That way we buy ourselves the longest possible breathing time before they know what we're doing. Come on.'

As they prepared to duck out of the corridor, the prince gestured to Asander to move first and to head along the left hand wall of the room. The scout frowned for a moment but nodded and, with a deep breath, strode from the passage into the brightly-lit vestibule. The guard barked something in his raspy, harsh language and spun, levelling a spear that had a strange, almost sickle-shaped, tip, at the scout. Asander stopped dead and turned to face the nomad, an expression of surprised innocence plastered across his face.

'*Sa'ath vahra uhdich gradhu?*' the scout asked, appearing perplexed.

The guard started to rattle on in the awful dialect, challenging him, and Quintillian briefly noted Asander's eyes flash up over his opponent's shoulder to pick out the figure of the prince silently emerging from the corridor, a human shadow detaching itself from the gloom. An almost imperceptible nod, and Asander was busy chattering in nervous tones to the guard again. Whatever he said didn't impress the nomad, for the spear dipped and flashed forward threateningly, coming within a hand's breadth of taking the scout's eye. Asander started to speak more urgently.

Quintillian was biting the inside of his lip. The nomad was a big man, while the prince was strong, but smaller and wiry. It had to be quick, and very, very quiet. As silent as any Pelasian assassin, Quintillian slipped close behind the guard and reached up. His left hand shot round the man's face and covered his mouth. His right grasped the nomad's throat.

The guard let out a stifled gasp and started to wrench his head this way and that. Quintillian fought to keep tight hold of the man. If his mouth became free they were lost. Yet he could feel his grip slipping. The nomad was both big and powerful. As he clung on for dear life, trying to squeeze the man's throat apple for a silent kill, Quintillian saw Asander take a step forward and grab the wavering spear just below the blade. With relative ease, given the big man's distraction, he yanked the spear from the man's hands, turned it and tried to match the weaving of the man's head with the gleaming sickle-tip.

'Hold the bastard still,' he hissed.

Quintillian, desperate and struggling still, threw every ounce of strength in his body into holding the man for just a moment and, as the nomad's thrashing temporarily lessened, Asander thrust forward with the spear.

The prince felt a thin, hot line of pain across his hand as the spear tip whispered past his flesh and slammed into the nomad's face. He could hear the crunch of bone and the shudder-inducing meaty sawing noise as the blade entered the man's face and drove deep, dividing his brain. The body clutched in his arms was shaking now rather than struggling, quivering in its death throes. He heard the spear being pulled back out and felt the wash of blood and brain matter flow down over his hands. Still he kept tight hold, fearing that even in death the man might scream. Only when the nomad fell still did he remove his hand from the mouth. The ruined face was the stuff of nightmare as the guard fell onto his back in a pool of his own ichor.

'We can't take him with us,' Quintillian hissed, wiping his hands on the man's tunic once he'd found the cleanest spot. 'But we can't just leave him here.'

Asander shot him a scathing look. 'You don't think the huge pool of blood will be a giveaway anyway?'

'True. All right. Speed over stealth, then. Problem is, that means we don't have time to wait for the guard to be relieved. There goes the idea of jumping the relief and taking his place.'

'Not quite. You don't have to look too far to find a nomad's war gear you can don!'

Quintillian grinned. Thanks to the attire they had been given in the palace, all he would need to do was slip on the heavy boots instead of their leather shoes, then strap on the weapons, the fur headgear and the heavy cloak and he could easily pass for one of them in the gloom. The man had no bow, which was unusual for one of the nomads, but then what use would a bow have been in the corridors of the palace, so that was no surprise, really.

'Who gets the gear?'

'You do,' Asander said. 'You're the one with the fair hair. I'm nice and dark, but you could never pass for a nomad without the hat.'

Quintillian nodded and quickly slipped on the outer gear of the fallen guard, belting the sword in place. 'You'll have to take all the blankets then, and stay behind me in the shadows until I give you the signal.'

'Would the signal by any chance be the death rattle of a clansman?'

'Something like that. Keep your eyes and ears open.'

The two men left the open vestibule, the body of the dead guard, lying in the pool of viscera, a grisly centrepiece. Quintillian tried to decide between keeping the blade sheathed at his side for the appearance of normality and drawing it to carry bared in preparation for trouble. Subtlety won out and he left the blade in its sheath, pulling out the dagger instead and hefting it as Asander tested the pole-arm and prepared himself to use it in more open combat.

Together, the pair scurried along the passages, trying to maintain a steady balance between speed and stealth. Once, at a junction, they had to recoil into the shadows as a slave with a bleak face and an arm full of platters passed across the end. Praying to the goddess of fortune that the hapless thrall didn't stumble across the ravaged body of the guard, the two men waited for the man's footsteps to fade and then ran on, turning one more corner and finding themselves in the small room with the table and the water cask. Pausing for a moment, Quintillian rinsed the worst of the crimson goo from his hands in the keg, and doused the knife to clean it. Asander did the same with the spear point. The two men stopped, looked each other in the eye, and both nodded. This was it.

Quintillian crossed to the heavy wooden door and, temporarily sheathing the dagger, heaved the large wooden bar from it, resting it on its end against the wall as before. Slowly, carefully, he inched the door inward. The space between the palace and the settlement wall was so much less distinct at night. The gloom was oppressive and very obscuring. In fact, it took precious long moments for their eyes to adjust enough to pick out the shape of the refuse pit outside the door.

'Come on. Just stay at the edge in the deepest shadow.'

'You mean rather than throwing myself forward into the pit?' hissed Asander, rolling his eyes.

Quintillian threw a withering look at his companion and slipped from the door, leaving the palace for the first time in five days. The air was cloying and thick with the smell of urine and rotten food, and the entire pit steamed gently. The prince felt around the side of the door and grasped the timber surface of the palace's outside wall as best he could, shuffling out along the lip of the 3-foot drop into sucking nightmare.

It was not far – just three paces – but it felt like a thousand miles, with the slowness and difficulty involved in not falling into the murk. Once he reached the wide grass, Quintillian stepped out onto it and heaved several deep breaths in and out, despite the reek. Behind him Asander slipped along the outer edge of the palace, suffering a heart-stopping moment when his foot slipped and he almost plummeted into the unpleasantness. Finally, the two men were both on the open grass in the shadow of the palace wall.

'Now comes the bit for which I couldn't plan. Who knows how the man at the top will react. Be ready. As soon as he's down or all hell breaks loose, you need to be climbing that ladder with the blankets. At that point, it becomes all about speed. All right?'

'We've been over this twenty times this afternoon, Quintillian. I know what we're doing.'

With a last look at his friend, the prince breathed slowly three times – in, out, in, out, in, out – and trotted from the shadow across the grass. The wall was perhaps between 40 and 50 feet in height, formed of the tallest logs possible from the sparse forests of the upper steppe – slim full-grown *iron-wood* trunks, in fact, rather than branches. Observation or fighting platforms rose behind it every 50 paces or so around the circumference, and each platform consisted of a single wooden walkway behind the parapet, standing atop a timber scaffold, with just about enough room for three people to stand side by side, and no railing to prevent a man tumbling into the darkness. Quintillian wondered idly how many drunken nomads had died on guard duty, all from a simple fumbled step.

The ladder that rose up the gantry to the platform was actually a series of three separate ladders, one atop the other, each pegged and roped to the timbers that supported the walkway. Quintillian had never had trouble with heights, but looking up the vertiginous scaffold to the nomad atop it was heart-stopping even for him. The guard had not noticed the new figure moving across the grass in the shadows far below, but Quintillian realized with relief that, even if the man or his neighbours happened to be looking down there, it was highly unlikely they would spot a man moving across the grass in the darkness. Subtlety would likely be forgotten entirely very soon, though. Biting into his lip in an effort to stay loose and steady, he crossed to the ladder and wrapped his hands around the rough timber.

He began to climb.

Every five rungs without their world crashing down around them seemed a monumental achievement, and – to add pressure to an already tense situation – even five rungs reminded him how far there was to fall either side of the wall. The ascent seemed to take forever, and the closer he got to the summit the more he simply couldn't believe that the man at the top had not yet spotted or heard him.

Then, almost without warning, the nomad guard came to the edge and peered down. Fortunately the creak of his footstep on the timbers as he turned gave Quintillian just enough time to lower his gaze to the ladder in front of him, so that from above he would not be so obviously clean shaven – well, with several weeks' growth, but still far short of the norm for the clans.

'*Chun hval?*' the nomad said quietly, with curiosity but not concern.

Quintillian clenched his teeth for a moment. He'd been half-prepared for this. He had three responses playing around his head of the few words he had learned, depending upon what the man sounded as though he'd asked. The problem was that he had no idea what *Chun hval* meant, and the tone had been so level he could glean nothing from inflection. He breathed levelly and paused in his climb for a heartbeat.

'*A'atum!*' Quintillian replied in a hissed tone, trying to load it with sarcasm on the assumption that the lack of timbre and the heavy inflection would mask his undoubtedly poor pronunciation.

A'atum. It was the first word he had learned in their tongue and had a thousand uses. It was also, therefore, the most flexible of all replies. It meant, simply: shit.

The guard at the top of the ladder let out a low guffaw and stepped back from the edge. Quintillian continued to climb, grateful for his acute hearing this past week and his apparent easy smoothing of a dangerous situation because of it. A thought occurred to the prince, and as he climbed the last few rungs he glanced left and right. The two adjacent platforms were far enough away that the figures on them were indistinct in the darkness. The nomads knew their business well enough to not position torches at the top of the rampart in order to preserve the night vision of the lookouts, but that also made the various platforms fairly hazy at distance. Neither of the figures seemed to have noticed the brief exchange. If that was the case, he might be better risking one short noise than the potentially prolonged sound of a struggle. Settled on his course of action, and casting up his thousandth prayer that things go his way, he clambered up the last few rungs and, attaining the level of the platform, rather than climbing up onto it, he reached out and grasped the ties that wrapped the guard's leggings. Gripping them as tightly as he could with his left hand while holding on to the top rung for dear life with his right, he jerked back.

The guard was taken enough by surprise that he failed to adjust his balance in the tiniest moment available to him, and he fell like a sack of turnips. At least one of the more influential gods must be listening to Quintillian's prayers, for as the nomad fell, rather than arcing out wildly over the edge, his lower half went out into space but his torso hit the timbers hard, the brunt of it being borne by his face. He had let out a stifled squawk as he dropped, but it was cut off by the solid platform before it could become a scream and he was, blessedly for him, only half conscious as his upper body slid slowly backwards and out over the edge.

Quintillian hung on to the ladder and watched the man fall. The drop was far enough that the body had time to flip end over end before he hit the turf below head-first with a faint thud. The prince could see only the faintest outline of the figure in the shadow, and even then only when he squinted and concentrated. He then saw Asander's dark shape detach from the gloom and cross to the fallen guard. There was a pause and some movement around the body, which would clearly be the scout making sure the nomad was dead, and then Asander was over to the ladder and beginning to climb.

Quintillian hauled himself up to the platform and stood upright, trying not to get too close to the vertiginous edge. Instead, he peered over the parapet, which turned out to be little better, and filled him with a dull terror of what was shortly to come. So far things had gone much better than expected. How long, though, could such luck hold?

His answer came a moment later with a shout in the guttural nomad tongue. He swung round and looked down towards the palace. The slaves' pit door was brightly illuminated by guttering torches, and the figure of Ganbaatar was clearly visible amid them.

'Shit!' muttered Quintillian and looked down the ladder to where Asander was climbing as fast as he could. '*Come on!*' he hissed.

'Oh, like I'm dawdling,' snapped the scout as he heaved himself up at speed, arm over arm, the rope blankets dangling around him causing him extra weight and difficulty.

Ganbaatar sidled round the pit with surprising ease and yelled something else, gesturing to one of his men.

'What was that?'

'He's called… for his bow,' managed Asander between heaved breaths as he climbed.

'Then we have to go now. You know he'll be able to pick us off.'

'Will you stop… stating the fucking… obvious… our Highness,' grumbled Asander as he climbed the last few steps. A thud drew Quintillian's startled glance and he turned to see an arrow protruding from the timber next to him, vibrating gently from the impact. Along the rampart, on the next platform, a nomad was nocking a second arrow to his bow.

'This is getting shittier by the moment.'

Asander heaved himself up onto the platform, gulping in breaths, and the two men began to try and secure the blanket ropes. Quintillian dropped the prepared loop over the pointed tip of the enormous tree trunk, while Asander attempted to tie the two lengths together.

'Is it secure?' Quintillian asked, as he peered back down. Ganbaatar seemed to have given up on waiting for his bow and was now starting to climb the ladder behind them. Another arrow swept past from the same direction, nicking a small chunk from Quintillian's ear, and another whispered from the far side, pinning the blanket rope to the wood. Asander dropped his half-finished knot and wrenched out the arrow to free the rope.

'We have to go, now,' he said.

'Is it secure?'

'No.'

Quintillian stared in mounting panic as Asander threw out the two ropes over the far side. The prince looked down. Between them the ropes descended more than a third of the way, almost a half. That *would* make a difference. Also, due to the curve in the circular palisade, once they were over the edge they would be hard to target on their descent. 'Who go…' Quintillian began, but Asander pushed him to the parapet and, needing no further prompting, Quintillian swung himself out into the 50-foot space that descended to freedom.

The rope slipped and gave alarmingly, and Quintillian felt himself drop several feet three different times before the rope seemed to anchor itself. Just as his heart began to steady a little, Asander cast his spear down into space and swung out over the parapet above him. Arrows hissed through the air from left and right, though neither of the adjacent nomads could get a clear shot around the curve. After heart-stopping moments, Quintillian reached the end of the blanket rope. The remaining drop still looked terrifyingly far to him, but this was no time for doubt. Clenching his teeth and tensing himself ready to try and hit the ground as flexibly as he could, he let go.

Despite the fact that he moved straight into a roll on impact, the reverberation up through his legs and echoing across his whole body made him feel instantly sick. Plus, his sword had caught badly against his ribs on landing, and his organs all felt jumbled up, as though they had been swirled around inside and left in new positions. He felt utterly bruised. He forced himself to his knees and tried to rise to his feet, but had to pause to vomit copiously into the grass.

Recovering, he turned and looked back up in time to spot three things, each more alarming than the last.

Firstly, the ropes were stretching rather worryingly as the knot connecting the two unravelled a few feet above Asander. Secondly, the two adjacent archers were nocking arrows and sighting down towards where the prince now floundered, where they stood more chance of success. And, thirdly, Ganbaatar had reached the top and was bellowing furiously from the platform.

Then the ropes separated. Asander gave a brief sharp curse and fell awkwardly. He landed with a thump and lay motionless. Quintillian stared in horror and disbelief, and then his heart began to beat again as his friend rose slowly to his knees declaring all the gods to be bitches and bastards. Above him, Ganbaatar had climbed out and was beginning his own descent. Somehow Quintillian couldn't see the powerful giant being fazed by the drop.

Now Asander was up and running, though Quintillian was dismayed to see that one of his legs was injured and he was limping, which slowed him drastically. The prince dithered, in a minor panic as to what to do. That was when an arrow struck him in the shoulder so hard that it spun him to the side and sent him flying to the grass again.

'Don't wait for me,' Asander barked. 'Run!'

Hissing with pain, the prince rose swiftly to his feet and, with just a momentary glance at Asander, started to pelt away across the turf, up the slope towards the distant, looming figures of the rocks. As he ran, he reached round and grasped the shaft stuck in his shoulder. Thankfully the head had punched into muscle but scraped on his shoulder blade, causing the impact that had thrown him, rather than lodging in. It was a quick task, though a mighty painful one, to yank the shaft out and throw it away.

As he ran, he detached the heavy cloak and let it fall, recognizing it as an encumbrance that outweighed its protective value. His fur hat went the same way, though he kept his sword and dagger belted in place in spite of them thumping repeatedly against the massive bruise they had caused in the fall.

Slowly, he noted the incline as he began to hurtle up the side of the huge grassy bowl. He paused after a few more moments to take a breath and turned. Another arrow thudded into the grass a couple of paces from him, indicating that he was not yet completely out of the archers' range.

His heart fell at what he saw.

Asander was way back and dropping further behind all the time. And the most horrifying sight of all: Ganbaatar was stomping speedily and purposefully across the grass, catching up with every step. Could Quintillian do this? How could he leave Asander behind after all they had been through together? He felt a duty of kinship, of comradeship, of mutual respect. But in his heart it battled with the duty he knew he owed to the empire to warn them of the threat that was coming.

Tears began to flow as he turned and struggled up the slope towards the nearest of the stone stacks. The war raging in his heart threatened to tear him in two so that half of him at least wanted to go back and help.

By the time he reached the weathered stone and threw his hands against its welcome surface, he felt hollow and broken inside. He disappeared from view, sliding round behind the rock, then moved through the shadows from one gnarled shape to another.

Then he stopped and looked back.

And his heart broke all over again.

The figures were too distant now for him to make out too much detail, but Asander was on his knees with Ganbaatar behind him, gripping an arm. The tiniest gleam of moonlight from between the obscuring ribbons of black cloud happened to filter through at that moment to gleam on something in the huge warrior's hand.

Oh gods, make it quick.

'Prince of Velutio, hear me!' called out the sonorous voice of Ganbaatar in good, clear tones.

Quintillian swallowed nervously. The big champion was scanning the rocks and clearly didn't see precisely where the prince was.

'I offer you one chance. Come back and submit to my father, and I will spare your friend the delicious agonies I have planned and grant him a clean death.'

There was a pause. In his soul, Quintillian cried out his acquiescence a hundred times. His mouth, along with the rest of his body, belonged to the empire and remained closed.

'Then it will take two days for your friend to die. We depart for your empire in two days. Any hour between now and then you can return and put him out of his misery.'

There was the merest of pauses and then a blood-curdling howl from Asander. Quintillian closed his eyes and lowered his gaze.

'Bastard,' he whispered to himself.

'D...argh!' Asander shrieked. 'Don't do it, my prince. Run!'

His words were given horrendous punctuation by another spine-tingling scream.

Quintillian stood slowly, purposefully, his hands clenched, his eyes closed. Still in the shadows, hidden among the rocks, he took a deep breath and called out in a steady voice.

'Prepare yourself, Ganbaatar Khan's-son. In my family we believe strongly in retribution. Your downfall will be hard and terrible, and I will be the man who brings it to pass.'

His only answer was another dreadful scream from the two figures down in the bowl, which split the night. Quintillian's jaw hardened. It went against his principles to leave the poor bastard back down there to the tender mercies of the Khan's son, but Asander had known what was at stake. That was what had driven him to tell Quintillian to run, not some personal desire to see his prince free. They were both soldiers, and they both knew what was required of them. Duty and sacrifice.

Wishing his friend a quick death, Quintillian turned and ran from rock formation to rock formation, heading around to the southeast, where he would finally make a true run for it. He felt comfortable that at least until dawn he would be safe. He would hear any horsemen in pursuit long before they would see him, and the grass of the steppe was long and tufted. At the first sound of pursuit, he would just have to drop to the dirt and he would disappear in the mile upon mile of identical grass. By dawn he would be far away, in a direction he didn't think they would search, at least at first.

That was it. He was free. Now all he had to do was run hundreds of miles through barren, enemy-held territory and convince the soldiers of the Third Army near the imperial border that he was their commander-in-chief so that he could ride swiftly back to Velutio and warn them of the coming storm.

What could be easier?

PART TWO

THE SOUTH

'Family is the heart of all life. It is also the cause of most sadness.'

Germallan dramatist Haulius

CHAPTER IX

Of Ripples and Consequences

Titus Tythianus, Marshal of the First Army, commander of the emperor's guard, Lord of Munda, tromped along the corridor with a sense of resigned irritation. For weeks now, since the disappearance of Prince Quintillian, his first duty each day had been to visit the emperor and keep him apprised of progress. And each day the summary had been the same as the day before.

There *was* no progress.

They had traced the prince's movements as far as his exit from the palace with ease. And he had taken a horse through the city's Forest Gate, which was his wont on his less busy days, since the prince loved to ride along the shoreline to the north of the city. His trail ended there, though there had been one established sighting after that and half a dozen odd unconfirmed reports that had thus far turned up nothing. The prince had been recognized by an off-duty guard in the great trade fair below the city, though it had been only a glance in the middle of a crowd, so the man could state nothing for certain other than that Quintillian had been there early in the morning.

There had been conflicting sightings after that. Serfium. Munda. Some hole by the Tyras River. Quite apart from the fact that those three locations were in entirely opposite directions, the prince had been variously described as travelling in a dark cloak with the hood cowled low – one wonders how the man could know it was the prince thusly attired, also attending a travelling theatre, which seemed unlikely given Quintillian's contempt for the theatrical art, and dressed as a mercenary with a trade caravan. None of them seemed likely, though the other three sightings were even less credible. Scouts had been sent out to all locations and had yet to pick up the threads of a trail. Parties of scouts and soldiers scoured the countryside seeking word of the prince or sign of his passing.

Nothing.

Weeks of this, now. The emperor, usually so ordered, careful and in control of events, was starting to fray around the edges. He was holding things together remarkably well, really, given the closeness he shared with his brother. But the strain was showing to those who knew him well. He held court. He attended to the business of rule. And then, as soon as the public eye shifted from him, he paced and tapped, paced and tapped, sought out Titus for updates, advice and questions. Then paced and tapped, paced and tapped, paced and tapped.

They had attempted to keep the news of the prince's disappearance quiet, but the investigation the day or two following his vanishing had been too difficult to keep under wraps, and word had inevitably leaked out. A thousand rumours now circulated in Velutio and beyond, few of them good, none of them likely to even approach the truth.

The one thing they *had* managed to keep secret thus far was the fact that his absence was a deliberate flight. That first night when he failed to return, the emperor and empress had been concerned, and questions had been asked. The prince's room had been searched with the emperor's assistance, and what had been found to be taken confirmed the prince's deliberate flight and lack of intent to return.

'Another shitty day,' the marshal muttered to himself as he rounded a corner and made for the emperor's rooms.

The attack came so quickly that he barely had time to register his assailant's existence before he was on the floor and rolling. Only instinct – an instinct mostly inherited from his father – had prevented the top half of his head from leaving the rest of him. He'd felt the presence of the man in the split second the blow came and had thrown himself down and forward.

As he came out of the roll, noting idly that his knees and elbows hurt more than usual and that it was likely to be a wet day, he turned to see his attacker desperately trying to wrench the axe blade out of the wall, where it had bitten deep into the painted plaster and brick where Titus's head should have been.

Titus hit the man in the midriff, barrelling him to the floor, his hands sliding from the haft of the axe which was still wedged into the wall. For the first time in living memory the marshal wished he'd travelled the corridors of the palace armed. But quite apart from the fact that that would be utterly ridiculous, it was inviolable sacred law that no man brought a weapon into the emperor's rooms.

This man was armed, though.

Quite apart from the axe, there was a short dagger sheathed at the man's side. Even as the assailant struggled to regain his breath, pinned on the marble floor underneath Titus, he was already reaching down for the dagger. Titus caught sight of his searching hand. Adjusting his position slightly, he jammed an elbow into the man's neck, keeping him down, while he reached with his other arm and grabbed the man's questing wrist. The man was strong. The hand pulled the knife most of the way from the sheath. Titus noted with interest the unusual northern nature of the dagger, carved with some sort of boar design. Then he was struggling to control the blade. The knife came free from the scabbard and the two men fought for control.

Titus was no weakling. He may be plagued by joints that creaked in cold, damp weather. He might be scarred and missing a finger. But he was fit and strong despite that, with a daily training routine that matched the men of his army, and surpassed some. And yet the man beneath him, despite being pale and wiry, was stronger. Titus could feel the man's hand even now beginning to gain control of the knife. The marshal was losing. If the assassin managed to gain the blade, Titus would die.

There were times when those who cared for Titus Tythianus made their concern known over his drinking and gambling habits. They had cost him three promising relationships in his time. But whatever they all said, gambling was inevitable. Life was a gamble. He was going to have to gamble now – on his speed against the attacker's.

For just a moment, he released his pressure on the man, lifting his weight, struggling still to control the knife. The change of balance gave the assassin the advantage he needed and the man's grip won out, the knife slipping away from Titus's hand. The assailant brought the dagger back for a blow into the marshal's side. But he never finished the swing.

Instead, Titus dropped back into position, putting every pound of his weight into that one point – his elbow that now descended back to its former position on the man's neck. However, last time it had been lowered into place to pin the man. This time it smashed into the man's throat apple, crushing it, the windpipe and the cartilage in the man's neck. The dagger fell from his assailant's hand and as Titus rose again and stepped back, the man began to die. His neck was not broken, and in bone and muscle he was generally intact, but no air was reaching his lungs. Titus had utterly crushed his throat with the elbow and nothing could save him now. The pale man struggled, clawing at his neck and mouth, his eyes bulging in terror as he thrashed, unable to breathe, not a squeak emerging from his ruined voice box.

Titus watched the man die with quiet dispassion. It irked him. He would have liked to question him. Assassins in the palace were unheard of. Such things had not happened since the days of the interregnum – maybe even the reign of Quintus the Mad before that. But this man would tell no secrets, except to the lord of the dead.

Finally the man, his face a blue-grey colour, stopped thrashing about and lay still, his limbs giving a last few involuntary twitches.

His face grave, Titus bent and lifted the body – he may have been strong but he was surprisingly light – and threw him over aching shoulders. As an afterthought he reached up and with some difficulty yanked the axe from the wall. He lifted the weapon to the lamplight from the wall niche and examined it. Again, a northern weapon. One of the tribes of the northland mountains. The very tribes that had supplied the blood that ran in the emperor's veins, in fact.

Grunting with the effort, he traipsed through the corridors, ignoring the various gasps of horror from the odd servant he passed. Finally, he arrived at the imperial quarters. The last wide vestibule, lined with delicate statuary and lit by the morning sun that poured through high leaded windows, ended in a T-junction. Left lay the emperor's apartment – a suite of rooms with a bathhouse attached. Right lay the mirror image that belonged to the empress. While the two often stayed in the emperor's rooms, it was only fitting that the empress have her own suite, especially bearing in mind that she was not only the wife of an emperor, but was a Princess of Pelasia in her own right.

The two men of the guard who stood at the junction to protect the imperial family stared in surprise as their commander approached with a corpse over his shoulder and an axe in his hand. They gave him a belated salute and Titus simply grunted, turning and heaving the body from his shoulder. The assassin thudded to the marble flags of the corridor at the guards' feet.

'Find out everything there is to know about this man. Either he works in the palace, in which case there will be records, or he doesn't, in which case someone knows how he got in. I want to know everything down to the colour of his mother's underwear by sundown. Got that?'

The guards nodded, still in shock. One of them bent and lifted the man's body, scurrying off with it. The other remained at attention until Titus thrust the axe at him and he took it gingerly.

'The emperor's in I take it?'

The guard nodded. 'Yes, sir.'

'Today is shaping up to be a shitty day, soldier, and I have a feeling in the pit of my stomach that it's far from over.'

Without waiting for a reply, the commander rounded the corner and strode along to the imperial apartment. Three raps on the door and a servant opened it wide.

'Good morning, Marshal. The emperor is on his balcony.'

Titus nodded and walked past the man, who was busy tidying up the main room. He emerged onto the colonnaded balcony a moment later to find the emperor in a simple tunic and breeches leaning on the railing and looking down over the lawns.

'Good morning, Majesty.'

The emperor gave him a tired smile. 'Drop the honorifics when we're in private, Titus. We've known each other since you were old enough to wound yourself on a spoon.'

'Habit. A good habit too, I might say. Both our fathers would have approved.'

'Morning report, Titus?'

'Look, can we skip the part where you question me in detail on everything that we already know in preparation for asking me for news that we both know I don't have? I've just nearly had my skull split in two by a mad northerner with an axe lurking in the palace corridors, so I'm not really in the mood for an inquisition.'

Kiva turned wide eyes on him.

'You jest?'

'You know my jokes, Majesty. They're funnier than that, and usually have more boobs.'

'You were attacked in the palace?'

'Yes. I've got my men looking into it. Sadly, I was forced to kill the bastard so we won't learn as much from him as we could. But I'd like your permission to double the guard in the palace, institute a lockdown of the doors and gates and put armed men in the parts where weapons are currently forbidden.'

'Whatever you think is necessary, Titus. You know you have my full trust and authority.'

'One more thing, Majesty,' Titus said quietly. 'You should start carrying your own blade even in the palace, unless you'll consent to 24-hour protection?'

'You know I can't work like that. You think I am in enough danger to go armed in my own palace? The last emperor who had to do that was Quintus, and he was universally reviled.'

Titus shrugged. 'Until we know more I can't say anything for certain, but there is always the possibility that I was not the man's true target and I just happened to bump into him. He was not far from the imperial apartments. He may have been after you or the empress.'

Kiva rubbed his neck and stretched. 'Who could be behind such a thing? There are no revolts or usurpers out there at the moment, are there?'

'There will always be those who are dissatisfied, Majesty. Even you, popular as you are, cannot please everyone. Remember how when you succeeded there were some who thought Quintillian would make a stronger emperor?'

Kiva chuckled. 'True. Very well, look into it and find out what you can. I cannot afford to divert my attention from the business of imperium, especially now that I am lacking Quintillian's support. We should go and see the empress, tell her of these matters.'

'She was my next port of call.' Titus nodded.

The two men passed back through the apartment and into the corridor. The servant busily mopped the floor behind them as the door clicked shut. Ahead, the soldier remained at attention at the junction. He saluted sharply, almost concussing himself with the axe, as the two most powerful men in the empire passed by. Moments later they reached the empress's apartments and Kiva reached up and rapped smartly on the door.

Only silence greeted them.

Frowning, Kiva knocked again. No answer.

'Perhaps she is bathing?' Titus asked quietly.

'Perhaps, but Nisha or Zari should answer if so.'

The empress's two personal maids were never far from her sight, and even if one were helping Jala bathe, the other would answer the door. Titus felt the hairs stand proud on the back of his neck. Something was wrong. 'Wait a moment, sir.' He turned and jogged back to the guard at the junction.

'Give me your sword.'

'Sir?'

'Just do it, man.'

The soldier drew his blade and passed it to his commander in confusion.

'Neither the empress nor her maids have passed you this morning?'

'No, sir. And no one's been in. But then I've only been on watch since dawn call.'

Titus nodded and ran back to the emperor, his sword respectfully lowered. Kiva peered at the blade and raised an eyebrow.

'Just in case, Majesty. I've already been jumped once today.'

The tension was building in the corridor as Kiva bent to the door handle and turned it. The door swung in easily on oiled hinges. The key remained on the inside. The apartment was eerily silent and Titus's skin was rippling with nerves now. 'This is not good.'

The emperor moved into the room alongside his general, who raised his borrowed blade, anticipating danger.

'She's not here,' Kiva murmured.

'I'll check everywhere to be sure, Majesty. You're unarmed. You wait here.'

The emperor looked for a moment as though he might argue, but finally seeing the sense in the matter, nodded and stood with his back to a wall. Titus moved carefully through the empress's bedroom, dining room, sun-room, balcony, bath suite, changing room and finally her closet, checking behind everything that could conceal a human being. Finally, he re-emerged into the main room, his eyes serious.

'No sign. Would she have gone out early? When did you last see her?'

The emperor began to pace, a return to his most common nervous habit. 'Jala wouldn't go out in the dark. She hates spring nights. Says it's too cold for her Pelasian blood. She only likes the darkness in high summer. Besides, you know as well as I that it would take a natural disaster to tear her from her bed before dawn.'

Titus nodded. It was true, but he'd needed to hear it nonetheless.

'So when did you last see her? She was at the state dinner last night, I remember.'

'She was here when I checked on her last night. I had a few things to do and retired to my own apartment rather late, but I called here on the way.'

Titus nodded thoughtfully. The emperor rarely went to his bed before midnight, and mostly later even than that, claiming his mind was at its most productive in the hours of darkness. It was then that he attended to the minutiae of statecraft. 'Times?' the marshal prompted.

'She retired after the meal, which would have been in the fourth hour of the night. I checked on her between the sixth and seventh hours, I suppose.'

'And it starts to get light these days at around the tenth hour. I've been up and about since then, and the guard outside hasn't seen any movement. That suggests she vanished during those three hours or so. At least I'm content that axe-wielding assassins didn't break in here. I'd rather she wasn't here than she was, under those circumstances, if you get my drift. She didn't say anything to you last night?'

The emperor shook his head. 'Nothing in particular. She was guarded, though. A little... off in some way that I can't quite describe. But then you know that something has been wrong between us for months now. I can't work out what it is, and I have no idea how to repair it. It seems to be something with Jala, though. In myself I am unchanged.'

'Whatever the case, the empress likely left her rooms between the seventh hour of darkness and the tenth. And it would appear that she went with both maids. I will need to talk to the guard.'

Kiva reached out and grasped Titus's arm. 'Do you think someone has her? Someone with a grudge against the family, perhaps? I mean, it seems too much to be coincidence – first Quintillian, now Jala, and assassins in the palace to boot.'

'I don't know, Majesty, but I will find out. What we need to avoid right now is a panic. Rumour could be crippling. We need to keep the empress's absence completely secret for now. We failed to do so with Quintillian and the damage to palace credibility was immense. Until we know more of what's happened, tell no one. I will keep my guard silent, but I must speak to them first.' He rolled his shoulders. 'You'd better get to your morning business, Majesty. There are important people waiting for an audience.'

'To the netherworld with them, Titus. This is my *wife* we're talking about.'

The marshal huffed at the emperor, who was pacing madly back and forth and tapping himself like a maniac. 'And this is doing you no good. The empire needs its emperor. Go to your people. I will speak to the guards and the servants and find out everything I can, then I will find you straightaway. Try to act as though everything is normal. But make sure you're armed wherever you go, and if you feel danger closing, make sure to be near the guard. Within the hour they'll be armed and all over the palace.'

As the emperor departed with a last look that told of a man at the top of a slippery slope into despair, Titus stood in silence, tapping the tip of the sword on the marble at his feet and thinking. It was just like Quintillian – there was no denying it. The empress had gone before anyone knew it. While he couldn't yet say for sure she wasn't taken by force, it seemed unlikely. The imperial guard were the best of the best, raised from the main army. Even the lackest-wit among them would have sounded the alarm at someone abducting the empress, and leaving anywhere but by the gates was all-but impossible these days. She must have gone deliberately, just like the prince.

Which raised at least one ugly question.

Could the departure of the prince and the empress be directly linked? A horrible idea popped into his head and he fought to drive it back out. No. Never. Quintillian was better than that. *Jala* was better than that. But the emperor had been correct in that there had been a strained distance between the two of them for perhaps half a year now. Anyone who spent almost every day in their presence could see it – could *feel* it.

It was not that love wasn't there. Kiva wore his heart on his sleeve as always, and his love for his wife was visible and undeniable. And Titus, a man who knew how to read others whether across the dicing table or in a fight, had seen into the empress's eyes. She loved her husband – of that he had no doubt. But there was something *else* there too. Something indefinable. Damn that Parishid family. The monarchs of Pelasia, from whose line Jala had sprung, were an inscrutable lot, practised at guarding their thoughts.

Ducking back out of the room, he jogged along to the remaining guard.

'Has the emperor left?'

'Yes, sir.'

'Good. Then you're not needed here right now. Find the duty officer from last night. Have every man who was on guard at an entrance or interior door woken and brought to the Gorgon Hall as soon as possible.'

The man saluted and hurried off, and Titus rolled his shoulders again. It would take time for the guards to assemble and in the meantime he might be able to narrow down the options by searching her rooms again – this time not for the empress, but for evidence of her departure. And if he couldn't clarify anything here, by the time he was done the guards would be gathered in the hall. Then he would have the palace servants brought in for questioning, too. Someone, somewhere, would know about Jala.

But then, he'd said the same about Prince Quintillian...

He returned to the closet, this time examining the room rather than searching it. Sure enough, her clothing lay strewn across the chests and tables as though she had hurriedly been through everything deciding what to take. Like Quintillian, then, she had left of her own accord. Had she been snatched away by enemies they would have been unlikely to spend time letting her select specific clothing. No. This was definitely deliberate.

A quick search of the whole apartment failed to further enlighten him in any way and he finished, frustrated, standing in the empress's bedchamber. There had to be something here. He could almost *feel* the presence of some unseen evidence. It was the same feeling he'd get in a game of dice when he knew – he just *knew* – that his opponent had rolled snake eyes and not yet revealed it. There was something here somewhere. And if it was not in open evidence then it would have to be somewhere hidden.

But where?

When he and Kiva had been young, they had slid the prince's bed to one side, levered up a board in the floor and fitted it with a hinge. They had been so proud of their secret cache. It had been barely discernible to the unknowing. Of course, Quintillian had found it, but then the younger prince's mind was almost as sharp as his brother's.

Where would Jala's secret place be?

Not an underfloor stash. The empress's perfectly manicured nails would have shown betraying marks had she been messing with floorboards. And it would be somewhere the servants wouldn't be all the time, changing and cleaning, tidying and organizing. Not the floor, the bed, the hearth, the chests, the table. Not behind a drape.

His eyes played round the room three more times and then, without conscious intent, stopped on the shrine. Close to the hearth of the fire stood a small shrine on a 3-foot-high pillar carved into the traditional Pelasian lotus flower capital. The shrine itself was made of perfect white marble in the form of an ornate Pelasian temple. Most of the inhabitants of the empire – the house owners anyway – had such a shrine to honour the gods of the household and the family. Not the great gods of the empire, of course – there were plenty of public temples to them. But the family's private gods were kept with such shrines. And they were inviolable.

Muttering an apology to the star goddess of Pelasia, who he knew to be the empress's favoured deity, he stooped slightly and opened the perfect replica doors of the temple. Inside, the goddess Astara sat on her moulded throne, glaring back at him with painted, regal eyes. The interior was shadowed, but there was clearly no room for anything else. Not in there, then.

Yet his spine was tingling, and somehow he knew that here, somewhere, was what he was looking for. He peered inside again. The temple itself was empty of aught but the goddess. He rose, scratched his chin and then began to feel around the edge of the temple roof. The pediment was solid, the architrave around the edge masterfully carved. No. Nothing there. Another frown.

Perhaps he was thinking along too intricate a line? Sometimes subtlety was much more basic.

With pursed lips he leaned forward again and grasped the temple, lifting it gently. With a slight clunk, it came free of the column. He'd not imagined this to be likely, given the weight of marble, but it seemed that the sculptor of the shrine had been a master of the art, creating the temple so delicately and finely that it weighed surprisingly little. Certainly Jala would have no trouble lifting the shrine on and off the column. Sure enough, as he looked at the nearby table he could see scrape marks where she had repeatedly placed the carved shrine. The servants had tried to polish them out but had failed. He slipped the marble structure on the table with a sigh as his back twinged as it sometimes did if he moved wrong. A plague of bodily complaints and weaknesses had been one of the most prominent hereditary gifts from his father, the Marshal Tythias.

Unburdened, he turned back to the column, entirely unsurprised to find that it was largely hollow, a stylus and a number of parchments resting inside, some blank, some loose, some rolled and sealed.

Secret correspondence?

Feeling curiously like an eavesdropper, the marshal reached down and pulled out a collection of the parchments, wandering over to a table beneath the window. Had it been one of the servants or guards prying in this manner, they would have lost their hands, or probably their head. The letter of the law would call for the same for him, in truth, but he could hardly see the emperor calling for such punishment, even had he not been here on Kiva's business.

Discarding two blank parchments, he unrolled a third.

It was a letter from a cousin by the name of Arya. Despite his gruff manner and military nature, Titus Tythianus had learned young that he had a facility for languages, and Pelasian had been one of the first he had learned. He could still remember the envious looks he'd received from Quintillian, who failed repeatedly to master any other language at all, beyond a few words, and most of them curses. Briefly, he ran his eyes down the writing, feeling intrusive and wicked for doing so. He read just far enough to convince himself that this was unconnected, an outpouring of a young girl's heart to her close relation. Just looking at it made him feel uncomfortable.

The next letter was in Jala's own hand. He recognized the flourish and the elaborate, almost anachronistic nature of her archaic script. He scanned the lines, noting the opening words and once more feeling dangerously voyeuristic. It was an unfinished letter to her brother Ashar, the God-King of Pelasia. Prying into this could well see a man executed in two nations. The Pelasians would have to fight Kiva for his head.

Biting down on the discomfort of what he was doing, Titus scanned the letter.

His back, arms and neck began to tingle with gooseflesh that had nothing to do with the temperature. Eyes widening, he let the scroll furl again and leaned on the table, breathing heavily. In disbelief, sure that his eyes had somehow deceived him, he opened the letter once more and re-read it. No. It was definitely there. There were no names. *Of course* there were no names. Even in a secret letter, the empress could hardly risk applying names. But the *meaning* was clear even to Titus.

Could a person live a life *loving* someone, if they were *in love* with another?

That was the essence of the letter. A carefully vague outpouring of the soul. Titus stared. Phrases like *eternity of heartache*, *the sour taste of duty, the tearing of a heart that wants two different things*, leapt from the inked page and struck him repeatedly like a club.

Again, he let the page furl and leaned heavily on the table once more. It was becoming increasingly difficult to consider the two people's disappearances to be mere coincidence. And if he thought for a minute… No. Despite how it looked, he had known Jala since she first came to Velutio, and had known Quintillian all his life. Jala would never betray her duty, even if her heart drew her. And Quintillian? No, he would never put a knife in his brother's back that way. In fact, Titus mused, the prince would move the world itself to avoid doing so. He felt a momentary thrill of realization. Was that what Quintillian had done? Had he known what was happening? Had he known what was in Jala's heart and removed himself from the equation? Gods, that would be stupid, but it would be so very, very Quintillian.

He sighed. Was there any way he could resolve this without the emperor seeing the letter?

'No, you fool,' the marshal whispered to himself. 'It is your duty to show him.' Just to be certain, he pushed that document aside and went through the others, each and every one from the hidden compartment in the column. There were no other such letters, though a missive from the god-king, her brother, dated around a month ago, hinted that Jala had shared some unhappiness over her marital situation even then. Grasping that, he added it to the unfinished letter and, his heart beating fast, scooped up a leather bag from the table near the window and thrust the damning documents inside. Leaving the room, he paused at the suite's door and removed the key, locking it from the outside.

With a dreadful sense of growing doom about the day, Titus hurried through the palace corridors and down to the Gorgon Hall, a grand former audience chamber now used by the guard for training sessions and therefore far from the prying ears of the rest of the palace's residents.

With a floor patterned of different coloured stone flags, the room was surrounded on all sides by two tiers of columns carved into the shapes of unfolding naked females with hair formed of serpents with sharp fangs that twisted and writhed.

The hall had always made Titus squirm. He hated snakes.

Already the duty officer had 30 or 40 soldiers lined up waiting. They stood to attention, despite all being clearly exhausted, dragged from their beds little more than an hour after they had ended their shifts. All had managed to struggle into uniform, though they could almost all do with bathing, he noted, sniffing gently.

They shuffled straight and raised tired gazes to the fore as the marshal emerged from the doorway.

'My apologies for calling you back like this. I know you've had a long night. But it seemed the most expedient way of answering my questions. What I am about to tell you is classified information. It does not go beyond those of you in this room. Understand?'

There was an affirmative murmur.

'Good. If even a hint of this reaches ears in the streets, each and every one of you will be manning a mountain outpost on the northern border within the week and for the rest of your lives. Be assured I am not jesting.' He paused to let the importance of the matter sink in.

'The empress is not in the palace.'

The news clearly shocked the men, whose eyes widened with surprise and then with heightened nerves. After all, if there had been an incident, they would be the ones accountable. Titus coughed and paced back and forth for a moment.

'She disappeared sometime between around the seventh and tenth hours of the night. I know this palace is sealed tighter than a Germallan's arse-crack, so she did not leave the palace without being seen. That means that one of you knows what happened. Tell me now.'

A guard near the front stepped a pace forward. 'I was on duty at the empress's apartment, sir. She left her rooms not long before the seventh hour. It was unusually early, sir, so I noted the time out of interest. But she seemed content enough. The maid was carrying an armful of clothing, but nothing seemed amiss, sir.'

Titus nodded and the man stepped back into line.

'So where did she go at the seventh hour? How did she leave the palace? Or *did* she leave the palace at all?'

There was a long, uncomfortable pause, and finally a guard raised his arm and stepped out of rank, marching to the fore.

'I may have the answer, sir.'

'Go on.'

The man's eyes dropped for a moment, then came up to meet the marshal's steely gaze.

'Three servants left the palace this morning, not long before dawn. That would be I reckon about quarter of an hour after the ninth. All three were swarthy, Pelasian-blooded girls. They had documents signed by the empress, granting them permission to leave and they were carrying folded laundry. I thought nothing of it, sir. Servants come and go at all hours of the day and night, and they had the correct authorization.'

Titus nodded. 'You did nothing wrong, man. Two of the women will have been Nisha and Zari, the empress's body servants. The other will have been the empress herself attired in common clothing. At least we know she was not abducted now. I will check with the chamberlain, but I am content that we will discover those two girls to be absent too. Where were you on guard?'

'By the Gold Tower postern, sir. It's the most commonly-used gate for servants.'

Again Titus was nodding. The Gold Tower gate led directly out into the city's mercantile area. Within two streets were the spice market, the vegetable market, the meat market and the flower market. Beyond that were warehouses and mercantile compounds, streets of manufacturers and artisans. And past those, down winding streets and narrow staircases, descending to the lowest level of the city, was the commercial port, often filled with Pelasian traders.

He was now almost certain where Jala was bound.

'Get back to your cots, all of you, and rest. If I need anything else, we'll call on you individually. And remember: tell no one of this until you hear from me. Not even your mate when you're playing dice. Ice-cold border outposts surrounded by cannibal mountain men await those with flapping tongues.'

As the men dispersed, Titus took a deep, steadying breath. At least, unlike Quintillian, the empress seemed to have left a trail.

CHAPTER X

Of Departures

Titus pushed open the door to his apartment. Unmarried and with a strange status that hovered somewhere between courtier and soldier, he had a suite of rooms in the palace, but had made sure they were away from the emperor's private quarters and close to the offices and headquarters of the guard. The rooms lacked what others would probably call a 'womanly touch'. Used clothing was scattered in heaps. Swords lay on the cupboards. His bed was unmade. Old wine jars and cups and platters were stacked here and there. Servants did not clean Titus's rooms. He didn't let them. It was a matter of principle. To accept the palace skivvies picking up after him would state that he was a courtier, not a soldier, and *that* was a step he was unwilling to take. And it wasn't that he didn't tidy up every now and then. It was just that there never seemed to be time. He was only in his rooms to sleep and occasionally to eat. Other than that, duty kept him busy at almost all times, and when he wasn't required to work, the emperor or his brother always needed his presence for one reason or another.

It was an organized mess, though. He knew where everything was.

Crossing the room, he began to strip off his uniform tunic. The medals and torcs he'd earned throughout his time hung on the wall. Not only was he not one for ostentatious displays of superiority, but they were also unnecessarily bulky and heavy. He habitually wore his officer's tunic and breeches, with high quality boots and a nice belt. His one concession to rank had been the wolf blazon on the tunic and the gold-threaded stripes around the hems that denoted between them his rank (the stripes) and his unit (the wolf of the imperial guard.)

He peeled the tunic over his head and slung it across the bed. This was not the time for Titus Tythianus, Commander of the Guard. His breeches were utilitarian, but he quickly pulled on his riding boots that were more work-a-day. Crossing to his wardrobe he selected a plain grey tunic and slipped it on. His next job was one that required a little subtlety.

He had drilled into the guard the need to keep quiet about the empress's disappearance. The same message had now been passed to the chamberlain and the major domo, who would make sure the servants and various staff who might have noted her absence held their tongues.

The disappearance of Quintillian had alarmed the populace, and rumours of what had become of him were rife, but despite that, confidence in the court and the emperor was still high. Kiva was as popular a leader as the empire had ever had and it would take a great deal more to shake his people's support. But if the people were to discover now that the empress had similarly disappeared, they would start to wonder and would almost certainly link the two events. The damage that could be done to the line and to governance did not bear thinking about.

So, if he went into the city to make enquiries, he could not go in the guise of imperial guard commander or courtier. He would have to be an ordinary citizen. But, given what had happened in the palace corridors, an *armed and armoured* one, lest he wished his skull to play host to an axe.

His hands closed on the handles of the closet that was rarely opened and he slowly pulled the doors wide. There were ordinary citizens and *ordinary citizens*, though.

The closet contained a panoply of armour and weapons. A cuirass with segmented shoulder plates. One arm was similarly plated all the way down. The other: not so. But then its previous owner, Titus's father, had been missing an arm for most of his time as marshal. The sword was a soldier's blade – utilitarian and solid with little in the way of ornamentation. Titus reached out and took the armour from the hook, struggling a little to don it without the aid of a companion.

He rolled his shoulders, letting the segmented plates settle into place. The leather padding attached to the inside rested well on his shoulders. He was of a size and shape with his late father. He contemplated the helmet for a moment but decided against it, relying on the cuirass and arm plates, belting the sword in place.

Satisfied, he crossed to the mostly flat bronze mirror on the far wall. He looked oddly like his father now, barring the fact that he had thus far retained both eyes and all four limbs. One thing was certain, though: he did not look like an officer or official of the court.

Fine.

Leaving his rooms, he locked the door once more and placed the key in the pouch at his belt. He ignored the strange looks he received as he passed through the corridors of the palace and arrived at the Gold Tower postern gate. The guard there frowned as he approached, and then snapped to attention at the last moment as he realized who the armoured stranger was. Titus nodded at him.

'Open up.'

'Sir.' The guard would speculate about his passing through, but Titus would not be long, and the same man would be on duty when he returned. Having seen him re-enter the palace exactly the same, the sight of the senior commander in scruffy, mercenary kit would be relegated to drunken bar conversation at most.

Titus emerged into the street. It was still early. His hand on the pommel of his sword and his eyes scanning the seething crowds of Velutio, he moved through the streets, crossing the huge market square without paying the slightest attention to the stalls or the myriad shoppers, his ears open to any suspicious warning sound he might catch over the din of hawkers and citizens.

It took perhaps a quarter of an hour for the marshal to descend to the city's commercial port, which was one of the busiest in the world. With berthing for 50 ships of good size, over a hundred warehouses, six administrative buildings, its own guard and an endless sea of people of many nations loading, unloading, transporting, storing, arguing, shouting and singing, it was chaos on the grandest scale imaginable. Usually, if Titus had cause to come here, he would be in uniform with a military escort. The general populace would normally peel back like the tide to make room for the soldiers.

He was not used to having to fight his way through the crowd.

Beginning to get rather huffy with the whole situation, he pushed and shoved his way through the melee until he caught sight of the tall, red-brick offices of the port authorities. Not just any office, but the one he specifically sought: the shipping records office.

After taking an errant elbow to the gut and with a throbbing foot from where someone in the crowd had accidentally stamped on it, he reached the steps of the building. A queue of merchants and sailors stood impatiently waiting their turn to speak to the administrator. Acutely aware of the importance of the time that was passing, Titus marched past them all, pushed through the doorway to the main office and peered at the front of the queue. There were three desks in a small room filled with documents all in neat cubby holes. The queue was waiting for the first free desk and then filtering forward. Titus, ignoring the angry shouts as he pushed past people, spotted the clerk on the left furling closed a document and, the very moment his visitor turned and left the desk, Titus leapt in.

The big, dark-skinned man with the golden earring who was currently at the front of the queue barked an angry demand that he step back. Titus turned, tapping the pommel of his sword meaningfully.

'I am having the worst day in the history of bad days. I highly recommend you overlook my rudeness this once.'

The big man, who was entirely unarmed, frowned at the fingers pounding the top of the sword, and subsided with an irritated nod. Titus gave him a smile with the warmth of a dead lizard and turned back to the desk. The clerk cleared his throat, glancing nervously at the scarred and armoured man, rather incongruous in a queue of richly attired merchants or dirty, ragged seamen.

'How can I help?'

'I need to know about Pelasian ships that departed this morning. The vessel would have to have sailed…' he paused for a mental calculation of the time it had taken him to travel from his room to the dock, '…sometime after half past the ninth hour of the night. Probably after the tenth, but let's be thorough.'

The clerk pursed his lips, scratched his temple, and then collected four documents from the shelves, spreading them across the desk and pinning them down with small lead weights designed for the purpose.

'Eight vessels meet your criteria.'

'It would have taken on passengers. You keep a note of that, yes?'

'If they *declare* them. There are a surprising number of captains who take illegal passengers without documenting them.'

Titus frowned and nodded. He'd not thought of that. All life was a gamble, but he knew his odds and he knew what he was about. He'd not considered the possibility of such a subtle move, but Jala was Pelasian, and while they were a subtle people, she was cleverer than most. He would be willing to place money on the fact that she would be aboard a ship that officially carried no passengers. If she wished to travel unimpeded and feared that she might be followed, that would be her way.

'All right. Let's allow for the "clever bastard" quotient. How many were passenger-free?'

'Four, sir.'

'Hmm. How many were bound for Pelasia?'

'Three, sir. The other was moving on to Germalla from here.'

'How many of those three were heading for Akkad itself?' She was going home. He was certain of it. And Akkad was the home of the Pelasian god-king, her brother.

'Two, sir.'

On board one of those two ships were the Empress Jala and her servant girls. Could he catch up with them?

'When did they sail?'

'One at the tenth hour, one half an hour later.'

Neither was far ahead, then. Of course, Pelasian ships were built to be fast, and the one in question would be moving at top speed, for he was certain Jala would have paid her captain extraordinarily well to get her home in record time. The imperial fleet had some pretty fast ships, too, though he would have to report to the emperor first. *That* would be an unpleasant conversation. Perhaps he could keep the worst of the reasoning secret?

Nodding his thanks to the clerk, he left the counter and smiled alarmingly at the big, dark man, who glowered in return and then moved to the desk.

Titus pushed back through the corridors and out into the busy port.

The crowds were immediately around him again and he fought the frustration that threatened to take hold of him. He felt the irresistible urge to start kicking and punching to make some space, but he could see two of the harbour guard standing on a low dais nearby, keeping an eye on the crowd. He didn't want to attract their attention.

Speed was of the essence. He had to get back to the emperor, explain as little as possible while laying out the salient points in the kindest conceivable manner. Then, as soon as the emperor gave him permission, he would take a unit of the guard, commandeer the fastest vessel in the military port on the other side of the headland, and chase the empress down. He felt certain he could persuade her to come back and face Kiva. She was far from stupid, after all. He was convinced, now, that she had fled for the same reason as the prince: to avoid an unpleasant confrontation that they all could feel coming. But if the truth was out in the open, then she had no more reason to run. All could be sorted and maybe they could then even manage to find Quintillian and bring him back, too.

All he had to do…

Titus's world went swimmy and the din of the port was suddenly overwhelmed by the strange combination of an ear-splitting whistle that seemed to emanate from his own ears and the deep pulsing throb of his own blood. His eyesight went black then shattered into a thousand shards like broken glass.

He had been hit over the head. It had happened a few times in his life so he knew the feel of it well. This had been a particularly hard blow, too. His hand went up and after a few failed attempts touched the top of his head. It came away wet and sticky. The world was dark now, and it gradually filtered through the wool in his brain that that was because he was on the ground, surrounded by the legs of a thousand people.

He faintly heard the shouting of an official-sounding man, and suddenly he was being helped up. He caught a brief, wobbly glimpse of the uniform of the harbour guard, and then his eyesight went completely as he threw up copiously over the poor soldier. His last thought before unconsciousness claimed him was that he should have worn his father's damned helmet after all.

A faint light insisted itself on Titus's consciousness.

For some time he fought against its intrusiveness, but it seemed he couldn't drive it away, and in the end he surrendered to it. Then it went dark for a moment, then light again.

He blinked.

Sound came bubbling up like some kind of oozing lava spout, flooding into the world.

Every noise hurt, hitting him like a hammer to the centre of the brain.

'Should… full recovery…*real* damage… lucky… harbour guard… port.'

'Fagh,' was all he could he manage.

'You're awake?'

His eyes opened properly now. A blurred, grey shape against the white slowly resolved into the shape of a man. Kiva?

'Gnurgh.'

'Thank you, Doctor. Now all of you out, please. I need to speak to the patient alone.'

The shapes were starting to resolve into real forms all round now, and Titus could see the various features on the emperor's face. He heard the footsteps as the room's other occupants left, and then the click of the shutting door.

'Can you hear me, Titus?'

'Yerr.'

'You gave us a fright. The harbour guards who brought you in thought you would die. The doctor, though, tells me that you are fast on the road to recovery. Your head will be delicate for a few days, mind.'

'Port. I…hit in head.'

'Yes. Sadly, in the press the guards lost sight of the man who hit you. They can tell us nothing other than that he was wearing a brown hooded cloak. You were on the trail of Jala?'

Titus felt the memories come rushing back in. He felt cold all of a sudden.

'Kiva…'

'It's all right, Titus. I know. I read the documents in your bag. Forgive me for prying, but I thought they might be important and didn't know whether we could wait for your full recovery.'

'I...so sorry.'

His head felt as though it had been driven over by an iron-wheeled cart.

'That's not important right now. In fact, I am faintly relieved to at least know why things have become so difficult recently. But the matter of prime concern remains bringing back my wife and my brother.'

'Sure...*want* them back?'

The emperor gave him a sad, indulgent smile. 'Of course I do. How small you must think me if you believe I would be driven to such rage. The human heart is a strange thing, Titus, and cannot be guided by logic of the mind. There is much to discuss and resolve, but none of it can be done when I am here alone. I need Quintillian and Jala back here with me. My brother remains problematic in his ability to remain hidden, but Jala? We *know* where she is, don't we?'

'I can still catch her if I leave now.'

Kiva frowned at him, and then chuckled. 'I think that boat, to pun rather poorly, might have sailed, Titus. You have been unconscious for three days. Jala's ship will likely be almost at Akkad by now. Thus, timing is now less of an issue. I need you hale and hearty. The doctor wants you bed-bound for another week before he will even contemplate your departure from this room.'

'No... I... *three days? Really?*'

'Yes. And do not try to sit up. I am reliably informed that will probably make you vomit and faint, and not necessarily in that order.'

Titus sagged. Three days. Madness.

'I can't believe... this probably wasn't accident,' he said, gesturing at his head and only missing by a foot or so.

'No. I doubt it, too. The palace and the city are on high alert. I have informed the council that the empress is visiting her family, which will account for her absence, and your subaltern has made it known that we have received some vague threat, which is the official reason for heightened security across the city. In fact, with assassins in the streets and in the palace corridors, that's not stretching the truth very far!'

'A week is too long, Kiva. A day and I'll be ready to go.'

'And the moment a feather lands on your head you'll be out for the count, throwing up and passing out. No. You will do what the doctor tells you. And as soon as he clears you, you can take a unit of guards and go to Akkad. Bring Jala home so that we can repair this mess. But for now, I must attend to business. And you must sleep and heal.'

'But…'

'Sleep,' the emperor said, crossing to the door and opening it.

'And heal,' he added with a smile, slipping out of the room and closing the door behind him.

Titus stared at the closed portal for a moment and felt as though he were starting to spin gently in slow circles. With little preamble, he rolled painfully onto his side and threw up over the edge of the bed. Empty and feeling slightly better, he passed out.

CHAPTER XI

Of Deepening Trouble and Dangerous Waters

Titus Tythianus moved to the bow of the ship at the captain's gesture. On the fighting platform in the vessel's stern his unit of 24 hand-picked veteran guards gathered their kit ready for disembarkation. The great seething metropolis of Akkad, capital city of Pelasia, loomed ahead on the high promontory, made oddly unreal by the shimmering waves of heat radiating off the land. Pelasia was, it was said, the birthplace of the sun.

'What do you make of that, Marshal?' the squint-eyed sailor muttered, leaning on the rail casually.

Titus peered out across the bay. A small fleet of black-sailed Pelasian *daram* were moving swiftly towards them from Akkad's military harbour, spreading out into a line as they came. They looked... threatening. Titus frowned. Not the sort of welcome he'd expected. What had happened in the two weeks since the empress had come home, he wondered?

His own recovery had been fast, but then he had always been a quick healer, and the actual physical damage to him had been minimal, thanks to the timely intervention of the harbour guard. Once his brain had achieved equilibrium and he stopped throwing up every time he moved, he had advanced on the path of recovery at speed. And in less than the doctor's stated week, Titus had been back to business, selecting a unit of guards and commandeering the fastest ship in the harbour.

Then, leaving the emperor in Velutio, Titus had set sail south, down the eastern shores of the Nymphaean Sea, then a short hop across the mouth of the Eastern Sea and to the Pelasian coast, where they had turned east and made for the capital.

Leaving Kiva behind had weighed on Titus's mind and heart for, though the emperor maintained his façade of administrative care and imperious control, Titus had known him all their lives, and he could see that a shattered man hid within that tough shell, lamenting the flight of all those he loved. And for Titus to have to abandon him too… At least he would be safe. The marshal had selected the three best prefects in his army and put them in specific roles in his absence: controlling the city walls, guarding the palace and protecting the emperor. Of course, they were the stated duties of the imperial guard anyway, but they were being given more specific focus now, taking into account the potential threat of assassins.

He hated being away from duty. But the emperor had been adamant. Find Jala and return her to Velutio.

Was he going to be allowed to speak to her, though?

The line of black ships spanning the bay looked an awful lot like an interdiction rather than a welcome. 'Looks rather unfriendly, doesn't it?' he replied to the captain. 'Better slow down and see what they do.'

As the captain gave the orders and the ship backed-oars until it slowed to a crawl, Titus peered at the ships approaching. They were military vessels, all right. The fleet of the god-king, each with artillery mounted in the bow. The black-sailed ships closed on Titus's vessel and the centre of the line began to slow, the wings coming round and enfolding the stationary imperial ship like the wings of a great dark eagle. Titus resisted the urge to shout the order for his troops to make ready. It all looked extremely threatening, but Pelasia had been at peace with the empire for decades. As the lead ship closed further, the rest taking up a defensive ring cordon, Titus couldn't help but note the fact that the artillery on board was loaded ready, even if it wasn't actually pointing at them. Within moments the black vessel had come to a halt a few dozen paces away, the two ships drifting slightly in unison with the tide as the sun beat down mercilessly, turning the deck boards blistering hot beneath the men's feet.

'What are your designation, cargo, and intention,' called the daram's captain in thickly-accented imperial tongue.

Titus frowned. 'Since when have such things been of concern between us?' he shouted back.

'Answer the question.'

The marshal turned to the captain beside him. 'I don't like the sound of this.'

Turning back to the Pelasian ship, he cupped his hands around his mouth again. 'I am Titus Tythianus, Imperial Marshal, on a diplomatic mission from Velutio on behalf of the emperor himself. Why have you impeded us?'

There was a brief discussion on the other ship, then the captain shouted again. 'Prepare to be boarded and searched.'

Titus narrowed his eyes. 'Boarding a diplomatic vessel could be considered a belligerent act, captain. You might want to rethink that request.'

'The order stands,' the Pelasian replied.

'We could just comply,' the captain muttered next to Titus. 'We've no contraband, after all.'

'I am an imperial marshal, Captain. I'm damned if my ship is going to be boarded and searched like some low smuggler.' He turned back to the black-sailed ship. 'I am a personal friend of Mehrak, the *huvaka* of the god-king's navy – *your* commander! Unless you'd like an international incident on your hands, perhaps you'd like to escort me to port and allow me to speak to him.'

Again, there was a brief confab on board the Pelasian vessel. The imperial captain leaned closer to Titus. 'You really a friend of their commander, Marshal?'

'Well, I've met him a few times. He's a good man. He should be able to resolve whatever difficulties have arisen.'

'Very well,' came the shout from across the water. 'Follow us into port and dock where we tell you. Only you, Marshal. No soldiers.'

'That is highly irregular,' Titus grumbled.

'It is your choice. Submit to boarding or accept my terms.'

'This is starting to piss me off,' Titus grunted, but raised his voice. 'All right. Lead us in.'

As the captain gave the orders and the Pelasian fleet manoeuvred to return to port, Titus gestured to his unit's officer, who came jogging down the walkway between the rows of benches and halted with a salute.

'We're going into port and I shall be visiting the commander alone.'

'I don't like that, sir. Especially not with the way they're behaving.'

'Nor do I, but that's what's going to happen. Once you're docked and I've disembarked, run out the ropes a little so that you're not tight up against the jetty, and retract the boarding ramp. No one boards or leaves the ship at all. If the port authorities make any attempt to board, you have my authority to prevent them with the minimum force necessary, but they do *not* board this ship. Something mighty strange is going on here, and I'm not going to play their game until I know the rules. Got that?'

'Yes, sir. Shall I load up the bolt-thrower, just in case?'

Titus shook his head. 'That might provoke them. But make sure the thing is oiled and free and the ammunition is close by. Never hurts to be ready.'

Quarter of an hour later, the imperial coast-runner slid through the calm waters alongside the jetty in Akkad's military port. The daram that had escorted them mostly returned to their berths, though Titus was unsurprised to note that six remained at sea, bobbing around the entrance to the harbour. It seemed the Pelasians were taking no chances.

But of what?

The situation eased in no way as the boarding plank was run out and the marshal, dressed in his full uniform and armed and armoured appropriately, dropped to the timbers of the jetty. Ten of the god-king's soldiers were lined up at the far end of the planking, clad in black silk and shining steel, vicious-looking barbed pole-arms held high, small circular shields coming to a dangerous, spiked boss. The captain with whom he'd been conversing met him on the jetty and motioned for him to follow with no preamble. The ten black soldiers fell in and moved to escort them.

'Is all this strictly necessary?' Titus grunted, gesturing at the soldiers.

'*Strictly*,' the Pelasian captain retorted, 'I was under orders not to let you land at all. Now, please, follow.'

Up from the dockside they marched, past warehouses of military hardware and units of marines busy about their routines. Though Titus was no great sailor and had only peripheral experience of the imperial fleet, it was hard to see the heightened activity in the military port as anything other than preparations for war. His pulse quickened again. What was going on?

The headquarters of the huvaka of the fleet stood on the higher ground overlooking the numerous jetties. It was a delicate building of white arcades and graceful balconies, windows of coloured glass and roofs of glazed tiles. More soldiers met them at the entrance and reluctantly admitted the new arrivals after the Pelasian captain explained the situation to them. Once inside, half the escort dropped away and the captain and four remaining soldiers led Titus through the vestibules and halls of the headquarters – which seemed oddly empty and serene compared to the port outside – to the door of the commander. A knock, and the captain entered. There was a brief muffled conversation within, which, although Titus had a good command of the language, was too muted to quite hear. And then the door opened once more and the captain emerged, gesturing for Titus to enter.

The marshal stepped into the room and pushed the door shut behind him.

Mehrak Huvaka sat behind a wide desk, upon which was stretched a huge map. A model of a daram, complete with weapons and crew, sat at one edge of the table, and a tray bearing a jug of water with fruit floating in it rested at the other. Between them, the two weights held the map flat. Mehrak rose as the marshal entered and waved to a seat opposite him. He looked a lot older than Titus remembered, but then it had been almost a decade since they had met regularly.

'Huvaka,' he addressed the man politely by rank. 'It is good to see you again,' he added in seamless Pelasian.

'Please,' Mehrak replied in unaccented imperial, 'let us use *your* tongue. I may be lord in this palace, but nowhere in Pelasia is truly free of questing ears, so let us not make things too easy for them, eh? You are looking well, Titus Tythianus.'

'You politician.' Titus grinned. 'I look shabby and drawn and a good ten years older.'

'And you lost a finger,' the man laughed.

'Long story. And not over-interesting.' Titus sank into the chair and folded his arms. 'What's this all about, Mehrak?'

'Specifically?'

'Don't dissemble. Refusing to let an imperial vessel dock? Demanding to board us and search us? We're supposed to be allies, aren't we? What's going on? I came to speak to the empress, and attempt to persuade her to return to Velutio with me.'

Mehrak, who had been gently, rhythmically, tapping his stylus on the tabletop, stopped sharply.

'What?'

'Jala. Don't tell me she didn't come to Akkad, because I'll discount that as a lie.'

'Titus, do not play games with me.'

'I'm not, Mehrak. What is going on? Can I speak to the empress?'

'The empress is not here, Titus.'

The marshal straightened and unfolded his arms, his gaze becoming hard. 'I told you not to lie to me, Mehrak. I traced her movements to Velutio's port, and I'm sure beyond doubt that she took ship for Akkad.'

'Titus, I know you of old. You are not a man of lies or untruths. Are you seriously telling me that you do not have the empress at Velutio?'

The hairs on Titus's neck rose. 'What?'

'The empress? She is not in Velutio? Then where is she?'

Titus shuddered. Something was horribly wrong. 'She's here!'

'No, Titus. She never reached Akkad. Your own people took her.'

'Don't be ridiculous,' snapped the marshal. I would know if we had.'

The Pelasian commander pushed back his chair with a scraping noise and rose, pacing along the edge of the table in a way that reminded Titus rather disturbingly of the emperor.

'The empress never reached Akkad, Titus. Her ship was overcome and sunk somewhere in the northwest. Miraculously there were survivors who managed to live two days at sea until they were rescued by a passing merchant. They came to port here days ago now. They are witnesses to the imperial crime, Titus.'

'*What* crime, Mehrak? You're blathering.'

'Titus, the empress's vessel was sunk by an imperial warship. And with purpose of malice, for the witnesses say that the empress and her maids were the only prize taken. The ship, its crew and cargo were abandoned to the deeps. And you tell me you know nothing of this?'

'Shit.'

'That is hardly an answer, Titus.'

'It's the only one I have, Mehrak. I know nothing of the matter, and neither does the emperor. I came directly from his palace at Velutio, with his instructions to find his wife and bring her home.'

'This is very bad, my friend,' Mehrak hissed. 'Come to the balcony. Fewer ears there.'

As they stepped out into the sunlight, the Pelasian officer suddenly switched to old Germallan, a language only spoken in certain eastern provinces and used in ancient literature.

'You know this tongue?'

'Yes,' Titus replied. 'I'm surprised you do.'

'Few in Akkad will manage. It will grant us extra security. Titus, the immediate future looks troubled.'

'I get that, yes. Why in the name of the gods would an imperial ship capture our own empress?'

'There is some dissembling of motive here,' Mehrak murmured, 'but the truth of the matter is that the god-king believes your emperor to have imprisoned his majesty's sister.'

'You're spouting nonsense now,' Titus snorted. 'Why would he do that?'

'There is some notion of infidelity within the imperial family. The king believes that Emperor Kiva perceives such fault with his wife and has imprisoned her. What else was he to believe, given the fact that we have numerous witnesses to the imperial military capturing the Lady Jala as she attempted to escape to her brother's lands?'

'Oh, shiiiiit.'

'Titus?'

'The *letters*. She's been pouring out her heart to her brother, hasn't she. And he thinks… oh, shit. We haven't got her, Mehrak. The emperor didn't even know she was missing. We assumed her to be safely in the royal palace up that hill.'

'Then we have a problem of enormous proportions, Titus. The king is furious beyond belief. Yesterday he dispatched a missive to the emperor demanding the return of the Princess Jala, and threatening hostilities if she is not delivered to Pelasian forces. *Nahmad!'* he cursed. 'The messenger and your vessel probably passed in the night.'

'Mehrak, we cannot return her to her brother. We don't *have* her!'

'With respect, Titus, *someone* does. Someone with an imperial warship. That rather damns you all.'

'Don't tell me,' the marshal grunted, pinching the bridge of his nose. 'You're already gathering the military aren't you? That's why there's so much activity in the port. That's why this headquarters is so empty. Because every officer with a job to do is out there doing it.'

Mehrak nodded unhappily. 'The fleet is assembling along the coast. The army is gathering in three places, to cross by ship and by land if the empress is not returned. Our only hope to avoid conflict is that the empress is brought back to us. Hence the fact that every imperial vessel found is being boarded and searched.'

'In Pelasian waters,' added Titus.

'No. Anywhere they are found. A sizeable sector of the fleet is at sea, hunting imperial shipping and searching them. It is likely a futile gesture, but the god-king demanded that I do all I can.'

'Mehrak, even if gathering your military on the empire's southern border doesn't prompt conflict, boarding imperial vessels is tantamount to an act of war anyway, especially in open sea. This is madness. You've got to call off your fleet.'

The officer shook his head, his face bleak. 'I cannot refuse my king, Titus. Just as you cannot refuse your emperor.'

'You'd be surprised how often good men have refused bad emperors in the past.'

'And look what happened. Twenty years of civil war. We are not the same in Pelasia. We cannot refuse the king. He is a god, Titus.'

'If he's so divine, he should be able to see the truth of this matter.'

Mehrak's gaze hardened. 'By standing order in Akkad, I should now impound your vessel and question everyone aboard.'

'Don't be ridiculous. And we are a diplomatic party. You do that and war will come surprisingly quick.'

'Which is why I am going to allow you to return to your ship, Titus, and put to sea unmolested. But you need to get far from Pelasia as fast as you can. You were very lucky not to have met my fleet on your way here as it is.'

'Mehrak, we have to resolve this. I can't just go home and watch things deteriorate. Can you get me an audience with the king?'

'No. He will not see you. And if he finds out you are here, he might well have you questioned and broken. Did I mention his fury?'

'Then what can we do? We can't let this descend into conflict. There hasn't been war between our peoples in centuries. Remember the tales of the bad old days? None of us want a repeat of that.'

'If war is to be prevented, the Princess – the *Empress* – Jala must be returned to Akkad.'

'I told you: we haven't got her.'

'*Someone* has. Someone with an imperial warship. Find her, Titus. Bring her back and prevent the disaster that is coming.'

'Find her?' Titus snapped. 'Are you mad? Have you any idea how many imperial ships ply the seas? And not just merchants. There are old warships owned privately by lords and cartels. There are pirates, there are mercenary vessels hiring out to guard merchant convoys. Then there are actual merchant vessels and couriers that have been fitted out to stop pirates that could easily be mistaken for warships. It would be like searching for a needle in a wheatsheaf. A nightmare.'

'But, with respect, it is *your* nightmare, Titus. An imperial ship took her. Find her, and you might avert what is coming.'

Titus fell silent, looking out over the balcony. Far below he could see his ship, sitting in the water some ten paces from the jetty, loosely roped. Black-clad soldiers lined the dock defensively, and six daram splashed back and forth across the harbour mouth. It looked bleak. Jala had been taken by someone under an imperial flag. To find her seemed an impossible undertaking. But what choice did he have? He simply had to do it. Mehrak was correct.

'All right, my friend, but I need two favours.'

The Huvaka of the Pelasian fleet nodded encouragingly.

'I need to send a letter back to my emperor, and I cannot afford the time to do it myself, nor spare my ship, since I have immediate need of her. Can I put a few of my men on one of your scout ships to take word back to the emperor, and explain what I am doing?'

Mehrak winced. 'That will not go down well when word gets back to his divine majesty.'

'Nor will the fact that you had me here and let me go. You're already in for it.'

'Very well,' the man agreed unhappily. 'I shall do as you ask. What else?

'Can I speak to the survivors of the attack? I might just be able to narrow down my search. Certainly better than scouring the open sea for any and all armed imperial vessels.'

'Of course. They are being quartered in the port for now. I will have you escorted to them. And the captain who brought you here will take your letter and your soldiers to Velutio. He is a good man, and he will be relieved to be out of Akkad after having broken the rules to bring you here.'

Titus sighed and sagged. 'You realize just how small my chances of success are, Mehrak.'

The officer smiled sadly. 'Yet you have a reputation for surviving the most ridiculous of situations, Titus, like your father before you. Your luck goddess, I suspect, rides upon your shoulder.'

'Then I hope she's paying attention at the moment.'

CHAPTER XII

Of Troubles Seaborne

The black sail was growing in size by the moment as the Pelasian daram gained on them.

'So much for the damned fastest ship available,' Titus complained to the captain, who stood next to him at the stern rail, watching the dark blot in the endless azure blue knifing through the water towards them.

'It's a matter of draft and water depth, not ship speed, Marshal.'

'Sailor jargon,' dismissed Titus.

'It's quite simple. This part of the sea, off the north coast of Pelasia, is an underwater plateau. Most of it is quite shallow and the only way a proper vessel can get through is by navigating the deeper areas and channels in it. It's almost as though the ship runs on rails, you see. In fact, if we didn't have good Pelasian charts we'd have been high and dry over an hour ago. Back in the old days when we were at war with them a whole imperial fleet came to grief in these waters. Our draft is quite deep, while the Pelasian daram have a very shallow draft. While we are limited to the deeper channels, they can race across the shallow areas of the plateau.'

Titus frowned. 'So why don't we do what they do?'

The captain gave him a look as though he'd asked why cats couldn't bark.

'Pelasian vessels are only made for activity in the Eastern and Nymphaean Seas. Even then they tend not to operate in the middle of the sea and rarely roam more than a few hours from the coast. Their draft makes them unstable in rough waters, you see?'

'No. Not really.'

'Well, our ships with a deep draft are hard to knock over sideways, so they can roam out into the Western Ocean, from where we get all our tin and amber and the like. The Pelasians are shallow. One big wave like you get in the Western Ocean and the whole thing would be upside down. It all depends what the ships are made for. Ours are suitable for all waters, you see.'

'Except these,' noted Titus bitterly.

'And yet these are the safest waters to ply to get where you want to be, Marshal. Better than risking the twin monsters or the harpy rocks in the open sea.'

'I don't believe in sea monsters.'

The captain's eyebrow jacked up a notch. 'Better that way, I can assure you. When you've felt Scautha clutching at your hull and trying to drag you down into her lair while your oarsmen pull for their lives, there are moments when you'd give an arm not to believe in sea monsters. The fact remains, I will be boarded by a thousand Pelasians before I risk my ship to the swarming depths.'

'I'll remind you of that in half an hour when those bastards have caught us.'

'We could have gone directly north from Akkad,' the captain noted in a level tone, 'made for Barada and then coasted it to Rilva. It would have been safer and little chance of being caught by Pelasians out that way.'

'And it would add days onto our journey. We're already too far behind and time is of the essence. Just see if there's any way you can get to open water and outrun this black-sailed shitbag. The delay will make me fret.'

As the captain bent over his charts once more and tried in vain to find an alternative that wouldn't scrape off the keel of their vessel, Titus returned to watching the daram that closed inexorably upon them. He was limited in terms of destination by the small hope he had gleaned back in Akkad.

The naval commander had shown him to the survivors of the attack, and he had very politely and gently drawn from them every small detail they could give him.

They had been only a day and a half out from Velutio. Though the survivors hadn't a solid grasp of imperial geography, given the likely speed of their ship – a fast one – and a few of the features of the coast they could describe, Titus placed the attack somewhere off the southwestern point of the central provinces, around the port of Haphoris, though out of sight of it, since they were in open sea and heading south. That gave him a location for the ship's sinking, though such would be of little help in tracking Jala.

However, while all but one of the survivors were oarsmen with only passing knowledge of what went on around them, the other was a lookout, and his information had been a lot more elucidating. He gave them a solid description of the attacking craft.

It had been taller than this one, and wider, with three sails, rather than the more common two – an extra small lateen at the stern. That made it a ship designed specifically for the wide ocean, which put it somewhere in the western provinces. Moreover its imperial flag bore a green stripe down the edge of the fly, and *that* confirmed a solidly western origin. Given the flag and the shape of the vessel, it was a reasonably safe assumption that the ship had come from the outer edge of the empire, along the Western Ocean shores. It wasn't much, but it was a start.

He had, in truth, been a little dismayed to learn that the huvaka had been telling the truth and that it *had* been an imperial ship that sank the empress's vessel. The lookout's description was just too credible to be faked. Such ships were rarely seen in the inner seas, so it was almost certainly the first time the man had seen such a vessel.

And so Titus had formulated his plan. They would sail back towards the open arms of the Nymphaean Sea and once the twin archipelagos came into sight they would turn west along the outer coast. What then, he didn't truly know, and was still thinking through that part, but at least he would be in the right quarter of the empire. Not much, but a start. If all else failed they would sail along the coast until they reached Burdium Portus, the largest coastal installation in the west, where, if there was any information to glean, it would be found.

They were already many days behind the empress and her captors, and every hint of a delay irked the marshal.

The black sail was closer still, now.

Titus ground his teeth and took a deep breath. 'Slow the ship.'

'Sir?' the captain looked up from his map.

'It's all about speed. And if we faff around looking for ways to outrun the bugger, we'll just cause extra delay. He's going to run us down in the end anyway. We might as well let him catch us, get this over with and then get moving.'

The captain nodded with a look that rather unsubtly suggested that had been his opinion all along, and gave the order to slow the vessel.

Once they stopped plying the deeper channel in the underwater plateau, the black daram raced towards them with impressive speed, pulling out to port and coming alongside. Titus was unsurprised to see the artillery in the bow loaded and turned to face them. He'd given no such order aboard their own ship. Better that this be dealt with peacefully and very quickly.

'Prepare to be boarded, imperial vessel,' shouted a deep voice in the northern tongue, laden with a southern Pelasian accent. A desert nomad by heritage, then, and now sailing the wide seas. Odd how things work out for some people.

'We are a diplomatic party,' Titus shouted back in faultless Pelasian, 'four hours out of Akkad and making for Burdium Portus. We have nothing to hide and no contraband. Send your party aboard quickly and get this over with, as we are on a tight schedule.'

The daram closed and grapples were sent out, biting into the rails, the ropes tightening and drawing the two hulls close together.

'I hope he's going to pay for that damage,' the captain growled.

'Don't make trouble. I'll see you right for it,' Titus hissed back as the ramp was run out of the daram and across to their vessel. He turned back to the Pelasian captain.

'Before anyone boards, and given that we have peacefully agreed to your "request" to board us, I would take it kindly if that artillery piece was pointed somewhere else. We're not at war yet, you know.'

There was a brief discussion aboard the black ship and the huge bolt-thrower swivelled ponderously until it pointed off across the water.

'Thank you.'

Four Pelasian sailors in black tunics and trousers, with their heads covered in dark cloth to ward off the worst of the blistering sun, trotted across the plank and dropped into the imperial vessel, nimbly stepping between the oar benches. Once aboard, the

Pelasians split into two pairs. One went to the bow and began to move back along the ship, peering into each space between the benches. The other moved to the hatch and dropped down into the belly of the ship, where the cargo hold was almost empty in order to grant the ship all the more speed. Their search shouldn't take long.

The captain hopped across to their ship and bowed to his opposite number, who gave a sour, half-hearted salute.

'You are a senior officer,' the Pelasian noted, addressing Titus.

'An imperial marshal, yes.'

'Then you have my apologies for the necessity of this.'

'I understand. I just want to get on with my journey.'

The man nodded. 'You speak my language well.'

'And you mine.'

The two men fell silent, with little else to say. Titus stood still, pensive, irritated, as the air filled with the sound of the sea lapping against the ship sides, the creak and groan of rocking timbers and the thud of canvas as the half-reefed sails caught the occasional whisper of wind. All was eerily quiet, the Pelasian crew watching with a strange mix of boredom and expectation, the imperial crew simmering at the indignation of being boarded.

'Where does the plateau…' Titus began, but was cut off sharply by an urgent shout from below.

He and both captains exchanged startled glances and started to move down the ship towards the hatch with a sense of urgency. Titus felt his heart lurch. What could they have found? Surely the captain hadn't been stupid enough to bring anything suspicious with them?

As they neared the hatch, a figure emerged from it, and the marshal felt his world falling apart around him. One of the two Pelasian sailors who'd gone below was staggering up onto the deck, clutching his head. Blood was sheeting down from his scalp, and he looked distinctly unsteady.

'What happened?' Titus barked.

The other Pelasian appeared now, dragging an imperial sailor by the throat, the lighter-skinned man's face pulverized and bloody.

'He wanted to search my sea chest,' the sailor growled through split lips.

'What have your sailors done to my men?' demanded the Pelasian captain, despite the answer to his question standing plainly before him.

Titus rounded on the foreign captain. 'I understand you are searching ships for the Empress Jala. Do you really think to find her in a sailor's sea chest?' He almost spat the words with anger.

'You submitted to a search,' shouted the Pelasian captain.

'For a *person*. Not to have this ship scoured for anything of value. Get the fuck off my ship and take your legalized pirates with you.'

The Pelasian bridled, his eyes flashing dangerously. 'It is my duty to search this ship and I will do so.'

'No, you will not,' Titus snarled. 'You lost that right when you started looking to pillage instead.'

Out of the corner of his eye he could see the artillery on the Pelasian ship starting to swivel back towards the imperial hull. Before he could say anything, there was a scream from the hatch. Turning, he saw that the bloodied imperial sailor had taken the opportunity in the confusion to jam his knife into the thigh of the hitherto intact Pelasian sailor. The man was shrieking as he fell, clutching the hilt sticking out of his leg.

'Shithead,' snapped the bloodied sailor, just before he was hit in the midriff by the man with the battered skull and the pair went down on top of the leg wound.

'Oh, shit,' Titus murmured, then turned to his remaining 15 guardsmen, who were standing tense at attention in the stern, simply awaiting the command. 'Get that artillery piece loaded and train it on the Pelasians. The next time any of them touch an imperial citizen, put a 10- pound shot through their hull and sink the bastards.'

He turned back to the Pelasian beside him. 'We're teetering on the brink here, Captain. One word from me and we're fighting. Now, I'm politely, as an ambassador of the court of Velutio, giving you one last chance to get off this ship and take your pirates with you. If you refuse we will have no choice but to force you.'

The Pelasian sneered, his hand going to the hilt of the blade at his side.

'I think that answers that question. Prefect Torus? Take three men and secure the enemy artillery.'

Even as his own men finished loading the heavy rock into their own artillery and turning it to face the daram that bobbed alongside, half a dozen sailors at the rear had hauled the two bloodied Pelasians up and were pushing them back down the walkway towards the boarding plank. The two who'd been searching among the rowing benches were nervously edging back towards their only means of exit, their hands on their weapons.

'Last chance,' Titus said in Pelasian. 'Leave or fight.'

With a roar, the Pelasian captain ripped his blade from his sheath. Before he could bring it to bear, Titus punched him in the face with every ounce of strength he could muster, sending the Pelasian floundering into the oar benches, where two of the imperial rowers grabbed him and began to throttle him.

The prefect in command of the guards was now leaping across the dangerous narrow gap between ships with three of his men. The entire Pelasian crew were grabbing swords and rising from their benches. Similar activity was taking place on the imperial ship. Titus sighed. Why was nothing easy? And he was fairly sure he'd broken a finger on the captain's jaw, too.

A thud and a scream announced the release of the Pelasian bolt-thrower. The marshal caught the scene from the corner of his eye. The last of the three guardsmen leaping across to the enemy ship took the blow full in the chest. The 2-foot iron bolt exploded his torso, showering both ships and their crews with blood and gore. The blow plucked him out of the air and threw him back against the foremast of the imperial ship, which he hit with a wet thud and then slid down. Most of his chest was gone, and Titus could see the mast through it.

The Pelasians were busy loading the weapon again, ratcheting back the firing mechanism, but the prefect and his remaining two men were there now. One man took his blade to the bound sinews of the artillery, hacking through them and ruining the weapon with every blow. The Pelasians reacted immediately, half a dozen sailors running over and swamping the prefect and his men.

Even as poor Prefect Torus fell under the rising and falling blades of the angered Pelasians, the first shot from the imperial stone-thrower hit. The men, loosing the weapon as quickly as they could without taking too much time to aim, had released it too high. The huge stone ball failed to hole the hull, instead smashing the Pelasian ship's rail and bouncing across the deck, where it took the leg clean off a sailor in a shower of bone and red spray before passing through the far rail and off into the turquoise waters.

The Pelasian artilleryman dropped a bolt into the groove of their weapon and turned it to face the centre of the imperial deck. Then the man made a dreadful mistake. He ratcheted the mechanism back one more time, and the twisted sinews that created the weapon's tension, weakened by the sword blows of the guardsman, gave. The entire weapon folded in on itself and exploded in a shower of wood and splinters. The bolt itself arced up gracefully and passed through the imperial ship's foresail before plopping harmlessly down into the sea. The entire enemy artillery crew were pulverized, sprayed with deadly shards of wood and splinters of iron. Indeed, half a dozen of the nearby Pelasian sailors were hit by the agonizing cloud of death.

Titus stared in shock. All about him, fighting had erupted. The imperial sailors were up now, running for the boarding plank with swords drawn. The Pelasians were doing the same, though there were fewer of them, given the nature of the imperial vessel's passengers.

Down in the oar benches, the Pelasian captain was thrashing about as the two sailors throttled the life out of him with a length of rough rope. Ah, well. Titus had thought this would be relatively routine. He should have known better. Hefting his own blade, he moved to the edge of the ship and prepared to jump across.

There was a creaking noise and a kerchunk and suddenly a large section of the black daram's starboard hull disappeared. The 10-pound shot from the imperial artillery passed easily through the timbers and down through the hull then, from the sound of it, out the other side.

Almost immediately the Pelasian ship lurched and the boarding plank bucked and crumpled. The men busy struggling on the plank to try and board each other's ship screamed as they were upended and dumped into the water between the two vessels. Then the inevitable happened. With the stability of the Pelasian ship ruined, the two vessels collided, their sides crashing together, crushing those men who'd fallen from the ramp and grinding them to paste. The turquoise water started to change colour around the ships as more and more blood filled it.

The daram lurched back the other way and the grapple ropes all strained taut. The imperial ship jerked with the motion and Titus, who had been standing at the rail, found himself tipping over it. For a dreadful moment he thought he was in the water, where the next wave would send the ships together again and crush him. But at the last moment his questing hand found the rail and instead he was hanging precariously over the side, his sword in his other hand. The fiery pain lancing up his hand from the rail confirmed that he had, indeed, broken his finger on the enemy captain.

He looked around for a moment. With one hand he was never going to be able to haul himself back up. But the sword in his other hand had been given to him by the emperor's father. It was the very blade Darius had borne with him on that day he had been proclaimed emperor and the interregnum had ended. He *couldn't* drop that sword!

An ominous sail shape suddenly streaked through the water nearby.

Sharks!

Drawn by the huge cloud of crimson flooding the waters.

Suddenly, the heritage of his blade seemed of considerably less importance. He was about to let go when hands closed on his clutching arm, and two burly sailors hauled him back into the ship. As he landed on deck once more, shaking with nerves, nodding his thanks to his saviours, he turned to take in the scene. The daram was done for. At the rate she was taking on water she would be under the surface in a hundred heartbeats. Precious few of his own men were aboard that ship, which was a good thing, since there was little chance of them getting back to their own vessel.

The daram was rolling off to the far side, the sails mere feet from the water.

'Lower the ladders. Let any of our lads who can swim back get aboard!'

'What about the Pelasians, sir?'

'Sod 'em.'

It was a brutal thing to do and he knew it, but there was no choice. Thanks to the draft of the imperial ship, they were in one of the deeper channels of the plateau, which meant that there was plenty of sea for the daram to sink without trace. The dorsal fins streaking through the water, circling around the scene, signalled the inevitable demise of anyone who couldn't make it to the imperial ship. In fairness, the poor Pelasian bastards might be better off drowning.

Men were now swimming through the gore-filled water, desperately making for the lowered rope ladders. They were a mix of Pelasian and imperial, their feud forgotten as they all sought the safety of the remaining ship.

Titus felt his heart grow heavy as the first black-clad, soaked Pelasian who started to ascend the ladders was plucked off with a long wooden pole and sent back down into the water with a disbelieving shriek. Behind him a lucky imperial sailor started to climb. The same scene happened time and again, the Pelasians pushed back into the water. Then they started to pull the imperial sailors off the ropes.

And the sharks moved in.

Titus watched the first attack but, sickened, turned away and stepped back from the rail. As the last two imperial sailors were brought aboard, he saw the Pelasian daram disappear beneath the waves, bubbling and groaning, flotsam bobbing up to the surface. Screams echoed up from the water, often cut agonizingly short.

'That was a hard thing to do, Marshal,' the imperial captain muttered, shuffling over to stand next to him.

'That was an act of war, though I'm not sure on whose behalf. Either way, we could leave no witnesses. If one of them made it back to Akkad and told what had happened, that would be it. No diplomatic solution would work. We'd be at war with Pelasia. Sometimes we have to sacrifice a few to save the rest. If you are short of oarsmen, my guards will take their place.'

The captain nodded. 'Let's just hope that's the last we see of Pelasian shipping.'

'Indeed. Square away everything and get us underway, Captain. Take us to the western provinces. No time for the men to rest yet. I want to be far from this carnage before we take a break.'

As things settled and the men returned to their benches, Titus saw the body of his prefect bob to the surface of the water for a moment before it became the subject of interest for three sharks.

'I cannot wait to get back onto dry land.'

CHAPTER XIII

Of Troubles Airborne

'The corner of the sail's come loose, you shower of shit!' bellowed the captain in the face of a wind that stretched and distorted his face. The few men not bent hard at the oars leapt to the rope to deal with the furled sail.

Titus eyed it nervously. He'd never been a bad sailor – didn't get seasick or anything – but this journey was starting to put him off ships in a somewhat permanent manner. Drownings, crushings between two hulls, shark attacks, and now…

He tore his gaze from the sail and the feverishly-working crew and peered with dismay at the black clouds that were boiling in the sky like ink dropped into a bottle of water, churning and billowing, sending out lashing rain that had yet to touch the ship but was tearing the surface of the sea close enough to view. They had been sailing for five days since the incident at the Pelasian coast, and the marshal had begun to think they were out of danger. Certainly they'd not seen any more black sails, and this far northwest, so close to the Western Ocean, they were unlikely to do so. He'd not counted on spring storms, of course.

'Are you sure we can outrun it?' he asked the captain, trying – and failing – to keep a hint of nerves out of his voice.

'No.'

'But there's a good chance?'

'No.'

'Is there *any* chance?' he prompted nervously, looking back. An hour ago the storm had been little more than a black smudge on the eastern horizon. The captain had watched it carefully, trying to judge the direction and speed of the tempest and had announced after a short time that it was matching their bearings and moving at almost twice their speed. It didn't take a mathematician to calculate the results of *that*.

The captain grunted noncommittally.

The marshal's gaze slid from the churning clouds to the surface of the sea as his stomach lurched sharply to one side and the prow of their ship rose and fell, crashing into the next trough. The storm might not quite be upon them, but it had sent a vanguard of high, powerful waves ahead of it. The captain had shrugged them off with the comment that even a light squall had that effect this close to the Western Ocean.

To add to the unpleasantness of the situation, the only clear part of the sky, out to the west, was filled with the orange dome of the sinking sun. Soon they would be at sea, in a storm, in the dark. A three-way battering of hideousness.

Yet the only land within sight was the Vinceia Peninsula, the elongated arm of the western provinces that both encircled the Nymphaean Sea and began the coast of the Western Ocean and the edge of the empire. And the Vinceia Peninsula was infamous enough with sailors that even a landlubber like Titus knew of its reputation. A 200-mile peninsula that rose from the water on high, craggy cliffs with only jagged coves filled with rocks that rose like teeth from beneath the surface of the sea, waiting to tear open the hulls of unwary ships. Two hundred miles of inaccessible, rocky nightmare. The only boats that made it in or out of those coves were small, flat-bottomed fishing vessels from the local villages, piloted by men who knew every rock and shallow well enough to float over the top of most of them. And even then, those fishing fleets only went out in the calmest of weather. Not on nights when *Pluvus*, the god of storms, was heaving his breath into the wind and stirring the sea with his thunderbolts.

Burdium Portus was still 200 miles away, and most of that consisted of these unforgiving cliffs.

The ship suddenly lurched to port and swayed, the bow rising sickeningly high, hiding the dome of the setting sun.

'What do we do?' Titus asked the captain as stinging salty spray slapped him across the face with the force of an oar, compelling him to brace himself or slide across the deck.

'Any gods look favourably on you, Marshal, you might want to start praying.'

'Very helpful.'

The captain had been planning to take the unusual step of staying at sea for three nights in a row until the coast was accessible, further north. Rarely did captains do so, though out here it was something of a necessity, given the lack of available anchorage. The hold contained enough rations and fresh water to see them all through. But that had not taken into account the black boiling clouds closing on them from the east. Titus couldn't imagine them making it through the night in that.

'We're going to have to find safe haven.'

Titus stared at the captain. 'And where, might I ask, will you do that?'

'On the Vinceia Peninsula.'

Titus shook his head. 'Even I know that's not possible. Those rocks are ship-killers. Even the fleets of the imperial navy stay away from them, let alone merchants. We'll be smashed to pieces long before we get in close.'

'Not necessarily,' the captain said, and Titus couldn't help noticing that the man was not quite meeting his gaze. He narrowed his eyes.

'Explain.'

'This is, strictly speaking, a private vessel, Marshal, not a military one. We are *part* of the imperial courier system – the fastest ships on the sea – but we're all private vessels, nonetheless. And we take on secondary commissions when business is slack. You know – sometimes we can run wine for a desperate merchant, or act as a ferry for a caravan or the like, just to keep the money flowing when courier business is slow.'

'You're a smuggler,' accused Titus in a hiss.

'No, Marshal. I am a courier captain with a sideline in mercantile voyages. But I will admit to knowing of a few generally secret anchorages along the peninsula that *are* used by those with less legal business to take care of.'

Titus's eyes stayed narrow. 'You could get us into one of these places?'

'Yes, but you'll have to bear in mind that the place might just be filled with lowlifes. Our insignia and passengers might not be welcome.'

'I'd rather be unpopular than drowned,' Titus snapped. 'Where's the nearest place?'

'There's a village called Nessana only a mile or so away. You can just see the lights twinkling.'

Titus squinted into the gloomy sunset.

'I personally can't see shit. All right, take us to this Nessana, but if we hit a rock and drown, then I'm going to pursue you through the afterlife with a sharp stick until I can ram it up your smuggling backside.'

The captain gave Titus a grin that he thought looked a little too deranged for his liking, and then began to shout out orders to his crew – orders including, oddly, the taking down of imperial colours.

Titus glanced back along the ship. A dozen crew dashed around the deck, stepping from narrow walkway to narrow walkway, slipping on the treacherous wet timbers, nimbly moving across the oar benches where necessary. The whole guard unit were now on those same benches, alongside the sailors, heaving on oars like pros, their muscles straining as they tried to drive the ship on ahead of the storm.

The captain turned to him with a dangerous cast to his expression. 'My advice, Marshal, is to strap yourself to something and hold on tight.'

Titus frowned, but at a loss for a reason to argue, he unfastened the second belt from his midriff, relying on his sword belt to keep his tunic in place. Hurriedly, he scurried over to the rail near the captain and pushed the tip of his belt through his sword belt, linking the two like a chain, and then fastened the belt around the rail. He tried not to contemplate the possibility of the rail splintering and both he and the section of timber going over into the churning water together.

'Brace!' the captain bellowed out across the deck, and Titus watched the sailors desperately grabbing onto things and holding tight, hunkering down as low as they could. As soon as everyone was as safe as they could manage in so short a time, the captain gritted his teeth and pushed hard against his steering oar. Titus watched with confusion and worry as the great, heavy timber protrusion gradually shifted in the roaring waters.

He frowned.

'What are you doing?'

'I'm steering with the storm.'

Titus mentally calculated their trajectory and his confusion grew. The way the captain had shifted the oar would send the ship further out to sea, *away* from the land.

'Gaius and Ufius?' the captain gestured at the two nearest sailors sharply before grabbing hold of the steering oar again and holding it steady as it fought to free itself from his grip.

The two men looked up.

'Get below and move the cargo. I want all available ballast shifting to the starboard side and roping tight.'

The two men nodded and let go as soon as the deck momentarily righted itself, scurrying across and down into the hatch.

The captain, his jaw hard with clenched teeth, his muscles rippling as he barely maintained control of the steering oar, caught Titus's frown. 'The landward side of the tempest will be the roughest seas. We'll use the power of the storm to pick up speed in the safer waters, getting just far enough ahead to make a run for land. Then I'll turn her sharply across the front of the storm and, using the speed we've built up, make a run for Nessana. If I time it just right and the gods are kind, we'll shoot into the cove just ahead of the worst of the storm.'

'And if you don't time it right or the gods are unhappy?'

'Then we hit the rocks on the way in and tomorrow morning the locals will be hauling bodies from the water. Or maybe we'll not manage to cut across the storm and the waves will take us as we turn. Or maybe I'll have judged the ballast wrong and we'll tip over just in time for the storm to hit us. There are a dozen ways this can go horribly wrong and only one way for it to go right.'

Titus closed his eyes for a moment. 'And there's no other chance?'

'Not leaping to my mind.'

The marshal took a deep breath and unfastened his belt.

'What are you doing?'

'Well if we're betting everything we own on one roll of the dice, I'm going to be the one rolling the damned things. That oar's fighting you back. You could do with a hand.' As he rushed over and slid into position opposite the captain, grasping hold of the huge timber arm and pulling it in the same direction as the captain pushed, lending his own prodigious strength to the task, the captain nodded at him. 'Then you'll have to react instantly when I tell you to do something. Got it?'

'Got it.'

Titus looked back over the rail. The storm was almost all around them now, rather than chasing them down. The great black clouds formed a churning wall that blurred with the sea so that it was hard to make a distinction between the two.

The rain hit the ship.

'The storm will have us any moment,' the marshal muttered unhappily.

The captain gave him an odd smile. 'See this wave?'

The ship bucked once more, the prow rising.

'I am faintly aware of it, yes.'

'Watch what happens now we've changed bearing.'

The ship's prow rose and rose until Titus lost sight of the sunset ahead and was sure he was staring vertically into the sky. Then, in a sickening, stomach-yanking moment, the vessel crested that huge wave and the ship teetered as though it were held aloft by a god. Then it began to tip forward. Titus's eyes widened as he stared down what looked like a mountainside made of water.

'God shit and battered testicles!' he yelled.

'That is more than a possibility, yes.' The captain grinned.

The ship descended. Titus gripped the steering oar tight, more in order to hang onto something than out of desire to direct the vessel. The captain next to him was laughing like a madman again, which did little to instil further confidence in the marshal.

'Steering to broad off port,' the man shouted. Titus stared at him. 'I speak five languages, but *sailor* isn't one of them!'

'Ease up your grip.'

Titus let go of the oar, and the captain straightened the oar to a more gentle turn. 'Now hold her tight again.'

The ship spun slightly so that she was exactly stern-on to the crest of the wave behind. As the vessel plummeted down the steep, watery incline, she picked up tremendous speed, and Titus felt the gods watching as he held tight, sweating despite the cold, his backside clenched so tight he feared it would be summer before it loosened.

'Ship oars!' The captain bellowed and, as the crew pulled in their oars, which were now doing little to affect the vessel's speed, he looked across at the hatch. 'How's that ballast?' He shouted so loud that his voice cracked.

'All good, Cap'n,' came a hollow call from below.

'Almost time,' the captain murmured. Titus looked off to the right. The rocky coastline was now almost twice as distant as it had been before and while the waters they were currently knifing down into at horrifying speed were terrifying enough, the waves between here and the coast were much more worrying. He glanced back and was surprised to see that the storm was now considerably further behind.

The captain grinned at him. 'We used the storm to get ahead of it. Now comes the dangerous part.'

Titus, against the odds and defying apparent physical possibility, felt his backside clench even further.

'All right,' the captain said, 'we're almost down. Now we're going to straighten the oars for dead ahead. Then we're going to count in bundles of five, and every five we reach, we're going to move the oar one point to starboard until we've come through a right-angle and are off our starboard beam.'

'I wish you'd talk normally,' grumbled the marshal.

'Count five and let me move the oar, then five and oar, five and oar and so on until we're making straight for the lights of Nessana.'

Titus nodded. He felt cold and frightened. No amount of axe-wielding northerners on a bloody field would worry him, but this was something wholly different. He sent up a fervent prayer to Pluvus of the storms and Galinus of the wild waters that they reach this strange village unharmed.

'Now,' the captain shouted. 'Dead ahead.'

Aware of what that particular direction meant, Titus helped the man shift the heavy oar until the vessel was using the last of its descent to run ahead of the storm. He'd seen ships at ramming speed in small conflicts with pirates before now, and he'd seen this particular vessel race across the seas to Pelasia in fruitless pursuit of the empress, but until this moment, he'd never have believed a ship could travel *this* fast. It was exhilarating. And terrifying. The sailors had driven her as fast as their muscles allowed, and the last great wave had added a god-like impetus to the hull.

'Let's hope that ballast is adequate,' the captain muttered. 'Now count with me and then release. Ready?'

Titus nodded, freezing water dripping from the tip of his nose and spraying from his wild hair.

'One... two... three... four... five!'

As the marshal stopped guiding the oar, the captain jerked it through a small angle and then held it tight again. Titus added his own grip once more as the ship turned a little so that it was cutting slightly towards land.

''One... two... three... four... five!'

Again, he released, and the captain moved the oar a fraction before they both locked their grip once more. The ship changed course slightly again. Now, he could feel the pressure starting to build on the starboard, storm-ward side of the hull. That was why the captain had shifted the ballast to that side – to counteract the force of the water trying to push them over.

'One... two... three... four... five!'

This time, Titus was prepared and actually helped the captain move the oar and then grip it. The man nodded his approval.

'One... two... three... four... five!'

Again.

Four more times the captain made the count and they moved the oar, and finally he declared that they were done.

'What now?' Titus shouted over the blowing of the gale.

'Pray.'

He could feel the ship struggling, the ballast barely counteracting the pressure the advancing storm water was putting on the starboard side of the hull. But the ship was still moving at speed, and the cliffs of the Vinceia Peninsula were coming closer and closer. Now, for the first time, Titus could actually see the lights of Nessana to which the captain had been referring. They did not fill him with confidence. He'd been expecting beacons and dockside guide lights. What he could actually see were the lights in house windows. Maybe five or six such lights flickered atop the cliffs, and a small cluster of them emanated from a shadowy area of the crags. It looked about as port-like and welcoming as any other part of the peninsula – to wit: not at all.

'Have you been to this Nessana before?'

The captain, still gripping the oar tight and gritting his teeth against the pressure – the current was trying to turn them *with* the storm again – hissed between clenched jaws. 'Not for some years.'

Titus watched the lights getting closer. They were starting to lose their momentum now, rushing across the front of the storm rather than racing with it. But the captain had known his stuff and if Titus was any judge of speed they would make the cliffs just before the storm overwhelmed them.

He *hoped…*

There was an ominous groan and a cracking noise, and he felt the steering oar lurch.

'Shit,' the captain said, with infinite feeling.

'Shit is not a good thing. What is it?'

'The oar's cracked. Way down, where I can't see it. We'll just have to hope it holds.'

'And if it doesn't?'

The captain snorted. 'Then we go wherever the storm wants to take us. Most likely straight down.'

Titus started to churn out prayer after prayer, aiming them at any god or goddess whose name he could recall. He wasn't an overly religious man. He respected the gods, though he was never entirely sure how much their hands were truly involved in the world of men. But the fact remained that when death was sharpening his blade, no man denied the gods.

'We're going to make it,' he said with heartfelt relief as he saw Nessana racing towards them. The ship was miraculously – or at least due to a stunningly adept captain – aimed directly for the centre of a narrow opening in the cliffs that led into a sheltered cove full of twinkling lights.

'Don't tempt the gods, Marshal,' snapped the captain.

But they were almost there. The storm was on them again now, and the rain that heralded it was battering the ship, but the roiling waves would not get them before they were through and into safety. Titus laughed.

And the steering oar snapped.

He watched a full third of the great wooden shaft, tipped by its wide, flat blade, rocket out of the water and bounce off across the waves. The ship lurched sickeningly to port, and in dismay, Titus watched their course change so that they were no longer making straight for the cove.

'Port oars out!' the captain bellowed. 'Row for your life, ramming speed.'

There was precious little chance of anyone hearing the tune of the piper that would normally set the pace, and instead, as the oars were run out, the leading man started yelling the timing, which was picked up by every rower until they were heaving their oars in time and chanting the pace. Titus watched with bated breath as the ship, which had spun left off target, gradually clawed its way back towards the narrow gap in the cliffs, the oars fighting against the storm-driven currents.

'Will we make it?' he shouted, but the captain was busy, his lips moving constantly in silent prayer as they closed the last hundred paces to the cliffs.

There was a horrible tearing sound from somewhere below, announcing the meeting of timber and rock, and a strange sound that Titus could only assume was the sea beginning to flood the hold. Still, they pressed forward, so the submerged rock must have barely touched the hull in passing, just enough to tear through the planking.

They were not going to make it. The safe harbour entrance was getting closer, but the storm current was fighting the power of the oars, and the ship was bearing down on a particularly sharp spur of rock at the left edge of the cove entrance. Titus added his own silent prayers to those of the captain, and very likely the rest of the crew too.

Despite the fact that the rowers had been pulling with all their might and matching the impressive ramming pace, they were now, somehow, finding an extra turn of speed. Men from the starboard benches were dashing across the ship, endangering the delicate balance of the ballast. There they grabbed hold of any oar space they could find and added their own strength. Titus was impressed. Within four heartbeats, three quarters of the ship's rowers were on the port side, heaving the oars back and forth in their oval manoeuvre at such speed that if one man lost the rhythm, they would all clatter into chaos and the ship would be lost. Yet the vessel turned very slightly and Titus winced as they bore down on the rocks. *Five*, he thought to himself.

The ship was almost clear. It might just make it through the gap.

Four.

It would be close. So close.

Three.

'Clear the benches!' the captain roared. Titus frowned. Now? At this last moment? Surely they needed the oarsmen pulling against the current to the last?

He had no time to question the command, though.

Two.

The rowers were throwing themselves across the walkway and back to the starboard side.

One.

They *might* still make it. The oarsmen were almost all away from the benches now, barring a few stragglers, who'd been slowed in the press of men.

The imperial courier vessel *Sea Eagle* launched from the open sea into the narrow, hidden anchorage of Nessana, scraping along the side of that brutal rock as it went. The sounds of timber tearing all along the port side were clearly audible, but that was not what horrified Titus and drew his eyes wide with shock. It was what happened on board. That was why the captain had given the order to clear the benches. The oars had splintered and shattered like balsa sticks against the rocks, but the force of the impact had sent the sections of oar that projected along the benches on board jerking this way and that. The few poor bastards who'd not managed to clear the benches were shredded, broken, torn and pulverized by the flailing beams. Titus had seen men die in battle, by execution in extreme cases, and once, memorably, under torture. But he'd never seen men die as badly as this.

The ship coasted across the eerily calm lagoon towards a single wooden jetty. Every 10 feet it progressed, Titus could feel it dip slightly and he had the horrible feeling it wouldn't quite make it. There must be four or five breaches in the hull now, and water was pouring in at an alarming rate. He glanced back over his shoulder. The storm was upon Nessana. Though the brutal waves were now rushing past the cove, only small swells were making it through the gap, disturbing the calm within. The rain began to lash down into the secluded harbour, sizzling on the surface of the water. Titus gripped the shattered remains of the steering oar tight, though it made precious little difference. It was more for a personal sense of security than out of hope of steering.

He almost passed out with relief as the ship suddenly lurched to a stop with the sound of scraping gravel, and then tipped to one side, throwing everyone against the port rail.

They had beached.

The rain washed the deck in huge torrents, swilling away the sheets of blood from the unfortunate rowers who'd been killed by the oars. The captain straightened with some difficulty, gripping the stern rail for support. He grinned like a lunatic.

'What now?' Titus managed to ask, shaking wildly.

'Now we go ashore and make it through the night. Then in the morning I assess the damage and try and decide whether the *Sea Eagle* is salvageable or whether you owe me the price of a ship.'

Titus stared at the man, but the captain simply jacked up his mad grin and began to shout orders to his crew. The marshal turned and looked over Nessana. The entire place couldn't number more than forty buildings, including the shops, artisans and what looked suspiciously – and welcomingly – like a tavern set back from the shore.

'I need a drink.'

CHAPTER XIV

Of Unexpected Connections

'Is this strictly necessary, sir?'

Titus turned to the guardsman who was holding up a spare sailor's tunic with an air of distaste. The grey garment was patched in three places and covered in old stains. Not that the tunic the soldier was currently wearing was in much better shape. It was fully intact, with no patches or darning, but in respect of dirt and stains, the long sea voyage had taken its toll.

'Yes, this is necessary. The captain knows his stuff, and we're in *his* world right now, so what he says goes. There might just be villagers here, but there could be smuggler crews riding out the storm, and I have no wish to start a fight against a larger force just because we couldn't be arsed to change our clothes. And when we get in there, it's first names only, remember? No ranks and no "sirs" and all that. We're just ordinary mercantile sailors caught in the tempest. All I want to do is wait out the night somewhere warm and with food and wine and then in the morning, when the captain's had a chance to look at his ship, we can decide what our next step is.'

A heavy droplet of water hit the marshal square on the forehead and he grunted irritably as he peeled off his wet tunic, his mat of curly body hair plastered to his flesh. He looked up at the thick branches above him and a second drop hit him in the eye, bringing forth a virulent curse.

The *Sea Eagle* lay 25 paces away, looking forlorn and broken. The captain had tutted over his initial assessment and wasn't convinced she was salvageable, but the morning sun might cast things in a different light. The ship's crew were busy wading through the water, carrying crates and barrels and sacks, ferrying them from the ruined vessel into the shelter of the trees where other men were unfolding giant canvasses with which to cover the retrieved stores and protect them from the worst of the weather. The meagre shelter of the trees was shared by the guard unit while they changed out of their uniforms and into the spare clothing from the ship. A few of the men had miscellaneous tunics in their packs, but most carried only a spare uniform tunic and had been forced to rely on the sailors' charity. Titus was convinced that the captain, who had begun mumbling surprisingly high numbers with respect to the value of his ship, would also charge them an inflated price for the old tunics.

Young Appius had already donned his borrowed, dry tunic and belted it on, slipping on the tight dark-blue breeches beneath, and was now staring with clear disdain at the borrowed sword – a slightly curved effort with a grip carved into the shape of a naked mermaid. The poor young fellow had been the only one of the guard whose kitbag had been lost in the storm, and he had to rely entirely on borrowed goods. He looked peculiar, and quite unhappy.

Another drip hit Titus, announcing the end of the trees' efficacy as cover. The storm had now rolled over the village and settled in for the night, and the saturation of the shoreline woods had begun.

'Come on, lads, hurry up. Time to go for a drink and get out of this rain.'

He turned as the ship's captain plodded into the meagre shelter, his clothing plastered to him, his hair stuck down to his face. 'Are you coming with us, Captain?'

'Yes, since we're done here. Have you given thought to what you will answer when you're asked difficult questions?'

Titus shrugged. 'I was planning to improvise.'

'Poor choice. What happens when you and three of your men all say you come from different places?'

'I was planning to be rather reticent and not reveal much. Surely that would be in keeping with smugglers.'

'Don't overextend yourself, Marshal. Don't try and play smuggler. These people will see through you. You're too legal to pull it off, and they know smugglers well. You're just a merchant and his men caught in a storm and washed here by chance. That way you won't get tripped up so easily. You were coming from Haedaris with a cargo of lead, bound for Burdium Portus. A lot of lead goes that way, and tin comes back the other, so that was probably what you were planning on buying in. But now you're worried about being destitute, since we had to heave the lead overboard at sea to prevent sinking. There's a few ingots among our goods, so there's some evidence if you need it. But if you play the role calmly and don't draw attention to yourself, you should be fine. You might even be able to buy a horse and cart to travel west again in the morning if you don't cause any trouble.'

Titus frowned. 'I thought we'd sail west again?'

'How, Marshal?' Even if the *Sea Eagle is* repairable, it'll be weeks of work. If not, then we have to start the trek back east. Either way, you're on foot from here given the urgency of your task. And don't bother asking any of the locals about ships. There'll be none willing to take unknown passengers.'

'Shit,' grumbled Titus as he settled the cloak about his shoulders and adjusted the hang of his sword belt. 'I hadn't thought of that. Burdium is, what, five days away by horse?'

'Bet on seven or eight, especially if you're taking kit in a cart.'

Titus hissed his disappointment. 'Bastard gods and their storms.'

The captain made a warding sign against ill luck and glared at Titus. 'Bear in mind that those gods you're cursing saw you safely into harbour. You could easily be floating face down out on the ocean right now.'

The marshal merely grunted his acceptance of that fact and pulled the hood of his cloak up to stop the rain that was now beginning to filter through the tree branches in force.

'Come on. Let's go get a drink.'

The party emerged from the trees and the sodden sailors converged with them so that one large group moved on up the slope towards the houses. Titus tried not to feel self-conscious as every window they passed framed a suspicious face, peering out at the shipwreck in their harbour and the fortunate survivors moving into their village.

'Friendly place.'

The captain snorted. 'The authorities almost never get out here. Your officials and soldiers just pass by on the main roads a little inland. They have no real interest in the tiny fishing villages of a harsh and dangerous coast. That's why it makes such a good place for underhand transactions. Be wary, Titus. Don't, for the love of the gods, let them think you're officials.'

'All I want is to get warm, fed, drunk and rested. In that order.'

'And you've money?'

Titus jangled the heavy purse at his belt. 'There's more in the kit back under the trees, but this should be ample.'

'Good.'

The building that sat slightly apart from the houses, with warm, glowing windows and smoke curling up from twin chimneys at both ends of the structure, bore a sign that declared it to be the Drunken Harpy.

'My kind of place,' grinned one of the guards.

'Have a drink, by all means,' Titus addressed his men, 'but remember the tale the captain concocted for us. Watch your tongues and be on your guard at all times. These will not be the friendliest of people.'

Titus let the captain push open the tavern door and followed the man in, the guards and sailors all filtering in behind, grateful to be out of the torrential rain, the sailors dripping wet, the guards removing their soaked cloaks, largely dry beneath. Half a dozen locals glared at them as they filled the tavern's large common room to the seams.

'We've nae room for your whole crew,' the innkeeper snarled, his eyes flinty and suspicious.

'Unfortunately we can't stay on board,' the captain replied levelly, 'what with half the ship filled with seawater and the gravel of your beach. My men can make do with stables or barns or whatever shelter you can offer. My friend here is – *was* – a wealthy merchant. He can pay you handsomely.'

On cue, Titus jingled his purse. The innkeeper, and the rest of the room's occupants too, looked the marshal up and down, taking in every detail. Titus was unusual for a high-ranking military man in that he was rarely shaven, his hair was long and unkempt, and he looked generally much scruffier than one would expect of an imperial marshal. Of course, the same had been true of his father. On this occasion, it would work in his favour. He couldn't imagine that he looked very official.

'There's two barns out back. Your men can sleep there. Upstairs, we've two bunk rooms what can sleep six each, an' one room wi' two singles. Sort it out 'owever you wish, but it'll be twenty-five corona for the night.'

'*Twenty-five*?' snapped one of the guards in astonishment.

Titus glared at him. 'Twenty-five is a little much, given that I just lost a very lucrative cargo to the deep. Would you take eighteen?'

'Twenty-one.'

The marshal crossed to the bar and counted out 20 gold corona onto the stained wooden surface. 'I'm a merchant. Odd numbers don't sit well with me. But bear in mind we'll need food and a lot of drink.'

The room still held a palpable air of suspicion, but at least the locals had now seemingly dismissed them as uninteresting.

'You lot out to the barns,' the captain gestured to the wet sailors. 'Dry yourselves off best you can. I'll have food and drink sent out to you.' He turned to Titus. 'Your men joining them?'

'No,' the marshal replied, looking at the nine men that remained of the 24 he'd brought from home. Six had gone with the message back to Velutio, one had gone in the storm, and the rest had fallen during the set-to with the Pelasian ship. For a moment he'd considered sending them out back with the sailors, but the idea of him and the captain being outnumbered in this room by unfriendly locals was not an encouraging one. 'They can stay here.' The sailors, sodden to a man, cast disgruntled looks at the guardsmen, who were dry and now were being allowed to stay in the tavern while they were banished to the barns.

'How many for wine and how many for beer?' Titus said to the guardsmen once the sailors were gone. 'The first drink's on me. The rest are your problem.'

Each man spoke in turn, and Titus leaned on the counter, from which his 20 corona had already disappeared. 'Seven wines – the best you have in stock, mind – and four beers, if you will. And can you do us food?'

'Lamb stew,' the innkeeper said curtly. 'An' bread. Nothing fancy.'

'I'm not looking for fancy. Just hot and filling. We'll have eleven of them in here, then. And can you arrange to send a jar of wine and a small cask of beer out to the barns, and to have food taken out there too?'

'Their food'll be late. Can't cater for so many at once,' the man said gruffly.

'That's fine. If they have wine and beer they won't care.'

'Another twelve corona an' six pennies.'

Titus gave the man a hard look, but counted out 13 gold coins. 'I haven't brought small change.'

The innkeeper narrowed his eyes and reached into his money belt. With no preamble he slapped 14 bronze coins on the counter and moved to the rear of the bar, straining to lift a large stoppered jar of imported wine bearing the stamp of the Rilva port. Undoubtedly slipped through here without even a nod to the taxman. Titus smiled at the thought and reached for the coins.

He stopped.

Frowning, he extended a finger and shuffled the coins around, separating three from the rest. As the innkeeper worked at lifting the jar and filling a row of beakers, the room buzzing with low conversation among the new arrivals, Titus leaned closer to the captain and spoke in quiet tones, pointing at the coins.

'Pelasian *scudai*. Unusual here, I'd wager. Do the Pelasians smuggle through here a lot?'

The captain gave him a warning look and motioned for him to lower his voice. 'Don't be so loud and stupid, Titus. And no. The Pelasians don't have to, given the beneficial trade deals they have with the empire. In order to keep ties between the countries tight, their merchants barely pay any tax anyway. It's our own traders that suffer.'

Titus nodded, his eyes narrow with calculation.

'Do the locals bring goods in from Pelasia, then?'

'Will you be quiet?' the captain hissed. 'And no. The Pelasians have more sense than to endanger their favourable deals by messing around on the wrong side of the authorities. Besides, don't you think Pelasians and their goods would stand out a bit here? Not good for subtlety. Now shut up before you get us all into trouble.

You might outnumber the men in this bar, but there's a whole village out there.'

Titus, though, cared less about maintaining their fiction than about the suspicion growing in his mind. 'So, if the Pelasians have nothing to do with this place, where did three Pelasian scudai come from? They're not even found in general circulation in Velutio, let alone in the backwaters.'

The captain shrugged. 'They're coins. Just coins.'

'No,' Titus said, a thrill of suspicion running along his spine, 'they are not *just* coins. They are *unexpected* coins. They are out of place. Odd. Suspicious.'

The innkeeper returned to the bar with a circular tray full of wine cups, each slopping with thick, dark red liquid. He placed the tray on the bar and was about to turn and find the beer keg when the marshal gently slid the tray of cups away from them, along the grubby surface and leaned forward, tapping the Pelasian coins.

'Where did these come from?'

The barman clearly had no intention of answering and turned to fetch the beer. Titus's arm shot out and grabbed his wrist in a vice-like grip, hauling him roughly back. The local's eyes flashed with anger and his hand scrabbled towards the gap beneath the counter upon which the drinks and coins sat.

'If that hand comes back out with a cosh in it, things might go very badly for you, my friend,' Titus growled.

The hand reappeared slowly, empty, but there was fury in the innkeeper's eyes. Somewhere behind him there was the scrape of a wooden chair sliding backward.

'Same goes for your friends,' Titus added archly. 'My men know how to handle themselves and they're all armed. Now, why don't we all settle down for a nice little chat?'

He risked a glance over his shoulder. Two of his men had moved to block the inn's entrance, and others had sealed off the stairs and the door out back to the barns. The rest were standing in the same place they had been, hands on the pommels of their swords as they looked meaningfully at the few angry locals.

'Now,' Titus said again, donning a smile with all the warmth of a glacial crevasse, 'why don't we talk about coins?'

'I dunno what you mean,' snapped the innkeeper.

'You gave me my change in Pelasian coinage. Month upon month can go by even in Velutio without me seeing a *scudar* among my change, and here I have three at once in a small village out in the west. Unusual, I suspect. And while it's strictly speaking viable currency with the appropriate metal content, I have to wonder how you came by them? Perhaps you might have more in your purse?'

'Nothin' wrong with Pelasian coins,' spat the local.

'Indeed, as I just said myself. But you have not answered my question. How did you come by them?'

'What's it to you?'

'I am a man of only middling patience, armed with a very sharp sword and accompanied by very mean men. Let's leave it at that. Tell me where they came from.'

Releasing the man's wrist, Titus slowly drew his sword, making sure to scrape the flat of the blade against the metal mouth of the scabbard so that it grated with a bone-chilling sound. He then lay the blade on the counter in front of him and fixed the innkeeper with a look. Behind him there was another scraping noise, but the innkeeper peered past Titus and cleared his throat. 'Leave it, Jonas. I ain't gettin' dead for the sake of a bit o' coin. Besides, we don't owe that freak an' his men nothin'.' He focused on Titus again. 'Bunch o' northerners came through a few days back. All blond-haired lads from the northern mountains, I reckon. Not a Pelasian among 'em. But they 'ad plenty of their coins, mind.'

Titus felt his spirits fall. No Pelasians.

'They came from the sea?' the captain prompted.

'Yeah. Their ship 'ad been damaged, an' the sail was useless. Must've been slow goin' gettin' 'ere. There was more'n a score of 'em, an' they'd a few horses an' a carriage too.'

Titus perked up. 'A carriage?'

'Yeah. Whatever they was guardin' they looked after it careful, like.'

'It's them,' Titus hissed to the ship captain. 'I was wrong about the gods. They brought me exactly where I needed to be. I wonder what happened to them at sea to so wreck their ship, but whatever it was, it slowed them down. We're only a few days behind them.

Holy bell-end of *Juvis*, what a stroke of luck. The girl must be in the carriage, and her maids probably, too.'

'They was a rough lot,' the innkeeper said, though his expression made it clear that the same description would later be applied to Titus and his men. 'They was cagey, too. Hidin' somethin'. They stopped for food an' then went on.'

Titus leaned on the bar, his face coming close to the innkeeper. 'Where did they go?'

'Up the hillside path.'

The marshal rolled his eyes. 'Very helpful.' For a moment, he wondered whether to reissue his threat, but instead, with a smile, he fished in his belt purse and retrieved ten more gold corona, stacking them on the counter in two piles of five.

'Bet your memory's improving by the moment.'

The innkeeper licked his lips in a combination of nervousness and greed, his eyes on both the sword before him and the coins within his reach. His hand snaked out towards the piles of gold.

'Ah, ah,' Titus said, his own large hand slapping down on them. 'Information first. Coins later.'

'Calacon,' the man muttered.

'What?'

'Calacon. It's a fortress town in…'

'I know where Calacon is. How do you know they went there?'

'I don't,' the man admitted, 'but I 'eard three of his men mention the place.'

Titus smiled. 'Three is too much for coincidence.' He turned to the captain. 'Right. One night's rest, then the lads and me have to be on the chase. I take it you're staying with the *Sea Eagle*?' As the man nodded, the marshal clapped a hand on his shoulder. 'Thank you for everything so far, Captain. If you get back to Velutio, see my people,' he urged as vaguely as he could, remembering the potential ongoing local threat. 'My people will see you right for your ship.'

The captain nodded again, and Titus focused an intense look on the innkeeper. 'We will be gone at dawn, but I will be back this way very soon, and if anything has happened to my friend and his crew, I will be *very* upset. Look after him. I've paid you plenty to do so, after all.'

He turned back to the sailor. 'I don't think you'll have trouble.'

'We can handle ourselves, Titus.'

'I know. We have to go at first light. We're days behind them, but they'll be moving slow with a carriage. If I can secure horses for the ten of us, we can be on them by the time they get to Calacon.'

The captain smiled. 'The gods seem to stand by your shoulders, my friend. I pray they continue to do so and you find the lady. But for tonight, you need to rest and prepare for your journey.' He gestured to the innkeeper. 'My friend here will pay for the night's drinks. Keep the wine and beer coming and get that lamb stew on.'

Titus collected his sword and sheathed it once more. The innkeeper hurriedly swept the coins from the bar into his pouch and scurried off to get the ale as the marshal lifted two cups of wine and passed one to the captain, clonking his own beaker against the other. 'Cheers, Captain. To the goddess of luck.'

'To luck.'

CHAPTER XV

Of Trails and Their Ends

Titus reined in 50 paces from the gatehouse, his horse sweating and fatigued. It had been another hard day's ride, the latest in a series since they had purchased the best horses available in Nessana and ridden for Calacon with all haste. They had travelled day and night, allowing only frequent breaks to rest the horses, since there had not been enough beasts to purchase in the coastal village to allow each man an extra mount. Instead, the three spare animals carried all the baggage to spread the load and spare the animals.

The marshal had fretted over each break, though he knew they were required. It would be no good riding hell for leather and only covering half the distance before the horses dropped with exhaustion or went lame. It was just one of many things that played on his nerves, mind and conscience during the journey, not the least of which had been leaving the captain and his men at Nessana under the suspicious eyes of the locals. Yes, the man had retained most of his crew and they were burly and armed, but nagging images plagued Titus whenever he paused to think. Images of the captain waking up among a murdered crew, of the local smugglers roping them and selling them to slavers. After all, the sailors had a small but significant quantity of cargo under the trees near the water.

Now, though, he could start to rectify things.

Calacon was the second most powerful fortress in the west after the great imperial city of Vengen. Along with the latter, and the city of Burdium, it played host to a sizeable portion of the Fourth Army. Calacon had once – many centuries ago – been the capital of a powerful native western tribe and its fall into imperial hands had sounded the death knell of western independence and the final conquest and settlement of the region. This was only the third time the marshal had visited the place. He was commander of the First Army and so his jurisdiction out here in the west was minimal. As

Quintillian commanded the Third in the east, and Partho the Second in the north, so it was Marshal Sciras who commanded the Fourth here in the west. There was a small chance of him being in Calacon, though he would far more likely be in Vengen – his home.

The fortress city was an impressive sight. The region, inland, and roughly equidistant between the southern and eastern coasts, was a network of rippling hills and ridges and narrow, hidden river vales. Nestled in a deep valley – a gorge really, at this point – Calacon clung to the cliff on the north side of the river like a lizard to a rock. Atop the crags, heavily fortified towers and walls protected the site, and a double circuit of the same ran from cliff to cliff at the valley floor, encircling the town and running along the river. It boggled the mind how one might even consider trying to take the city. Sadly, while the general who had taken Calacon from the natives back in the early days of the empire had kept a record of his campaigns, three of the books had been lost over the centuries, so no details remained of that particular siege. One thing was certain: Titus was glad *he* didn't have to attempt it.

Beyond the gate and the low, thick, powerful walls he now faced, he could see the second circuit rising higher, with square towers topped with artillery. Then, behind that, the city climbed the cliff. There were no vehicles in Calacon and precious few beasts of burden. Almost every street in the place consisted largely of steps, snaking up the cliff side between buildings and through arches, and sometimes actually underneath those structures too. Nowhere in the place was flat. Half the buildings were nestled in niches and half-formed grottoes in the cliffs, their interiors an odd mix of natural cave, hand-chiselled hollow and purpose-built wall.

The gate stood open.

The land was not at war and there was no threat to Calacon – hadn't been for centuries. Yet soldiers still lined the defences, for all their bored expressions. Calacon may not be sealed tight and defensive, but it was still the province primarily of the military.

Titus turned to his men.

'Be watchful. We cannot be more than a day behind these villains, and they may still be in Calacon. Do nothing to betray your true nature.'

The men nodded their understanding. The marshal had made the decision, upon leaving Nessana, that they would continue to dress incognito. Better to be more or less invisible, for that way there was less likelihood of spooking their prey. 'Come on, then.'

As they trotted slowly towards the gate, he turned and looked over his shoulder. 'Anyone here familiar with Calacon?'

One of the men waved a hand. 'I know it, sort of.'

'Know the Crossed Swords tavern?'

'On the Street of Blind Butchers. I know it.'

'Take the lads there and arrange rooms. I'll meet you in time for dinner.'

The guards at the gate barely registered the newcomers. Travel-worn horsemen would hardly be an unusual sight here. Passing through the outer gate, the small party crossed the killing zone between the two walls, and clattered slowly beneath the heavy twin inner gate under the watchful eye of more guards who failed to stop or query them.

They were in Calacon. The question was: were the enemy?

'See you soon,' Titus called to his men as the one who was familiar with the city led them off in the direction of the tavern. Titus, instead, made for the Way of the Gods, the most direct route up the cliff. Although it lay on the edge of the town, rather than at its heart, this zigzagging route was one of the most important in Calacon, connecting the valley floor with the clifftop with the minimum of fuss. Its name derived from the altars that dotted its length. At every turn in the path – and there were *many* of them – the priests of Calacon had set up an altar to one of the gods. It was said that a century or so ago the stairway was extended and some of the slopes altered to allow for extra bends just to incorporate more altars. After all, it didn't do to leave a god out of such an affair, even if they were lesser gods. Gods had long memories and held grudges.

At the bottom, Titus dismounted and led his beast from there on foot. His horse was tired, while he was relatively fresh, even if his backside felt as though it had been beaten repeatedly with rods from the ride. The marshal nodded his respect to the gods that held a direct connection with him as he climbed – the gods who watched over the military, the imperial family, his home town. Vengeance and justice in particular, given his current task.

Perhaps half an hour later, wobbly-legged and heaving in breaths, the Marshal of the First Army crested the top of the Way of the Gods and emerged into the upper city. The fortress that controlled Calacon was sited here and a wide plaza lay between the edge of the city, clinging to its cliff, and the walls and gates of the army's domain. With a quick glance around the marshal rode to the gate. Unlike the city's gateways below, this one was firmly shut and guards above watched him suspiciously.

'State your business,' one of them called.

'My business is with the fortress prefect.'

'Name?'

The marshal glanced this way and that. So much for incognito, but then a strange, hairy horseman with no credentials was unlikely to gain entrance to the citadel. 'Titus Tythianus, Marshal of the First Army.'

His announcement was met with initial disbelief, bordering on hilarity, and then, as he held their gaze, his own serious, they shifted to doubt.

'Do you have identification?'

Titus stroked his horse's nose. The beast was becoming restless. 'Prefect Aurelian knows me well. Open the gate.'

There was a brief discussion, but as they erred on the side of caution there was soon a wooden clonk and rattle as the gate swung ponderously inward, revealing four soldiers, one a captain.

'If you would follow me, my men will take care of your horse,' he said curtly. Titus couldn't help but notice that while one man took his reins and another closed and fastened the gate once more, the third followed him and the officer, his hand on his sword at all times. The marshal was pleased to see such adherence to the rules, and smiled as they passed through the courtyard of the fortress, past the barrack blocks and the small regional hospital, and into the headquarters building with its colonnaded front. Inside, he was requested to hand over his weapons, which he did without complaint. The captain then took him on alone, leaving the other watchful soldier in charge of the marshal's blades. A moment later, the captain knocked on an office door leading off the long hall with its statues of the emperor and of Martus, the war god.

'Come.'

The captain pushed the door open and beckoned the marshal to follow him. Coming to attention inside, he cleared his throat.

'Good afternoon, Prefect. This man approached the citadel gate claiming to be…'

'Titus!' boomed the man behind the desk, rising with a grin. 'In the name of all the gods what's happened to you? I mean, you've never been the tidiest of men, but still!'

The marshal chuckled as the captain, wide-eyed, stepped back.

'Sorry about this, Aurelian. I'm travelling incognito with a few men. Something quite important, so I'd appreciate it if word didn't get out that I was here?'

'Of course, old fellow,' the prefect laughed. 'Captain, fetch us some wine.'

'I'm afraid I've not time to socialize, Prefect,' Titus apologized. 'I have to dash straightaway, but I had a couple of things to ask and I've a request to make.'

'Go on?'

'Have you had any trouble in Calacon the last few days?'

'Trouble? No, nothing worth mentioning.'

'Any unusual visitors?'

'Titus, we're a major town on a major road. The emperor himself could pass through, painted purple and dancing on the back of a horse, and we'd probably not find out for days. No one interesting's come up to the citadel, that's all I can confirm.'

The marshal nodded. 'Fair enough. A favour, then? There's a village called Nessana on the coast a few days from here.'

'Never heard of it.'

'I'm not surprised. The locals are involved in avoiding your taxmen, though seriously it's not worth your effort trying to sort it all out. I'd just write it off. But there's a sea captain there named Sorvio, a friend of mine, who's been shipwrecked in the line of imperial duty. Not only do I owe him for his ship, but I'm a little concerned for his safety in that place. Can you send a small unit out there to help him, and escort him and his men wherever they need to go. Oh, and pay him whatever ridiculous figure he names. I'll sort it out for you when I get back to Velutio.'

'I'll see to it this afternoon.'

'Thank you.'

The conversation turned swiftly to more personal reminiscences, and Titus was forced, after a short while, to remind the prefect that he was in something of a rush. As he stood to leave, he turned with a smile. 'I'll be gone in the morning, and I may not be back this way in the near future. Oh, and next time you see Marshal Sciras, pass on my regards, will you? I keep missing him whenever he's in Velutio.'

The prefect's brow folded, and his expression soured immediately. 'Have you not heard, Titus?'

'What?' Once again, the hairs stood proud on the back of Titus's neck in anticipation.

'The marshal's dead.'

'How?' Titus slumped back into his seat.

'Poor bugger got a knife in the back. He'd been at the theatre to celebrate his daughter's naming day. His wife was killed too. The daughter got away, but she's traumatized. They never caught the assailants.'

Titus's mind dredged up an image of that man in the palace corridor, yanking desperately to pull an axe back out of the wall plaster. Somehow, this did not sound like random thuggery. Quintillian gone, Sciras knifed, and an axeman trying to take his own head? That was three of the empire's four senior generals.

'Can you get word to the fortress at Cercina? Just check that Marshal Partho is all right, and if so, tell him to be on his guard. There is something at work here, and I don't like it, Aurelian.'

A few minutes later, Titus left the concerned and slightly befuddled prefect, collecting his weapons at the headquarters arch and his horse at the main gate. He took a different route back down, despite the zigzagging Way of the Gods being the most direct path. For some reason, the news of Marshal Sciras's death had him examining every shadow as he passed, and those shadows were growing in number, depth and size by the minute as the sun disappeared behind the cliffs. In the gorge where Calacon lay, sunrise came late and sunset early. With a swift pace, he led his horse down the stepped streets between and beneath the strange buildings, descending the vertiginous city until he reached the street upon which the Crossed Swords tavern lay. The gloom was already oppressive by the time he arrived, and torches and lamps were being lit around the city.

Two of his men were in the main room as he pushed the door open, along with eight locals, all of whom carried themselves in such a way as to suggest to Titus that they were off-duty soldiers. Bars like the Crossed Swords existed across the empire, catering largely for the military.

'You got rooms?' he asked the men.

One of them nodded. 'Three four-man bunk rooms.'

Titus crossed to the bar and ordered himself a drink.

'Get that and come upstairs,' the other man said quietly. Titus frowned at him, but the guardsman was almost twitching, stopping just short of waggling his eyebrows conspiratorially. The marshal paid for his cup of wine, and then followed his men as they led him upstairs and along a corridor. At the end of the passage, they knocked on one of the doors marked with a number three, and it was opened. The men entered and Titus saw four of his guards sitting at the room's table drinking wine and playing dice. They stopped as he entered and the others closed the door behind him.

'Your room is number two, sir, but you're going to want to hear this first.'

The marshal crossed to one of the bunks and sank onto it, sipping his wine.

'Go ahead.'

'There's a rumour that a Pelasian girl was seen in Calacon yesterday. I haven't been able to find specific details, but I overheard a man talking about it in the wine shop across the street. One of the others agreed, which I guess is confirmation. No specifics, as I say, but it seems a Pelasian is rare enough in Calacon to be noteworthy.'

'A girl on her own?' Titus frowned.

'I can't say for sure, sir. I didn't want to pry, since you told us to be really careful, but the way they talked it sounded to me like she was on her own. They certainly didn't say she was being held or escorted.'

'That's damned odd,' Titus murmured. 'I think we might need to do some more prying. After dinner, though. I'm ravenous. It seems to have been a long time since we've been anywhere we could have a proper hot meal.'

'Did you hear that, sir?' one of the guards said sharply.

The marshal paused, confused. Then a muffled curse was clearly audible from elsewhere in the inn, accompanied by a dulled steely clang.

'Damn it,' Titus grunted, leaping up from the bed, his wine cup discarded and falling to the floor. The others were already drawing their blades. The man who'd closed the door behind them gripped the handle and looked to Titus for confirmation. The marshal nodded.

The corridor outside was in chaos. Men with scarred, mean-looking faces were right outside the door. Titus could see across the corridor to the room on the far side, where a fight was already underway, his men battling against these unexpected opponents, and the other room's door, further along, was also open, the sound of fighting emerging from there too. Titus was the second into the corridor.

The man in front of him thrust his blade into the press of the enemy in the passage. He could hardly miss, and the blow brought forth a cry of pain from someone. A head among the crowd dropped out of sight in response to the unseen wound, but the victorious guardsman was immediately made the target of the enemy's fury and was hewn down by half a dozen blows, his cries of agony filling the corridor as axes and swords hammered into him, carving his muscle and smashing his bones.

Titus stared in shock, but recovered at speed and edged out of the doorway jabbing out with his sword and taking one of the attackers in the chest. As he twisted his blade, cracking ribs, and ripped it back out with a gout of blood and a sigh of escaping air from a ruptured lung, one of his men stepped out of the door and lunged, taking down another of the enemy.

The press was awkward, with so many men in such a confined space, and Titus parried two blows with difficulty, finding himself too busy defending himself from the crowd to make in-roads.

There was a dull thudding noise, and the marshal turned at the sound to see the tip of a crossbow bolt emerge from the back of the other guardsman's skull, sending shattered pieces of bone, blood and hair across the corridor where they spattered the marshal. The guard turned, still alive, his empty hand reaching up in disbelief and touching the shaft of the bolt that transfixed his head before the enemy hacked him, too, to pieces.

The marshal's gaze rose for a moment across the top of the dying man and a shock of recognition rang through him. The man at the far end of the corridor, who was even now lowering his light crossbow and fetching another bolt from a belted quiver, was a familiar one. So pale as to be almost translucent and with moonlight-white hair, he caught Titus's eye and held it for a moment.

'Get back,' someone shouted, and Titus felt himself being dragged backward into the room again. Even as two of the enemy tried to stab at him, he was hauled to safety and the door slammed shut and locked just as a second crossbow bolt thunked into wall where he had just been.

'What the shit is going on?' the marshal shouted as two of the room's other men jammed the table against the door, which was already reverberating to the blows on the far side. The white-haired man outside had been so desperately familiar, though he couldn't quite remember from where. A few moments later the noise in the corridor stopped, and instead there was a brief shout from the street outside. Titus ran across to the window and peered out. In the alley below, the enemy were pouring back out of the inn, carrying the bodies of their dead comrades. Among them, he could see the white-haired man directing them into various different alleys, and in moments the street was empty again and eerily silent. The marshal's jaw hardened as he remembered that moment months ago when he had seen that same man from almost this same angle. The man had fought a Gota champion in the hall at Velutio during the emperor's feast. He had dispatched the powerful, impressive barbarian with seeming ease. He had been the servant of one of the northern lords, though irritatingly, the name of that lord wouldn't quite come to mind right now.

What in seven hells was *he* doing here? The idea that he could be here and attacking an incognito marshal and a unit of imperial guard without there being some connection to the disappearance of the empress was simply unbelievable. Clearly, this man was the one who had taken Jala from her ship, and the notion that they were somehow also linked to the death of Marshal Sciras and the attempt on his own life back in the palace was hard to put down.

'Do we pursue?' the man by the door asked quietly.

'No,' Titus muttered. 'They clearly couldn't have had the empress with them while they were here, and by the time we get down into the street, they'll be long gone. They obviously know the place, too, and we need to take stock of our situation. I want to know how they knew we were here.'

The men pulled the table away from the door and out in the corridor his men were busy checking on each other.

'Casualties?' Titus called out.

'Four dead, one badly wounded,' answered the man just outside the door.

'We came out better than I expected, then,' Titus snarled. 'They took us completely by surprise.'

'I reckon they were after you, sir,' murmured the man who'd pulled him back into the room.

'How'd you figure that?'

'I think the bolt that took Parsas was meant for you. He was just unlucky enough to get in the way.'

'Perhaps,' Titus conceded, remembering once more the axeman in the palace corridor. His memory slid to images of the white-haired ghost and the man he'd served, sitting in that great hall. 'Either way, we now know who we're dealing with,' he smiled viciously. 'Aldegund. That pale killer serves Lord Aldegund. And Aldegund has a small fleet of ocean-going ships of just the sort the survivors described from the sinking of the empress's vessel.'

'Why attack us?' the guardsman mused.

'What?'

'Why attack us now, sir?' he repeated. 'I mean, they had the advantage. We didn't know who they were and we were still behind them. Why risk it?'

'Because we've caught up with them,' Titus said quietly. 'They didn't expect such dogged pursuit, and we're right on their tail. That ghost is trying to put us off following him – trying to deter further pursuit. I suspect he's making the most of Calacon, because he knows the place and they can disappear easily here, which they couldn't if we caught up with them in open country. I wonder if they've been further slowed by their prisoners? If the empress or one of her maids managed to get loose in the city, the way it looks, then they may have been trying to bring her back in when they came across us. It's all moot, anyway. The fact is that there are still seven of us, and we know who we're dealing with now. We won't get jumped the same way twice. We've no call for subtlety any more, though. Time to get back into uniform. Then we're off up to the citadel to see the prefect. The gates of the city should be closed after dark, so unless that white bastard is some sort of magician, they're trapped in Calacon. I can have Prefect Aurelian seal the city, and then we have them.'

The men sagged with relief at the thought of wearing their uniforms once more, and Titus looked down into the empty, dark street blow.

'Now, you pale shitbag, I'm coming for you. I know who you *are* now. I *know* who you are.'

PART THREE

THE WEST

'Sometimes it is not the destination that counts, but the journey.'

Ancient saying

CHAPTER XVI

Of Betrayals and Consequences

Jala Parishid Augusta, Empress of Velutio and Princess of Pelasia, slapped at the rough hand that shoved her urgently up the step and into the carriage. The hard northerner cursed her, but she had survived worse than curses, and she would survive this too. Her former handmaiden Nisha sat in the rear of the wagon already, her face turned from the doorway to hide her hideousness.

Nisha would survive this, too.

Clambering into the seat, Jala cast a sympathetic look across at her companion as the same rough-handed villain threw her cases in, bruising her leg in the process.

'Keep that *desert bitch* voice down until we're safe. Boss says you've got to have all your limbs when we get there, but he never mentioned your tongue.'

Jala swept her gaze back across to the unpleasant soldier and fixed him with a look of implacable, imperious revulsion. 'I am quite aware of how to deport myself in any situation, thank you. A talent sadly lacking, apparently, in many of my subjects.'

The man frowned as though trying to work out whether he had been insulted, and the dawning of realization across his face was like the progress of a glacier. Finally, at the end of the slow dawn, he raised an angry fist, only to have a slender, pale hand with perfectly manicured nails wrap around it in a vice-like grip. The ghost, who seemed to be in command of the party of kidnappers, shook his head at the thug, tutting.

'Use that brain, Corris. If you administer casual beatings all the time, then when we have real cause to punish, we will have to escalate just to make the point. Take your poor addled brain back to the house and use it to make sure we've left nothing.'

Halfdan – the awful ghost's name was Halfdan – leaned into the carriage doorway as his hireling left, muttering.

'I do apologize for the quality of my men. They are the best of a poor lot, but then I did not select them for their manners and knowledge of etiquette.'

Jala wrinkled her nose. 'Where are we going?'

'My dear princess, you ask me the same questions every day. Have I ever given you cause to believe I will answer them? No. The same holds true today. Within an hour we will be safe and far from Calacon, and then you may scream and rail and holler, should you wish. Until then, I would take it as a favour if you hold your tongue, as my colleague demanded. Shouting will not affect the end result, but it will likely cause a scuffle and these carriage walls are hardly crossbow resistant. Any unpleasantness will endanger you as much as it will us. Do we have an understanding?'

Jala was about to nod when she spotted the shape of Zari, her other maid, lurking in the darkness just behind the strange, white figure.

'Only if you do not saddle me with that creature once again.'

Zari flinched as if she had been struck, and Halfdan gave her a strangely sympathetic smile. 'I'm afraid that is not an option. I must keep her as well concealed as you at this time. Make the most of things. Reminisce about your homeland.'

The ghost pulled back, and Zari began to clamber into the carriage. Her expression shifted with the ascent from wary apprehension to smug self-importance.

'My lady.'

'Zari,' Jala acknowledged coldly.

Behind them, Halfdan once more leaned into the doorway. 'And when we have more time, tonight, I wish to discuss recent activity with you, Zari.'

Before the maid could reply, the ghostly figure closed and latched the door.

'Am I correct,' Jala addressed her maid haughtily, 'that there are fewer men out there this morning?'

'There was an… incident… last night. A few casualties. Halfdan assures me it is not a matter for concern. Soon we will be out in the countryside and safe once more.'

Safe. From whom? Who was the ghost so concerned about that they had tarried in Calacon for three nights? The empress added it to the list of things she needed to pry out of Zari in due course. She eyed her darker-skinned maid once more with distaste.

How was it possible for a girl to be so devious and yet so utterly vapid at the same time? Yes, most of the planning of this must be laid upon the shoulders of Halfdan, but how long had Zari been living this double life?

The empress had long since stopped kicking and cursing herself for the impetuous actions that had led to her flight from Velutio, the disastrous voyage, the capture and now their captivity. It had been the work of Zari, she now understood. For weeks – months possibly? – the maid had been manipulating her moods and her intent with a skill unexpected in one so credulous. And Jala could recognize with irritation how utterly foolish this whole thing had been. The Jala who had left Pelasia and married Kiva was bright and clever, and would never have been so rash. It was a sign of how totally her heart had been in turmoil that Zari had managed to persuade her into flight back to her brother. Idiocy. The maid must have discovered her private letters months ago and learned of her troubles. All this time she had been working to push Jala into a position where she could be taken. All this time, she had been working for Halfdan the ghost.

The empress caught the disgusted sneer on Nisha's half-hidden face as the other maid observed Zari. The pair had once been such close friends, they had been inseparable. Indeed, all three of them had been. Jala had been more of a friend or even sister to the two girls than an employer. Nisha and Zari had done everything with the empress, from hawking to attending great occasions, to enjoying theatrical performances and so on. But now, if the opportunity ever presented itself, the empress knew full well that Nisha would tear out Zari's throat with her teeth.

That first time Zari had come back to them it had almost happened, too. Nisha and her mistress had been kept in confinement on Halfdan's ship, and there had been no sign of Zari. Then there had been the set-to with the pirates that had almost sunk them. All these complex plots the pale northerner had hatched, and he had almost been undone by simple chance piracy. Fortunately – really? Fortunately? – the pirates had been fought off, though the damage to the ship had been catastrophic and the ghost had abandoned his plans to sail to Burdium Portus and put in at some unfriendly coastal village instead.

There, in the early morning, Zari had been bundled into the commandeered carriage with them and the other maid's betrayal had become apparent. She had not died in the sea action as they had thought, but had been with the enemy the whole time.

For Zari was Halfdan's whore. She was hopelessly smitten with the white ghost, that was plainly obvious to anyone with eyes. And anyone with both eyes *and* brain could see that the affection was entirely one-sided, though Zari was naïve enough to hang on to the delusion that Halfdan was her lover.

That morning, as the carriage set off from the village, rattling north towards Calacon, the true depth of Zari's betrayal had been revealed, and Jala had tried to kill her. Nisha had urged her to stop as the empress tried to beat Zari's face concave on the carriage's timbers. Sadly, Halfdan and his men had stopped the coach and pulled the empress off the maid before she could do any serious damage, though there was still bruising apparent on Zari's cheek and forehead from the attack. Jala shuddered, remembering the result of the scuffle.

The carriage had stopped on the clifftop, just above the village and the cove that huddled it, and Halfdan had had the three women brought back out of the carriage. He had told Jala that Zari was not to be harmed and that he would give her just one lesson to that effect. And on that clifftop, in response to the empress's attack on her maid, the ghost had produced a sharp eating knife and had removed Nisha's left eye, leaving a network of scars on her cheek into the bargain. It had been questionable who had shrieked more: Nisha or the empress. Even Zari – deluded, betraying Zari – had watched in cold, numb shock. As he wiped the eye matter and blood from his blade on Nisha's dress, Halfdan had calmly informed the empress that the next attack on Zari would leave Nisha without her left ear.

So Zari had since travelled with them in the carriage in an uncomfortable silence, but untouched. And Nisha had taken to sitting in a certain seat to hide her ruined face from the others. But by the time they had reached Calacon, Jala had decided that this situation could be of use after all.

She had been calmly accepting of her captivity so far – barring the incident with Zari. She was clever, and knew it. And she knew that uncharacteristic precipitous action was what had landed her in this position in the first place. Besides, on board Halfdan's ship what chance of escape was there? A chance to drown in the briny deep instead? And since then, they had been very carefully conveyed, with threats to Nisha's remaining appendages generally enough to keep the empress compliant. But the time would come when she would make her move and escape. She just knew enough to recognize that such action would have to wait until the time was right.

Of course, she also knew her own value and was not naïve enough to believe that this kidnapping was a small matter. She was an empress and a princess, and her worth as a political playing piece was immense. So there was always in the back of her mind the stark knowledge that if it came right down to it, it would be more important that she take her own life than be used as leverage. She owed that to her wonderful husband and to her dear brother. But that option would have to be saved as a last resort.

Zari's presence could turn out to be a boon, despite everything, for she was as suggestible to Jala as she was to Halfdan. She would do anything the ghost asked of her through her fawning delusion. But she was so glowing in her belief that she would be Halfdan's love forever, and that she would come out of this whole mess smelling of roses, that information was easily prized from her. She had already revealed the name of their captor – this Halfdan – though it seemed the ghost worked for someone else and that name as yet remained a mystery. She knew that they were travelling north from Calacon, which limited the number of destinations, since there were few cities of any size out there. Vengen was the only great metropolis, and being the province of the imperial military it was highly unlikely that the great fortress city of the Fourth Army was their destination. So that left smaller provincial settlements. And Zari had revealed how many men there were – a total of 27, including Halfdan himself. Mind you, there seemed considerably fewer this morning. What calamity had befallen them, and who was responsible? Whoever it was, there was little doubt in Jala's mind that the attackers had been her allies, for her captors had delayed in Calacon in order to deal with some sort of pursuit. Had they succeeded, or had they failed? Were all Jala's allies now rotting in the vertiginous alleyways of the city, or had Halfdan bitten more off the steak than he could chew and been forced to retreat? Certainly, he couldn't now have more than half his former unit.

And what was this 'recent activity' that the ghost wished to discuss with Zari? Not the attack that had cost him his men, surely. The ghost was not the sort of man to discuss such matters with the maid.

The carriage began to rattle across the cobblestones.

She would hold her tongue, as ordered, for calling out to potential saviours might get them all killed, but at the very least it would cost Nisha her ear, and the empress had already lost the maid an eye. But the imposed silence meant there was danger to her captors. Which suggested that either their pursuers were still alive, or perhaps that the authorities in Calacon were likely to come crashing down on them in an instant. How, then, were they to get out of the city?

Now to manipulate Zari the way the maid had managed to manipulate *her* those weeks ago. Direct questions would not work, but subtlety was beyond the girl. Visibly ignoring the presence of the traitor, she addressed Nisha in the knowledge that the other maid would not be able to resist interfering.

'Calacon will be sealed. It matters not what time we set out – darkness will not save Halfdan or his men. The gates will be shut and the army in control of the city. There will almost certainly be some sort of trouble. When the noise kicks off, I will peek through the door and work out how to make a break for it. You throttle the life out of Zari.'

The reaction was instant and totally predictable. Nisha was bright enough to know what she was doing, though she was still unable to keep from her face the leer of desire at the thought of strangling her former friend. Zari, on the other hand, flashed red with anger and self-importance, and wagged a finger at the empress.

'You will do no such thing, or Halfdan will tear Nisha in two. He will not let you hurt me. And anyway, there will be no such scuffle. He has men in the military – has had them there for more than a year, just ready for such occasions. You have no idea how deep this goes, Jala, or how prepared he is!'

No, Jala thought to herself with a sly smile, I don't. But every outburst from Zari was enlightening her a little. Now she knew that Halfdan or his shadowy master had men infiltrating the Fourth Army, and had done for some time. He was a northwesterner, as were all his men. And they were travelling north in the western provinces. The Fourth Army was the force based in this region. Everything pointed towards his master being someone from the northwest, which meant that such infiltration among the other three armies of the imperial military was unlikely. They were further away and manned by folk of much different backgrounds.

Sure enough, listening out in the relative silence, Jala heard the horses of her captors slow to a halt, and the carriage rumbled to a stop a moment later. There was a muffled exchange between Halfdan and a man with a northern accent and a rather official tone. A gate guard, almost certainly. There was the slow, deep creak of timber doors being swung open, and the procession began to move again. A few moments later, the procedure was repeated at the gate in the outer walls, and then the kidnappers and their prize were out of Calacon and in the countryside.

Damn it. If she *did* have allies in the city, they were being left behind, and probably wouldn't even be aware that their prey had left the place. She would have to believe. She would have to assume that whoever was pursuing them was not only still alive, but competent enough to quickly realize what had happened and find their trail. After all, whoever it was had managed to track her across the sea, through a small coastal village and all the way to Calacon. If they could follow her trail that far, they would not be stopped by this small hiccup.

She smiled to herself.

'Your lover will soon regret leaving Calacon, Zari.' The maid frowned in consternation and incomprehension, and Jala smiled indulgently. 'This is a narrow gorge, following the Triobis River. Whoever thinned his ranks last night has a ready-made trail to follow. As soon as they realize we are not in the city any more they will simply have to ride north along the valley until they catch up with us. Then the rest of Halfdan's men will meet their end and you will be mine to deal with at last.'

She almost laughed when the smug expression appeared on Zari's face again. This really was easy.

'They will never catch us,' the maid replied haughtily, 'for they will be riding north following the river, whereas we will cross it at the next bridge and climb the far slopes in a narrow gorge. Your precious friends will follow the valley, while we cut across the hills above.'

Jala tried to look defeated. It was difficult, when what she wanted to do was laugh and slap the stupid wench for her idiocy. Instead, she gave one of the prearranged signals to Nisha. They had developed four such tells during their time alone without the other maid, and Nisha nodded slightly, knowing exactly what was required of her. There was a long pause – long enough that Zari's small mind would not connect the two exchanges – and then Nisha turned to her former friend.

'When this is all over, Zari, and I have you to myself, I am going to do to you what your boyfriend did to me.'

Zari, predictably, reacted with a mixture of recoiling anxiety and smug disbelief that such a thing could come about. Then she started to launch into a quiet tirade about how Nisha would have to be careful over her tongue if she wished to keep it attached. Nisha responded with accusations of treachery and so on, and their argument, albeit a stifled quiet one due to Halfdan's threats, railed with spite and bile.

Jala left it a moment to make sure Zari was busy, but the poor dumb girl had only enough mental capacity to devote to one thing at a time, and right now she was aiming it at Nisha. Trying again not to smile, Jala reached down and started fiddling with the hem of her over-dress, a beautiful, expensive piece that lay atop her under-tunic. It was a purple and white garment – the imperial colours – although it was now dirty, stained and torn almost beyond recognition. Finding a piece of the material that had been snagged during the journey, as slowly and quietly as she could she tore a small strip of purple from the garment by the low-pre-dawn light, and then let the hem drop again.

In case Zari was being unusually observant, she sat back for a count of 20, but the girl had not even looked her way. Biting her lip, Jala nibbled one of her fingernails until it became jagged and sharp, and then, keeping it hidden from the exchange, though Zari was totally oblivious anyway, she used the sharp nail to draw blood from the soft flesh of her wrist. Once a couple of tiny crimson beads were bubbling up from the small wound, she used that same sharp fingernail to draw a fairly good representation of a bridge and a slope on the material. She had always had a talent with images, perhaps born from her skill at calligraphy – an art taught to, and required of, all Pelasian nobility.

Satisfied that her image was the best she could do, she paused again to be sure of Zari's lack of attention. Still the argument went on. The empress's eyes scanned the carriage floor until she spotted the crack that she'd seen days earlier.

This was the gamble. Not that Zari would find out. The empress could probably paint herself and jump up and down on the carriage roof shouting 'Here I am!' and the maid would be oblivious. But almost half of their captors – six or seven men at the least – would be riding behind. If they noticed the article fall, it would be of no use. It would be gathered up, and any future attempt at leaving clues would be forestalled.

'Will you two stop arguing?' she snapped with fake anger, and left her seat, kneeling by her cases. She opened one and rummaged in it until she found the book of Pelasian poetry she knew to be in there, thrusting it at Nisha. 'Here. Keep yourself occupied.'

As the two girls glared at each other, Zari wincing at the empty socket in Nisha's face, and the latter grasping the book, Jala took the opportunity to push the scrap of purple cloth through the hole, prodding it until it disappeared, fluttering down to the muddy ground below. She returned to her seat in the unpleasant, uncomfortable silence, and listened carefully. Every set of hoof beats maintained their pace. There was no comment. The scrap had gone unnoticed by those behind.

A lot of this rode on chance. Any one of those hooves could have churned the purple material into the mud and out of sight. It could be blown away, though there was barely a breath of a breeze on this temperate spring morning. And then, even if it stayed there as a marker, some local could find it and pick it up. Or her pursuers could ride straight past it and on, uselessly, up the valley.

She just had to hope that it stayed there and that the men who had such skill and luck as to be able to track her even across the waves would see the marker and know to cross the bridge and climb the hill in pursuit. It was a gamble, but one that she needed to take.

Half an hour later, as the sun finally put in a full appearance, they rattled across a high-arched, narrow stone bridge and began a steep ascent. The rest of the day was spent in sullen silence, and Jala knew that evening was coming as the cracks of light around the carriage door faded to orange and then to a deep indigo. Finally, many, many hours, and many, many miles from Calacon, they stopped for the night.

As they were released from the carriage, Jala wished she had spent more of her time as empress touring the western provinces. She could tell her north and south, but her familiarity with the region was so scant that beyond the knowledge that she was somewhere north and a little west of Calacon, she had no idea where she was in relation to anything else.

They were on an area of plateau and far from civilization, and their captors had reined in by a copse of trees close to a stream, which, between them, would provide shelter, protection and water.

The men went about putting up four tents, gathering wood and lighting a fire, while the three women stood shivering in the growing gloom under the watchful eye of one northerner with a wickedly-pointed spear. Within half an hour the camp was up and the women were made secure once more. Nisha and the empress were each cuffed on the left wrist to a long, sturdy chain that was secured to the carriage's heavy timber wheel. The chain was plentiful and allowed them to move about their tent that had been erected next to the vehicle, but there was no chance of them removing either cuffs or wheel, as they had quickly determined during those nights between the coast and Calacon. The only way they would free themselves would be to remove a hand, and the ghost had clearly considered that, refusing them anything sharp even to eat with.

Resigned to the fact that they were spending another evening with their enemy, Jala and her companion sat close to the tent door, watching the camp as the evening meal was cooked and guards posted. Then, Halfdan appeared, calling for the other maid, and the two captives perked up with interest.

'Zari? Come here.'

The young Pelasian sauntered over, all-but fluttering her eyelids inanely at the man. Once again, Jala wished with all her heart that she could risk slapping the foolish girl.

'My love?'

'You almost cost us everything last night, Zari.'

The maid stopped in her tracks, clearly surprised by the tone of the comment, and the tone of her master's voice. 'Halfdan?'

'You are aware of the delicacy of our task, Zari, and the need for care and stealth?'

'Of course, my love.'

'And yet you decide, without even consulting me, that it is perfectly acceptable to leave your place of concealment in Calacon and go swanning off around the town as though this were a simple shopping trip?'

Zari recoiled slightly as she realized her error.

'I was… I just… I thought…'

'No,' the ghost said, his voice little more than a sibilant whisper and yet carrying in a shudder-worthy manner even above the noise of the camp. 'No, Zari, you did not think. You *never* think. It is clearly beyond your capacity.'

In an almost humorous way, Zari's brow furrowed as she worked through the insult. Jala felt a moment of glorious satisfaction that her former maid was being upbraided, and she could feel the same thing emanating from Nisha beside her.

'I thought we would need a few extra supplies,' Zari spluttered out. 'After the shipwreck we lived on such meagre rations all the way to Calacon, that I thought while we were in a large town with a market…'

'And it had not occurred to you how unusual a Pelasian face would be in Calacon? Fortunately one of my men alerted me to your foolishness and I was able to track your movements, which led me to discovering the location of our pursuers. Hopefully, our little engagement has made them more cautious and they will delay and lose our trail. But the fact remains that I was forced to leave the city by clandestine means and utilize some of my carefully-placed hidden allies because of your desire to shop. What have you to say for yourself?'

'Halfdan, my love… I…'

'You are an utter liability to my mission, Zari. I find you vapid and pointless. I have seen better use of skin and bone among village idiots. I am past protecting you from your spiteful mistress now, I think.'

'My… my love?' stuttered the girl in confused shock.

'Oh, do try and break through that veil of self-delusion, Zari. Had you not been so well-placed I would have sooner trysted with the stable boy than with you. He is considerably brighter, and better-looking for that matter.'

Zari stared at her master in total shock.

'Now, my little Pelasian moron, I have to teach you a lesson about following my instructions, but I am mindful of the fact that our relationship is now changing nature, and I must give you a choice. I still may have use for you, since you are well-versed in the habits and abilities and thoughts of your empress, and that could be handy. Thus I would like to keep you around, though in a more subservient role. But I am a practical man and not given to sentimentality. If you are not willing to submit to my justice, I will grant you quick release instead. Choose now.'

'You'll just let me go?' blabbered Zari, and the empress shook her head and rolled her eyes in the shelter of her tent.

'No, Zari. Release from this mortal realm. Honestly, if you were any slower on the uptake, I would wonder if there was sheep somewhere in your parentage.'

Again, the maid took a moment to think this through. Anger flashed quickly across her face before it was replaced by fear. 'I… I submit to you, my lo… Halfdan.'

'Good.'

The ghost's hand, which had been hidden behind him in the shadows, appeared holding a length of timber with a leather grip at one end. Zari's eyes widened in terror just before the first blow hit her across the upper arm, accompanied by the sound of breaking bone. She screamed.

'I will not tolerate the kind of foolishness that you have brought to this endeavour,' Halfdan said sternly as the girl recoiled, whimpering, clutching her upper arm. 'I will now deliver you one blow for each night you have accompanied me on this journey with your incessant chatter and your dangerous and useless idiocy. And when I am done, if you live, you will travel with the prisoners and you will keep that pretty and stupid mouth firmly sealed. Do you understand?'

Zari stared at him in panic and horror, and the ghost simply gestured with the rod. 'Nod.'

When she continued to stare, clutching her broken arm, he changed his grip on the timber and stepped forward and to one side, delivering her a powerful, driving blow to the gut that sent her to her knees, doubling up and choking out vomit.

'That's better,' the white-haired man said without the trace of a smile. 'Twelve more blows and you may retire for the night.'

Jala found suddenly that her elation at the thought of the traitorous maid being punished was not as to her taste as she had expected, and she winced as the third blow took the girl around the back of the head and sent her scattering across the floor, sobbing through the vomit and blood.

'Oh, Zari, you stupid girl. Now look what you have wrought for all of us.'

She turned away, unable to watch the rest. Nisha, she noticed, was less put off, an air of sickened satisfaction sating her need for revenge.

'The time is coming to leave soon,' Jala said quietly. 'But before we go, I want to know who is behind all this. Who is pulling Halfdan's strings and making him dance. Be prepared, Nisha. Soon, we go.'

CHAPTER XVII

Of Plots and Designs

Jala felt the carriage rattle across ruts, suggesting that they had moved onto a more major road, and a brief muffled murmur of conversation between the accompanying riders told her that there was some discussion, presumably about the route. Every jolt brought a whimper of pain from Zari, who lay upon the carriage floor on a bed of blankets taken from the bags and scavenged from elsewhere. The beating she had taken from Halfdan had not killed her, though Jala was fairly sure the maid wished it had. Miraculously she seemed to have suffered only three broken bones, in her upper and lower left arm, and her right collarbone. Nisha was familiar with basic medicine, which was an art oft taught in Pelasia, and she had set the arm as best she could and made their companion comfortable. She did not like doing so, of course. That was clear. Zari's face was a mess: scrunched up, misshapen and discoloured, like an old windfall apple in an advanced state of rot. Neither of her eyes had opened the next day, and only one the day after. Nisha was clearly hoping that the eye was permanently damaged, which would grant her a little of the vengeance she sought. But finally the maid saw clearly again this morning, on the fourth day out of Calacon.

Zari slept. She slept most of the time, healing slowly, and even though she whimpered now with the jolting of the carriage, still she slumbered, murmuring her pain in her dreams. Jala glanced down at her and then across at Nisha, who sat as usual with her ruined face to the carriage side.

'We need to get away, mistress,' Nisha said quietly. 'Every day we move north is a day further from safety and a day closer to Halfdan's master.'

Jala nodded her agreement. The delay was making her twitch, too. She had rather hoped that whoever it was who had so rattled their captors back in Calacon would catch up with them in short order and deal with the traitorous scum, but either they had been dispatched in the city, or had missed the clue and ridden off the wrong way, or – at best hope – they had been delayed and were still on the chase some distance behind.

‘I still want to find things out. I have a feeling we’ll know when we’re close to our destination. Soldiers always change attitude when a journey’s almost over, have you ever noticed? And they still seem settled and weary, so there are a few days left yet at least. Besides, we’ve yet to make any kind of headway with an idea, and now that *she’s* with us, I’m loathe to talk about it openly. But I need her to come round properly so I can pry a few answers out of her.’

The wounded maid’s eyes flickered for a moment. She had been conscious a few times over the last few days, but her mind was still rattled and fugged from several blows to the head, and Jala had not yet deemed her recovered enough to question.

‘I’d say ask her now,’ Nisha prompted. ‘You’ll probably get more truth out of her while she’s brain-aching. She won’t be able to dissemble properly. Not that she was ever much good at that.’

‘I would say that our predicament suggests otherwise,’ the empress replied archly. ‘But I take your point. No, I want clear, precise answers. This is too important. If I manage to get away and back to my husband, I need to have every last detail I can discern at my fingertips to help him put this trouble down, whatever it might be. I need more information.’

‘Ask away, Majesty,’ muttered a cracked, tiny voice from the floor.

‘Zari?’ Jala leaned forward. The maid’s eyes were open, and though they were still pink and bloodshot, there was more clarity in them than these past two days. Sudden alarm thrilled through her that the girl must have been aware and listening to her damning conversation.

‘Ask your questions, mistress. I will answer them with perfect truth, I swear on the name of Astara, most high and most powerful goddess. I have wronged you and I will pay with my everlife, but I will do what I can to set things right here.’

‘Don’t trust her,’ Nisha huffed.

‘She swore upon Astara,’ Jala noted. The senior Pelasian goddess was the keeper of oaths and punisher of wrongs, and an oath to her was the most binding that one of the faithful could ever make.

'For a traitor like her, oaths are as easily broken as a glass.'

Jala peered at Zari's face. Though it was difficult to look into those reddened, damaged eyes without squeamishly looking away again, Jala focused on them. She knew people, and she could see one thing clearly here that overrode any other possibilities or aspects: Zari was broken. Utterly and hopelessly broken. It was plain to see for those who knew how to look.

'She's not lying, Nisha.'

'So you say, mistress,' the other maid replied, unconvinced.

'Ask your questions, Majesty,' Zari said again, 'and if I can answer them, I will.'

Jala flexed her fingers and then steepled them. 'Who is Halfdan's master?'

'He's a northern lord. I've never met him or seen him, but I've heard Halfdan and his men talking about him. He's someone called Aldegund.'

The empress frowned for a moment, casting her mental net wide and fishing for details in her memory. 'He's one of the newer lords. Only one generation, if I remember correctly. My husband's father made him a lord. Before that he and his people were just a semi-civilized tribe on the northern border. Darius gave him a title and imperial support and set out his domain. He has quite a lot of land and is fairly wealthy. He's in a fine position. He could gain little from taking me, unless he means to try for the throne itself, but he would never manage that. He is not an idiot – I remember him from the celebrations of my husband's coronation anniversary. He's far from stupid enough to think he could take the throne. So what could he hope to gain from my capture?'

Zari tried to talk and the result was a coughing fit that lasted for some time. Once she subsided and relaxed, she took a calming breath. 'From what I understand, mistress, Aldegund is not the master in this. They talk of him as a king in his own right, as though he was independent of the empire, but they also talk of him paying lip service to some other lord. Not the emperor, though, mistress. Some *eastern* warlord.'

Jala's eyes widened. 'He serves someone from the east? I presume, then, that he has been promised his own little kingdom in return for his support. If Aldegund were no longer bound by his oath to the emperor, he could easily overwhelm his neighbouring lords and create a sizeable domain.' She tried to picture the map of the provinces hanging on the audience chamber wall back in Velutio. If Aldegund was based where she believed, then it would be within his power to create a kingdom that stretched from the Western Ocean to the Nymphaean Sea and from the mountains to the southern peninsula. More or less the whole of the western provinces. He would never stand a chance with the imperial government and army in place, though. Unless this eastern warlord…

'Why me, though? What use am I to him?'

Zari looked worried now. 'I cannot say for sure, mistress, but I have heard things, and if I assemble them like a puzzle, it forms a horrible picture.'

'Go on.'

'Well, mistress, they say that two of the marshals are dead, and that the other two are missing.'

'*Quintillian* is missing. Who else?'

'Titus Tythianus, mistress.'

Jala tried to picture someone abducting the scruffy, unbearably down-to-earth Titus. The idea seemed somehow absurd. Titus was surely indestructible? She'd certainly heard both Kiva and Quintillian opine as much. Not *dead*, though. Just *disappeared*. A small smile crept across her lips. Could he be the cause of Halfdan's troubles? It was an attractive idea.

'So the army is without its senior generals, and this Aldegund has the empress in his grasp.'

'I think, mistress, that you are lucky.'

'Lucky?' snorted Nisha, her first words in the conversation. 'Lucky *how*, precisely?'

'Lucky to be alive,' Zari replied quietly. 'I get the feeling that Halfdan was supposed to sink the ship and kill everyone aboard. I believe he took you instead of killing you, because of your potential value as a bargaining tool.'

'Then I *am* lucky,' Jala murmured. 'And my husband, the emperor, is in Velutio, utterly alone, facing insurrection and possibly further trouble from the east. He is missing his brother, his generals and his wife. My poor Kiva.' A further thought struck her. 'What do you suppose my brother is doing?'

'Mistress?'

'Oh, sacred sand devils, I just realized what will happen – why Aldegund took me.'

'Why?' Nisha asked, edging forward.

'My brother will blame the emperor for my disappearance. You know Ashar. He's hot-blooded and quick to anger. Even now the Pelasian army and fleet will be preparing. Gods above and below, can you imagine it? My husband is alone in the capital without his advisors and generals, and facing disaster on all sides! The north rebels against him, some eastern warlord is interfering, and now my brother will go to war with him too. Pelasia *alone* might well destroy the empire if it is not prepared, let alone with war on other fronts. And the empire will *not* be prepared. The military and the government will be in chaos!'

Nisha's one eye widened in horror, and the look on Zari's battered face below was terrible as the maid realized how much of a part she had played in potentially bringing down the empire and ruining centuries of peace between the two nations.

'Oh, no. No, no, no,' the empress said, the line of her jaw hardening. 'This will not do. This will not happen. I will get out of here and back to Velutio and warn my husband. If the gods are with me, I will be in time to help. We must go, and we must go immediately. As soon as it is dark, I think, and the soldiers are settled in for the night. But first, we need a plan.'

'I think, mistress, that I can help there,' Zari said quietly, a new look of determination in her bloodied eyes.

CHAPTER XVIII

Of Freedom

Aulus Wulfstan was underappreciated. Signed on to serve with the army of Lord Aldegund, he followed three generations of his family in that service. Of course, his grandsire and great-grandsire had been tribal warriors of note, rather than imperial subjects, but the principle was the same. His father had begun as a tribal hero fighting alongside Aldegund the chieftain and, after the agreement with the empire and the resettlement of lands, had become an officer in the lord's personal guard. Aulus had followed in his footsteps only a year before the old fellow's demise. He'd almost joined the imperial military, since he felt he could get far, but something in his tribal blood had called him to Aldegund. He felt sure that within the first year of service he would be made an officer as his father had been.

But no. Instead, he had been selected by that creepy monster Halfdan to take part in this backside-pummelling journey through the wilderness escorting three difficult, snobby women through horrible conditions for no greater remuneration. Of course, Halfdan had declared that they were all chosen because they were the best, but being the best should net you more in return than danger, soggy clothes, catty women and a sore arse.

He pulled his wool cloak around him as the spring rain came down like javelins from the night sky, pounding him and pushing him ever further into depression. The cloak was now so wet it was hardly worth calling protection from the weather and may well in fact be making him *more* sodden.

He grumbled and cursed Halfdan – an old curse his grandsire used to use on men who cheated at dice. The camp was silent. Oh, there would be snoring, farting, murmuring and probably chitter-chatter from the women in the tent, but with the constant hiss of falling rain and the clatter of the heavy drops battering off leaves, such noise was a hidden thing. Another curse at Halfdan, this time not for his general situation, but for his immediate one. Drawing the middle watch was irritating. The only thing that made it bearable was that Halfdan's most favoured man had drawn the same watch and was suffering just as much on the far side of the camp. And, of course, that Halfdan himself was wandering about somewhere in the downpour. The man never seemed to sleep. Aulus couldn't remember ever catching the boss aslumber during the entire trip. He couldn't possibly sleep more than an hour or two a night.

Perhaps that was what made him so pale and unhealthy-looking?

And evil tempered.

It didn't affect his speed or skill, though.

Aulus shrugged into the cloak and turned at the sound of a broken twig, loud enough to sound even over the rain. The taller maid was walking across towards him from the tent – the one with the missing eye, who'd been quite pretty until Halfdan started to work on her. Still she was quite a looker if you tried to ignore the eye. Aulus felt stirrings and wondered if he would be allowed to have her when they got back and the maids were no longer important. That would go a little way to making up for this onerous duty.

The maid – Nisha, he remembered – was smiling at him, which was slightly disconcerting with that empty orb. The smile only reached one eye. He shivered, but the sensation was not entirely unpleasant.

'The mistress sent me to speak to you,' the maid murmured quietly in her sultry Pelasian accent. Aulus felt suddenly quite warm, despite being soaked with cold rain. He smiled warily and opened his mouth to reply when something sank through his soggy, spongy, sleep-deprived brain and forced his brow to crease.

How did she get here when she was supposed to be manacled and chained to a piton with her mistress? Brow still furrowed in tired confusion, his eyes lifted to her shoulder and then widened. The empress was visible only as a rapidly-retreating figure in dirty purple and white, sprinting from the tent in the opposite direction, making for the river.

Aulus felt panic enfold him. The empress was escaping and it would be his fault!

He knew what Halfdan did to punish failure…

The first two times he shouted the alarm, his throat was too scratchy and hoarse to be heard above the rain, but he put two fingers in his mouth and blew a shrill whistle that drew the attention of the whole camp.

'The empress!' he bellowed. 'The empress is escaping!' He looked back and forth in worry between the maid and her mistress. He should run after the empress, but would he then suffer for leaving the maid free?

He almost shat himself as Halfdan appeared seemingly out of nowhere, right next to his shoulder, his face thunderous. 'Where?'

Shaking uncontrollably, Aulus lifted his spear and pointed to the distant figure even now descending the river bank. The white-haired monster fixed Aulus with a look of angry disgust. 'Stay here. Watch her!' Then he waved an arm to the general company who were now all up and grabbing weapons. 'After her. Ten gold coins and a night with the maid to the man who recaptures her!'

Aulus felt the last shreds of hope dying away. Now he would not get extra money, he would not get the girl, and he would probably be beaten for letting the damn Pelasian bitch get away. He still couldn't figure out how she'd got the chain off.

As the entire camp pounded off after the empress, Aulus, utterly despondent, turned to the one-eyed maid. 'Show me your hands.'

She did as she was bidden, raising them, and he was both horrified and fascinated. The maid had broken her thumb and all her fingers more than once so that her mangled paw would fit through the manacle. That took some guts. How had she not screamed enough to wake the entire camp? He opened his mouth to speak to her, but then everything went wrong.

Jala padded lightly across the wet grass, feeling the odd restriction of Zari's dress, for the traitorous maid was thinner than her and the clothes were just a little restrictive. A quick glance towards the river and she could just see the guards racing away into the darkness. Ahead, the man left to watch them was close to Nisha, examining her hands.

As Jala closed on the man, her movement masked by the constant hiss of rain, she raised her manacled hand, the long chain wrapped around her forearm to prevent it dragging and clanking, and brought down the heavy iron piton – the spike that had anchored them to the grass until Zari managed to dig and lever it out with the piece of timber she had stolen – hard across the guard's skull. As he fell to his knees, gurgling and swiftly passing from consciousness, she contemplated wrapping the chain around the man's neck and throttling the rest of the life from him, or driving the point of the piton into his brain, but she instantly dismissed the idea.

'Come on,' she hissed, grabbing Nisha and making a beeline for the trees nearby.

'Kill him,' replied Nisha, a vicious edge to her voice.

'No time. Come on.'

Ignoring the maid's protestations, Jala yanked her on to the relative safety of the woods. The oppressive, gloomy edge of the forest loomed and the canopy was visible rising up the side of the wide valley. It was their best opportunity to lose the guards, for Halfdan and his men would soon learn their folly. As if on cue to remind her of what Zari had sacrificed, a blood-curdling scream rent the night from the direction of the river. The treacherous maid had paid the final price for her deceit. As she ran, Jala cast up the briefest of prayers to the goddess Astara that Zari be redeemed in the afterworld. Nisha's face showed less compassion as her feet pounded across the sodden grass, her jaw set angrily, her one eye burning with vengeful ire.

It was with a great sigh of relief that Jala passed the gnarled trunk of the first old oak tree and entered the almost pitch-dark gloom of the woodland.

'Where do we go?' Nisha asked. 'Where will we be safe?'

'Nowhere,' Jala replied darkly. 'Halfdan is too clever by half, and both he and several of his men seem to be trackers and hunters. They'll be familiar with following trails through all sorts of terrain. Our only bonus is that they will not be able to enter the forest on horseback, so we have a little head start. We try and confuse our trail and then find the most secret place to stay until it gets light, since it's treacherous moving in this place in the dark.'

Nisha nodded her agreement. Woodlands were anathema to her, as they were to the empress, having been born and raised in the scrub and desert lands west of Akkad. There a forest was any place with more than four trees, and green was an almost magical colour, it was so rare in nature. They may all have been in the empire for years now, but still they tended to avoid forests. Plus, these superstitious old northerners were always telling legends of monsters and half-gods in their woods, and neither woman had the desire to meet a half-goat, half-man creature and be beguiled into living their life as part of a tree.

'How do we confuse the tracks?' the maid enquired as they carefully picked their way over roots and through scrub.

Jala wasn't entirely sure. She had little enough experience in this terrain. Peering down and back, she noted with dismay the obvious trail they had left through the leaf mould, tangled plants, sticks and mud. It would not require a hunter to follow that. A confused donkey could follow that.

'Water,' she said with certainty. 'If we can find water, we cannot leave a trail through it. It will wash away signs of our passing.' Another thought struck her. 'And rock. If we can find rock, we'll pass across it with just footprints that the rain will clear for us. So keep your eye out for water and rock.'

The two women ran on up the gentle slope in almost darkness, regularly pausing to extricate themselves from tangles, floundering against trees or slipping and falling, each helping the other back up so they could run on blindly. Where they were going was a moot point. For now they just had to get safely away from their captors. Still, Jala had selected the woods for more than just protection. They lay to the east and, far beyond them and the Nymphaean Sea, so did Velutio and her husband. It would be easy to get turned around in the forest, but as long as they kept climbing they were going in the right direction. When they reached the top of the great hill, they would try to get their bearings.

Suddenly, Nisha disappeared with a cry and Jala teetered to a halt. The maid had crested a rise in the darkness and found herself suddenly stepping into space. Below, a long scree slope descended to a stream which fell in short cataracts from high up before meandering off through the trees, presumably to feed the river where Zari would now be lying, dead. Nisha managed to arrest her fall a third of the way down the slope and carefully rose, using her good hand, now badly scraped. She tottered for a moment and almost fell again, but steadied herself.

'Good,' called Jala. 'This should help. Try and make it along to the third fall. Can you see it?'

Nisha peered off at the stream and focused in the shadows. The scree slope meant that here there were no trees and the gloom was less oppressive, though the constant driving rain made it almost as difficult to make out details. Finally, the maid nodded and began to carefully pick her way around the gentle curve, stones skittering away constantly from under her feet. The noise on a good day would carry far enough to make them easy to track, but the blessed rain would help cover such sounds.

With great care, Jala began to descend the slope until she was perhaps 15 feet below the lip where Nisha had fallen. Happy that she was far enough down, she began to slowly pick her way along, wincing at every slide of scree that clattered down to the stream below. Several times she lost her footing and almost fell, recovering her balance at the last moment with bellows-breath and wide eyes.

It felt like the work of a lifetime, slowly – so slowly – making their way around the scree slope. Nisha had something of a head start from her fall and was ahead, though every time she slipped and almost fell it took her long to rise and move on, and each time the shriek of pain cut through Jala like a knife. Because every fall she had to put one or both hands to the scree to prevent tumbling away down the slope. One of her hands she had ruined to free them from their chains, and the other would now have been shredded by the scree in her tumble. Jala would owe Nisha for the rest of her life for all she had done.

Abruptly, galvanizing her into further speed, she heard noises back across the woodland. A momentary lull in the rain – just 20 heartbeats – revealed the distant sound of shouted discussion. She could identify the rough direction and with sinking spirits realized they were directly behind. Clearly Halfdan had good trackers, for she was sure they were already on her trail.

She slid suddenly, dropping another ten feet down the slope before regaining her balance. The sound of pebbles and dirt tumbling on down the steep slope to the stream below was to her almost deafening. Fortunately the rain had picked up in pace once more and she could only hope that it had been loud enough to cover the sound of her slip.

Gritting her teeth, she moved on carefully, but as fast as she dared. It felt as though she had been stepping across scree the entire night by the time she finally felt solid stone beneath her feet. Even then, the stone was wet and treacherous, and a single slip could send her tumbling on down the waterfalls. Nisha was waiting a few paces away, leaning back against a wet rock, breathing heavily and with relief.

'It's not over yet,' Jala said, not unkindly, and gestured up the slope. The maid's eye widened.

'You can't be thinking that, mistress?'

'They will assume us to have crossed the stream or descended the valley.'

'Because only a madwoman would attempt to climb it.'

'Precisely.'

Though Nisha was shaking her head, Jala felt sure it was the only way. They needed to keep ascending the hill, and a logical pursuer would follow the stream down, looking for where the tracks started again. Clenching her teeth, the empress began to clamber up the slimy rocks, moving to the centre where the water fell and battered her as she struggled, her limbs heavy with cold, her fingers numb to the point of insensibility as she felt for edges to cling onto, hauling herself ever upward, her tracks non-existent as the torrent of water all around her cleared them. Behind, Nisha was now pulling herself up the steep cataract.

Like the scree slope, the ascent was interminable. The tumbling stream was louder even than the endless rain, and Jala could hear nothing but the roar of water and the rhythmic, all-too-fast pounding of her heart. Even shouted conversation between the two of them would be impossible, which unfortunately also meant she could no longer hear their pursuers, which added a nerve-wracking uncertainty to the whole thing.

They passed the first fall and paused to get their breath before even attempting the next two. The empress glanced across the slope to the lip where they had both first appeared. From this position, there were tracks in the scree that seemed horribly obvious, but she could only hope that they would be less visible from above, given the angle.

'Let's move,' she said, half expecting Nisha to argue, but the maid simply nodded. How she was managing with her mangled hand, Jala couldn't imagine, but sure enough, as they climbed the second-highest waterfall, the maid gave a cry of pain and slipped. As she fell back, Jala reached down and caught her good hand. The jerk as the maid's fall was arrested almost pulled the empress from the rock too, and her fingers, cold though they were, felt as though they were on fire as they clung onto a lip in the stone and her other hand gripped Nisha's bloodied palm, embedded with grit from her fall. How she had managed thus far was astounding. Jala felt proud of her Pelasian friend, but also worried for her.

Slowly, she helped Nisha upright once more and when the maid gave her a nod of confirmation, she finally let go and paused to let strength return in small measure to her arms. Perhaps it had been foolish to climb the falls? Still, they were almost halfway there, now.

Jala flattened herself to the rock at a shout that cut through the hiss and roar. Her roving eye caught a figure at the top of the slope, exactly where they had crossed. Beneath her, Nisha stilled, recognizing that something was wrong. The empress could see the figure only as a vague shape in the gloom, visible between the spray and fall of water that hopefully hid her from view. It hovered there for a moment, then shouted and gestured down the slope with a waving arm before retreating back into the gloom.

'What does that mean?' Nisha hissed from below.

'I think he's seen our tracks. We have to go. Now. Fast.'

Ignoring the numb cold in her limbs, Jala threw herself into the climb, scrambling upward, passing the spout of the next waterfall and scurrying up to the final ascent. Nisha somehow managed to keep up with her, struggling along behind, and the empress began to count her heartbeats as she rose, 137 signalled the top of the torrent. She pulled herself over the last rock and reached down to help Nisha up, the two of them falling to the wet stone and huddling together in relief, shaking in unison with cold and nerves.

Another call, and suddenly there were three figures at the far side of the scree slope. There was no doubt that they were on the trail, then. Jala pressed herself back against the rock, hoping that the combination of distance, falling water and shadow would keep them from view. More figures appeared at the lip, and the familiar shining white hair of Halfdan was among them. The leader gestured several times with his hand and two men began to descend the scree with difficulty, another two edging around the top and the rest descending the hill the other way, around the upper edge of the scree. Halfdan was taking no chances, clearly. Fortunately, most of them were concentrating on the bottom end of the cataract vale, and only two were moving upward, but they might well end up cutting off the two women if they didn't move.

'We have to go.'

'What if they see us move?' Nisha hissed.

'If we don't, those two will get ahead of us.'

Nodding, the maid rose unsteadily, and the two Pelasians began to hurry up the wet stones and scurry, keeping as low as they could, into the treeline. Once more, after another 20 heartbeats, they were in the relative safety of the trees.

'What now?'

Jala looked around her. In truth, she wasn't sure. Now they would start to leave a trail again, and with two men closing on them, that was a dangerous thing to do. She was so dispirited and uncertain that she missed it the first time, and it was only on her second circle that she spotted the cave.

'There!'

Nisha turned to where the empress's finger pointed. It wasn't much. A dark hollow beneath the gnarled roots of an old tree, high enough and wide enough to accommodate two people hunched over or kneeling, and deep enough, hopefully, to conceal them from casual view. Better still, it was close enough to the rocks of the stream that there was hardly space to leave a trail. The maid nodded and the two women crossed to the place and peered inside. Her initial fears that the cave was home to wolves or a bear, or even some dreadful legendary forest monster, proved to be unfounded. The cave was only a dozen feet deep and showed no signs of habitation and, most relieving of all, no hint of gnawed bones. Carefully and quietly the two women squatted and edged back into the darkness.

Over the din of water falling both from the sky onto the leaves of the trees and down the sequence of falls into the vale below, Jala caught the sound of shouts. Motioning to Nisha she shrank back into the black of the cave as best she could. Sure enough, the two men who'd gone round the top of the slope emerged from the trees some distance away, deep in discussion. Jala held her breath, shivering like the maid beside her.

'...says we're to head back to camp,' muttered one of the figures.

'Now?' asked the other in surprise.

'We might have missed their trail in the dark and the wet. When it gets light we'll pick up their tracks. They'll not lose us for long. Come on. We don't want to piss off Halfdan.'

'I've no wish to be face to face with the boss so soon,' shouted the second man, and Jala realized with a start that this was the guard she'd hit over the head with the piton. Clearly Nisha had been correct and she should have finished the man off after all.

'Well, I'm going back.'

'I'll be along in a moment,' called the one with the head wound. 'I'm just going to check the stream edge just in case.'

The empress felt her heart begin to race as the first man turned and disappeared into the woods again, but the second made almost straight for the cave, close to the stream. Jala held her breath once more, and could hear the whispered sounds of Nisha praying beside her. Outside their tiny haven the rain continued to lash down between the trees, accompanied by the sound of the guard tramping through the undergrowth and then sloshing into the stream in search of their tracks. There was something else, too – a louder noise, but further away, something she couldn't quite identify.

The guard stopped at the edge of the stream and leaned over, peering at the wet stones. Surely not? How could he know someone had passed that way? Even if she'd left mud, surely the water would have washed it away? The strange, unidentifiable noise was getting louder. It was a rumbling, like thunder, muffled by the forest. The empress felt a chill through her veins as she watched, in seeming slow-motion, the guard with the bloodied, matted hair slowly straighten, his eyes following some kind of trail until they came up to the level of the cave. The knuckles clutching the spear at his side whitened and his eyes gleamed as he spotted the two figures hunched in the cave.

The thunder reached a cacophonous climax as the guard began to change his grip and level his spear, his mouth twisting into a triumphant leer and opening to shout a warning.

And the boar hit him.

The crescendo of thunder must have been the huge beast running towards them along the forest floor above the cave. The guard screamed as he fell back, the protruding massive canines ripping twin gory lines across his belly. Jala could do nothing but try and shrink ever further back into the darkness, her horrified eyes locked on the bloody conflict mere paces away.

There was no hope of the guard bringing his spear to bear. The usual defence against the charge of these creatures, Jala knew from dull hunting talk at court, was to prepare with a braced spear that took the creature in the heart as it ran. The noise of the water had disguised the monster's approach, though, such that the guard had not been aware of the danger until it was upon him. Now he cast his spear away, trying to draw his sword despite the agony in his midriff, his other hand questing for the dagger at his belt.

The boar was merciless. With the man down and pinned beneath it, it began to ruin him, its powerful hooves pounding ribs into splinters. Then, as the desperate, agonized guard finally managed to get his dagger free, the animal finished it. Lowering its head, it dropped its tusk-like teeth to the man's chest and ripped up as though shovelling dirt, the huge, powerful muscles in its neck and shoulders driving those awful teeth through bone and muscle as it carved a huge ravine along the man's body from heart to nose, smashing the collarbones, shredding the neck and ripping away the lower jaw. The man went from guard to ravaged meat in moments. Blood sprayed the trees and undergrowth and bits of meat and bone catapulted up into the air as the monster raised its head. A keening sound was all that was left of the guard who she'd thumped earlier, and even that faded as the vocal chords were crunched and eaten.

The other guard, drawn hurriedly by the din, emerged from the trees opposite, his eyes wide and white.

'Fuck!'

The commotion caught the attention of the boar, which looked up at the newcomer, its pink eyes filled with rage and hunger. But *this* man was prepared. He levelled his spear, stepping to the side by a tree, even as the boar ran at him. At the last moment, the man ducked behind the tree and held the spear firm as the monster hit it. It was not a proper boar-spear, with a cross bar, so the creature ran on, impaling itself more and more in a frenzied effort to get at the wielder, and it almost reached the tree, close enough to gouge the man, before its brain brought it the message that it was dying.

The second guard stayed behind the tree, his boot still anchoring the butt of the spear little more than a foot from the animal's head, even after the boar stopped convulsing and lay still. Finally, shaking like a leaf, the guard stepped out, staring at the animal who'd almost had him. Had it had a good run at him, it would have slid all the way along the spear and now there would be one dead animal and *two* dead men here. Only the fact that it had already killed the other man had saved him, by removing all the momentum.

'Aulus you poor, unlucky bastard,' the man muttered, his eyes still rolling wildly, chest still heaving as though he'd run a race. He never once looked at the cave, where two women watched on in horror. Finally, the man gathered up his friend's fallen spear, stripped him of sword, dagger and money pouch, then turned and left.

Jala continued to stare in shock at the bodies so close to her. Man and pig, both deceased mere paces away. At length, she turned to see Nisha with a matching expression and, deciding that the man was far enough away to risk noise, she breathed deeply.

'I think we're safe here for now.'

'S...safe?' wheezed Nisha, staring at the dead boar, which was still transfixed with a spear.

'Safer than out there, anyway. You heard the man: they're heading back to the camp. They'll start to look for our trail in the morning, but I have no intention of accidentally bumping into another of those things in the dark. We stay here until it begins to get light, then we start to move east. Hopefully we can get an hour or so on them and be gone before they locate our trail. I have a feeling we're going to be tracked doggedly for some time. They're good at it, and Halfdan cannot go back to his master without me.'

'I wish we'd never left Velutio, mistress.'

'I'll second that, Nisha. But in the morning we'll begin the journey back.'

CHAPTER XIX

Of Pursuit and Safe Havens

Jala and Nisha struggled up the hill in the golden light of the descending sun. They had been running now for more than 12 hours with only infrequent breaks to gather their breath. They had emerged from the forest perhaps two hours after dawn having found a viewpoint at first light that gave them a clear picture of what lay ahead.

The first task of the day had been to deal with Nisha's hands. At the maid's suggestion, they laid her ruined hand flat on a rock and with a great deal of whimpering and tears, tried to arrange it such that the fingers were in the correct position and might stand some chance of knitting together once more. They then tucked the hand into her side and bound it to her with a strip of material torn from the empress's over-tunic, so that it would be as comfortable as possible and safe for the journey. Then Jala found a stick and honed it on a rock to a point, which she used to prize the gravel out of the maid's wounded other hand. Once this was done and the scrapes had been thoroughly washed, the empress bound that hand tight too. Nisha was dismissive of that damage, claiming it would be workable in a day or two. The other would never be usable again, and they both knew it.

But they were alive and free and moving.

Beyond the forest, the landscape had changed. It had become scrubland and hills and valleys with odd yellow-brown strata lines everywhere, so that it looked as though the world had been laid down by the gods one thin layer at a time. Only the bottom of the valleys were green, where rivers and streams meandered, and even some of these were seasonal and had now dried up after the spring thaw. To some extent, it was more comfortable terrain for the pair than the forest or the rolling green of the northwest, as it more closely resembled the hot, brown lands of their home.

Still, it seemed to go on forever, yet somewhere beyond lay the shore of the Nymphaean Sea and the hope of home; that knowledge drove them on.

Thus far, they had seen only two settlements and they had avoided both carefully. Nothing left a trail more readily visible than interaction with other people. Had they come across a farmstead or such, Jala would have contemplated stealing a horse or other rideable animal to help them along, but the only farms they had seen were on the edge of the two villages, and she'd not risk being seen by those who could report to pursuers. Other than that, only olive groves and vineyards showed signs of life. Jala had been surprised. She knew they cultivated olives and made wine down in the south of the western provinces, near the Vinceia Peninsula, but she'd have thought it to stop before this latitude. Still, it was warm, even in spring – now that the rain had stopped, anyway.

They had passed through an orchard unexpectedly just after noon, just as their bellies began to complain over lack of fulfilment. With no sign of the orchard's cultivators in sight, they had fashioned a bag from Nisha's over-tunic and filled it with oranges, plums, pears and peaches.

Nisha had complained at the relentless pace her mistress set, and Jala was sympathetic enough not to push as hard as she'd like, given how the maid's hands must be paining her, but while Nisha felt they must be safe now, and that no one could have followed them through that woodland, Jala remembered how easily they'd been tracked to the cave and she knew Halfdan's mind. He would have been mere hours behind them by noon, she was sure. And once they had picked up the trail on this side of the forest, which she was convinced they would do, they would move fast, mounted as they were.

Consequently, she had chosen their route carefully. They had not travelled directly east during the day, but had meandered, crossing rivers where they could, avoiding soft, impressionable ground, climbing valley sides, and dropping back down, keeping away from well-used trails wherever possible.

Finally, as the sun was beginning to sink towards the western horizon, Jala and her friend made for an old tower atop a high hill.

Shelter out here seemed to be particularly sparse, and they would need somewhere to hole up for the night. The tower had a crumbled top and was accompanied by the ruined shell of a low building, clearly derelict. To be sure they left as sparse a trail as possible, they had skirted around the south of the hill, far from the path that ran along the north side, and climbed the slope in a zigzag.

Now, weary, they neared the crest, sweating and huffing. The place had been some kind of watchtower, rather than a windmill, which had been Jala's first thought. It appeared that the fallen outbuilding had been the main edifice, including living area, storeroom and stables, while the tower had been little more than an observation structure. A careful, slow investigation in the fading light confirmed the place to be deserted, and both women heaved a sigh of relief at the discovery.

The main structure was too ruinous. Not only did it lack any form of roof, but the walls crumbled to the touch, mortar blowing away like dust, and even a gentle prod had brought down an entire section of wall, so they had ruled the place out as a potential refuge. The tower may be crumbled at the top, but it was more solidly constructed than the outbuilding, and two floors remained intact, smelling only of dust and the urine of some wild animal that had recently used the place as a home.

Best of all, some other wayward traveller had recently been in the place and had left a small pile of blankets in a corner. They were a little dusty and threadbare, but intact and warm enough to help them make it through the night. Moreover, a water butt outside still functioned and had gathered fresh rain during the night, so they had plentiful drinking water. In the upper room, windows overlooked the dusty hillside road in both directions, and so they decided to make this their home for the night. Greedily, they tucked into the last of the fruit Jala had carried all afternoon, Nisha's hands not being up to the task.

Finally, they settled in for the duration. Neither of them had slept more than a few winks the previous night in their cave, still terrified by their ordeal and the sudden appearance of the boar. Both women were exhausted, but Jala insisted on taking the first watch, knowing that the maid with her wounds had suffered much more over the past day than her.

And so it was that Nisha was fast asleep beneath her blankets when Jala first noticed the riders. It was still only evening, the world was a glowing violet fading to black in the east, and the low level of light meant that she heard them before she saw them – 9 horses made a lot of noise on a track of stones and hard-packed earth.

The empress dropped from her place at the window, her heart racing, so that just the top of her head would show, allowing her to peer over the stonework and out at the hillside trail. It was almost certainly dark enough that she'd not be seen, and they had had no way to light a fire in the tower, but eyes would be drawn to the ruined structure and she didn't want to take chances. Tense, she watched, unsure, but her worst fears were soon realized as one figure in the middle of the riders pulled back his hood to reveal silvery white hair.

Halfdan.

The man was like a bad smell, turning up unexpectedly and unwanted, and far too often. His trackers *must* be good. As the small party walked their horses along the track, Jala quickly padded across to the other window to keep them in view. She contemplated waking Nisha, but to do so would take precious time, and she didn't want to take her eyes off the riders.

The other window looked east along the valley, but a little stretching and craning revealed the dirt road below. With no sign of Halfdan's horsemen! Her heart lurching in her chest, Jala scurried as quietly as possible back to the first window. The riders had reined in below the tower just out of sight of either aperture. How had she been so stupid as to choose an obvious landmark in which to pass the night? Of *course* it would attract other attentions too. Willing her heart to slow and quiet a little, she leaned closer. The men were talking.

'…could be anywhere by now. We don't even know for certain she's heading east.' It was a voice she didn't recognize, but the reply came from a very familiar one in a snarl.

'She came this way. And she is going east, though she meanders in an attempt to obfuscate. She fails. Gierbert and I could track a bird across the sky if we set our minds to it. They crossed the stream an hour back, certainly, and though the trail is scant at best in these rocks, unless she decides to double back and go the wrong way – which she will not, as it would cost her precious days and she knows time is of the essence – then she will have to cross either the Duria or Urbanus River, and there is no way she can do so without leaving some mark I can pick up. Besides, most of this land is loyal to Aldegund and no one will help her. Within a day, two at the most, she will be ours again. Stop wasting your breath fretting over nothing. Concentrate on the task at hand.'

There was a tense silence, and then finally Halfdan spoke again. 'Very well, ahead is the village of Raetis. I can secure comfortable lodgings there for the night and move on to cover the rivers in the morning. Gierbert? Take three men back to that last crossing and stay at that farmhouse. In the morning, see if you can pick up any more signs we might have missed in the failing light, and meet me at Corbas by lunchtime. Rief? Take three and scour this valley for signs, then come down to Raetis after full dark.'

'We'll not find anything in this light, Halfdan,' complained the petulant voice she had first heard.

'There is always a chance, even for the mindless and unobservant,' snapped Halfdan. 'Just do it. I'm certain she passed through this valley, and quite recently. There will be signs. I will take the rest on to Raetis and arrange rooms. You all know your tasks?'

There was an affirmative chorus. 'Good. To work.'

A murmur of low conversation was given counterpoint by the sound of riders departing. From the window Jala could see four men riding off back into the dim glow of post-sunset evening. More horses were leaving for the east. She listened intently, her heart racing again.

'How in shit do we search in this light? I could fall over the Pelasian bitch and not notice her.'

'Halfdan is punishing us,' another man grumbled.

'Well, shit on him. I'm not picking through rocks and falling over in the dark looking for something that might not even be there,' the petulant leader grunted. 'I'll take Burrus and Erlend down to the end of the valley. We can stop at the shrine there and rest for an hour, then head down into Raetis and tell the arsehole that there was nothing to find.'

'What about me?'

'You get to the top of that tower and have a look. If there *is* anything to be found in this valley, our best chance of spotting it now is from there. Once you've had a quick scan of the place, follow on east and meet us at the shrine. Halfdan's gone far enough now that he won't see us following.'

The sound of three men clattering off across the stone was a welcome one, but the knowledge that a fourth was to climb their tower forestalled any joy. Jala crossed the room and crouched by Nisha. Outside she could just hear grumbling and the sounds of someone dismounting and tying up their horse. With her heart in her throat, she gently shook the maid. Nisha's eye shot wide and her mouth opened, but the empress pressed a finger to her lips in warning, then pointed to the stairs and held one finger up. Nisha nodded, nerves showing in her face. Grabbing the blanket, Jala crossed the room again to one side and dropped to a crouch, beckoning. Nisha joined her and together they pulled the ragged blankets over them, trying to look like nothing more than a heap of refuse. Given the extremely dim light in the tower and the fact that the disgruntled soldier was making for the top, he might well just pass them and not notice.

Still, just in case, Jala slid the spiked iron piton she carried from the makeshift sheath in her over-tunic. Moments later she heard the sound of footsteps approaching in the stairwell. The empress wished she could see, but had no desire to attract attention with movement. The footsteps paused, clearly at the doorway to this room, and then began once more, echoing as they ascended to the top. Jala let out a gentle, slow breath and shivered with tension. It was pitch black under the blanket, but she could feel Nisha's nervous one-eyed gaze upon her. She listened as carefully as she could and caught brief snatches of sound from above where the man moved about amid the rubble-strewn top, peering into the gloomy valley for any sign of the two women who were, unbeknownst to him, mere paces away on the next floor.

She heard a muttered curse, and then the footsteps began descending towards them. Again, she hunkered down under the blanket with the maid and again the footsteps stopped at this floor. Then, bringing panic to both women, the heavy boots clomped into the room. There was another pause as the man surveyed the circular chamber in the almost dark, trying to discern anything of interest. Jala held her breath and the silence was so intense that she could hear the guard's breath as he scanned the room. Then the boots approached them.

Jala gripped the heavy, long iron spike tight and tensed.

The soldier grasped the blankets and yanked them away.

He was far more surprised at what he found than they were to see him. His eyes bulged and he fumbled for the blade sheathed at his side. Clearly he'd not expected to find anything, let alone the very thing he'd been tasked with. Before he could recover from his surprise and leap into action, the two women were on him.

Jala had listened to endless sour and unpleasant conversations between Quintillian and Titus on swordsmanship and killing blows. She knew enough to know how to kill, even if she wasn't practised in the art. The neck. The armpit. The groin. However, the man wore a shirt of mail sewn onto leather that hung to halfway down his thigh, protecting most of his torso, and the empress was crouched on the floor. Unable to reach a killing point, she settled for the most certain blow available.

The spike jammed down through the leather of the man's boot, through the soft foot with the crunch of fragile bones, and into the leather sole beneath, only stopping as it struck the stone floor. Even as he screamed and looked down, Nisha snapped her teeth shut on the hand that was reaching for the sword. The man's panicked, agonized eyes ripped away from the maimed foot to the mad, one-eyed woman hanging off his hand like some sort of giant, maddened rodent. Howling, he shook his savaged hand, but the teeth gripped firm into bone and muscle. Nisha wasn't being moved. He slapped at her head with his free hand, still unable to move her, but his attention had shifted from Jala, and that would be a fatal mistake. The empress ripped the spike from the foot, blood bubbling up through the hole in the leather, and rose, unfolding like the fury of sand devils. As the soldier realized his peril and his gaze turned back to her, the glistening, sticky iron piton slammed into his left eye, driving deep, deep into the brain.

He fell, gasping, and lay on the stone flags shaking and gurgling. As he collapsed, Nisha had the presence of mind to unclench her teeth and spit out the severed digit.

'Now get ready to move,' Jala breathed.

'What? Why?'

'Because when this man doesn't join his friends at the end of the valley in half an hour they'll know something's wrong and this valley will be crawling with Halfdan's men. We have to be long gone by then. I heard where the man's going and about two rivers, one of which we're going to have to cross shortly. I want to be across that river tonight. I know you're exhausted. So am I. But we can't sleep until we're on the other side of that river.' She gave a hard grin as she crouched by the body. 'At least now we have a sword, a dagger and a purse of money.'

CHAPTER XX

Of Journeys and the Future

The sun glowed a hot orange low in the western sky. Jala and Nisha climbed a slope rather reminiscent of the one beneath the old watchtower with now-practised, weary ease. It had been a fraught three days following one of the most heart-stopping nights of their lives.

Leaving the watchtower, they had descended the way they'd arrived, along the southern, unwatched slope. It had been a swift flight and a panic-filled one, despite the lack of immediate pursuit. In Jala's opinion, it would not have been more than an hour before the three men waiting at the shrine at the valley's eastern end decided to head back and search for their missing man. Another quarter-hour riding, then a quick search, and she could only estimate that within an hour and a half the enemy would be looking for them in force again. The big question was what the petulant one would do. Would he immediately race off to report to Halfdan and bring the majority of the group back into the search, or would he and his small party scour the hillside and valley first. The latter seemed the most likely possibility. A man like that would not want to report to his master as a failure, and would only do so as a last resort.

In the end, it seemed that must have been what had happened. Surely, if the man had run to Halfdan, the enemy would have been waiting at the river. As it happened, Jala and Nisha ran like madwomen with the swirl of sand devils after them, down the slope, along a dry streambed curving around the southern end of another hill to stay as far from the valley as possible, then over a hilltop where a ramshackle farm had been built amid the ruins of some ancient long-gone settlement. Fortunately, the farm's owners were abed and the fugitives passed by unnoticed. From there they were afforded a view of a small town – more of an overgrown village, really. This they presumed to be Raetis, where Halfdan and his men would be waiting. Two sizeable rivers met at a confluence just beyond the settlement, forming one great snake, silvered in the moonlight, writhing its way east to the sea.

It took two hours from that hilltop to reach the river, now a total of three-and-a-half since they had fled the tower. Crossing the great torrent had proved to be more than just troublesome. There were boats, but they were all tied up at ramshackle jetties by houses belonging to fishermen and it would be far too risky to take one. There were no bridges, and the ferries that would be found in the larger settlements would leave an obvious trail. Now that Jala knew they were in Aldegund's allies' lands, she couldn't trust a single human they came across. That left only one possibility, and it was not an attractive one. She could only hope that when Halfdan had said they would leave evidence at the river he had not counted on their willingness to try the impossible.

Swimming.

Both she and Nisha could swim – had learned in the great baths of the imperial palace in Velutio. But only a lunatic would attempt to swim a wide and fast-flowing wild river, especially at night, exhausted and – in one case – with wounded hands. And that was what she had relied upon. But even then, it was all about obfuscating. She was under no illusion that Halfdan would lose her trail. Eventually, he would pick it up, but every hour she bought them took them an hour closer to home.

And so they doubled the danger. They took an impossible task and made it worse. The two women walked out onto the riverbank at an area of stones where they would leave no prints for the morning, and gingerly plunged into the cold water. It took only two or three strokes for Jala to realize how little chance she had of making it with the sword, so she unbuckled it, letting it sink into the black depths where it would leave no trace to be found by the hunters.

Then the two of them swam out into the middle of the great river. The current was worse even than she'd expected, and her and Nisha were dragged along and battered from side to side, smashed by lapping water as they struggled to stay afloat. Swimming became more a matter of staying up and taking a breath than actually attempting to move in any direction, but that was fine by Jala, for that was her plan.

If Halfdan *could* bring himself to believe that they had swum the river, then he would assume they would take the narrowest crossing and stay as far from potential viewers as possible. To do so they should now be swimming against the current. Instead they had surrendered themselves to it, choking, coughing, floundering, battered and oft-submerged, carried relentlessly downstream. Only as the lights of the large village became visible through the endless struggle did they try to propel themselves, moving across the central flow of the river with painstaking effort, such that if the current carried them to the edge it would be at the far side, and not the jetties of Raetis.

And so, half drowned and in desperation, the two women were borne by the spirits of the great rivers into the confluence, where they found themselves dragged into the depths half a dozen times, needing every ounce of their strength to pull themselves back up into the air for a breath. And somehow, after a few minutes in the water that felt like a century, they were past the meeting of two rivers and being carried by one of the empire's greatest watercourses down to the east. Nisha tried to make it to the shore, but Jala stopped her and they foundered and panicked on along the river until the lights of Raetis were little more than the twinkle of fallen stars in the distance.

When they finally washed up on the southern bank of the great river, neither of them had enough strength even to crawl out of the water. Both lay there, submerged still from the hips down, flat on their backs, gasping for air.

The sun had already climbed some way into the arc of the sky by the time they awoke, still half in the water, the gentle clonk of bells announcing the presence of a herd of goats that wandered the low slope munching on what little vegetation they could find.

The women had survived. And, given that they had spent the first few hours of the day unconscious in the wide open and had not been caught, it seemed that Jala's gambit had paid off and the pair had bypassed the ghost and his men. They would be impossible to track along the river itself, and the enemy would be highly unlikely to think of looking right under their noses for signs of passage. Jala and Nisha had bobbed past their hunters by probably not more than a hundred paces, completely unseen.

The ghost would *eventually* locate their track. Within the day he would have found where they reached the river, she was certain, and then it would be a matter of spreading out and searching up to five miles of the far bank. It would be a miracle if they had left no sign for the man to follow, but it would take a long time for him to get back on the trail, and that bought them much needed leeway.

Despite only having slept for perhaps four hours in the water, the night had felt like the most blessed and reinvigorating slumber they had ever had, and their new reserve of energy as they rose had been surprising and welcome.

Once more Jala had begun her tactic of zigging and zagging, using the most helpful terrain. They stayed away from the river, running roughly parallel with it but up in the hills, in order to avoid any chance of bumping into Halfdan's scouts. And now, as they clambered up that hill on their third day from the tower, the two women were beginning to feel a glimmer of hope deep within. They had managed to scavenge food each day – mostly fruit – and had achieved at least four hours a night sleep each, taking turns on watch. Nisha's gravel-bitten hand was nearly healed, pink skin growing in the ravaged surface.

Another day of freedom.

Jala glanced at Nisha by her side, and the maid had a most unusual smile on her face. She'd hardly had cause to smile since their capture, but now she looked something of her old self, even taking the eye into account.

The hill was the shape of an upturned boat and rose slightly higher than those surrounding it, which would afford them a good view of the terrain to come. It also bore no structures, which made it safer. Atop were just a collection of rock stacks carved by ages of howling wind. Even now, despite the good weather and the warm season, the wind cut down the valley and hit the boat-hill, passing by in both directions and whistling over the top. The two women climbed the last few paces of the slope and rounded one of the huge weathered stacks, peering off into the east.

Jala drew a stunned breath and beside her Nisha's smile blossomed.

The hills stretched out the same as the ones they had passed now for days, built of stratified layers and cut through by dusty brown valleys. The great river still wavered and coiled east some way over to their left. A town lay maybe five or six miles away. But none of these were what drew their breath from them.

Far off – at least two days' walk yet if not three, but perfectly visible nonetheless – they could see the shimmering surface of the Nymphaean Sea glittering in the fading light. The lands around the sea belonged to the western provinces, but regardless, the ports and settlements on that coast would hold close to the emperor and to Velutio, and Halfdan and his master would hold little sway in the coastal lands. Plus, Pelasians would be more common there. Jala felt sure that once they reached the sea, they would be safe. From there, the return to Velutio and her husband would be a certainty.

Not to Quintillian, though…

She shook her head and pushed away that thought angrily. Her duty was to her husband, and she could not wait to see him once more.

'A view fit for kings, eh?' said a voice behind them.

Jala, startled, turned, half expecting Halfdan and his men to be standing behind them, though there seemed little chance of that. Instead, an old man leaned against the rock stack, idly gnawing on a chicken leg. The empress realized her hand had gone automatically to the dagger at her side, their only real weapon with the sword now at the bottom of the river.

The old man wore a tunic and long trousers in the style of northern barbarians, but his hair was shorn and he was beardless in the imperial manner. He did, however, have a strange tattoo on one side of his face that seemed to be made up of black whorls and patterns, and silver rings in his ears.

'They say this hill is where the great hero Aeduus, half-divine son of the archer god, is buried. He was a giant, you see.'

'Who are you?' Jala asked, trying not to sound nervous and suspicious. On closer examination, the patterns of his facial tattoo were made up of numerous stylized creatures and men.

'I am Api. And this is my hill. Well, it's *Aeduus's* hill if it's anyone's really. In truth the land doesn't belong to people – people belong to the land. Even the emperor only rents his tenure until the gods take him back, but the land will remain. We are nature's pets, if you like.' He smiled, and his teeth made an odd mosaic pattern of missing black spaces and square off-whites.

Despite herself, Jala found a smile rising to her face. She could imagine the expressions of the men and women of the court if she espoused those sentiments in Velutio. It was a position hard to deny, though.

'Api. Well met. I am Alaleh, and this is Fila.'

'If you say so.' The old man grinned with a worryingly knowing look.

'We were taken by slavers but managed to free ourselves. Now we are trying to make it back to the sea.' It was close enough to the truth, after all.

'I see,' Api nodded. 'Chicken?'

'What?'

'I have chicken. There's enough to share.'

Jala frowned, casting a sidelong concerned glance at Nisha, but the maid's face removed any possibility of refusal. Nisha was almost drooling.

'That would be wonderful, Api. Thank you. Though I do not wish to see you run short.'

'There is plenty. I felt sure I would have guests.'

The two women shared a glance as the old man turned and ambled past the rock. Jala and Nisha followed to find between this stack and the next a dip in the ground had allowed a cave to form. Bad memories of the forest and the boar leapt to mind, but overcoming it they followed the old man inside.

The cave was clearly his home. The interior had been decorated with multi-hued paint as though it were the dining room of a wealthy villa. A small square of bricks and mortar off to one side formed a pool, and looking up they could see a water spout jutting out of the wall top, which would bring rainwater in from above on wetter days than this. The pool was perhaps half full. To the far side of the cave, which was surprisingly spacious, a fire burned in a small hearth that had been constructed by a man familiar with the builder's craft. Meat roasted over the flames and the scent filled the space, bringing forth an endless chorus of rumbles from the stomachs of the two women. A low table sat in the middle, surrounded by cushions and rugs. It was oddly homely. As they moved into the centre, the old man lit three extra oil lamps in specially-carved niches on the walls and then returned to the entrance, heaving across a heavy brown drape that sealed them off from the outside, just a narrow gap at the top remaining to allow the gathering smoke from the fires to exit.

Jala tried not to feel trepidation at the sudden loss of the world beyond, but she was more concerned to see that three plates sat on the table, along with three cups and two jugs. She filed that away to perhaps enquire about later as Api returned, removing more chicken from the fire and pushing it out onto the plates, dividing it evenly three ways. He then added beans and some sort of tuber that had been cut up and fried in a skillet. Jala waited politely, and Api laughed.

'Sit. Eat. Only a poor host watches women starve to death at his table.'

The empress sat quietly, making a point of removing her dagger and the iron piton and placing them to one side out of reach. Api seemed to be harmless, and she didn't wish to offend him with weapons at her fingertips.

'Before you find some subtle, dissembling way of asking,' the old man said with a grin, 'yes, you may stay the night here. I would give you my oath no harm would come to you, but in these days when man rules and the gods are all-but lost to us, a man's word might as well be written on the water for all the weight it carries. But for what it's worth, I promise you a safe night on the names of Aeduus and his father, Aphollion. The old gods are still close for some of us.'

Curious, Jala thought that it took a strange hermit in a cave to espouse the values of the pious when it was now the norm in the forward-looking empire to only invoke the gods as a curse or when danger loomed. Pelasians, in her opinion, were considerably better at observing appropriate ritual and maintaining a true belief. Somehow, despite knowing nothing of Api, she felt sure they were safe.

Nisha, beside her, had not stood on ceremony, and at the old man's words had sunk to a cushion and immediately begun to dismember a chicken with her teeth. Api glanced at her and smiled, gently sliding a knife and a two-pronged fork across to her.

'Wine?'

Jala frowned, then nodded and smiled. Api poured for the three of them, watering it three parts to one, and when the empress took an experimental sip, she was most surprised and delighted to taste the rich, thick tones of a fine Germallan.

'Where, if you don't mind me asking, do you come by all your treasures, Api? You have well-built facilities, expensive cushions and rugs, a fine wine, and cutlery that would be at home in a nobleman's villa.'

The old man smiled.

'I perform the odd service for those with questions and needs, and people can be very generous when they are grateful.'

'Are you a seer?' Nisha asked quietly. 'An oracle?'

Api laughed. 'Who knows? I suspect *some* call me that. I just have the knack of looking past the surface at the heart of the matter and working out how to fix seemingly insoluble problems. There's nothing magical about it, though I like to think that the archer god is responsible for my speed of mind.'

Jala tried not to think about the fact that the old man had been prepared for two guests, and ate the chicken. One mouthful delicately taken led to a sudden ravaging of the succulent meat. She simply could not help herself, and wondered, as she ploughed swiftly through the meal, how undernourished they had become on their journey.

'I have coins, Api,' she said finally, looking down guiltily at her emptied plate.

'This is not a hostelry. I do not charge,' he laughed.

'But I do not wish to put you out.'

The old man leaned forward, gazing deep into her eyes and the empress almost flinched at the depth of wisdom in that look, which seemed to be picking through her mind, heart and soul like a library to find the scroll he wanted.

'You honour your gods as I do mine. I find that a satisfactory arrangement. Perhaps one day I will come to your home by chance and you will feed me a meal and find me a place to sleep.' Jala couldn't help but let out a sharp laugh at that, trying to imagine Api's face if he was confronted with the great octagonal dining hall of the palace with its gilded columns and marble statuary.

'I am not uncultured.' Api chuckled, and Jala started, her eyes tearing from his at the sudden fear that he was reading the words from her mind as though from a book.

'I have read many things in many languages.' He smiled. 'I have fought battles and sailed oceans. I have seen monsters and gods. I have shared the company of three emperors in my time.'

The empress shuffled back slightly, her brow folding suspiciously.

'Listen to me, child,' the old man said, leaning over the table. She flinched as he took her small hand in his and cupped it gently. 'You have suffered much, I can see, and even when your predicament is but a sour memory, you will still suffer inside. Even for me, yours is an insoluble problem. What is it that you want, child?'

Jala swallowed nervously. 'To return to my home.'

'Tripe. That is a transitory wish. What is it that you *truly* want? You have but two choices, I fear. A life of unbounded love and passion, tainted with regret and guilt, or a life with a clear mind and conscience, but a heart bound in chains. It is not a comfortable choice, I know, but sadly it is the one before you.'

Jala closed her eyes, her heart thumping inside. This man was unsettling in the extreme, and for all she felt that he posed no threat, still she could say nothing in reply.

'I understand.' Api smiled. 'But soon – all *too* soon, I fear, you will stand at a fork in the path, and you will be forced to look one way or the other. That look will seal your fate and decide your future. Be aware of this, for when you reach that fork in the road, you must be prepared for the consequences of your decision.'

Still, Jala could find nothing to say in reply, and the old man snorted. 'Do you like music?'

A moment later he retrieved a set of rural pipes from somewhere and began to play a strange, discordant, haunting melody.

The old man changed then, seemingly retreating into himself, and spent his time clearing up or playing soft, sad music. Jala and Nisha shared many a glance as they finished their wine, but not a word passed between them. An hour later, they were lying amid furs and blankets in a rear, shadowed corner of the cave, and Api retreated to his own blankets, where he played his pipes for a few moments more and then fell asleep fast, his snoring gentle and rhythmic. Nisha was soon to follow, her breathing light and even. Jala somehow knew no harm would befall them in the night. She could feel something about this place, as though the archer god himself were present, keeping a close watch on his son's grave. She knew they could sleep safe and sound through the night. Yet sleep would not come. For all her tiredness, the insightful words of the old man had woken in her something she had put to sleep weeks ago. The troubles of her heart had been swept aside to make room for her current peril. And yet now they were back, and seemed greater than ever.

Quintillian and Kiva.

CHAPTER XXI

Of Persistent Ghosts

Jala paused at the low saddle with Nisha, the two of them drinking in the vista ahead. The sea was so tantalizingly close they could almost smell the brine and hear the gulls. If all went well, they would be at the coast by nightfall. They could see a small settlement – a fishing town presumably – almost directly ahead, and that was now their goal. And between them and it, a long descent past a spur of land with a village perched upon it.

She turned, the strange night with the hermit in the cave still fresh and uncomfortable in her memory, his words riveted to her thoughts, immovable and ever-present. His cave should be visible – well, the hill within which his cave sat, anyway. Sure enough, as she squinted into the morning sun, she could just make out those rock stacks as a distant serration atop the high hill almost directly west. Was Api sitting in the entrance of his cave watching the landscape and wondering where the two women were? She had the uneasy feeling that he would know *exactly* where they were and what they were doing.

'We're almost there,' Nisha said. Jala smiled gently to herself. She had noted that every day saw the barrier in status between the pair of them degrade further. The maid had stopped calling Jala 'majesty' long ago, and 'mistress' had now all-but become a thing of the past. Now she spoke directly to her as one woman to another and nothing more. Adversity tightens bonds.

'We are. Do you think Api is watching us back there?'

Nisha turned, squinting into the bright light.

'I don't know. He was a strange one.'

'That he was.'

Jala turned. Nisha was scrutinizing her as she had done several times since the evening in the cave, as if she might be able to see into the empress's heart and unpick the puzzle that lay within. She sighed and turned back to look up at the cave.

A glint of sunlight flashing on something caught her eye and her gaze wandered from that high place, down to the hills between. For a while there was nothing to see, but then the sun caught a reflective surface again and glistened, leaving a greeny-yellow pinprick on her sight wherever she then looked. She frowned as she peered into the distance.

Horsemen!

On the hilltop less than a mile back, a small mounted party was cresting the rise, the plates of armour on some of them catching the sun's rays and betraying their presence in the endless landscape of arid brown.

'Is that Halfdan?' Nisha breathed, clearly having seen the same thing.

'It has to be,' Jala muttered. 'It would be too much of a coincidence for there to be two parties of riders like that out in these lands. Either way, we cannot stay to find out.'

'Oh, gods,' cursed the maid, and Jala felt her pulse begin to race as the riders suddenly burst into speed, the increase in their pace clear from the sudden clouds of dust the horses' hooves threw up. There was no doubt now, not only that they were Halfdan's riders, but also that they had somehow spotted the two women standing on the pass's high point between two hills.

'Sweet lady Astara,' Nisha hissed. 'What do we do?'

'We can't outrun them,' the empress replied, wracking her brain for options. 'They're too fast. They'll be on us in a flash. Until we get to the water we'll never be able to outpace them, so we need to lose them. We have to hide. There,' she added, pointing at the village on the spur.

'I thought we were avoiding built-up places?'

Jala nodded. Anywhere here might still pay service to Lord Aldegund, but perhaps not. This close to the coast, far south and east of the rebel lord's own homeland, perhaps these people would be loyal. But whatever the case, all other options seemed to be open hillside or craggy cliffs, and Jala couldn't see them evading the enemy for long there. The village was the only real choice, even though the enemy would also realize that.

'Unless you can pass for a rock or a carob tree, I think we're stuck with the village. Come on.'

The two women ran to their right, in the shadow of the nearest peak, beyond which the village lurked in the shade on its vertiginous spur. As they followed the curving contour of the hill away from the saddle, they passed into the shadow and out of sight of their pursuers. Jala was running so hard her breathing became little more than gasps, and she almost crashed painfully into the dirt when suddenly Nisha's better hand landed on her shoulder, arresting her speed. The empress jerked backward and came to a halt, confused and desperate.

'What are you doing? Come on!'

Nisha was standing, pointing at something. Jala followed her finger and picked out an old wooden sign that had half-fallen, the post upon which it stood broken and leaning heavily. The sign showed a skull drawn hastily in dark paint with a cross over it in white.

'This is a place of the dead,' the maid said, her voice little more than a terrified rasp.

'That is a plague sign, Nisha. Nothing to be afraid of.'

'*Plague*?' said the maid, her voice ratcheting up an octave. 'Nothing to be *afraid of*?'

Jala gestured urgently at the sign. 'Look at it. This sign has been here for decades. The last plague outbreak in the empire was under Kiva's father when he was still a young man.' She turned and peered at the village. Her suspicions were immediately confirmed. 'Look, Nisha. The village is deserted. There's no smoke, no sound, no movement. There aren't even any animals. No local farming. This place has been dead since probably before we were born. Any contractible plague has long since gone.'

The maid still looked unconvinced, but Jala grabbed her by the upper arm and all-but shoved her forward. '*Come on!* Better the ghosts of the infected than Halfdan and his knife.'

This rather stark appraisal of their situation seemed to galvanize the maid into action and moments later they were running again, making for a narrow road between two houses on the edge of the village. Sure enough, each house had a yard fenced in, but the slats of the fencing had rotted and fallen apart with disuse and the houses stood empty and broken. On a normal day, the very sight of the place would chill Jala to the bone, let alone the horrible soulriving feeling of standing in a place where all life had ended in the most unpleasant way possible. She forced herself to imagine survivors fleeing to the lowlands with their children and animals, so that at least the young survived. That would not have been the case, though. Those signs told the tale of a fate sealed. At the height of the plague, soldiers were deployed to quarantine the worst places, to keep the infection from being spread to larger population centres. This village would have died trapped and cut off from the world. And if the stories were to be believed, parents drove blades into their children's hearts to save them the agony of succumbing to the disease before dispatching themselves the same way.

The ghost was pursuing them into a town full of the same. Despite the almost non-existent risk of infection so long after the village's death, Nisha tore off the hem of her already shortened and ravaged tunic, using her less wounded hand with some difficulty, and wrapped it around her face, covering her nose and mouth. Jala was about to chide her for it, but instead followed suit. There was no reason to take chances, after all.

The streets of the village were narrow, wide enough for humans or pack animals, but not for carts and wagons, and as they passed a few side streets it became clear that the houses were now beginning to collapse in on themselves, as many of the narrow ways were filled with rubble and debris from the buildings facing onto them.

The street they were on doglegged, and then became a T-junction. Looking this way and that, Jala ignored the clear path to the left and turned right, clambering over a fallen wall. It would be harder for horses to follow them over such terrain. Rounding two more corners, they found themselves suddenly face to face with a building that had survived the ravages of time in better condition. A temple to the god of animals – likely an important deity to please in these lands. Constructed of perfectly squared grey stones imported from elsewhere, rather than the weathered sandstone, bricks or timber of the rest of the village, the temple would likely stand long after all the other buildings had collapsed. A tower rose proud at one corner, next to the domed roof, both intact, and a bell was still visible in the top.

'Come on.'

'Why?' the maid said.

'Because we can see far from up there, and I want to know what the ghost is doing. I don't relish the thought of bumbling around the village and bumping into Halfdan at a corner.'

Nisha looked less concerned, probably preferring to pass through the village and out the other side as fast as possible. Jala, on the other hand, knew they had to evade the enemy, rather than outpace them, and needed to learn all that she could. Turning the corner, she found the grand arch that formed the entrance to the temple. Within, a single gallery with high, empty windows displayed mosaics and paintings of gods, heroes and emperors. The value and quality of this place far outstripped the meagre settlement that surrounded it.

The naos of the temple with its beautiful decoration and a marble floor almost lost to dust and debris stood solemn, but Jala could see – damn it but she couldn't *help* but see – the roughly-carved altar standing incongruously in the centre of the floor. It was one of those made by the masons of the army, rough and practical rather than careful and artistic. It had been placed here at the end, and though the empress couldn't read the text as the pair passed and made for the stairs to the tower, she shuddered. It would be an altar to the memory of the hundreds of dead that the soldiers had had to bury in communal pits, or burn, or both.

At the stairs, Jala began to pound up the steps at speed, despite the breathlessness that caused. Nisha was at her heels and both women were grateful that the omnipresent debris of the deserted village did not afflict this temple. The stairs were clear and well-shaped. Moments later they emerged into the room with the small bell and its now shabby, threadbare cord. Immediately Jala dropped to the parapet, pulling Nisha down with her. The view from the tower was unobstructed in every direction, and she could see the horsemen at the edge of the village, near the road where they had entered. Nisha opened her mouth to whisper something, but Jala motioned her to silence. She could just hear voices. Frustratingly, she could almost make out the words, but not quite. She realized that her own pounding blood was overriding sound as much as anything, and she took a moment to force herself to calm, eyes closed and willing her pulse to slow. As her blood returned to normal and she felt a strange sense of relaxation despite all that was happening to them, she leaned on the parapet and listened, her gaze locked on the enemy.

It *was* Halfdan. His shockingly white hair and pale face stood out in the brown. Fourteen horses and their riders – each of the ghost's men, barring the one that lay in that tower with a hole through his brain. Halfdan was arguing with his soldiers, gesticulating angrily. Good. Anything that made the ghost angry was fine by Jala. She concentrated and caught a few words of the exchange, a satisfied smile creeping across her face. Many of Halfdan's men were refusing to enter the plague village. Good. Their loyalty went only so far, clearly.

The ghost seemed to reach some furious decision and gestured again wildly with his arms. Four of his men began to walk their horses, skirting the village to the south, passing beneath the peak and circling around the dead settlement, and another four followed suit to the north, along the main route through the pass. Sure enough, confirming what Jala had assumed, once those riders on each side passed one quarter of the way around, a single man reined in his horse and sat, watching the buildings. The other three rode on. They were setting up a perimeter. Although the village stood on a spur, they could still surround it. In a few moments there would be no way to leave the place without being seen by one of the pickets. And, sure as death to a plague village, Halfdan and his other five men began to ride into the streets, where they were quickly lost from sight.

Things were now becoming desperate. Jala knew they had been more than just lucky with that man in the woods who'd been gored by the beast, and again with the man in the tower. She was under no illusion about their chances against six strong, armed men who were expecting them. Halfdan was clever. He would want to search the place thoroughly, but he wouldn't risk his men being alone. There was a record of them dying when that happened. He would split his search party into two groups of three or, more likely, three of two, so they could cover the village better. And even two men would be too much for the tired, barely-armed women. And this place was untenable. It was too much a focal point for a search, as they had realized after the business with the watchtower. As quickly and quietly as she could, Jala began to descend the stairs, Nisha following on close once more.

Fortune seemed to be turning against them. As she reached the lowest steps, she heard voices outside. Footsteps approached the temple, and Nisha's eyes rolled white and wild. Jala pressed herself back into the shadows of the stairs and watched as two men passed beneath the arch and into the decorative gallery.

'I don't like this place,' one grumbled.

'It's only a temple.'

'The village, you moron. Not the temple.'

The two men crossed into the naos where the rough-carved commemorative altar stood, and for a moment the view from the stairwell was clear. The soldiers would certainly want to climb the tower for a good look, and when they did the two women would be trapped. Taking a deep breath, she beckoned to Nisha and stepped out into the hallway, tiptoeing lightly, her teeth clenched tight. Quickly, she moved to her right, where a small side chapel stood. It was hardly more than a niche, really – a tiny apse with a single window and a statue of some caprine deity. Time to gamble.

Entering the room, she ducked to the left of the archway, where there was almost enough space for a person. Nisha followed suit to the right, the two women pressing themselves back against the stone. If the men decided to be thorough, all would be lost.

A few heart-stopping moments later, the soldiers' voices rose once more as they emerged from the main naos of the temple into the gallery, talking in low voices of the plague. Both men had short blades in hand. No one was taking chances after the man in the tower, clearly. Jala bit her lip and tried not to shake as the searchers came closer. Then, when they were mere feet from the archway, they turned, apparently satisfied with peering in from the hall, and disappeared into the stairwell.

The sound of their echoing footsteps and ongoing conversation would hide small noises from below, and Jala quickly slipped out of the side chapel and padded across the gallery, Nisha behind her again. The two women emerged into the road, and turned sharply to the right, sidling along the temple wall and then turning the corner where the building's main bulk would hide them from the tower. Now that they knew they would be observed from the belfry, they would have to be very selective in their route lest they be seen.

But their route *where*?

Jala chewed on her lip again as she turned into an alley that ran at a sharp angle, which should hide them from the tower. 'Where are we going?' whispered Nisha quietly, and Jala slapped a finger across her lips. They were in the most dreadful danger right now, and even the tiniest sound might give them away. In the pressing silence as the maid looked sheepish and fell quiet, Jala listened. She could hear the muted conversation of the men in the tower as little more than muttered sounds. There were shouts further across the village as another pair searched buildings. And there was the sound of occasional shouts from outside the settlement, but nothing else. No birdsong, or animals…

…apart from a strange low rumble, so quiet you had to concentrate to hear it.

What was it? She frowned and listened hard. It sounded like a cart rattling over an uneven road, but deeper and slower. A rhythmic rumble. And something else – another noise almost hidden beneath that rumble, which itself was barely audible. Whatever it was, it signified a possibility. Dead, empty houses filled with plague ghosts held no chance of refuge from a thorough hunter like Halfdan, and simply fleeing the village would be suicide with the ring of men watching closely. *Anything* different had to be investigated. Not risking speech, Jala gestured for Nisha to follow, and padded on along the alley. At the end she paused again, listening until she picked up that odd, unidentifiable rumble, then turned towards it. Another junction, another pause, and a dreadfully dangerous moment where their latest road would put them in view of the tower for precious heartbeats.

They rounded a corner back into the shadows, and even as Jala caught the sound of a shout from the tower, signifying that they had been seen, she realized what the rumble was, now loud enough to hear even over the other noises.

A mill.

It sounded like a waterwheel turning. And that other noise, submerged beneath the rumble, was running water. A mill race. No matter that the village had been dead for more than a decade, the water in the race was still running, and still turning the wheel. Astara was watching over them, preserving her Pelasian daughters, for the wheel was one of the symbols of the goddess. Jala was suddenly sure that this was the right thing to do – that they had been given a path by the divine.

Beckoning Nisha, throwing caution to the wind and a prayer to the goddess, the empress ran down the alley, following the sound, certain that it would somehow harbour their salvation. By now the rumble of the wheel and the babble of the water was loud enough to hear even over the distant shouting and the pounding of their own feet.

The two women turned a corner and came to a halt.

The watermill was mostly still standing. From this angle, they could see into the second floor, where the internal mechanism had fallen apart. The heavy grindstones had collapsed through the rotting timbers, one tangled precariously in the rotting beams, poised to fall, the other broken in two on the street outside. Yet the spindle that drove those great stones was still turning with the flow of water. From here, Jala could just make out the glittering line marching off up the slope from the village, around the curve of the hill, where it could only emerge from some subterranean channel, given the fact that they'd not seen it before. Once more it smacked heavily of the goddess's intervention. Jala had no idea of the source of the water, but its destination was a certainty: the plain below and, finally, the sea.

'Nisha, do you trust in the goddess?'

The maid's brow furrowed, an unsettling sight above that empty socket, and she shrugged. 'Of course I do.'

'With your life?'

'What do you have in mind?'

The empress smiled. 'Following the path Astara has laid out for us.'

Nisha simply gave a single short nod, and Jala grasped her hands. 'Come on, then.'

The sounds of shouting were increasing in volume as the enemy closed through the narrow ways of the village. Despite the maze-like alleys and their endless intersections and the tight-packed crumbling houses, the village was not over-large, and they had to be close to the far side now, especially given the need for the water to exit down the steep slope of the spur. If the goddess was not being kind, they could be trapped against the encircling watchers. *Faith.* She had to have faith, despite all that had happened. For Pelasians faith was part of life, not some lip service way to blame gods for the failings of nature, or of men. The goddess would provide.

Ignoring the worryingly close shouts of Halfdan's men, the two women scurried across the street and in through a hole in the wall, just large enough to traverse at a crouch. Inside, the grinding and rumbling noises were suddenly intense, and the spindle continued to turn as did the horizontal shaft that drove it, the wooden gear, even with its broken teeth, still functioning well. The slosh and gurgle of the water was audible from the mill race, and without pausing to look at anything else, certain of why they were here, Jala crossed to the large wheel, which turned with surprising speed.

The wheel sat in a purpose-built mill race and what was probably a fairly sedate stream further up in the mountains had clearly been funnelled through a channel in the rock and down into this race, all constructed with the precision of a military engineer, increasing the flow and pressure of the water to best drive the wheel. Thus a small mountain stream here, by the mill, became a fast, deep torrent of water powering through the edge of the village. The channel had been carved in the bedrock of the spur, but had been subsequently lined with smooth stone slabs to ensure best functionality. Jala, aware of the ever nearing shouts of the hunters, looked critically at the channel, her mind filling with horrible memories of that plunge into the river at Raetis and the near-drowning they had both suffered as the current carried them eastward in the dark.

That time had been terrible and this time the water was shallower, narrower and lit by morning light. Yet the dangers would be just as great, if different. Moving to the edge of the torrent, she looked downstream. The water ran under the street then emerged briefly before disappearing once more under a house built curiously on a low bridge. Beyond that she had no idea where it went.

Faith.

It was all about trusting the goddess now.

'Are you ready?' she asked quietly.

'No.'

'Come anyway.'

Without waiting further, the empress lowered herself into the channel, gripping the sides, and then let go. The pull of the water, combined with the slope of the channel sent her immediately barrelling off downstream and she had to do nothing to propel herself, just use her hands and feet to try and keep herself straight and avoid banging her head. Once or twice as she was carried away from the mill and beneath the street, Jala felt her head clonk on the slabs, but never hard enough to damage, and once or twice she was submerged, having to hold her breath and suck in air when the opportunity arose. It was as though the river at Raetis had been a test run for this.

She tried to look behind to make sure Nisha was with her, but there was simply no chance of turning her head in these conditions, and quickly she resigned herself to only seeing what was immediately around her.

The world suddenly exploded into light between the road and the next house, then oppressive black again as she disappeared beneath the bridge house. As she was buffeted and battered, she suddenly saw the gleam of sun on the water below her feet, which, in a matter of two heartbeats, became the end of the tunnel and daylight, and in one of the most heart-stopping moments of her life Jala burst forth into the sun from beneath the house just in time to tip over the edge of the spur and pick up speed where the channel cut vertiginously down the slope. For a brief, panicky moment, voices were almost audible above the water, and she realized she was passing close to one of the mounted pickets. She had no idea whether he'd seen her in the channel and could only hope not as she shot past him, half drowned, at the speed of a diving hawk. She had no time to wonder how far down the slope the engineers had bothered with nice smooth paving, because suddenly there wasn't a slope any more.

With her heart thundering apparently in her throat, the empress shot from the end of the channel into the open air, where she plummeted for what seemed an eternity.

She hit the surface of the water toe-first, grateful that chance had granted her that form and not a belly-flop, which might well have killed her. For a moment the world went silent apart from the thumping of her heart, which, after the deafening torrent in the channel, was exceedingly odd. A strange blooof sound signalled a second form plunging into the water close behind her and she spun, using her hands to turn and holding her breath, to see Nisha, struggling with one working arm, trying to keep herself upright and move back towards the surface. Pride and relief powering her, Jala pushed her way through the water to Nisha and helped her. As the two broke back out into the air and heaved in deep breaths, Nisha laughed, and Jala hurriedly slapped a hand across her mouth, rolling her eyes upward. Somewhere above, Halfdan's men were still there.

Quickly, the two women swam to the edge of the pool. Here, another stream joined the mill race, and together they formed a small river that flowed from the pool beneath an old rickety bridge and off towards the sea in the east. The pair crawled up onto the dirt and Jala looked up. Atop the slope, so far above, no one was looking down. They had slipped past the pickets.

Astara had been kind.

And better still, just beyond the pool, a small wood covered the side of the shallow valley that led down to the sea. Trees sporting their spring foliage would hide them more than adequately from the plague village above as they once more gained some distance on their pursuers.

They were almost safe.

CHAPTER XXII

Of Gulls, Ghosts and Evasion

The two fugitives slipped between the buildings of one of the sleepiest little towns Jala had ever experienced. Built of warm, brown stone and mostly daubed with whitewash, the town was probably four times the size of the village they'd fled that morning and yet boasted no such monument as that great stone temple. The town, which the milepost just outside announced to be Burbida, simmered gently in the heat, the only sounds the wheeling gulls that filled the sky and the occasional bark of an irritated dog.

Jala and Nisha made their way swiftly through the streets down towards the port, and they had reached the central square before they saw another human being. Even then he only added to the sleepy feeling, since his fruit stall sat idle while he lounged back beneath a cypress tree, snoring gently while his dog lay curled beside him, occasionally kicking a leg out as he chased something in his dream.

It was easy to forget the desperation of their plight when faced with such almost unbearable ordinariness, and the two women were starting to relax without any conscious effort to do so. Nisha veered towards the unguarded fruit stall but Jala shook her head and motioned to keep moving. Down the gently sloping street they hurried. The first sign of real activity they experienced was when a door opened onto the street and a woman with a face like an old saddlebag ejected a bucket of excrement into the street. The two fugitives skirted around the mess, which ran down the channel outside the house and wedged against a stepping stone, and strode on.

A few more figures were out and about as they got closer to the water, but even these were generally silent, or at best involved in a little light conversation with one another, and they were still few and far between. Of course, it struck Jala that it was still more than an hour until sunset. The menfolk of the town would be out at sea, fishing in small flotillas, while the womenfolk were busy in their houses and with their families. And in a place like this, only the youngest of children would be free to play. Anyone old enough to help haul a rope would be out on the boats, which might be a problem for two women in urgent need of transport.

The road opened out onto a wide area of dockside, dotted with numerous small jetties that marched out into the glittering water. The overwhelming smell of dead fish made the women gulp and swallow nauseously, and the area of the waterfront was covered with the tat and debris of fishing wharves everywhere. At the centre of the square sat a well house, somewhat incongruous this close to the waterfront, a squat brown building with a low roof, one door and a basin on three of the four sides filled with water. The buildings curved around the dock area in an arc, their fronts given over to rope, sail, and net-makers and the like. At the far end of the long wharf a small team of men were sawing planks while a new fishing boat gradually took shape close to the waterline.

Jala felt her spirits sink at the sight of the empty jetties. While they'd come down the long, shallow valley unmolested as the ghost's men searched the plague village, she could hardly believe that Halfdan was not now in close pursuit. Certainly she didn't strongly rate their chances of passing a night in Burbida without being set upon once more. As soon as the hunters had convinced themselves that their quarry had somehow slipped through their grasp and fled the hilltop village, this fishing town was the natural next port of call.

With a glimmer of hope, Jala spotted a fishing boat at the opposite end of the wharf to the shipbuilders, neatly tied to the furthermost jetty. It was a small affair, and would certainly never make it across the open sea to Velutio, but that had never been Jala's plan. It was a matter of getting out to sea. Once they were gone from here, they could go anywhere and would be almost impossible to follow. Grabbing Nisha, the empress ran over to the boat. An old man with rheumy eyes and sagging skin was busy folding a canvas sheet in the boat and his eyes remained on his task as the two women hurried up to him.

'Would it be possible to hire your boat?' she asked directly.

The old man huffed and shifted his fingers, putting the last fold in the canvas and laying it on the jetty. Finally, his task complete, he looked up into Jala's face. 'Eh?'

'We two are in dire need of transport. We need a boat and I have money to pay handsomely.'

In truth there was not an awful lot in the purse she'd taken from the dead man in the tower. By the standards of the capital it would hardly keep a man for a day or two, but she'd be willing to bet that it would go a lot further somewhere as small and provincial as Burbida. To emphasize, she drew out the purse and shook it with a tinkling of coins.

The man shrugged. 'No.'

Jala straightened. 'I really will pay well.'

'Can't,' said the old man flatly.

'Why not?'

'I need another crewman. My son should be out on the water with me, but he's sick with the flux. Without him I can't sail. And I don't want to leave town with him sick, anyway.'

'Look,' Jala said, trying – and failing – to keep the edge of desperation out of her voice, 'we don't need to go far. Take us two villages along the coast in either direction, and I'll pay you well. We'll take another boat from there.'

'Can't.'

Jala heaved in a breath. This was not what she needed at all.

'Can we not help you?'

'Can you sail a boat?'

For a moment, the empress almost lied, but the lie would be uncovered the moment they untied from the jetty, so she stepped a pace back. 'No. But we're quick studies and we'll do whatever you say.'

'Still no. Too late in the day to sail now. And I'm not leaving my son.'

'Please,' pleaded Jala, and Nisha nodded vigorously next to her.

'The answer's no, woman. Now leave me alone.'

Nisha opened her mouth to upbraid the man, but Jala, sighing, grabbed her and pulled her away. As the two stomped disconsolately from the waterfront, the maid grumbled. 'We should have pressed him. Threatened him. If he only knew who you were.'

'But he doesn't. And we know nothing about boats. If he says he needs another, then who am I to argue? And he might be right about it being too late. Are we really prepared to sail in the dark? No. But we can't stay in Burbida. Maybe we should head along the coast a mile or two and find somewhere to shelter for the night. Then in the morning we can decide whether to come back or move on and find somewhere else.'

'I...' began Nisha and then stopped dead in her tracks. Jala frowned but a moment later she too saw the figure. White-haired and pale-faced, travel-worn and looking much more drawn than Jala remembered, Halfdan stepped out of an alleyway, sword in hand. The empress looked this way and that. Other armed men were emerging from the other streets into the open space by the wharf.

Her desperate eyes caught an alleyway that seemed empty and, grabbing Nisha's wrist, she ran for the dark aperture. Nisha was quick to agree and the pair were side by side as they reached the alley entrance. The enemy hadn't yet moved.

Something hit Jala in the forehead and she staggered to a halt, stumbling in confusion. The darkness was pushed back by afternoon sunlight as she reeled into the open once more. Reaching up, she tested her head, but her hand came away clean. No blood. Still dazed, she had to concentrate to think clearly. Nisha emerged from the alleyway a moment later, one of Halfdan's men holding her tightly by the wrists.

'You have led us a merry dance, Jala,' the ghost said almost amiably.

'You won't get away with it again, Halfdan,' Jala spat. 'There are witnesses here.'

'Oh, Jala, please don't espouse such feeble, trite sentiments. These people are nobodies. If there is the slightest hint of trouble, I will not blink at burning the whole fucking place to the ground and gutting everyone in it. Now stop endangering everyone else and come over here like a good girl.'

Jala was still backing away, but out of the corner of her eye she could see the furthest of Halfdan's men moving out to the waterfront, cutting her off so that she was completely surrounded. Still, no matter what happened, she would never submit to him again. In the best of worlds she would now be bobbing eastward over the sea, carrying tidings of danger and betrayal to her husband, but if that were not possible it was better to be dead than a pawn of this man's.

The guard from the alley shoved Nisha across the space towards Halfdan, who grasped the maid's wrist and smiled. He sheathed his sword and drew a knife. Jala was impressed by Nisha, whose face, rather than exhibiting the utter terror one might expect, showed only defiance and disdain. The tip of the knife came up and traced the scars on the maid's face before he reached the empty eye socket. There he sickeningly bobbed the tip of the knife inside and tapped it on the circle of the socket. Jala wanted to be sick.

'Don't make me hurt your friend again, Jala.'

'Don't worry about me,' Nisha shouted, and the knife suddenly slipped to her throat, pressing gently so that she had to pull back her head to prevent it cutting the flesh.

'Now, now,' Halfdan said pleasantly. 'Let's not have pointless heroics.'

Jala's hand went to the knife at her side, still sheathed. She'd never be able to fight them off. She would, in the last moment, use it to take her own life, but she hated to think of such a fruitless end. If she were to die, it would be worthwhile if she could somehow take Halfdan with her. She needed time to think, but the blow to the head had made that difficult, and she was still staggering uncertainly, no plan forming.

Something bumped into the back of her thighs and she ripped the knife from its sheath and turned to discover that it was the stone basin at the side of the well house. Her heart pounding, she edged along the trough.

'Come now. If you will just accompany me, no one needs to get hurt, Jala. Imagine how sad life will be for your friend here when her other eye goes. And maybe her tongue? I see one of her hands was mangled in your escape. How will she fare when I pulverize the other, I wonder?'

Jala was now pressed back against the wall of the well house, increasingly aware of the impossibility of her situation.

'I will not let you take me alive, Halfdan.'

'Then be aware I shall take your reticence out on your friend. I can keep someone alive for months and make every day a living hell for them. Are you sure you want to condemn this poor girl to that sort of fate just so you can slip a quick knife in your own throat?'

Jala shuddered. She was more than certain that the ghost meant every word. He was not the sort of man to boast or make idle threats. He was a cold, efficient killer. Was it her fate to spend every moment of her adult life torn between duty and desire? Duty to Kiva against desire for Quintillian. Duty to empire against desire to save Nisha from pain. Duty and desire.

But Jala was not only an empress, she was a Princess of the Parishid dynasty of Pelasia. Duty went far beyond simple desire. It was bone deep. It ran with the blood, pounding in the veins and informing every decision of the brain and the heart. It was why she knew deep down that if she ever got back to Velutio, she would have to choose Kiva and let go of Quintillian. It was why she would have to sacrifice Nisha to prevent becoming a political pawn.

Sidling along the wall, she suddenly felt the handle of the well-house door behind her, and gripping it, she swung it open. A moment later she was inside in the dark, pulling the door shut. The door had a latch, but it had not been used in many a year, and the actual bar was seemingly welded in the open position. Even gripping the handle tight, she would not be able to keep it shut for long.

At the centre of the room – its only decor, in fact – stood the well itself, complete with chained bucket. The only light in the dim interior came from four small windows, one in each wall. Each window was perhaps a foot square and covered with an iron grille that made it poor as a source of both illumination and visibility. Still, unable to keep from watching, Jala moved across to the closest window and peered between the iron bars through the dirty, poorly-made glass.

Halfdan still held Nisha, and the maid still looked defiant and angry. The ghost tapped his foot impatiently for a moment and then yanked Nisha's arm upward, displaying her good hand.

'I'm going to count to five. The sooner you open the door, the more fingers you will save your friend. Are you ready, dear princess? Here we go.'

Jala closed her eyes – screwed them tight. She couldn't relent, but she also couldn't watch. A leaden pause descended.

'One.'

There was a faint clunk and a hiss. Jala, confused, expecting a scream, opened her eyes again. Halfdan was holding a knife and a finger in one hand. In the other he still held up Nisha's now four-fingered hand. The maid had not even screamed. The empress felt her heart become even heavier. Her friend was braver and stronger than she had ever imagined.

'Don't open that door,' snarled Nisha, earning her one slanted, quizzical eyebrow from her captor.

'I shall now resume the count, Jala.'

The empress squeezed her eyes shut again. How could she endure this?

There was another hiss and a faint thud. Unable to stop herself, Jala opened her eyes.

Nisha still had four fingers. The empress frowned in confusion and peered through the dirty glass at the scene, trying to work out what was happening.

The ghost let go of the maid and turned, trying to look at his own back. Jala stared at the arrow sticking out of Halfdan somewhere around his kidney. Nisha fell away and scrambled across the ground. The other men were staring at their leader in confusion. Halfdan himself was peering at the arrow in utter perplexity. His brow still furrowed, he straightened once more and opened his mouth to speak. All that came out of it was the barbed tip of an arrow, crimson with blood. In shock, the ghost turned, and Jala stared in wonderment. The arrow had hit the vicious bastard in the back of the head, at the base of the skull and just to one side of the vertebrae, passing through the neck and out of the mouth, and was now transfixed there, lodged at the flights. Even as she stared, another two arrows hit Halfdan, one in the chest and one in the sword arm. Peppered with shafts, the man turned, unable to speak. Blood was starting to pour from him. Still his men stared, mesmerized at this unexpected turn of events. Only when two more of the men suddenly sprouted deadly shafts did the group start to move in a panic, running for the alleys from which they'd emerged. Nisha was clambering along the ground, heading for the well house and, unsure whether there was danger or not, Jala pulled open the door and helped her inside.

Returning to the window, she could see that their now fleeing captors had themselves been caught. The alleyways for which they had been making each disgorged a man in armour bearing the livery of the imperial guard. Never had she been so happy, or more surprised, to see that grey wolf symbol.

The hunters might be efficient killers, but they were also panicked and desperate, and the men who now had them trapped made short work of them, cutting them down mercilessly. One managed to get free and ran for the waterfront, only to suddenly sprout three arrows from his back as he slammed face-first into the dust. In a matter of heartbeats it was over. Halfdan and his men, who had followed them so ruthlessly for so many days were, to a man, worm-food.

In the now certain knowledge that they were safe, though still gripping her knife for security, Jala pulled open the door once more and stepped out into the light. Nisha followed her, nursing her newly-maimed hand with the missing digit.

The empress stared around the square. Guardsmen were busy administering the mercy blow to men who were gasping and bleeding out their last. Those not so occupied bowed low. She was still staring in shock as Titus Tythianus, marshal, commander, nobleman and friend, stepped out of the alley near Halfdan's immobile corpse, still scruffy and hairy despite his uniform, busy slinging a bow back over his shoulder as two more archers followed him.

'Majesty, you have no idea how hard you make it to find you.'

Jala wept with relief, and the marshal, grinning like an idiot, hurried over and hugged her tight, driving out some of the horror and returning a modicum of her warmth and humanity.

'We have to get home, Titus.'

'You're preaching to the priest, Majesty. I've seen Aldegund's army, and they're already on the move.'

PART FOUR

THE CAPITAL

'War is the crucible in which the future is forged.'

Imperial proverb, unattributed

CHAPTER XXIII

Of Solitude and Unexpected Visits

Kiva Caerdin, Emperor and Lord of Velutio, Father of the Nation and Chief Priest, rapped his fingers rhythmically on the arm of his throne – a subtle, understated affair. The great golden throne of the ancient emperors had been melted down by his father due to the inescapable connection it held to the corrupt and insane dynasty that had previously occupied it. The gold had been minted into commemorative coins that had been distributed to the poor in a great show of largesse. Now, Kiva sat on a simple wooden affair. Well-made and with a purple velvet cushion, but simple for all that.

The prefects standing before him were looking up expectantly – due to the throne's position on a dais, they were below him, even though he sat and they stood. Five of the most senior military men in the empire. Men who might one day become marshals and command the armies when the current marshals stepped down or – as more often happened – passed away in office. They looked pensive. Nervous. They had good cause.

'It must be a mistake. The reports are wrong.'

'With respect, Majesty, the reports are quite correct. In the Lion Courtyard one of my captains is recovering from a breakneck race to bring us this news. The wound on his shoulder is mute evidence that the war has begun.'

Kiva's rapping fingers picked up pace. He was, it was said, and he knew it to be true, one of the ablest administrators ever to sit on the throne in this hall, but he was no military tactician. In times of peace he could achieve treaties and deals that advanced the empire. He had instituted so many new laws and amendments to improve the life and economy of his world. And he had managed to maintain good relations with all his neighbours – even the fractious and warlike northern barbarians. But once the empire found itself in a military dispute, as it now did, he was blind. Without his advisors, he was blind.

For a month now he had waited for word of Titus, of Jala, of Quintillian. And instead, all he had heard were worse and worse tidings. The other two marshals had met with grisly ends and, with Quintillian missing and Titus out in the provinces hunting the empress, the army was effectively leaderless. The prefects were doing an admirable job in the absence of their superiors, but it took years of training and a certain slant of mind to make a good marshal. Some of the prefects would be there one day, but as yet they were too rigidly bound by their rank to think outside the lines.

Pelasia.

The empire's ally of centuries had turned on her. Now Kiva and his people were staring at the bleakest of futures: a return to the ancient days of constant war. And Pelasia was no poor enemy, either. If there was a force in the world that stood a chance of bringing the empire to its knees, it was Pelasia. Despite everything that had happened and the military build-up in the south, Kiva had never truly believed it would boil over into war. How could any sensible leader allow that to happen?

Four days ago, the border fortress of M'Dahz, a port town close to the Pelasian border, had fallen to enemy forces. The wounded captain in the courtyard outside had sailed in a courier ship, skipping fast across the waves day and night, to bring the tidings of the first action of the war. It seemed that there had been some kind of naval altercation off the coast. A mistake or misunderstanding had led to a Pelasian ship being sunk. The response had been overwhelming. The satrap of the nearest Pelasian region had flooded the borderlands with men and taken M'Dahz.

'Respectfully, Majesty, our army sits drawn up less than a day west of Calphoris, awaiting the order to march and retake M'Dahz. The fleets are gathered in three positions, one guarding the western reaches of the sea, the others awaiting the command to begin their blockade of the ports. Only the marshals or the emperor have the authority to declare war.'

'I would say that King Ashar has already done that.'

'Not officially, Majesty,' one of the other prefects reminded him. 'We have had no official notice of the opening of hostilities. The current trouble is a regional dispute caused by a misunderstanding. However, we will look weak if we relinquish

M'Dahz to the enemy. We cannot let them simply sit in our fortresses. We must make the first official move in response to this unacceptable situation. If you will give your command, then we will cast the spear of war into the sand before their ambassadors and march on M'Dahz to recover the city.'

'And where does that leave us, Prefect?'

The officer frowned, apparently confused by the question, and Kiva sighed and leaned forward. 'The empire has not been at war for centuries. Not properly. Border scuffles, barbarian incursions and the like aside. Are we really prepared to cast that spear and with it carry the world into a war that could last for decades and ruin the empire? Think about what it means beyond the battles themselves. I have no wish to be remembered as the man who destroyed the empire, when my father was the man who restored it. No, I am not comfortable opening hostilities.'

'Majesty, the eastern satraps of Pelasia have been hungry for our lands for long years and they are angry, violent, and almost autonomous. The god-king keeps them under control largely by letting them rule their own little domains as they see fit, just in his name. Those satraps will see the unanswered taking of M'Dahz as a sign that we are unwilling to stand up for ourselves. If we do not retake M'Dahz, then they will swiftly annex the other coastal towns until they reach Calphoris.'

'You sound very sure of yourself, Prefect?'

The swarthy man huffed. 'I have been based in Calphoris for years, sire. I know the satraps of the borderlands. They *will* move on us further, regardless of orders from their overlord. And when they get to Calphoris, we will then be left with a simple choice: deploy the army and fight, or withdraw from the southern lands entirely and cede them to Ashar.'

Kiva's drumming on the chair arm was becoming frantic.

'Leave me to think.'

'Majesty, this is most urgent.'

'One more day will not mean the fall of Calphoris. Return tomorrow morning and I will have an answer for you. For now this audience is over.'

The prefects shared a look and bowed, turning and making for the large bronze doors at the rear of the room. The two men of the imperial guard that stood to either side pulled the doors open to reveal a small group of men outside. More of the guard with a man in dusty, travel-worn clothes. They shuffled aside to allow the prefects to leave, and then one of the guard hurried into the room, approaching the throne and bowing. The departing officers paused to look at the dusty man, but apparently his clothes or insignia made him uninteresting to them, and they left, muttering to each other about the coming war.

Kiva pinched the bridge of his nose. He could feel a headache of epic proportions coming on.

The guard before him cleared his throat. 'A courier from the Argaela Fort, Majesty. He has no letters of authorization and he is not expected, but he claims to be bearing important news for your ears only. Standing orders in times of war, Majesty, are that no one gets into your presence without appropriate authorization, and normally we'd have ejected him immediately, but he claims to have news of your brother the marshal, sire.'

Kiva's drumming fingers stopped dead and he sat straight suddenly.

'Quintillian?'

'Yes, Majesty. We've searched the man and he is unarmed, but you hear stories of Pelasian assassins, sire, and I am loath to admit a potential threat.'

Kiva pursed his lips as he chewed on the bottom one, thinking hard. 'What would King Ashar have to gain from my death?'

'Majesty?'

'I mean we are already in the worst position we can be militarily, without any of the senior commanders. My death would just make war sure, and despite the actions of certain border satraps I know Ashar well enough to know that if he can avoid outright war, he will. Killing me would seal it. No, I don't believe the Pelasians will send assassins.'

The guard looked less than convinced, though he respectfully held his tongue. After all, word was that Marshal Sciras had met an assassin's blade, and Marshal Partho had drowned in his bath mysteriously. And an axeman had tried to kill Titus in this very palace. Maybe it was not the Pelasians, but *somebody* was removing the imperial high command.

Kiva's father, Darius, had been a great proponent of standing up for oneself. He had not become master of an empire, he used to say, by hiding behind people.

'Show him in.'

The guard threw him a look of utter disapproval, but bowed and backed away to the doors. There he held a brief discussion with his peers and finally four guardsmen escorted the courier into the hall, one at each side and two to the rear, each with spears out and levelled, such that the slightest unexpected move from the visitor would result in skewering.

Kiva watched the dusty courier approach. The man was thin and drawn with a haunted look about his face. He had a pronounced limp on the left foot but held his head high. Kiva tried to recall what he knew of the Argaela Fort. It was on the great east road, still in the central provinces, but only just. It stood beside the Tyras River and watched over the crossing, which delineated between the central and eastern provinces. It had never had a strong garrison, since it was well within imperial territory and was only really occupied for policing and taxation duties. And now that the bulk of the army was concentrated in the south on the Pelasian border, there would be little more than a skeleton garrison there. The east? What might Quintillian have been doing in the east?

The man stopped where the guards indicated, a good spear length from the emperor, and he bowed.

'They say you have news of my brother,' Kiva said quietly.

The courier trembled for a moment. 'I have a great deal of news, and most of it bad.'

Kiva frowned at the tone in the man's voice. The guards were staring with angry astonishment at a courier who might address the emperor so casually without even an honorific.

Something was niggling at Kiva's mind, nagging at the back of his scalp like a tic. 'Who are you?'

'Have I changed that much?' the courier asked, a sly smile suddenly splitting his dusty face.

The emperor's brow folded a little more, and then his eyes widened. 'By all the gods, no!'

'Yes.'

'How?'

The guardsmen were staring at the emperor and the courier both, in confusion.

Kiva spluttered out a disbelieving laugh and fell back into his chair, gesturing to the guard officer.

'Do you not recognize the marshal? No, that's unfair. Neither did I, and he's my brother.' The guard's eyes widened too as he realized and stepped a pace back.

'Quintillian! You have no idea how pleased I am to see you. People said you were dead, but I've never believed it. Where have you *been*?'

'It is,' sighed the marshal, 'a *very* long story. But unfortunately I am the courier of bad tidings. You've a war on your hands, brother.'

'I am well aware of that. Even now one of Ashar's satraps has taken M'Dahz and threatens Calphoris.'

Quintillian was shaking his head. 'It's worse than that. Whatever's happened there, it's just a diversion to split our forces. The horse clans of the east are coming, Kiva, in their tens of thousands. They've united under a lord who calls himself the Khan. Some kind of easterner from the Jade Emperor's lands. And he has his sight set upon your empire.'

Kiva exhaled heavily, shaking his head. 'You're certain of this?'

'I escaped from their army. They're coming. They're disorganized and fractious, but what they lack in discipline they make up for in both numbers and in bloodlust. And the Khan claims to have agents in the empire already paving the way. They're presumably responsible for your trouble with Pelasia. How are the forces disposed, Kiva? Where are the other marshals?'

The emperor sagged. 'So much has happened, Quint.'

'Tell me quickly, Kiva.'

'Partho and Sciras are dead. I haven't had the chance to promote anyone to the role, as I needed either you or Titus to advise on who could do it.'

Quintillian tapped his lip. 'What of Titus, then? Where is he?'

'Quint, Jala disappeared. We thought she'd gone back to Pelasia, but she was taken by some western imperial ship not far from Velutio. Titus is somewhere in the west, tracking her to bring her home. I've been alone, Quint.'

Quintillian began to pace back and forth, and the guards backed away to give him space.

'So where are the four armies now?'

'About two thirds of the military are in the south, facing Ashar's forces. We kept a few cohorts back here and on the northern and eastern borders, and much of the western army is still there and in the north, making sure the barbarians don't take advantage. We need to pull the border guards back from the east, if what you say is true.'

Quintillian shook his head. 'They will already be gone. The Khan and his men are days behind me. A week at most. They will already be in imperial lands, and any men on the border are gone. There isn't much time. You need to send word to the western army and to our barbarian allies in the north. Bring them here. And have the bulk of the army withdraw from Pelasian borders. Leave just enough cohorts to make the satraps think twice, and bring the rest home. We need them here, or the heart of the empire will fall even while we try and save the borders.'

Kiva shook his head in despair. 'There's not time, Quint. It'll take too long.'

'We've no choice. We just have to hope we can pull enough men back to the central provinces to hold against the Khan and his men.'

Kiva rose from his seat and stepped down the dais to the mosaicked floor, striding over to his brother. Ignoring the dust and muck, he threw his arms around Quintillian.

'It is good to have you back. So good. Now tell me what happened to you!'

'In good time,' Quintillian sighed. 'Have the couriers sent straightaway, and can you have someone rustle up some food and wine. I've eaten pretty badly for many weeks and I've not tasted wine since I left. I'll go and bathe quickly, and find some clothes. Then I'll fill you in on life out east, and you can catch me up on what's been happening here.'

Kiva smiled. Despite the fact that the empire was seemingly now facing two-fold danger, somehow it seemed easier with Quintillian returned.

CHAPTER XXIV

Of the Growing Threat

Quintillian tapped his chin thoughtfully, took a sip of wine and leaned over the map once more, sweeping up a wooden horse with an XI marked on the top, shuffling it across the surface and dropping it next to four similar pieces, each bearing a numerical legend.

'We can take the Fourth cavalry from Emona. They're doing little more there than idling in the background as distant support to the Calphoris force. If Ashar's forces crushed the army in the south and rolled across Calphoris, they'd be of little use then anyway. And being light auxiliary skirmish cavalry, they could be on the Tyras River and in the way of the Khan maybe two days after they receive the orders.'

Kiva huffed as he peered at the force gathered on the map at the river that formed the border between the central and eastern provinces. 'That's not fast enough, Quint. The scouts say the clans passed through Lappa yesterday. They'll be at the river before the Fourth could possibly reach them.'

'But they could be held there long enough for the Fourth cavalry to reach them and add their weight to the defence. This is about slowing the enemy until we're prepared, Kiva. Any unit we send to the Tyras are running to their deaths. We all know that, even the men doing the running. But it's going to be days and days before we can gather enough men near Velutio to even think of facing the Khan. And don't forget, the enemy are not moving with the pace of light horsemen. They're moving at the speed of siege engines, which is little more than a crawl. They could be in Velutio in around a week if they really push it, but certainly no sooner than that. And every day we can stop them crossing the Tyras with their machines buys us more time to assemble a proper army.'

Kiva sat back in his chair. He looked tired and drawn. 'I still find it hard to believe that Ashar will really go to war with us.'

'Don't underestimate the importance of Jala, brother.'

'He must understand I've not done anything to her. We've known each other all our lives.'

Quintillian sighed. 'Ashar has the same problem as the Khan. His empire is built up of satrapies, each of which has its own lord. They pay obeisance to Ashar through tradition that he is descended from the line of the sun god and nothing more. Some of the satraps are militarily more powerful than the god-king himself. But the Parishid dynasty have always been masters of the game. They play each satrap off against the others and manoeuvre so that they maintain ultimate power. But no matter what Ashar thinks personally, the fact is that Jala was taken by an imperial warship and disappeared, and if he doesn't challenge the empire over it, he will appear weak. Some of the satraps might start to think they could do a better job, and I don't need to remind you how bad things could get if we had a non-Parishid on the throne of Pelasia?'

Kiva shook his head. Some of the satraps were violently anti-imperial, an enmity that remained from centuries of warfare between the two nations. He eyed the rather sparse wooden figures scattered around the southern end of the map. They were considerably fewer than the Pelasian models.

'But do you really believe the troops we've left in the south will be able to hold Ashar?'

'It's a matter of playing for time in every respect, Kiva. Pelasia threatens the south, but as yet things are still simmering. The Khan threatens Velutio itself. He is coming here for this city and your throne, brother, and there is no question about *those* hostilities. We have to do what we can to build the army here. The men we send to the river we're sacrificing to slow the clans. And we just have to pray to the maiden of luck that things continue to simmer in the south and that the meagre forces we have there can hold the stalemate until we've dealt with the Khan.' He sighed again and threw a lopsided grin at his brother. 'One disaster at a time, Kiva.'

'If only the Gota would answer the call,' the emperor muttered unhappily. The great northeastern barbarian tribe would have added precious numbers to the imperial forces, but the riders sent to the Gota had not returned yet, and they were not truly expected to. The Gota king might have deigned to join them at the celebration earlier in the year, but that was still an early, tentative meeting of age-old enemies. Even telling them that the empire sought their aid was a gamble. They may well see an opportunity instead to take advantage of the empire's temporary weakness.

'No use counting eggs not yet laid. We just have to hope and pray that we'll have enough men, and enough time to gather them. I'm counting on the fact that they have the siege engines, but precious little experience in siege warfare. They're horsemen – skirmishers. If an *imperial* force were coming, they'd be able to crush us pretty quickly, but for all the Khan's abilities and swiftness of thought, even *he* cannot change a people's nature overnight. The clans will be slow and disorganized and that is where we gain the advantage. Our men are prepared for sieges and we know what to do. There's enough food stored in Velutio to feed the populace for half a decade, and these walls have never been breached.'

Kiva smiled nervously. His brother sounded so confident, and certainly his words made sense. And yet Kiva had caught Quintillian's expression when he thought no one was looking, and the prince was worried – that much was clear.

At the very least, it was good to have a tactician back in the capital. The absence of all the marshals had been a blow, but within a day of Quintillian's return couriers had been racing from Velutio to every corner of the world with orders and missions – summonses to war, transport and travel orders, new dispositions, even auxiliary levies. Enough money to buy a small kingdom had left the city in chests to facilitate the emergency raising and equipping of new auxiliary units. They'd be untrained – little more than peasants in smocks with spears and shields – but every body might make the difference in the coming conflict.

It was possible. Kiva could see that. Even though the numbers were against them, as long as the Pelasians didn't yet open hostilities in the south, they might just be able to pull together enough men to beat back the Khan. It *was* possible.

There was a knock at the door and the brothers looked up from the map. From the corner of the room, a servant appeared with a bucket of charcoal, which he carefully shovelled into the brazier that was beginning to fade.

'Come.'

Two of the imperial guard opened the door and admitted another of their number, who was clad in uniform but had left his weapon outside as per custom. The man crossed the room, his heavy soldier's boots clumping across the marble, and came to a halt in front of the two men, bowing.

'Majesty, lookouts have sighted a ship approaching the city bearing the ensign of the Marshal Titus Tythianus.'

Kiva's eyes shot from the messenger to his brother, who met his gaze.

'Titus!'

'By the gods, that's timing I can approve of,' Quintillian laughed, but Kiva's face was less certain.

'That depends on whether he's alone.'

The prince's face slid into pensive concern again as he nodded. 'Where is he making for?' he asked the soldier.

'The military harbour, sir. The ship will dock very soon.'

'Come on,' the prince said, launching himself from his seat and almost upsetting the carefully positioned wooden markers on the map. Kiva rose in response and gestured to the guardsman. 'Lead on, man. To the harbour.'

Leaving the room, the two men hurried out into the corridor. Two more guardsmen joined them there as an escort and, at the exit to the suite of imperial apartments where they collected their cloaks, another two men added their presence. Ever since the attempt on Titus's life those weeks ago, Kiva had barely had privacy even in the latrines, with guardsmen ever in close proximity. Out of the building they hurried, shouting for horses. By the time they had reached the palace's main gate, their steeds had been brought for them, and they had accrued another eight guardsmen, each of whom mounted alongside their masters in the late morning sun.

The gate rattled open and the two men rode out into the city, anticipation and nervousness vying for control of their expressions. The open courtyard outside the gate led to the Imperial Way that led off down the slope into the heart of Velutio, columns and triumphal arches lining it proudly. And if one moved along the centre of the street, one could just see, through a succession of astonishingly lofty arches, across the forum and the lower reaches of the city, the great walls of Velutio and the greenery and shanty towns outside.

From here the city wall looked a frail and easily overcome obstacle. It was barely even visible. But like Quintillian, Kiva knew better. He had walked those walls plenty of times in his life, around their complete circuit, even. From the palace down the slope above the water to the private palace harbour, then back up and across the Hill of Croton, marching along the coast above the rocks that made the sea here so treacherous, then down to the Forest Gate, around the land walls to the Hill of Tellus in the south, then back around the commercial harbour and the military harbour and above the rocks once more to the palace. A grand circuit of 14 miles. And while the sea walls were granted the added defence of cliffs and rocks and the tough naval approach, the land walls were more defensive still. The main walls were 40 feet high, punctuated by heavy projecting towers, each of which bore artillery. A walkway separated these impressive fortifications from a lower outer wall, around 25 feet high, with its own towers, the entire circuit peppered with arrow loops. Then there was the moat, which had been cut down through bedrock so that the sea flooded it from both sides, effectively turning Velutio into an island. In places the moated ditch was only 8 feet deep, but in others it was up to more than 20, though any depth, when combined with bedrock, made mining the walls more or less an impossibility.

Velutio was well protected. A century ago, during the reign of one of their most powerful kings, the Gota had crossed the border in response to some perceived imperial sleight and had come against Velutio in force. At the time, due to the dispersed disposition of the armies, there had been little force to oppose the invaders, and they had reached Velutio with little trouble. What the masters of the empire had learned to their chagrin was that the old original walls of the city had been less than useless, buried as they were among the streets of the ever-expanding city. Velutio had burned and the population had been almost halved before the armies reached the capital and expelled the enemy once more.

But Velutio had learned the danger of overconfidence. The city was given a permanent limit and that boundary was fortified with the most powerful defences in the world. Never again would the empire's capital fall to the barbarian.

At least that was the theory, Kiva thought, swallowing noisily as he rode alongside his brother. They passed from the wide, impressive Imperial Way through the forum and down onto the Street of Iron Horses, making for the military harbour. The forum fell into surprised silence as they passed. It was a rare enough event for the emperor to appear in the city without formal warning that many people even forgot to bow until he was past, not that Kiva really cared for such formal ancient custom. He would rather people got on with their lives and kept the city working than they all stopped what they were doing to pay him respect.

But as figures appeared from doorways and faces at windows as they passed, Kiva could not help but become aware of an air of nervous tension all about him. He had been so wrapped up in the problems of governance and his own family that he'd not given much thought as to what the coming conflict meant for the ordinary folk. Silently, internally, he chided himself for such an oversight and sat straighter in his saddle, affecting an air of noble confidence, with even a half smile in there. His gaze caught the pensive, dangerous look on Quintillian's face and he cleared his throat and addressed all those accompanying him quietly enough to not reach most of the public.

'For gods' sake, try and look confident and noble. These people are looking to us for reassurance.'

In response, he saw Quintillian straighten and the guardsmen become more proud and alert. There was little they could do to make the coming days easier for the people, but a little confidence went a long way. There was an endless supply of clean drinking water from the city's wells, and enough food to last them years without hard rationing, but fear and despair could lose a war just as thoroughly as military failure or broken walls.

Through the sea of nervous faces they passed, trying to exude a confidence that in truth entirely eluded Kiva, and he was more than grateful as they emerged from the Gate of Swords into the wide span of the military harbour, protected by its encircling walls and the twin artillery-topped towers that guarded the harbour entrance.

Three ships sat at jetties, each a small coastal galley, built for speed and not strength. Almost the entire fleet was currently active somewhere in the Eastern Sea, which the Pelasians called the Sea of Winter Storms. It was a depressing sight when facing an imminent siege, even if the Khan's forces were entirely land-based and he could do nothing about blockading the ports. If all else failed, they could ship the populace out of the city slowly, but if the city was in danger of falling, the empire would go with it. Without Velutio, the emperor and the senate, what *was* the empire, after all? No, they had to hold Velutio. If the city fell, then the heart and soul of the empire would fall with it.

Even as they reined in close to the dock, a light courier vessel bearing the wolf insignia of the imperial guard with the radiant crown of Titus Tythianus rounded one of the great harbour towers and came skipping across the water towards the wharf, its oars rising and falling in perfect unison. Kiva found that he was holding his breath.

'Can you see?' he whispered nervously to his brother. Quintillian didn't answer and as Kiva glanced at him, he saw something of the same fear reflected in the prince's eyes. His heart twisted as the long-suppressed knowledge of what had passed between wife and brother resurfaced. He fought it down. This was not the time.

He stood, almost vibrating with nerves, as the ship closed on them. Finally, he could make out the figures standing at the stern of the vessel where there was plenty of deck space. Titus was a figure that stood out in any circumstances, his wild hair and untamed beard looking often more lupine than the wolf-pelt shoulder-cloak he habitually wore. And a small party of guardsmen stood with him.

Kiva almost collapsed as he picked out the two female forms amid them, their swarthy skin clearly identifying them. Both were dressed in ordinary clothing, and not the imperial finery he was used to, but that was hardly a surprise. What they must have been through…

As the ship pulled up alongside the jetty and the sailors began to throw out lines and secure them, Titus crossed to the captain and spoke to him urgently. The port master was crossing the dock now with a clerk, converging on the jetty's end where the emperor and his entourage waited. The official bowed low and waited patiently.

The first figure off the ship was Titus, who vaulted across the narrow gap between there and the jetty without waiting for the boarding ramp to be run out. Landing heavily and cursing, rubbing his knee vigorously, Titus straightened slowly and threw a cursory salute to Kiva and Quintillian, frowning in surprise at the presence of the latter.

'Well, well, well. The prodigal brother returns. Had enough of wandering in the woods?'

It was lightly said, but Titus's expression was not one of mirth or pleasure, and Kiva felt a curious tightness in his chest. Marshal Tythianus was one of their oldest friends, son of their father's closest ally, and a man not given to over-seriousness. Something was weighing upon Titus, and that realization made Kiva's breath catch in his throat.

The marshal cast a look around the port.

'All the ships in the south, facing off against Ashar, I take it?'

Quintillian nodded. 'Good to see you, Titus. They are, though I've sent for the lion's portion of the army to return. We're facing another threat, worse than the Pelasians.'

Titus stretched. 'Some eastern warlord, I understand?'

'Yes. You're oddly well-informed, Titus? A new Khan who's united the horse clans. They're closing on the capital even now. I've mustered all the forces I can spare at the Tyras River to slow the enemy, since they're moving with siege engines. Hopefully it'll give us time to gather enough manpower to hold them off. Between the forces pulling back from the south, the army and the allied tribes from the north, we should be able to stop them if we can delay them long enough to muster everyone in the city.'

'I think you need to start replanning,' Titus said darkly. 'Don't count on the northerners.'

'What?' Kiva, whose eyes had been on the women at the rear of the ship moving slowly towards the boarding ramp, ripped his gaze round to the hirsute marshal before him. 'Don't tell me the tribes aren't coming?'

'Oh, they're coming,' Titus said, his eyes glinting. 'We caught sight of them moving around the northern shore of the Nymphaean Sea about three days from here. A massive force, they are.'

'Then we…'

'Kiva, they're not coming to help you. They're marching under a rebel lord called Aldegund, who bends his knee to this eastern invader of yours. You're about to get squeezed between the horse clans and a rebel army.'

Quintillian rubbed his face wearily. 'Then there'll be nowhere near enough men to hold off the Khan. And worse still, the northerners will be familiar with siege warfare in a way the horse clans aren't. Shit. Even if we pull in every loyal man and arm every farmer we can find, we'll be nowhere near strong enough to hold Velutio.'

'But we can't *evacuate*. Can't let the city fall.' Kiva, from the corner of his eye, saw the two Pelasian women being helped ashore a few paces away by Titus's men. Jala and Nisha – no sign of Zari. As they stepped onto the solid boards of the jetty, Nisha looked up in relief and caught sight of Kiva with a smile and a respectful bow of the head. The emperor could not help but note the bandage around the maid's hand, the arm tucked carefully in at her side and, worst of all, the missing eye and the scars that surrounded it. He shuddered. Behind the maid, Jala alighted, but her eyes remained on the ground before her and she did not look up and meet the eyes of those awaiting her. Kiva felt another lurch of nerves.

'…so this ship will be prepared to leave again within the hour,' Titus was saying, and Kiva pulled his gaze from his wife back to the conversation of which he had missed part.

'For Pelasia?' he said, catching a thread.

'Yes. If I take the empress and we explain to the Pelasian high command that the empire was not responsible for her plight, but rather a rebel, then Ashar might be willing to throw his support behind us.'

Kiva felt a sudden thrill of realization. If the army could all pull back from the south, and the Pelasian forces came with them as allies rather than enemies, they could still win this.

'But it will take too long,' Quintillian said in a hollow tone. 'Within the week we will have both the Khan's army and

Aldegund's at the gates. And there's every chance that the northern rebels will have ships coming from the west too. Even at the fastest speed possible and even if Ashar and his generals fall over themselves to kiss and make up, you'll not be able to get back here for almost two weeks with any force to be reckoned with. If there's anyone among them with a working knowledge of siegecraft, Velutio could be rubble and ashes before you get here.'

Kiva's eyes were back on Jala, who still looked at the ground beneath her feet. What was wrong with her? He gritted his teeth and turned back to Titus and Quintillian.

'No. It *won't* be too late. Don't underestimate Velutio, brother. If we can rouse the resistant spirit of the people, with the walls that have never been breached, we can hold until the Pelasians and the southern army come. You and I. We are the sons of Darius. Grandsons of Kiva Caerdin. We've taken our father's empire and given it a new golden age and I *will not* see that age end now under the hooves of some eastern warlord or some rebellious pseudo-barbarian.'

Quintillian took several slow, deep breaths, his forehead creased as he pondered matters. Finally, he straightened, and when he looked once more at Kiva, he was the old Quintillian again – the man who had fled Velutio months ago.

'Everything happens for a reason, Kiva. The gods abhor blind chance. I went east shrouded in doubt and solitude, and despite everything that happened to me, I brought advance warning of the Khan and his men. Jala and Titus – and Nisha – have clearly been through a lot out west, but they've brought us warning of this Aldegund and his rebel army. Hardship has given us a tiny advantage. We have not been caught with our breeches down as was so clearly the intention. And two of the marshals have survived the purge the enemy planned. Moreover, with Jala returned, we have the solution to our problem in our hands. Jala can defuse the tensions in the south and bring back our allies to save the day.'

He grinned. 'You're right, Kiva. We *can* do this. And we will. I can look to the defences of the city and the placement of the forces we have. You can rouse the city and organize everything else. And when the time comes, we will stand side by side on the battlements and show the Khan what the sons of Darius can do. The empire will not lie down and offer its throat to the invader.'

Kiva's answering smile faltered as he saw Quintillian's eyes flicker up and over his shoulder. He turned. Jala looked back down in an instant, and the emperor felt his heart break once more. Jala couldn't look at him? But she *could* with Quintillian? And as if some barrier had been broken or some decision made, now Jala looked up again and fixed Kiva with a warm smile. A moment later she was in his arms, clutching him tight, as though anchoring herself to him against the storm winds of fate. Had he not caught that tiniest moment between her and Quintillian, all would now be right with the world.

Forcing his shattered heart into a deep, secret place, where it could desiccate without being seen, the emperor shared a moment of reunion with his empress that raised smiles from even the hardy guardsmen Titus had brought back with him from the west.

'Don't get too attached,' Titus snorted. 'I need the empress again within the hour.'

'And we have a war to plan,' Quintillian said, stretching.

Kiva held tight for a long moment and when, finally, Jala released him and stepped back, turning to Titus and the ship that was already resupplying for the desperate journey, he sighed and whispered, inaudibly under his breath.

'Goodbye, my love.'

CHAPTER XXV

Of Enemies New

The two brothers stood atop the Eyrie – the tallest tower of the city walls by a clear 20 feet – each gazing off in a different direction. The late spring weather, usually so predictable and pleasant in the central provinces, had turned sour last evening, with black clouds from the north bringing a torrential downpour that washed the streets of Velutio and left the stonework of the walls slippery and glistening. The torrent had let up just after dawn but had left in its wake a leaden grey sky and that fine constant drizzle that soaks a man to the bone as surely as any downpour.

Pushing back the hair plastered across his forehead, Quintillian watched the new arrivals. The army of Lord Aldegund was an impressive and curious sight. Formed from roughly even numbers of imperial troops that had been swayed by the renegade lord's gold or promises, and of barbarians from beyond the border, it bore the signs of an imperial army at war, but with the chaotic form and lack of organization of a barbarian warband. Clearly the Fourth Army, which had been based in the northwest and was the only sizeable military group not committed against Pelasia, had succumbed en masse to Aldegund's pay wagon, for Quintillian would be willing to bet that over half that army was now bearing down on Velutio, a neat, ordered column amid whooping groups of warriors waving axes and spears, some stripped to the waist to display the designs etched upon their torsos.

Aldegund's force alone would be enough to overwhelm the poor defenders of Velutio in due time. They travelled without siege engines or a supply train, and Quintillian had to nod to Aldegund's plan there. Lands that owed fealty to him as a lord stretched most of the way from the northwest to this end of the Nymphaean Sea. With enough time and organization, his army could – and almost certainly did – have supply drops ready at the end of each day's travel, making a slow wagon train unnecessary and allowing the army to move fast. And that last two days from the other side of marble-sheathed Danis to the capital could be done with supplies carried by the army itself. Aldegund, the prince would wager, had worked everything so that he had to move only at the very last minute in order to join up with his new overlord. Had he moved earlier he would have risked giving the game away and landing himself with his *own* war in the north.

Quintillian wondered what had happened to the troops from the Fourth Army who had remained loyal. It seemed highly unlikely that they were still hale and intact.

He heard a grunt from Kiva and turned to look.

Kiva, clad in fine armour over a tunic of white and purple, and every bit the warlike emperor, was watching the other enemy. The huge space below the walls and beyond the moat had been cleared of shanty towns and tents and shacks over the past few days, all free citizens being brought back inside the walls for safety, and the first of the horse clans had arrived yesterday before the rains came, casually setting up their great circular tents in place of the demolished structures as though on some sort of summer outing. The enemy had quickly learned their folly when Quintillian had given the artillery their orders and stones and missiles rained down on those tents, killing and wounding hundreds before the riders pulled back out of artillery range and began to set up camp once again. Then, gradually, the bulk of the horse clans had arrived, joining their vanguard and assembling in a huge gathering that seemed to be organized by clan with tiny gaps between them, as though none wished to be entirely associated with their neighbours. And between the moat and the horse clans' camp lay a sward covered in abandoned tents, loose horses and the pulverized and impaled corpses of those who'd been so overconfident.

It had given Quintillian some hope for the coming days that the clans had been so completely unprepared for what they were facing. They had never seen somewhere like Velutio, and even with the Khan telling them what they would find, they were still clearly completely baffled by such a place.

Then, this morning, almost synchronized with the arrival of Aldegund's vanguard, the Khan's baggage train and artillery had arrived.

Kiva had felt his heart skip as he peered off through the rain at the seemingly endless shapes of timber monstrosities being wheeled across the low rise in the distance beyond the camp. He could feel the resentment emanating from Quintillian, who had unwillingly contributed to the construction of these nightmares that would shortly be brought against them.

For the briefest of moments, both brothers glanced off to the south, as though something had drawn their attention. The sea was just visible from here as a lighter grey smudge between the land and the glowering clouds. The sea was empty, of course, but somewhere beyond the horizon, Titus and Jala raced for Pelasia and with them sailed all the hopes of Velutio and the empire.

'What will happen first?' Kiva breathed, turning back to the assembling hordes before them. Quintillian dragged his attention back from the endless stretch of water.

'Unless the Khan considers a parlay, then it'll be a few trial sorties. The barbarians at least know what they're dealing with, but even they will want to know what Velutio is like compared to the smaller border fortifications they've faced in the past. The horse clans will have no idea, and I doubt even the Khan, for all his care and stratagems, will be able to resist an initial attempt just to see what we can do.'

Kiva nodded. 'And our response? Full? Measured? None?'

'Depends on exactly what they try, but I want to keep our strength and numbers as an unknown quantity to the enemy. They now must realize that we had at least a little warning, if not enough to be prepared, and will be wondering just how many men we have. I want our true peril to be a secret as long as possible.'

'I understand.'

They watched for almost an hour in silence as the drizzle gently saturated the world, the troops lining the walls stamping their feet to return life to cold toes, every pair of eyes locked either on the gathering barbarian army outside the northern walls or the fascinating and deadly nomad horde to the east. On a rise at the near side of the nomad horde, a large tent was being erected with banners and streamers outside. The Khan's own tent, presumably. Finally, Quintillian nudged Kiva, who'd been gazing out to sea again as though he could will Titus back. The marshal pointed off into the nomad camp, and Kiva frowned into the mizzle. A sizeable group of riders was gathering there, around a central party that seemed to be swarming over a wooden frame. The emperor chewed on his cheek as he watched, unable to determine what precisely was happening, though it clearly presaged some sort of foray.

Finally, the horsemen filed out into two groups, each of perhaps a hundred horses, and Kiva and his brother could see what they had been concentrating on. A ram. A huge tree trunk had been carefully adzed and tied around all along its length with ropes. Now, those ropes were held by riders. The trunk was lifted from the floor by thirty horsemen and secured so that they moved slowly forward, the ram bobbing between the lines of horses. It took a few moments for them to come into a concerted pace that allowed them to move without the trunk smashing into one of them. Kiva squinted. There was some kind of decorative head on the ram, but he couldn't quite see it at this distance in such grim weather.

Quintillian chuckled next to him. 'Every day they waste on such ridiculous ideas is another day for Titus to complete his task.

'Looks fairly reasonable to me,' Kiva frowned. 'That thing represents a danger to the gates.'

His brother snorted. 'It'll never *touch* the gates. They've not thought it through. Watch.'

Quintillian turned to the captain standing nearby, waiting for orders.

'I don't want a single shot or arrow loosed at them until they've decided they failed. The moment they start to retreat, hit them with the artillery. Loose shot and bolts. Same as yesterday. They already know we have the artillery, so it's revealing nothing.'

The captain saluted and passed the orders on to several runners, who disappeared off around the walls, carrying the messages to the men at the weapons and the various officers in charge of wall sections.

'Come on,' Quintillian urged his brother. 'Aldegund won't try anything until his camp's set up. Let's go watch the Khan make his first mistake.'

Kiva followed his brother down the three flights of stairs from the Eyrie, past the room full of artillery shot and the room with the huge map of the city surroundings, and out onto the wall tops. Quickly, they hurried around the perimeter of the city until they were roughly opposite the gathered nomad horde. There, they made for the Inda Gate, which would be the natural target for a ram.

The gate had once been the weakest point in the walls, but one forward-thinking emperor had had the entire structure strengthened, buttressing it, cladding the lower two thirds of the towers in an extra layer of thick stone blocks and raising the tops by two more storeys. Now, it represented one of the strongest gates in the walls. Below, in a huge arch carved with representations of the war god Martus and inscriptions commemorating the gate's builder and its restorer, a huge set of oak doors, 8-inches thick and banded and studded with iron was held fast with three bars each almost a foot thick. Then, if that should give, a second identical set of doors filled the inner edge of the arch, forming a second defence. And inside the gate a small barbican had been constructed with a third set of doors and archer platforms all around, forming a killing zone that would wreak havoc upon invaders.

The enemy were coming by the time the two of them took a place on the gate top. The captain of that section saluted them and Quintillian waved at him. 'Remember: no reaction until they run. All right?'

The man nodded and saluted again.

The enemy had managed to reach a reasonable pace, and Kiva was struck suddenly by how good these horsemen were. To manage 30 riders moving in perfect unison, tight enough that the great trunk between them hardly swayed, was a feat of horsemanship no imperial cavalry unit could hope to achieve. And the rest of the 200 or so riders were out in front and to the sides as though forming some sort of shield. Kiva couldn't quite figure what they were intending.

'I know that ram,' Quintillian said suddenly.

'What?'

'Sounds ridiculous, I know, but I've seen it before. It was on a painting in the Khan's palace back in Ual-Aahbor. It's either the one the Khan's father failed to take a city with, or it's a damn good copy of it.'

Kiva frowned down at the approaching riders. The great heavy bronze head on the trunk was a very stylized dragon, complete with wavering tongue and horns. It reminded him of the decorative jade dragons in the palace that had been gifts over the centuries from emissaries of the Jade Emperor.

'Now watch them realize how idiotic they are.' Quintillian grinned. Finally, the surrounding horsemen unslung their bows and, with incredible skill, guided their horses with knees and hips alone as they nocked arrow after arrow, drawing them from wide quivers on their saddles with almost mechanical speed and releasing them up at the battlements on the far side of the moat. As they reached the water's edge, they wheeled left and right, continually sending shaft after shaft up at the walls. Not one made it to the wall top, and precious few even crossed the water.

'They're not actually expecting to cause any damage, of course,' Quintillian explained. 'They're trying to keep any archers' heads down to protect the ram. As if I'd bother wasting precious arrows on that thing.'

Kiva continued to watch as the riders constantly wheeled their horses, racing back and forth along 20 or 30 paces of wall to either side of the bridge, continually loosing arrows at the parapet.

'They'll be mighty irritated when they return and have to restring their bows,' Quintillian cackled, then caught the look on Kiva's face. 'The bow strings will be getting wet,' he explained, 'stretched and ruined in the rain. Only an idiot has his archers out in the rain, which leads me to believe that the Khan isn't the one behind this particular push. He's not so stupid.'

Kiva returned his attention to the action below and watched it fail.

The ram reached the end of the bridge and the horsemen carrying it reined in suddenly, realizing that they would not fit onto the bridge in two files with the ram between them. As Quintillian howled with laughter next to him, Kiva couldn't help but chuckle at the farce unfolding below him. The riders had moved in perfect unison but, taken by surprise by their inability to fit on the bridge, such perfect organization had failed utterly and they had all skittered to a halt independently. The result was chaos. The huge tree trunk bobbed and dipped, then swung one way, smashing a horse and knocking it over so that the rider fell, letting go of the rope. The ram then swung back, smashing into another horse. Its rider howled as he fell from the steed over the bridge side and into the moat which, here, was a good 8 feet down just to water level. He would have to swim some distance to find a place he could climb out. Sure enough, the man swam perhaps 20 paces before the weight of his armour and furs dragged him under and he failed to reappear.

At the end of the bridge, the travesty continued as the log took out two more horses before the rest had the presence of mind to drop it to the gravel.

'Captain?' Quintillian said happily, 'You may now pass the word to the artillery. Tell them to have fun.'

There was a pause of about 20 heartbeats while the horsemen below milled about, trying to decide what to do next, and then they turned en masse to ride back to their camp just as the first thunks, thuds and clanks rang out from the towers. Maybe a quarter of the riders and horses were pounded and minced by flying stones or pierced through by 3-foot iron bolts before they were up to speed in their flight. Quintillian was chuckling as the second wave from the artillery took perhaps half the remaining force, and then the few panicked survivors were out of range and racing back to their camp.

'Well, now *that* was amusing.' Quintillian grinned. Then he sighed, and his face slipped to a more serious tone. 'Sadly, that sort of thing won't happen much, and soon we'll start to face proper threats.'

The two men stood quietly for a while as the men on the walls congratulated the artillerists to a background din of howling and shrieking from dying men and animals below.

'Aldegund is being cautious,' Quintillian noted, gesturing off to the left. Their view was less clear from here than from the Eyrie, but even Kiva could see that the northern lord had begun to set up camp on the near edge of the forest, at the top of the rise that faced the city. His men – at least the imperial ones, if not the barbarians – were setting up a proper fortification with a rampart and ditch, and pickets had been set with torches of pitch that burned even in the endless drizzle.

'Very defensive,' Kiva noted.

'He's just preparing himself.'

'I'm not so sure.' The emperor frowned. 'Watch him over today and tonight. I suspect he will make no move against the city, even in terms of tests and forays. Maybe Aldegund has committed himself to treason, but there will be allied lords in that army and commanders in the Fourth who took oaths to me. They will be less willing to commit until they can be sure of success. I think they will stay out of the fight until they can be certain of being on the winning side. And for all Aldegund's strength, a sizeable part of his force is made up of independents. The army may have been turned in principle, but an oath is a powerful thing, and they might be a lot less willing to put blade to flesh when they're face to face with the enemy and remember that they are all part of the same army. It takes a hard man to kill his colleagues.'

'I hope you're right,' Quintillian said, peering off towards the burgeoning fortress. 'That could buy us precious time.'

'Watch this,' Quintillian nudged him. The riders had returned to their camp and now that Kiva squinted, he could just make out two figures emerging from the large circular tent on a prominent rise.

'The smaller one will be the Khan. I can't make out the features of the other, but I can tell you even without looking that it's Ganbaatar, the Khan's son.'

'The one you told me about? The half-nomad?'

'That's the one,' Quintillian confirmed. 'He's far from stupid, but certainly doesn't have his father's wit. That being said, I'm not sure I'd want to face him in an arena. His skills lie in areas other than strategy.' He paused, a thought striking him. 'I would wager that it was Ganbaatar that sent that little deputation against the gate. Whether he was trying to impress the Khan or just getting over-enthusiastic, it smacks of nomad thinking, not the Khan, and I can't imagine any of the clan chiefs having the wherewithal to commit to that without their overlord's consent. That was nomad thinking, enhanced by the impetuousness of youth.'

Kiva smiled. 'I can imagine the Khan will be having some fairly severe words with his son, then.'

'Very much so. And if the Khan brought that ram here all the way from the Jade Empire because it has a family connection, then he will be less than pleased that he's lost it in the first hour of the siege.' Quintillian chuckled and turned to the section officer again. 'Do me a kindness, Captain. Send a party down to the bridge. If any horses are unharmed bring them inside, gather anything of value from the fallen nearby and saw the head off that ram. Bring the head inside and put the log across the far end of the bridge. Might help slow any advance down in time.'

The captain saluted and sent off his men.

'What will you do with the ram?' Kiva asked.

'Have it mounted above the gate. It will niggle at the Khan every time he looks at the city.'

'Might that not goad him into acting more viciously?'

'It might make him act precipitously. People who plan when they're irritated miss important things.'

Kiva nodded. 'I think it might be time to send a deputation out to Aldegund's army.'

'What? Why?'

'Because Aldegund has committed treason, but it is within my power to forgive such things. Perhaps an offer of amnesty might bring Aldegund and his men back to the fold?'

Quintillian stared at him. 'You must be *jesting,* brother. That man is leading a revolt against you. He's suborned your army. Besieged your capital. Fuck, he kidnapped Jala!'

Kiva nodded again. 'And I will never forgive him personally for those things, but I have to consider the good of the empire before my own welfare. If we could bring Aldegund or some of his men back to our side, we might be able to turn the tide or buy ourselves precious breathing room. I can't overlook the possibility.'

'Don't do it, Kiva. I don't care what you think, Aldegund is not sitting on the fence. He's opposed to us, and if he's staying out of it for now there's a good reason. Aldegund is a northern lord. He thinks he's our equal, Kiva.'

'And he probably *is* in truth, Quint. Grandfather started out as a barbarian recruit, after all, and ended his days as a marshal and the father of an emperor. Shit, he came from lands not far from Aldegund's own. We may very well be related. The point is: if it means a chance for the people of Velutio, then duty demands we make an attempt at reconciliation.'

'It's a mistake, Kiva.'

'One I have to make, nonetheless.'

'Then you're not going yourself. Send someone else.'

Kiva turned a lopsided grin on his brother. 'I'm not an idiot, Quint.'

Taking a deep breath, the emperor strolled back across the wall, noting with interest an altercation going on in the nomad camp where the Khan seemed to be berating his men. A quarter of an hour's walk brought him back to the Eyrie, below which was the Shadow King Gate. Here, since they had made the tower their headquarters this morning, their entourage remained gathered, a number of senior politicians and officers of the guard. Kiva gestured to a man in a senior uniform.

'Fetch me ink and vellum.'

As the equipment was brought over and a desk set up, the brothers watched the northerners' camp taking shape. It was a properly-constructed imperial temporary camp. Someone in Aldegund's force must have been a senior military commander. Taking a breath, Quintillian carefully scrawled a dozen lines of text on the vellum, dabbed the ink with the linen provided, then rolled it up and slid the vellum into a leather scroll case and jammed the lid on. He then dripped a blob of purple wax on the join, stamping it with the imperial seal from the signet ring on his left hand and waving it around to dry.

'Prefect?'

The officer hurried back over with a bow.

'Have a small deputation sent out to the rebel army. Only volunteers, but I'd like one officer and one member of the imperial court among them to maintain the appropriate levels of authority. They need to see Lord Aldegund or the most senior officer of the imperial army in that camp, whichever they can. They should deliver this scroll and wait for an answer.'

The officer saluted again and disappeared from the wall top two steps at a time. There was a pause of several minutes, during which the two brothers spent their time leaning on the parapet watching the enemy. Aldegund and his men were well organized. Finally, they heard the gates opening, and a group of ten horsemen sped away from the city across the open ground, leaving a trail through the wet grass as the gates closed behind them. Kiva and his brother watched, tense, as the horsemen approached the enemy camp and slowed. There was a brief discussion with the pickets at spearpoint, and then they were admitted. Once inside the northern camp, behind the ramparts and the defensive works and among the tents, the deputation was lost to sight. The brothers waited.

Finally, the guards at the enemy gateway parted and a single horse and rider emerged. Kiva felt his spirits sink at the sight, sure of what it signified. They watched as the rider returned and, as he neared, they descended the stairs and waited as the gates were opened. Kiva felt the breath catch in his throat as the horse and rider passed back into the city. The horse was a well-trained imperial military mount, and had returned of its own volition. The rider was still alive, but likely wished he wasn't. His eyes had been carved out, his legs pinned to his saddle with ten nails and his arms to his legs with six more each. Blood swathed both man and animal, and the courtier's face was rapidly greying as he bled out.

'I think you have your answer, Kiva,' Quintillian sighed.

Wordlessly the pair ascended the stairs once more, this time passing the wall top and climbing on up the Eyrie to the place with the best view of both enemy camps. There was activity now, and Kiva was further dismayed to see that it centred around nine tall poles outside the camp gate, each bearing the head of one of his deputation. That sealed it, then. There would be no negotiation with his former subjects. Aldegund and his rebels had set themselves irrevocably against the legitimate emperor.

The siege of Velutio had begun.

CHAPTER XXVI

Of Siegecraft and the Unexpected

The morning had dawned brighter than the previous day, though the ground remained saturated and the scent of fresh earth and damp grass clung to the air. The few clouds scudded high across the vault of the sky presaging no further deluge.

Kiva watched Quintillian leaning on the parapet of the Eyrie, chewing on bread and freshly churned butter and periodically taking a pull of fresh well water. He smiled. Barely an hour had gone by since his brother had returned when Quintillian hadn't eaten something. The privations of his months among the horse clans had left the man with a hole in the pit of his belly that never seemed to fill.

'Morning, brother.'

Quintillian looked over his shoulder and smiled, though there was no genuine humour in the expression. In fact, he looked extremely tense.

'What is it?'

'Something's going to happen this morning. Something big. I can feel it building, like the pressure before a thunderstorm.'

Kiva could feel no such thing and wandered over to lean on the rapidly drying stonework next to his brother. 'What do you think?'

'I cannot work out Aldegund, and that irritates me. He's not a complicated man. These northern lords are direct and not spiral thinkers. I'll admit he's unusually subtle, given the fact that he's kept his betrayal secret all this time, but now he's openly arrayed against us, yet doing nothing but sulking in his camp and beheading messengers. No,' he corrected himself, 'that's what he *seems* to be doing. I'm pretty sure it's not what he's *actually* doing. I don't like not being able to work him out. A large part of our chances of survival rely on our being able to predict the enemy's moves and react accordingly.'

'Well, as long as we keep a close eye on them…'

'But then there's the problem of the Khan.' Quintillian waved his hand vaguely at the nomad camp. 'He's preparing for something big. There've been men swarming all over those siege engines this morning and running around in preparation. But we know so little about their organization and their abilities I can't guess what they'll try.'

He huffed irritably. 'Then there's the problem of the *pair* of them. Bad enough not being able to work out what Aldegund's up to or what the Khan's planning, but why are they not working together? They're allies – we all know that now, and it's no secret, so why maintain such separate campaigns. The Khan cannot use those siege engines without Aldegund's men. His nomads would have precious little idea of what to do. And at the same time, Aldegund has the men with the ability to hurl rocks at us, but no artillery. So why aren't they working together? If it were you and I out there, those great onagers would already be throwing stones at the walls. But nothing's happening. I cannot predict what's going to go on this morning, and it's driving me mad.'

'Whatever it is,' Kiva replied calmly, 'it can only be good for us. Better to watch them sit and wait than watch them throw rocks at us. Every day we remain untouched is another day for Titus and Jala to bring reinforcements.'

'I'm not so sure,' Quintillian muttered quietly. 'I like to know what's going on. Something big is about to happen, and if we don't know what it is, how do we act against it?'

The emperor put a comforting hand on his brother's shoulder. 'We will persevere. I know that, and so do you.'

The prince merely grunted in reply and the two stood in silence for some time, listening to the subdued sounds of city life going on, somewhat muted by apprehension, and the various shouts and noises of the defenders along the walls. The two massed armies just outside artillery range sat gleaming under the morning light, patches of shade scudding across them as the high clouds periodically obscured the sun.

'There,' Quintillian said suddenly after such a long period of silence that Kiva had almost drifted off to sleep leaning on the parapet.

'What?' he said, starting back to attentiveness and peering off at both camps, trying to see what had changed.

'There,' the marshal said again, pointing this time. Kiva followed the gesture and could see a flurry of movement in the centre of the nomad camp. The two figures, clearly the Khan and his son, had emerged from their tent and were engaged in some sort of discussion on the hillside. At this distance they were little more than ants in a sea of other ants, and Kiva couldn't guess at whether they were planning, arguing or even telling jokes. Then he saw what had clearly attracted his brother's attention. Four groups of nomads on horseback were forming into lines, each one more than 20 beasts long. And nearby, other lines of nomads were taking shape, these ones dismounted.

'What are they doing?'

'I don't know, but it's some kind of assault, and it's coming now.' Quintillian turned to the captain nearby. 'Be prepared for anything. I want all the artillery facing the nomads loaded with short-range ammunition – scattering shot to use against large numbers of infantry. Have all the archers ready and pull in any you can spare from the other walls to that section. Be prepared for a major assault.'

The captain saluted and went about his tasks, leaving the emperor and his brother watching tensely, alone on the tower top.

Gradually, the enemy lines organized themselves. It must have been peculiar for the nomads to work in such a manner – truly against all their experience of war. The Khan had excelled himself in achieving such a thing with the fractious, disorganized clans. And whatever was about to happen this time had the backing of the Khan himself and not his impetuous son, leading Quintillian to believe it would be something that posed a proper threat to the defenders. Kiva shuddered.

The clans began to clear the way for the lines of men. These were no mere two or three hundred riders with a ram. This time their numbers were beyond counting, but at a simple estimation, Kiva reckoned they were facing two or three thousand men, all moving in oddly neat lines as they began to descend from their camp towards the city.

The four groups of nomads were dragging something. Each group had split into two lines in the same manner they'd carried the ram yesterday, but as they emerged from the press at the heart of the camp, Kiva frowned to see what they were dragging. Four long, flat timber structures. They each looked a little like a palisade that had been laid on its side, or… or one of those wooden walkways they installed in forts for ease of footing where the ramparts were too muddy.

In a flash, Kiva realized what they were.

'Bridges?'

Quintillian nodded. 'Four timber crossings for the moat. I did wonder how they were intending to come against the walls. It's still a precarious idea, but better than that idiocy yesterday. And look: the other lines are all carrying long siege ladders.'

Kiva swallowed as he saw dozens of lines of footmen coming along in the wake of the bridges, each carrying a heavy wooden ladder

'Now we'll see how good the intelligence the Khan received is. Are the ladders the right height for the walls? If he's underestimated them, this could be short and very costly for him.' Quintillian turned and looked for the captain, but he was gone, busy carrying out the earlier orders. The prince looked down from the tower top until he spotted an officer's uniform on the walls.

'You! Prefect!' The man looked up and saluted. 'Take every archer the walls can spare to the nomad front. Every last one. And any of the townsfolk who've reported for auxiliary duty… get them up there too. I want forked poles every ten feet along that wall. We're facing siege ladders. Oh, and have the baskets of rocks sent over too. Once their bridges are in position, I want hot sand, burning oil and a hundred rocks dropped on each one. The faster we can ruin, burn and sink those timber structures the quicker this will be over.'

The officer saluted.

'Shall we go over there?' Kiva prompted.

'No, I think not. The officers there know what they're doing, and having to keep bowing every time they walk past you would detract from their efficiency. I still can't believe Aldegund is sitting there and letting the Khan suffer the brunt of it all. And I can't believe the Khan's accepting that. The rebel probably thinks preserving his men will leave him as a power in the land when the Khan's army is diminished and the city's fallen. But without his help, I doubt the city *will* fall.'

As the walls swarmed with men preparing to take on the nomad assault, the brothers watched the enemy moving down the slope. Somewhere off to the right, an officer called for all the archers to nock their arrows. The auxiliary bowmen, mostly drawn from southern and eastern provinces, each set an arrow to their bow and drew back, holding tight and sighting, marking an approaching rider. They would have a range of perhaps 20 feet beyond the moat and no more if they wished any level of accuracy. The four groups of riders with the bridges were getting close now. Kiva could only estimate the length of those timber walkways at forty feet, and the moat was thirty feet wide in most places.

The timber bridges were leaving messy brown trails as they tore up the turf in their passage, and those muddy tracks were quickly lost beneath the feet of many hundreds of men. The nomads, unused to any sort of warfare that did not take place on horseback, kept losing formation, but it made little difference. Many of them carried long siege ladders, but others, previously unnoticed in the press, carried large wicker shields or huge timbers. Behind them came a huge mass of warriors brandishing weapons, eager to take the fight to the defenders of Velutio. As they surged across the grass and mud, those bearing the shields and timbers began to pull out ahead of the rest, closely following the bridges.

'Artillery!' came a call from along the wall. There was a pause and then the war machines began to sing their song of destruction. Thuds and crashes, twangs and whines brought forth the chorus of death. Sacks of stones had been shot from onagers, the bags shredding when fired, so that deadly rubble hurtled across the moat, ploughing into the approaching horsemen, pulverizing men and beasts alike, leaving shrieking and howling figures clutching what remained of their broken forms. Other catapults fired single rocks, which hit the ground, some ploughing long troughs in the turf, others hitting just right to bounce once, twice, thrice, and then roll to a halt. And the bolt-throwers launched their 3-foot iron missiles, seeking flesh to obliterate. Most missed their targets. An initial artillery volley was always a messy thing as even the best artillerists needed to find their range before they could hope to be truly effective. But here and there a shot had taken its toll. A scattering of stones had hit the rear of one of the bridge columns, killing three horses and their riders and causing mayhem among the footmen carrying the ladders behind them. Individual horsemen had been plucked from their saddles with iron bolts and hurled away to die in agony. One particularly large rounded rock had bounced just at the front of a bridge column, obliterating six riders and their mounts in a spray of pink and tiny shattered body parts. The second bounce smashed a section of timber in the centre of the bridge, ripping through dozens of running warriors at the back before rolling to a halt amid screaming infantrymen, leaving a long trail of crimson-smeared ground in its wake.

The defenders gave a rousing cheer at the sight, and Kiva almost joined in, but for the fact that his brother, still at the parapet, was pensive and worried. It had been an impressive sight, and spirit-lifting for the besieged city, but in truth the damage to the Khan's army was tiny. Negligible, even. And Quintillian was still expecting something else, clearly.

A second artillery volley was in the offing, men hurriedly loading the weapons and preparing them. Along the stretch of walls near the nomad assault, cauldrons of sizzling sand and bubbling pitch were being brought up to the parapet by four men apiece. Baskets of rocks were being positioned, along with forked poles, and the civilian levy, who had agreed to help defend their city, were moving into position among the soldiers, preparing to throw down rocks, skin-melting sand, and sticky fire. It was as thorough a defence as they could manage, and despite the Khan's serious numerical advantage, Kiva felt certain that they could fight off this assault with little actual damage. Perhaps this was just another test? Perhaps the Khan was not as clever as Quintillian seemed to think?

The riders reached the moat, having plotted their course in order to arrive at the lower areas of the bank. The Khan must have had men out during the hours of darkness, when the driving rain had made it hard for the defenders to spot movement. His scouts must have located the shallowest sections of moat and marked them somehow, for the riders plunged into the water with little difficulty, some directing their swimming horses, others fortunate enough to have found the lowest possible areas where their horses could even stand up in some places. And so they began to drag the bridges out across the water, their task easier the further into the moat they reached, the water taking more and more of the weight of the timber.

The second round of artillery shot ploughed into the enemy, the ranges more certain. However, the bridge columns were now too close, and the brunt was taken by the footmen – those carrying ladders, wicker shields, logs, or just weapons, running into battle. No shield could protect a man from these strikes, though, and Kiva watched as one iron bolt passed through the wicker as though it was naught more than butter, shredding the man behind it and continuing on in its flight to smash the leg of the man behind. The emperor winced as the shield-bearer turned and fell, daylight was clearly visible through his torso.

Another two heavy boulders struck, one carving a trench through men and turf alike, the other bouncing and leaving huge imprints of crushed and mangled bodies in its wake. A sack of stones failed to shred on loosing, and only scattered as it hit one poor bastard full on. He disappeared as though he had never existed, parts of his body joining the shrapnel of stones as the bag burst. The effect covered a smaller area than intended, but the damage in that place was just as intense.

Finally, as the horsemen struggled towards the end of their ride and the footmen began to reach the edge of the moat, the defending officers gave the call for archers. Hundreds upon hundreds of feathered shafts flew out from the walls, not in high graceful arcs as was the common sight on the battlefield. These bowmen had had plenty of time to mark their targets and follow them in their run, as had been the commander's intention. The many arrows whirred out from the defences in direct lines, plunging into figures both running and riding. Even as the artillery prepared for a third volley at the mass of warriors coming up behind, the archers were already loosing again at the men below them.

It was simple carnage. Most of the arrows found a target, some of the more unfortunate attackers having been marked by two or even three archers and sprouting deadly shafts from several angles. The air was filled with the whirr of arrows in flight and the resulting screams of the wounded and dying. Kiva's eyes read the tapestry of death along the turf before the moat. Stomachs were torn open, eyes exploded, necks pierced right through, legs and feet transfixed. Blood was everywhere and, though here in the high observation tower of the Eyrie they were too far away to experience it, Kiva knew all too well the stink of death and opened bowels that would now fill every breath of air over by those walls. He had to force himself to remember that these were the enemy and he must not feel sorry for them, though such empathy came naturally to him. Quintillian was less prone to it, and the look of satisfaction on his face even managed to surface through the layer of concern and uncertainty.

But for all the vast damage the artillery and archers had, and still were, inflicting, the enemy were getting closer. Three of the four timber walkways had been manoeuvred into position, though the fourth had broken apart where it had taken the blow from the bouncing boulder. Men were running along the floating timbers. The walkways would not yet hold much weight and even under the seven or eight men running on each they were bobbing down below the surface, but now those runners were securing it. As men with wicker shields held them up to stop the worst of the arrow storm hurtling down at them, others sank those huge logs into the water and tied the bridges to them, steadying the walkways even as others secured them back on the turf.

Again, one of the bridges failed here, the archers above managing to pick off both shield-bearers and log men, so that the walkway continued to float, held up only by the water and unable to support a great deal of weight. But two were intact and in position and now men were running along them, carrying ladders. Even as they closed on the walls, those ladders were raised. Others were splashing into the water and swimming with their burdens, and Kiva realized that some ladders had been made especially long in order to anchor them in the murk at the moat's bed. The Khan *was* clever, after all. Still, despite all this, Kiva could not imagine them securing any section of wall. This was a costly exercise for the nomads and would have precious little lasting effect on Velutio.

Already, ladders were dropping into place. More than half of them failed to reach the walls, courtesy of the artillery and the archers, but soon enough snarling, foamy-mouthed nomads were scaling the ladders, bearing down on the wall tops.

Half a dozen of them were quickly pushed away by the civilian volunteers with their forked poles and waves of cheering, the ladders crashing back down onto the bridges or splashing into the water, where other men immediately began to raise them again. Those who had been climbing the ladders plunged with cries of shock down into the cold water or onto the timbers, breaking limbs and floundering, some with heavier armour sinking from sight with horrified gurgles.

Kiva was elated by the success of his men and yet horrified at the sheer brutality taking place before the walls. He leaned forward on the parapet once more and turned to the serious frown of Quintillian, opening his mouth to speak.

The stonework shuddered. Just for a moment. Kiva frowned, but Quintillian was already stepping back from the edge. 'Oh, gods above and below,' he cursed, his head snapping this way and that, searching the walls.

'What is it?' Kiva asked under a questioning brow.

'The answer. The answer as to why Aldegund hasn't moved.'

'What?'

Quintillian lurched towards the far side of the tower, in the direction of the northern rebel army's camp. He squinted for a moment and then waved a pointing finger. 'Look!'

'What?'

'There. See the disturbed grass?'

Kiva peered down. There was, now that he looked, a series of trails through the wet grass that spoke of the passage of a number of people.

'The Khan had his scouts check out the moat during the night, when we could see nothing for the darkness and the rain, but Aldegund went one further. He sent men to our walls in the darkness and they've been there ever since, mining!'

Kiva frowned, feeling another shudder through the stones beneath his feet. ‘Surely our men would have seen them?’

His brother shook his head. ‘No. That’s the sigma. Plenty of angles there where they’d be hard to spot.’

Kiva’s eyes widened. The sigma was a stretch of the wall that had once been a gate, but had been rebuilt into wall at a later time. The result of the strange rebuild was a section of wall that bent through several odd angles, forming a ∑ shape. There would, as Quintillian noted, be several places where men could hide rather well unless they were being specifically looked for. He imagined dozens of men, half frozen in the cold water, hacking at the mortar between the stones with tools, the sound buried beneath the endless hiss of rain and the muttering of the men high atop the walls. They would have to have been quiet early this morning, but once the assault began, all eyes and ears had been on the horse clans, and no one would have noticed a muffled arrhythmic chipping down at the base of the walls beginning again.

‘But it would take them *days* to tunnel through the walls.’

‘All they have to do is remove enough stone to make the outer face unstable. They prop it with timbers and then set light as they run.’

Sure enough, even as the stonework shuddered again, Kiva spotted a small group of men swimming back across the moat, closing on the grassland, where they climbed back up and ran for Aldegund’s camp. As his gaze strayed back to the walls he could see a thin line of greasy smoke rising into the clear air just outside the sigma.

‘Pig fat,’ snarled Quintillian. ‘We’re about to be neck deep in the shit.’ He turned, searching out that prefect below and attracted his attention even as shouts of alarm went up from the sparsely-manned walls over by the sigma.

‘Change of plan. Leave the sand, oil, rocks and forked sticks to deal with the Khan. He’s only a distraction. Get every archer and soldier to the sigma now!’

There was a deep, unsettling groan, and the stones shivered again. Kiva looked down nervously. ‘Are we in danger? Maybe we should abandon the Eyrie?’

Quintillian shook his head. 'That's just a ripple. It'll be felt all the way along this stretch of wall. The tower's in no danger, but if the sigma goes, we're going to have a real fight on our hands.'

Kiva returned his attention to the endangered walls, his heart rising into his throat at the sudden realization of the scale of the danger. Black, greasy smoke was now belching up into the blue. It must have been an impressive feat of engineering in dreadful conditions, removing several of the large stone blocks just above the waterline in torrential rain and probably waist-deep in freezing water, propping up the stones with timbers as they chipped away. Then, this morning, when they felt the hole was wide enough, stuffing in brush smeared with pig fat. They must have brought it across the water with them during the night in a waterproof bag – probably also sealed with pig fat. No doubt the bag was stuffed in there as well.

And whoever had planned it had known Velutio's walls well. The sigma was probably the weakest section of the entire circuit, having been rebuilt from the stones of the gate and using pieces of old columns and the like to fill in the gaps. In most other places, the wall's stones would be too large and well-set to even consider this in one night. But the rebuild had, Kiva remembered, been a rather haphazard affair. His father had always planned on a new rebuild, but it had ever been put off due to the lack of any kind of threat to the city. Well, they were paying for such short-sightedness now.

Men were running along the walls, desperately making for the area where a column of roiling black split the sky. Before Quintillian even pointed it out, Kiva spotted the gateway of Aldegund's camp opening. The walls gave another shudder and there was another ominous groan.

The only bright spark was the independent thinking artillerist who took the opportunity without orders to loose a bag of rocks from an onager that utterly obliterated the small group of miners slowly making their way back up the slope, their frozen legs numb and giving them difficulty. It was small revenge, though. A last judder and groan, and there was a horrible cracking noise before suddenly, and most spectacularly, the entire sigma stretch of wall split away from the straight ramparts to either side and began to lean out precariously. Kiva watched in dismay as the walls reached that critical point of balance and finally gave way, smashing out into the moat where they more or less formed a causeway across the water.

'But we still have the inner walls,' Kiva muttered in a shocked tone as he stared along the circuit to where a huge gap in the outer defences had opened up, granting an access to the enemy that would hardly even wet their feet.

'Yes, it's not over yet,' noted Quintillian, his expression grim, 'but it's a major blow. And if they managed to get through the outer wall in just two days, what *else* have they got planned for us?'

Now, Aldegund's forces were pouring out of his camp. Down along the wall, officers were shouting orders and temporary obstacles were being brought forward to form a makeshift rampart in the gap. Archers were lining the higher inner walls two deep, preparing to deal with the coming assault. Kiva stared in horror at the sheer number of men coming down that slope from the camp at the forest's edge. He slapped his palm on the pommel of his sword and straightened.

'What are you doing?' Quintillian asked quietly.

'I'm going to go and take part.'

'No, you're not.'

'Quint, this is the life or death of the city… of the *empire*! I have to be part of it. Think of the boost in morale it will give the men.'

'Think of the knock to their morale when you get skewered by some rebel archer's arrow. Not a chance you're going down there. I'll knock you out myself if you try.'

Kiva sighed and sagged against the stonework. His eyes strayed back to the nomads at the far side. At least the Khan's distraction was now collapsing. The ladders had all gone and the bridges were burning under sizzling pitch and white-hot sand. The remaining clansmen were racing back towards their camp. Their work done, the Khan's men were running back to lick their wounds, happy to leave the next assault to their barbarian allies.

Kiva watched in dismay as thousands of rebel soldiers and barbarians poured towards the gap in the walls. He felt the dreadful possibility that he was watching the death throes of the empire playing out before him. And even if they moved at the fastest speed possible, it would be days yet before Titus and Jala returned with any kind of support.

The bulk of the defensive force of Velutio – currently the entire imperial army in the northern and central regions – were converging on the ruined sigma, members of the imperial guard alongside the regular army, auxiliary units drawn from every region and citizen levy raised from the city itself. Every man who could wield a spear or sword or loose an arrow with any level of accuracy was arriving, archers finding positions up high, the rest preparing to face the enemy horde or helping construct the temporary redoubt to fill the gap.

He watched, counting off the time first in minutes, then in quarters, then halves, then hours, as the enemy reached the sigma and began the fight to gain the outer walls. As the sun rose higher and the few scattered clouds faded from the azure sky, the fight for the sigma raged on and the dead piled up. And at every count he made, Kiva wished he could be there with his people, fighting for the survival of his empire. But Quintillian was right. For every spirit that would rise with his presence, there would be two that would break should he die in the fight, and Kiva knew his ability with the senate and the councillors of the court and the administration of empire, but he also knew the limit of his martial talents, and knew that if one man were to be a viable leader down there it would be his brother, not he. Yet Quintillian remained atop the Eyrie with him, endlessly giving out streams of orders to the various officers to reinforce certain sections, reposition archers, draw men from other areas and so on.

Away by the sigma, only 60 or 70 paces from their viewing platform, barbarians raised axes and brought them down in killing blows, smashing bones, severing limbs and crushing bodies. Soldiers lanced out with their short imperial blades, neatly and efficiently dispatching the enemy. Archers loosed missiles into any enemy they could pick out. Aldegund's army had a vast superiority in numbers, but their advantage was largely negated by their limited approach. The fallen sigma was just 50 paces wide, and the rubble causeway approaching it the same, such that the bulk of the enemy were still snarled up on the far side, where four artillery pieces on the nearest towers continually pounded them, leaving smears of flesh and blood on the grass. Better yet, given the positions, the enemy could not get archers in any place where they could effectively attack the men at the walls, and so the beleaguered defenders fought on with lions' strength against an army that would, in an open field, simply swamp them.

Finally, as the world began to take on an indigo hue and the sun became a dome of gold over the city roofs to the west, the struggle came to an end. Someone among the besieging rebels decided that the fight would be too uncertain in the dark, and the enemy pulled back from the breach, staggering and running across the turf to Aldegund's camp. The artillery continued to loose into the retreating army until they reached a safe distance, and Kiva stared at the world in the wake of the siege.

The green sward before the rebel lord's camp was littered with dead, mangled and torn. Spears, arrows and desperate, imploring arms reached up from the ground like a sickly forest, and carrion animals both flying and walking were beginning to feed among the dead, pecking even at the wounded who feebly flapped at them, trying to stop the dreadful torture of their dying bodies. There was little green to be seen on the grass at all.

Closer to Velutio, the moat was a horrible brown colour, formed of churned mud and seas of blood, bodies bobbing on the water so thick they could almost form a causeway themselves. And the sigma?

It had been held.

By all the gods, the sigma had been held! There was no jubilation among the exhausted defenders, though, as they moved about the rubble and the makeshift barriers, rolling hundreds of dead barbarians and rebels away into the moat, reinforcing the temporary wall and seeing to their wounds.

'We can plug that gap a little better during the night,' Quintillian sighed with relief. 'Certainly we can make it strong enough to give us a better chance tomorrow, depending on what the enemy have planned next. For now, you and I need to get down there and pat some backs. Those men achieved the unachievable today and they deserve to be honoured.'

Kiva nodded his agreement, all words dying in his throat, and turned to follow his brother. Before they descended, he cast a last look at the site of the battle in the increasingly orange glow of the sunset.

They had made it through another day. How many *more* could they manage?

CHAPTER XXVII

Of Words and War

'I'd not expected that,' admitted Quintillian as he peered over the parapet, trying not to lean on the damp stonework. Though the sky was once again clear and blue, the night had brought with it a two-hour downpour that had left the world smelling damp and earthy again. While Kiva had grumbled about it, Quintillian had pointed out that a damp world meant that if the enemy decided to use fire their task would be made all the more difficult, and rain made archery troublesome too, so he, for one, was hoping for even more of a deluge. And, of course, the rain had washed away some of the filth from the battlefield, reducing the stench of death.

The defending garrison had mostly slept fitfully in place, sheltered from the rain only by cloaks and in short shifts as they worked to plug the gap at the sigma, and with dawn they were ready once more for the next assault. Though tired, the men were alert, watching both camps as best they could to be prepared for whatever the enemy had in mind this morning.

But it appeared that what they had in mind was a conversation.

A rider from the nomad camp had raced towards the walls not long after dawn, a long spear in his hand bearing a white streamer, and had planted the spear in the earth just out of bowshot of the wall. Though none of the defenders knew the customs of the nomads, it seemed clear that this was a call to parlay, and now, as the brothers watched from their lofty viewpoint, a small party of riders began to approach from the nomad camp.

Kiva turned to the runner standing by the stairs. 'Have our horses brought round and have Prefect Secutus gather a small honour guard.'

The man saluted and jogged off down the stairs, leaving the brothers alone on the tower once more. 'I cannot see how he can have anything constructive to say,' Quintillian muttered, 'but I would like to look into his eyes. Perhaps I can glean a clue as to what he has planned.'

Moments later the pair were racing down the stairs and in short order the gates were opened and the emperor and his marshal, along with a prefect and 20 imperial guardsmen in their gleaming scale shirts and black tunics were pounding across the bridge and out onto the wet grass. Fortunately, this area had not yet been involved in the fight, lying as it did in the mid-point between the nomad front and the barbarian one, and so the turf was clear of the bodies and debris that littered other stretches of the defences.

After two days of being trapped within the city there was something liberating about riding across open grass, regardless of the circumstances. Kiva smiled. He was not a lover of riding for leisure like his brother, and he had spent weeks on end never leaving the confines of Velutio, but the moment it became impossible to do so, he'd never realized how much he wanted to be out in the open.

The nomad deputation were already sitting by the spear with its limp, unmoving white streamer. The Khan was there, as well as his son and a mix of warriors and old men. The Khan's advisors, Kiva guessed from his brother's descriptions, and a few of the most senior chieftains. Kiva kept his smile small and bland, though inside he felt like grinning at the sight. The old Khan, an impressive looking man for all his age, and his son, a huge brute of a warrior, were sitting with their horses turned slightly away from each other, their gazes not meeting. Clearly something had happened and father and son were not currently on the best of terms. Knowledge like that was always of use.

'Great Khan,' Kiva said in a cool, clear voice with a nod of the head as one noble to another. The Khan nodded back.

'Emperor of the West. You are younger than I expected. I had it in the eye of my mind that you were older than your brother here.'

'That I am, but not by a great deal.'

The emperor turned to the huge warrior who was gazing out across the grass at the walls. 'Ganbaatar.'

The Khan's son turned a look of utter hatred and disgust on him, and Kiva almost laughed. These two would never command an army together without quarrelling. Add Aldegund into the mix and there were likely already factions forming in the enemy ranks. And if Kiva could just insert a pry-bar into the cracks and widen them, perhaps he could buy time for the city while they fought among themselves.

'You will not turn my son against me, young emperor.'

Kiva, surprised, turned back to the Khan. The old man had an amused smile and his eyes twinkled. The emperor quickly reassessed. This man was every bit as sharp as Quintillian had said. He realized in an instant that whatever argument there was between father and son, the Khan would always win it. In fact, it seemed certain now that Aldegund was little more than a captain in the Khan's great force.

'I will not waste my time or yours, young emperor.' The Khan smiled. 'We are all busy men, are we not? I am here to offer terms, as that is the thing a civilized leader does, and I would like to consider myself a civilized man.'

'I will hear your terms and decide what level of unacceptability they reach,' Kiva said with a sharp smile.

The Khan chuckled. 'My terms are very simple. I will accept the surrender of Velutio and, with it, the empire and your throne. Your officers and nobles will be given their choice of slavery or a clean, quick death as their own fears or pride demand. In return for this, I shall ensure that the people of your city, and your empire as a whole, remain unharmed and continue to live their lives free and uninterrupted under a new ruling dynasty.'

'You are too kind,' Quintillian snorted.

'You are almost certainly correct,' the Khan said, his face becoming serious. 'My son, as well as a sizeable group of my advisors and chieftains, all despise capitulation. They see it as a weakness beneath the honour of even a slave. The clans do not have a word for surrender. The concept is utterly alien to them. The nomad way of war is to fight until you are victorious or dead, and then, if the former, to rape and pillage as is the conqueror's right. Be aware, princelings, that it is only my tenuous control over these men that allows us to prosecute this war in any kind of civilized manner. I advise you to accept my terms, naturally. If you do not do so, then I will be forced to acknowledge the failure of diplomacy and the end of civilized behaviour, and to accept the course of action my advisors advocate.'

He straightened. 'In short, take my terms and save your people, or I will let my son and his cronies set the tone for the war and every living thing in Velutio will be killed, after the nomads have had their fun with the survivors first. Do we have an understanding?'

Kiva nodded. 'I understand that you want me to hand over the empire to you without a fight. I think you are uncertain about your ability to take Velutio in the end, and so you attempt to do so by words alone. I think that your son and his friends are correct. You are weak, Khan, and the empire cannot be ruled by weak men. I refuse your terms utterly. Velutio will defy you to the last man. If all that are left are old women and babes in arms, even they will take up a spear and refuse you. You will never rule here. At best you will conquer and control the greatest charnel house in the world.'

The Khan's lip twitched and Kiva, looking around, was gratified to note a look of hunger on Ganbaatar's face. Good. Stir up the hornets' nest and see if they start to sting one another.

'Foolish,' said the Khan. 'You are making a mistake for your people, young emperor. For I have no fear of your city and it will be mine within mere days. I can assure you of it.'

'My decision stands,' Kiva said, rolling his shoulders. 'The empire refuses you. I deny you.' He reached out and plucked the spear from the ground. For just a moment the gathered nomads reached for their weapons, suspecting trouble, but Kiva held the spear level and snapped the shaft across his saddle horns, casting the broken shards down to the wet grass. He had no idea what the custom was among these people, or even if they had one, but the message that sent should be clear.

The Khan gave him one last sour look and then turned, walking his horse back towards the nomad camp. Advisors and chieftains followed suit. The Khan's son, however, remained where he was, his gaze on Kiva for just a moment before it slid across to Quintillian.

'Your friend the slave died badly, *Ba'atu*. He lost his eyes, his tongue and his ears. I left him his nose so he could smell his own shit when he fouled himself at the end.'

Kiva saw Quintillian tense and remembered his account of Asander, the former soldier who had helped him escape the nomad city. 'Quint…' he murmured in warning. The marshal was nearing the edge of his temper, Kiva knew, and he couldn't accept any chance his brother might break the terms of a parlay.

'He was screaming for his mother at the end, just before I cut off his manhood and stuffed them in his face.'

'You do not frighten me, Ganbaatar,' Quintillian said quietly, through gritted teeth. 'You *disgust* me, but you do *not* frighten me. You are a simple wild animal on your father's leash.

'I will kill you before this is over, *Ba'atu*.'

'You are welcome to seek me out, Ganbaatar. I would love nothing more than to put a sword through that flapping mouth of yours.'

The nomad prince sneered. 'The pair of you together could not defeat me, princeling. Before my army swarm through your palaces and rape your women, I will kill both of you. I will balance your head at my hip with your brother's on the other. I swear it on the horse father.'

In answer, Quintillian simply wheeled his horse, turning his back on the brute, and began to walk it slowly back towards the gate. Kiva gestured to the prefect and the honour guard turned to escort them back. The Khan's son sat astride his horse with an unpleasant sneer plastered across his face until the imperial party reached the gate. Somewhere up in the towers, there came the sound of artillery being prepared.

'No one looses a shot!' Kiva shouted up at the battlements. 'Leave him.'

By the time the pair had entered the city once more and climbed to their accustomed place in the Eyrie, with its all-round excellent field of vision, Ganbaatar had gone.

'That went well,' Kiva said with an odd grin.

'I didn't think so,' Quintillian grunted.

'There are factions among the enemy, Quint. They're only budding at the moment, but given time we might well find the

Khan and his son at odds. And Aldegund never even attended. Was he invited, I wonder? The Khan never even mentioned his northern allies.'

'It's moot, Kiva. There'll never be enough time for the enemy to fall apart. You're the expert on reading people. Did you see the Khan's face when you told him you thought he was uncertain about his ability to take the city?'

Kiva shook his head. He'd been mid-speech at the time, trying to goad the man.

'Well, I did. I looked into his eyes. There was no uncertainty there, Kiva. The Khan is absolutely certain of his success. No hint of doubt. And when he said he'd have us within days, he meant it. He has his next step planned. He only sought a parlay because he wants to conquer an intact city, not a ruinous heap.'

The emperor sighed as he leaned on the damp parapet. 'What's next, then?'

'That.'

Kiva followed his brother's pointing finger up to the nomad camp. It took a moment for him to realize what it was they were looking at, but when he spotted it, his spirits sank a little further. The tall shapes of the Khan's siege engines were beginning to move.

'How do we deal with them?'

Quintillian shot him a sour look. 'We don't.'

'What?'

The marshal sighed. 'Our artillery is smaller by necessity, since they've been constructed on towers. Even given their increased height, they won't be effective unless the enemy bring theirs close. The Khan's weapons, on the other hand, are designed for distance and weight, to bring down walls. They can happily sit them outside our artillery range and they'll still be able to hit the outer walls, though maybe not the inner. Under normal siege circumstances I would order sallies of men – probably light horsemen with pitch buckets and torches – to burn the damn things. But these are not ordinary circumstances. We've precious few defenders as it is and the Khan has men he can just throw away, and will be willing to do so. Any sally we make is doomed to failure and will leave us even weaker. We can do nothing about them.'

Kiva was incredulous. 'So we just sit here and let them demolish the walls?

'We don't have much choice. There's one hope, and that's a combination of lack of experience and poor construction. There will be precious few trained artillerists even in Aldegund's army, and none in the Khan's, so there'll be a lot of messing up, and it'll take them a day or more to attain any real level of accuracy. And though the Khan was familiar with what he was building – presumably he'd been given designs by Aldegund – his men had never built them before. I expect that one in three or four will break or fail in some way, and the others will probably exhibit odd deficiencies. I'm willing to bet they will be able to hit the outer walls but if they want to hit the inner walls they'll have to bring them close enough to put them in danger of our own artillery. So we should still maintain the *inner* walls, no matter what.'

The two men watched in unhappy silence as the Khan's war machines were brought forth. The range of Velutio's artillery was easy enough to identify from the damage still visible on the greenery. The enemy did not seem inclined to collect their dead for burial and had apparently left them for the birds.

The hours wore on and the sun climbed to its zenith as the siege machines were manoeuvred slowly across the battlefield from the nomad camp towards that of Aldegund. Kiva didn't have to ask why. They were making for positions where they could concentrate on the ravaged sigma area. Sure enough, by early afternoon they were being loaded and prepared, just out of artillery range from the towers. The first engine loosed just as the bell in the city's high temple of Jovinus rang out the eighth hour of the day. The stone fell dreadfully short, a good bowshot short of the moat, even. The second and third shots went equally awry. By the time every war machine had loosed at least one shot, three missiles had disappeared into the moat with a ploop sound, and the rest were scattered around the churned, muddy turf opposite, their resting places lost amid the scattered corpses from the previous day.

By the time the same temple bell chimed the ninth hour, they were beginning to hit the already fractured stonework of the walls that flanked the sigma. From their viewpoint, Kiva watched helplessly as time and again huge boulders pounded into the defences and squared blocks, sections of parapet and pieces of wall the size of carts fell away into the moat. The enemy artillerists were not good, but the machines were numerous enough that sheer quantity was having the desired effect. The temple's tenth bell came with the beginning of sunset. The great golden orb slid slowly down behind them, and the city walls were now throwing out huge dark shadows across the carnage-littered turf. Over the hours, Kiva had watched the machines slowly and methodically pick away at the remaining defences, and the breach at the sigma had now widened from 50 paces to around 80. Quintillian's considered opinion was that the Khan was widening the gap to allow his army to flood the walls in force. The previous day had taught them how costly it was to try and secure the breach with only a narrow approach. The next time they would be able to send in enough men to overrun the defenders.

But, thought Kiva, that still wouldn't give them the inner walls, and not one stone had come that far all afternoon.

As he watched the shadows lengthen, something new was happening in the enemy camp. Kiva leaned heavily on the rampart and peered, squinting, into the dim light of dusk. A new machine had been brought from the nomad camp and was now being dragged into position in a gap between the other onagers. He frowned. A huge barrel of what looked like iron, seemingly beautifully decorated along its length and settled amid a wooden frame on eight great wheels, it took a team of two dozen horses to heave it into position. What fresh nightmare was this?

Even as he watched, the engine was secured in position and a cart appeared from behind. Sitting atop the cart was a huge stone sphere, almost perfectly carved. The cart was positioned in front of the machine and a ramp was carefully secured. Then, with surprising speed, a dozen men climbed onto the cart and slowly heaved the huge boulder forward inch by inch until it reached the gradient of the ramp, where it rolled, guided by grooves, into the huge tube. The clong as the stone sphere rolled to a halt in the metal cylinder was audible even at this distance.

'What is *that* thing?' he asked Quintillian.

The prince was frowning. 'I don't know. But I remember seeing it represented on the painting in the Khan's palace. It was on the ground behind the Khan's father in the beheading scene. Whatever it is, it's important and it's old, and it's come all the way from the lands of the Jade Emperor, just like that battering ram.'

There was a great deal of activity around the strange device and it seemed to be jacked up at the front several times. The enemy's siege engines fell silent suddenly, and Kiva and Quintillian looked at each other, tense.

The boom as the weapon discharged echoed around the surrounding hills and valleys for some time. Initially, the brothers could do nothing but stare at the machine which, upon firing, had rolled back quite some way, apparently killing and wounding some of its own crew. The smoke pouring from it suggested that the machine had been ruined during the explosion and it took quite a while before the shouting on the walls drew their attention.

Kiva had assumed that something had gone wrong. The Khan's new weapon had exploded. It might even have been destroyed. But as they turned to the sigma, drawn by the calls, both men felt their hearts lurch. The weapon had not failed at all. In fact, it had been used with perfect and deadly accuracy.

The huge, round stone had struck the high inner wall of Velutio through the gap left by the sigma with such force that it had almost brought the whole section of wall down on its own. The depression in the stonework left by the blow was the epicentre of a whole web of cracks and ruptures that spread across the surface as far as the towers to either side. The boulder itself, as far across as a big man was tall, had shattered on impact and now lay in two pieces at the foot of the wall.

The brothers stared at the badly-damaged wall. The men atop that section were now fleeing it for the relative safety of the ramparts to either side.

'Gods, what *is* that thing?'

'Some kind of new onager, obviously,' Quintillian breathed. 'I knew he was up to something. The Khan was too confident for comfort at the meeting this morning.'

'Do you think it broke? There was a lot of smoke.'

'I don't think so. See?' They peered into the gathering gloom. 'They're readying it the same as they did when they arrived. They plan to use it again.'

'I don't see a second boulder.'

'No, but they must have one, else they wouldn't be readying it.'

Kiva peered back at the shattered stonework of the world's most powerful walls. 'Will the defences survive another of those?'

'Who can say? I wouldn't place good money on it, though. And if they can fire *two* shots, then they're probably prepared for more too. I can half imagine a row of those carts lined up at the back. It's too late in the day. They won't use it again now, as it'll be dark in half an hour. See how a huge force of Aldegund's men has come out to guard it. There's not even a chance of us getting close enough to sabotage it. And I wouldn't know how to sabotage an iron tube even if I got there.'

'So we can expect it again in the morning?'

'I'm afraid so. It looks disastrously like the inner walls will go tomorrow morning.'

Kiva swallowed nervously. 'Then we've lost Velutio.'

Quintillian turned to him, a hard, determined look in his eyes. 'We've lost the *walls*, Kiva. At this point *just* the walls.'

'But losing the walls means losing the city?'

Quintillian fixed him with a flinty look. 'What makes the empire?'

Kiva's brow folded at the question, but slowly he began to nod his understanding. 'The people, Quint.'

'Precisely. Land can always be recovered. Walls can be rebuilt. People are the only thing that matter. As long as you save the people, you preserve the empire. And we still have to believe that Titus and Jala have succeeded – that Ashar will come. Despite everything that's happened this year, he's our oldest ally. Once he knows Jala is safe, he will want the head of the man responsible, and that's Aldegund.'

'So we drag it out.'

'We drag it out, Kiva. We fight to the last to give our friends time to come to our aid. As long as the people survive.'

'So we get the people out,' the emperor nodded. 'Pull them back to… to the palace?'

'Yes. It's the biggest palace in the world. And since half the population left before the enemy arrived there should be room to shelter them within it. And the palace has strong walls. Maybe not as strong as these ones, but strong enough. The Khan couldn't possibly bring his monster or the big stone-throwers through the city. He'll have to take the palace the hard way – by steel and sinew.'

'And what happens when he does?' Kiva asked quietly. 'I mean, if Ashar doesn't come in time. We both know the enemy are numerous enough to overwhelm us quickly.'

Quintillian slapped his fist into his palm.

'We make the enemy pay for every street they take. Once the wall falls we get every armed man in to pull down houses and barricade streets. We make rat traps and killing zones for the archers. We make it impossible to get horses and bolt-throwers up the streets to the top. We slow them down by making them fight hard for every alley. And while we're doing that, the civilians begin to abandon the palace. They can leave one ship at a time through the dangerous straits to the island of Isera and the summer palace. They'll be safe there for days. That will hopefully buy us all the time we need. Even if all of Velutio falls, Isera can hold until Ashar arrives.'

Kiva nodded. 'I shall instruct the officials to start pulling everyone back to the palace and to begin shipping them to Isera immediately, along with adequate food and supplies for two weeks.'

Quintillian took a deep breath. 'And I shall obtain a plan of the city and begin working on blockading streets and turning it into a death trap for the Khan and his allies.'

Beyond the wall, torches began to spring to life along the line of the enemy. Now, between Aldegund's fort to the north and the camp of the Khan to the east, the enemy war machines and their enormous military guard filled the gap, sealing off the landward approaches to the city entirely.

Kiva peered at that huge iron tube, golden reflections of the torches dancing along its length like fireflies.

Tomorrow, Velutio would fall.

CHAPTER XXVIII

Of Final Preparations

The fourth day of the siege of Velutio dawned grey and miserable. Although the rain had yet to fall, the ground had been given a wet sheen by a heavy morning mist, and the air was hazy and filled with droplets. Fitting weather for the last day of an empire, in Kiva's opinion.

He and Quintillian had watched from the very first light as the enemy brought their ammunition carts from the rear of the camp. If the defenders had still harboured any hope of the walls holding and the city making it through another day, the sight of seven vehicles rumbling slowly into the war machine zone, each bearing a huge stone sphere, killed it. Kiva had felt a lurch of dreadful certainty then. Quintillian had said that the walls might take two more strikes but no *more* than that. Would the enemy, angry at the defiant city, just launch all their remaining missiles into the heart of Velutio?

He looked along the walls. They were almost empty. A sparse scattering of soldiers remained, purely to give the illusion of barely-adequate defence. The rest had been busy through the hours of darkness, sleeping in four-hour shifts in order to best use what little time they had. The civilians were all now in the palace at the highest point of Velutio, and ships were steadily ferrying 100 people at a time, crammed among the hold, the oar benches and the narrow walkway, from palace to island. The isle of Isera had served many purposes in its time. From summer palace of the emperors to prison during the civil war, it had become a retreat of learning and academia under Kiva's father. Now it would be a haven. Surrounded by an impenetrable ring of deadly rocks that barred all external shipping, the only access to the island was a narrow channel from the city of Velutio. Now the island was filling with citizenry, ships plying that channel back and forth time and again, despite the fact that only brave captains sailed the dangerous route even in the day, let alone during the hours of darkness.

The people of the empire would make their last stand on Isera. And if Titus and Jala and the might of empire and god-king combined didn't come, Isera would serve out its time in a new way: as a cemetery and a memorial to a vanished empire.

A crash from behind made Kiva wince, and he turned to see a mushroom of dust rise above the Forum of the Bull, some two thirds of the way up the slope to the palace. The once great Library of Carius was no more, its glorious brick and marble façade, which had been lauded by a millennium of architects, now scattered across the road as rubble, forming a barrier to the enemy. A tear formed in the corner of Kiva's eye and he wiped it angrily away. This was no time for misplaced sentimentality, though he wondered in passing if the officer in charge there had had the foresight to remove 100 generations of learning and literature from the building before destroying it.

Similar puffs of dust on a smaller scale were rising all over the city as street after street became a trap in the new labyrinth that was Velutio. The emperor heaved a sigh of regret and turned his back on his city to watch the activity among the siege engines. Even now a cart was being manoeuvred into position in front of the huge iron city-killer. The brothers watched from their lofty perch as a gang of men heaved the boulder down the ramp and into the tube and the cart was removed. A flurry of activity, and finally the crew stepped as far away from the dangerous weapon as they could. A pair of men stayed at the side of the tube and carried out whatever arcane procedure primed the machine. There was an ominous silence suddenly among the enemy, and an officer near the sigma breach called for the soldiers on the walls to stay where they were and be ready.

The enormous boom once more echoed around the hills but, unlike yesterday's first shot, this time the two sons of Darius on the parapet of the Eyrie knew what to expect. Rather than staring in befuddlement at the weapon, they watched the boulder hit the huge inner walls of Velutio. The effect was devastating. The rock hit close to the site of the previous shot, the machine not having been moved, just sunk slightly into the damp turf overnight. The impact struck the stonework about two yards below the previous indentation. Miraculously, the wall stayed up, though the top swayed alarmingly for a moment. Even from here, Kiva could see that there was a tiny fissure in the wall that went right the way through, as well as the two huge dents and the now omnipresent cracks that spidered across the surface. Kiva had been right. Another blow anywhere near centre and the wall was gone.

And when that wall went, the enemy would be in the city in force. The damage the lesser war machines had done to the outer walls had widened the breach enough that more than twice as many men would be able to assault the gap now as had in that earlier attempt. There was simply no hope of the beleaguered defenders holding the sigma. It was a lost cause.

Kiva turned and glanced across the battlefield. Again, the dreadful machine was wreathed in smoke and had rolled back an impressive distance. And yet already people were heaving it into position with the aid of teams of horses while the next cart was brought forward. A quarter of an hour was Kiva's estimate, based on the previous firing. Then the machine would ring out again and Velutio would be open to the invader. Echoing footsteps drew his attention to the opening at the top of the tower's staircase, and a man in a prefect's uniform, his black plume plastered to his bronze helmet in the damp air, emerged onto the tower top, heaving in breaths.

'It's time, sirs,' he said quietly. Quintillian nodded and gestured for the man to lead on before following. Kiva watched for a moment as that great iron tube was slowly trundled back into position, then his gaze slipped down to the walls by the sigma and along in first one direction and then the other. The men were leaving the ramparts. It was time.

'Majesty,' called Quintillian from the doorway of the stairs.

Kiva nodded, but his gaze swept on, taking in the remains of the city. Over it hung a pall of grey dust, and the grand roofs and delicate spires that marked 100 generations of construction were all but gone. The night had seen demolition on a scale undreamed of. Could Velutio possibly look any worse after it fell to the enemy?

'*Kiva*,' urged his brother from the doorway.

With a last sigh, the emperor tore his eyes from his ruined city and entered the stairwell, following Quintillian and the prefect down the seemingly endless flights to the ground. There, outside the tower in the Forum of Swords where military parades traditionally began and displays of martial prowess were the norm, a small party of the imperial guard awaited. There were no other soldiers visible, though the shouts of officers manoeuvring men into position around the city-labyrinth were omnipresent.

A hand grasped his shoulder unexpectedly – something unheard of for the emperor, since no one would dare try such a thing. He turned to find Quintillian beside him, a grave, determined look on his face.

'Time for you to go the palace and, when the time comes, to the island.'

Kiva frowned. 'Not a chance, Quint.'

'Kiva, you are the emperor. People look to you as the head of state. They need someone to follow and to feel is looking after them. That is your job – your responsibility. You are *their* emperor. And just as the people have to survive, if there is to be an empire, the emperor has to survive too.'

'Rubbish,' Kiva snapped. 'If the civil war, the fall of mad old Quintus and the rise of our father taught us anything it's that emperors can come and go. They can be found hiding under a bush or working in a tannery. There are a hundred men in this city alone that could rule as wisely as I.'

'Kiva.'

'No,' the emperor said with an air of finality. 'Say what you will but it'll fall on deaf ears. I will not stand in the background and watch empire and city crumble before me. If it must happen then I will do whatever I can to stop it. I can do no less.'

Quintillian narrowed his eyes at Kiva, grasping both shoulders. 'Then stay with me, brother, but stay *behind* me. I will not be the man who let the emperor die in our hour of need. Stay with us and bring heart to your men by presence alone, but I will not let you get close enough to the enemy to wet your blade. Do you understand?'

The two men locked eyes for long moments, engaged in a battle of wills. Finally, Kiva nodded. This was not the time. The time was coming, and it was coming today. Just not quite yet.

'All right. Where first?'

Quintillian turned to the prefect. 'Are the lines drawn up?'

The officer bowed his head. 'They are ready at the sigma, and each unit designated last night is in position, sir.'

'Good. All right, Majesty. We oversee the last defence of the sigma and the prefect will give us a nod when the lines are about to fail. Then we fall back to the next position, and the next, and so on until we reach the palace gates. Got it?'

'Agreed,' Kiva nodded, and the small party hurried through the streets towards the sigma. As they reached the Square of Stone Demons with its grotesque statuary poking from each building corner, their mouths jetting water from high gutters, Kiva felt his breath catch in his throat. Here had once been the Demon Gate. The outer gate had gone entirely and been replaced with the shoddy sigma wall that had been so easily overcome. The inner gate had simply been walled shut and reinforced. The only signs of it ever having existed were a roughly arch-shaped line of lighter stone in the smooth surface, and the marks of where twin turrets had been dismantled, their shape still visible in the stonework underfoot.

Only now there was a new mark. A hole halfway up, with cracks spreading from it across the stone surface. The square itself stood empty, ominously so. And then Kiva spotted the defenders waiting, gathered in the streets and alleys that led off the open space. Barely had the emperor and his entourage moved into position with the tense soldiery, when a deep booming noise heralded the third shot of the dreadful weapon.

Kiva watched the walls of Velutio fall in spectacular proximity. All he could see of the actual strike from this side of the defences was its effect. Huge shards of smooth stone flew out from the wall, followed by the compacted and mortared rubble that formed the core of the structure. Even this far back, Kiva felt the blast as a wave of stinging dust that swept across the defenders. The hole at the centre had not widened, but where there had been a cobweb of cracks across the surface before, now there were deep fissures, yawning in the stonework. There was a groan like the complaining of giants, as though the earth itself moaned, and then the wall shuddered. Kiva, a long-time student of architecture, found his sight drawn up to the joins at either side where the wall met each of the two adjacent towers. Sure enough the stones there were cracking and tearing away from the huge square bulks. There was another groan, and a sound like a paving slab being snapped, though magnified in volume a thousand times.

And the wall fell. It began so slowly, with the stonework tearing away to either side and the centre bowing towards them. Then, when the wall was leaning precariously enough that Kiva fancied he could almost see the outer parapet over the top, the sides gave way. The entire stretch of wall slowly toppled inward, the centre coming down faster, the fissures and depressions in it weakening the stonework there more than elsewhere.

There was a sound like an armoured god falling to the ground, and Kiva went deaf. For a moment it was as though he was lost in an all-consuming fog. All sound had gone except a whistling in his ears, and beyond the men to either side of him, all was a tan-grey colour as the cloud of dust billowed around the square. Gradually the aural whining began to die down and over the top of it he could hear the sound of hundreds of men coughing. He too was coughing, he suddenly realized.

The dust settled very slowly, but gradually the scene coalesced through the murk and Kiva's nerves twitched. The walls of Velutio had gone. A slope of stones projected from the two nearest towers, but all that remained of the defences in between was a sea of rubble, pock-marked by huge chunks of stonework that had survived the fall, some still displaying the crenellations of the battlements.

And slowly another shape resolved in the dust. A dark cloud beyond began to take the form of a tide of humanity flowing towards them, barbarians and rebel soldiers and nomad horsemen all massing around the hole in Velutio's defences. Men would be dying in the press, soldiers and barbarians crushed under the hooves of nomad horses, for this was a simple swarm of mixed enemies with no plan and no order. The Khan could organize his army only so far, but he was astute enough to recognize that when the city became open to them, no words in the world would be capable of instilling order in the resulting attack. The barbarians and the nomads alike would simply devolve into an orgy of death and rapine.

From the Square of Stone Demons issued six streets. Two led along the inside of the walls, and these had been partially blockaded, though the collapsing wall had largely sealed them off anyway. Two more led off north and south, parallel to the walls and one block further back. One of these was blocked thoroughly as a stables and a tavern had been pulled down to seal it off. The other was filled with worried-looking soldiers. Similarly, of the two streets that led west towards the heart of Velutio, one had been blocked with the rubble of a cooper's shop and a house, and the other contained Kiva and the forces of the city. They would not hold the enemy here for long, but every quarter-hour another ship left the palace taking the innocent citizens off to the island, and so every quarter-hour they held here meant that another hundred people might live.

The forces of the Khan and Lord Aldegund poured into the city across the still-settling ruins of the wall. Several were injured or killed by sliding or falling rubble in their desperation to bring death to Velutio. It was a chaotic invasion. Men simply swarmed wherever they felt looked best, which meant that every exit, blocked or not, was targeted by the enemy. A few tried to climb the blocked streets alongside the walls, but that quickly proved too troublesome, and they gave up, rejoining the mass. Others poured into the blocked streets. Kiva, standing near the rear of the force and atop a raised platform which granted him and his brother an excellent view of the action despite the dust cloud, felt a small surge of hope as he watched those doomed invaders.

Archers were not prized by the imperial army, or rather had not been so traditionally. Since the interregnum and the rise of the mercenary armies, the value of missile troops had become more recognized, and yet still archers were generally drawn from the lesser classes of the more provincial regions, with the hardy citizens of the old imperial centre forming the traditional heavy infantry. Yet the archers, for all their lesser status, were today proving their value.

Those two streets that had become blockaded dead-ends quickly filled with the enemy, attempting to climb the rubble and descend into the streets beyond. But as the first man – a spear-wielding barbarian with black, braided hair and a beard like a badger –

began to crest the mound of rubble, an arrow whirred from the upper storeys of one of the surrounding buildings and took him full in the face. He toppled, dead immediately, onto the detritus. Behind him, two more barbarians, both hungry for battle, suddenly looked up in surprise at the falling man. Arrows took one in the throat and the other in the chest, and both fell, adding their bodies to the barricade.

As if that had been a cue for the archers, arrows began to hiss and whirr through the air from all the high places, some in the streets leading off picking the targets and carefully holding back the tide, others simply loosing randomly into the crowd, where aiming was unnecessary and every missile would injure or kill, even if it was released blind.

And then Kiva could no longer watch the overall situation unfold, for the street that he occupied became a battlefield itself. Three hundred soldiers formed a barricade of their own, six-men deep with the front a shield-wall and the next two files jabbing over the top with long spears. The officers at the rear shouted orders and archers in windows above loosed into the press beyond, but the men at the front of the defences took the brunt of it. The shield-wall buckled and bowed repeatedly as the soldiers were pushed and buffeted back by the sheer weight of the enemy pressing against them. As spears lanced out overheard, striking eyes and temples, ripping into skulls and necks, the soldiers engaged in the shield-wall itself thrust out again and again with their blades, tilting their shields for a single heartbeat to allow the sword the space to do its work, then closing the wall again. The nomads, screaming their rage in their odd tongue, were falling like leaves from an autumn tree, and with every passing minute, the pile of dead grew, the attackers finding it a chore and a boon at one and the same time for, though it was difficult footing crossing the pile of dead, the height of the body pile was beginning to give them the slightest advantage over the men of the shield-wall.

Kiva watched from the back as gradually men in the front line began to die and those in the rear ranks shuffled forward to take their place. Each time the man in the second rank threw his spear over into the crowd and slipped into the line in front, drawing his sword and taking his place in the wall. Then those in further ranks began to shuffle forward too.

Time passed in a sea of carnage. The air filled with the tinny tang of blood and the stench of opened bowels that managed even to overcome the cloying cloud of still-settling dust. Kiva watched while the men in the rear lines started to thin out as they continually moved forward to plug gaps. He could see each and every death as he watched. A nomad smashed through the mouth with an imperial blade, fragments of white tooth and bone flying through the air with the spray of blood. And even as that ruined face fell away a barbarian who had lifted his arm to stab down at the line received an imperial blade in the armpit, the blow hard and deep, blood fountaining out. But the soldier had trouble removing his sword in time and as the corpse fell away it took the blade with it. The desperate soldier tried to recover, but a howling nomad with a short, curved sword jammed it to the soldier's neck and ripped it upward, yelling triumphantly as he cut the throat so deep he almost beheaded the man.

The soldier had barely hit the ground before another was in his place.

Death stalked the streets of Velutio, lapping up the carnage.

A hammer blow to a soldier's face that crushed his skull into his own brain.

A nomad taken through the neck by a spear from the second line, blood jetting from the wound around the shaft.

A barbarian stabbed between the ribs by a well-aimed blow that pierced the heart in a fountain of crimson.

A severed hand, still gripping a knife as it cartwheeled through the air.

Bone. Blood. Torn flesh. Severed appendages.

Kiva felt sick. He had seen battle twice in his life, both times from the comfort of the command position. Never had he experienced the horrifying gore and stench of real combat this close. Next to him, Quintillian was watching with a professional eye. Nothing seemed to faze the younger son of Darius.

'Time to go, Majesty,' a prefect said loudly from nearby.

'What?'

'We barely have enough men to plug a gap now, sire. This shield-wall will fall in minutes.'

Quintillian nodded and grasped Kiva's tunic. 'Come on.'

'Where are we going?'

'Through the maze.'

The next hour was the most fraught, heart-stopping, vomit-inducing and horrifying of Kiva's life. He only realized that they had held the enemy at the square for half an hour when Quintillian pointed it out. It had seemed like mere moments. He'd panicked that they'd fallen too quickly, but the knowledge that the grisly fight at the blocked street had saved 200 citizens gave him heart. Then, as they pulled back gradually through Velutio, he kept estimating the time and nodding to himself every time he pictured another ship sailing to safety with 100 innocents on board. Four more as the pair retreated up the slope. And during that hour they occupied three different blockades with the troops assigned there, the emperor's presence giving much needed heart to the defenders.

The blockade on the Street of Western Brewers had fallen hard, one of the city's most popular breweries having been torn down and felled across the narrow street along with two private houses. The enemy bodies there piled up in the hundreds as the 120 defenders fell to such an extent that the imperial party was urged on again before the barricade fell. Kiva had been sad to move on. After so long wallowing in the stench of blood and shit, the smell of the hoppy beer from the ruined brewery that ran endlessly between the cobbles and even managed to drown out the miasma of battle had been more than welcome.

The Street of Golden Statues fell quickly. With only 100 defenders, some wily enemy found a way into one of the adjacent houses and managed to circumvent the barricade, he and those who went with him falling on the poor bastard defenders from behind. Kiva and Quintillian were sent on by a captain, up the hill towards the palace once more.

The barricade in the Street of the Troubled God held well. Though it had been assigned only 70 men, it was one of the narrowest thoroughfares in the city with some of the tallest buildings, and the resulting barricade was impressive. There they had held for so long that Kiva had even begun to hope they could keep the tide of enemies back.

It was foolish, of course, for this was only one branch of the invading army. A sea of men flowed through every possible street across the city, and when he and Quintillian were taken to a viewpoint in an old belfry, the emperor stared in disbelief, only now recognizing the true hopelessness of the situation. The defenders had been pushed back two thirds of the way up the city, and still the enemy were crossing the walls far below, hungry to bite into flesh with their blades. It simply boggled the mind to imagine how many men the Khan and the rebel lord had between them.

'The palace,' Quintillian said quietly. 'The last barricades will fall quickly. We have to get to the palace and defend there before you and I get trapped. We can hold the palace for hours while the civilians leave. Then we will make our last stand. Half the military in the city are waiting there, and we have artillery on the walls.'

Kiva nodded, and the two men ran on, still accompanied by the imperial guard. They reached the great Imperial Way, which remained clear as it was simply too wide to consider blockading effectively. Kiva was hurried through the great gate and into the tenuous safety of the palace, the immense portal slamming shut behind him like the boom of a heavy tomb lid. Quickly, they hurried to the top of the gate tower. The palace grounds were filled with people – the ordinary folk of Velutio milling about in nervous tension, waiting in borderline panic for their turn to board the ships. The doorway to the harbour stairs was blocked with people trying to muscle their way further forward in the queue as officers held them back. That heavy doorway led to a long sloping staircase through the rock that descended to the bottom of the cliff and the sheltered, secure palace harbour where ships would be coming and going repeatedly. There were only four ships in the waterway between Velutio and Isera, and they would be on the move constantly.

The walls were filled with soldiers and artillery, auxiliary archers and those stalwart citizens who had answered the final call to arms and taken up bows, slings, spears and even handfuls of rocks to hurl down on the enemy. Here and there below on the ground, officers directed the milling public. It looked like chaos, but Kiva knew just how well organized it truly was, for he had planned the evacuation himself.

Turning, he looked down at his city and bit back a cry of dismay. Already the enemy had reached the Imperial Way. A last unit of a dozen soldiers fleeing for the safety of the palace were swiftly overrun by nomads and barbarians alike, their screams lost in the general din. Columns of smoke arose here and there where the more vicious and shortsighted invaders fired buildings, but even then those fires were being gradually extinguished by other men – those directed by the Khan or Aldegund, clearly – in order to make sure that the end of the day would see them victoriously occupying a city and not just a pile of ash.

'They're nearly here, Quint.'

'Don't worry, Majesty, we'll hold them outside the palace until nightfall. They can't bring artillery to bear and we can push back siege ladders. The only way they'll get in at the end is when they break down a gate. It'll take them hours to get a ram up here and in position, and more than an hour to break through a gate. And even now, all the palace gates are being blocked from inside, buying us more time. We're not done for yet. With the gods' favour we'll see another dawn in Velutio, even if we have to do it from a ship.'

The marshal straightened.

'Which leads me to my next order. It's time you went, Kiva.'

'What?'

'No matter how long we hold the palace, the emperor needs to be safe. And the only way I can run a solid defence here is in the secure knowledge that you're out of danger.'

'Quintillian, I'm not leaving you here to die on the walls.'

His brother gave him a wan smile. 'Now, Kiva, you know as well as I that someone in authority has to stay and maintain the last defence. It has to be a marshal, really, and I'm the only one in the city. And we both know that there's an unspoken trouble between us, too. This is a solution to that, if not an elegant one.'

Kiva stared at his brother, and Quintillian shrugged with an odd smile. 'We've never spoken about it since I returned, but we both know what I'm talking about. And when she comes back, the empire will be whole again, even if it has to be an empire in exile.'

'No, Quint.'

'Don't be an idiot, Kiva. You know that even if we win the day and save Velutio, there is no viable future with all three of us living under the same palace roof. What do you think drove me from the city all those months ago? What drove Jala back to Pelasia? It's a neat little solution, and it suits me. I've no family to leave other than you, and whether we win or lose, I'll go down in the histories as the last man in Velutio.' He chuckled. 'If you want to make it better, deify me afterwards.'

Kiva simply stared. 'I've not bloodied this in the defence of my own realm,' he said, tapping the hilt of the sword at his side.

Quintillian shrugged. 'One of us is the fighter, one is the thinker. It's always been that way.'

'It has,' Kiva admitted, drawing the blade and examining his distorted reflection in the cold steel.

'Careful with that. I don't want gutting before I can do my job.' Quintillian laughed hollowly, and turned as an officer shouted something about ladders.

Kiva struck fast. He was no trained warrior and had precious little experience of the fight, but he had experienced the same endless hours of boyhood training as Quintillian and, for all his lack of practice, he knew what the blunt end was for just as well as the pointed one.

The round wooden pommel with the bronze rivet smacked into the side of Quintillian's head with a sickening noise and for a moment Kiva panicked that he had killed his brother. But as the officers and men atop the gate rushed over to the fallen prince-marshal, Kiva knelt and checked. Quintillian was breathing. His pulse was steady. He was unconscious.

'Take the prince to the harbour. I want him bound for Isera on the very next ship. I want a guard of four men on him and his sword and dagger are to be removed. If he wakes and tries to leave the island, restrain him any way you can. Prince Quintillian stays on Isera until this is over one way or another.'

The guard officer gave him an uncertain look. 'Majesty, we have set orders from the marshal.'

'Who I outrank, if you remember. You are being given an imperial command from the lips of the emperor himself. In our final hours will you deny me, Prefect?'

The officer snapped to attention and saluted. 'Of course not, sire.'

'Good. Now take him.'

The emperor straightened as the guards gently lifted Quintillian's limp form from the stone flags and made for the staircase. Kiva watched with an odd feeling of relief. For a decade he had been groomed for power and then reigned as emperor of the greatest nation the world had ever known. And yet, despite the fact that his brother had always accepted their relative positions with comfort, Kiva had known that for all his organizational skills, the empire would have been stronger under Quintillian. And Jala had been a good empress and the perfect consort, but while Kiva loved her unconditionally, it was now clear to him that she had always loved Quintillian.

True, someone in authority had to lead the last defence of Velutio. But Quintillian had been wrong about one thing. It didn't have to be a marshal. And Kiva would, in the end, be the one to go down in the stories.

He smiled. It really was an unexpected relief. He gripped the sword still and examined his face in the blade. No longer the face of an emperor, now the face of a general. He rolled his shoulders, lowered the sword and strode over to where a prefect was tapping a set of plans of the palace and giving out orders to captains.

'Am I to understand that my brother has already organized the defence of the palace with you and the other officers?'

The prefect turned and saluted. 'That he did, Majesty.'

'Tell me everything. And do it quick. The enemy are at the gates.'

Overhead, unheeding of the troubles of the earth, the sun reached its zenith and shone down on an emperor organizing the last day of his life.

CHAPTER XXIX

Of the Fall of Empires

Kiva heaved in a breath, trying to prevent his knees from trembling. He'd not the heart to shout at the prefects and captains defending the palace, but it had irritated him more and more as the afternoon wore on that no imperial soldier would let the emperor into a situation where he might bloody his blade. He'd gone along with it, for the morale boost his mere presence gave the men was clear, but despite that, they needed every sword they could get.

There had been 1200 and some men on the walls of the palace when the Khan's army began to move up the Imperial Way. A number that was lost and insignificant against the enormous army the enemy fielded, but enough to hold for some time.

And yet they had to hold longer. The sun was sliding down the sky to the west, closing on the horizon across the Nymphaean Sea, and if people had followed Kiva's evacuation plans to the letter and the Lady of Fortune had been watching over them throughout, the last civilians should have been shipped away by now. But periodic reports brought to the emperor by sour-faced runners told increasingly unpleasant tales. One captain had lost a steering oar and his ship had foundered on the rocks. There were no details yet as to the casualties, but the awful truth was that no matter how many survived at the moment, clinging to the dreadful rocks in the last rays of the sun, the morning would see *no* survivors, for there could be no rescue mounted and the survivors would drown or starve. Then another of the four ships had suffered some kind of calamity and though it remained intact, it also remained docked on Isera. And so the evacuation had slowed to half the pace. The increasing panic among the remaining trapped refugees had led to numerous outbreaks of violence. Men, women and children had been injured and killed in surges as the mob tried to flood the ships. The forces down there in the harbour were struggling to maintain control and despite their own peril, Kiva had sent 20 more men to the ships to reimpose order.

So now, with the last of the day fading behind him, Kiva was faced with an impossible task. There were still over 1000 people – probably twice that – at the harbour, waiting for the next of the ships, which were now sailing only once every half hour. That meant they needed anywhere between five and ten hours to evacuate everyone.

They had held the palace walls and gates for eight hours against the most incredible odds, purely because the enemy were unable to find an easy way to get to them. They had been secure. And then, an hour ago, one of the lesser palace gates had fallen. It had not been unexpected, and in the preceding quarter of an hour the palace grounds had been secured, but it was a step closer to the end, and a huge one at that. The remaining civilians were now all down in the harbour and the door to the harbour stairway was very secure, so they at least were safe for now. But the palace grounds were as full of the enemy as the city outside. Over the afternoon the four stairways up to the wall walks had been demolished and all the doors leading from the grounds into the critical buildings sealed from the inside and blocked. The defenders were trapped on the walls above, and the attackers in the grounds below, but something would change very soon. The archers atop the palace had run out of arrows mid-afternoon, and even the civilian volunteers had run out of rocks to cast and were now throwing down roof tiles and the like. The Khan's men, on the other hand, were still well-supplied, and arrows from the excellent bows of the nomads repeatedly clattered against the battlements above. The wall height and the angles made the soldiers hard to target, but the enemy were good and so numerous that inevitably the defenders were being whittled away. Kiva could rarely count to 100 without hearing a scream somewhere atop the walls.

'Prefect, how are we doing?'

The officer, a drawn, serious face jammed between a dented helmet and a sweaty tunic, coughed. 'Last count we had three hundred and twenty-five, of which more than thirty were civilian levies. But there have been a number of casualties since then, Majesty.'

'And the situation.'

'Dire, Majesty. They've broken into the guardhouse, the servants' quarters and the Palace of Theodron. The guardhouse and the palace are both fairly well secured from here, but the servants' quarters are a problem.'

Kiva nodded. The servants, by the very nature of their work, needed access to almost everywhere. Consequently doors, stairs and passages left that complex to almost everywhere else in the palace. The defenders had blockaded what they could, but if there was a weak spot, it was there.

'Sire, they're on the floor below us. It's only a matter of time before they break through that last door, and then they'll be on the wall top. And once one man gets up here, the whole lot will follow.'

Kiva nodded again. 'Then we pull back again. Make our last stand on the roof of the imperial apartments. That's directly above the harbour, so we can watch for the last men leaving, and access to it from the rest of the roofs is just from two narrow wall walks. We can hold those longer than most places.'

The prefect nodded, though Kiva suspected from his expression he felt like arguing. They could hold as long as the fight came down to strength of arms. But if the enemy came up with their bows and decided to send an arrow storm across from one roof to another, the defending force would be halved in a heartbeat.

'I shall give the order, Majesty.'

Kiva took a deep breath. Heart or no heart, the emperor could no longer hold himself back from the fight. His arm and blade needed to be added to the forces for this last struggle. There seemed almost no chance all the civilians in the harbour would escape, but if the army fought like lions, another hundred or two might make it, and numbers were what counted now.

The emperor strolled along the wall walk as though he had not a care in the world. An arrow clacked off the stonework a few paces from him, but he ignored it, even though he shook inside. He would be strong to the end for his people. They were dying to preserve what they could of the empire, and he couldn't ask any man to do more than he was willing himself.

The roof of the imperial apartments was perhaps the best place to be if there was likely to be a cloud of arrows. Great fireplaces inside meant that chimney stacks rose here and there, and the rooms that were not host to such fires were heated with the circulatory hot air that rushed through cavities underfloor and through hollow tiles in the walls. The projecting hollows that released the air from that system meant further cover. Then there was the domed roof of the octagonal chamber, several raised skylights and a few other miscellaneous lumps and bumps. Agile and lucky men could escape a few arrows there.

Around him, as he found a good observation point, the last defenders of Velutio took their positions. The sun began to touch the horizon far to the west, and the channel from the city to the island of Isera was now thrown into deep shadow. Out across the lawns of the imperial palace, some nomad scum was standing atop the memorial statue to the emperor's grandfather and namesake, Kiva Caerdin, who had once been crucified upon that very spot. If only they still had archers, that bastard would pay for defiling the statue with his presence.

There was a distant cracking and splintering noise, and suddenly men were flooding out onto the roof of the palace. A wall walk of 50 paces was all that now separated the Khan's men from the last defenders of the city.

'Places!' yelled the prefect, and men fell into position at the end of that wall walk, shields locked together in one last shield-wall. Possibly the last the empire would ever raise.

The emperor took three slow breaths and started to walk forward, sheathing his sword.

'Sire?'

'My place is in that line.'

'Majesty, no,' he barked, stepping across and holding up his arms.

'I have the final say and ultimate authority in Velutio. No man can deny me, Prefect. Now get out of the way.'

'Sire, I…'

Kiva gently, but firmly, heaved the prefect aside and strode over to the end of the wall walk and the men there. He'd have liked to get it over fast – get to the front of the lines and take up a shield, but the press of men was tight and everyone was already in position. Instead, he found a place in the fourth line on a raised step and took up a spear, readying himself to use it. With the height advantage of the step, that line could strike at the attackers just as well as those at the front.

The enemy were coming, running around the wall, howling and shouting, waving weapons that gleamed in the golden rays of the setting sun. At least Kiva would die in the sunshine. This morning had been poor and damp, but the sun had burned off the moisture by noon, and the afternoon had been glorious.

The empire had been glorious. And now it was setting with the sun, and the emperor would do the same.

The first men hit the shields and slaughter erupted on the wall. The men's shields took the brunt well and their swords made short work of the first few warriors. With no rail on the inside of the wall walk, those who took sword blows or jabs from spears simply toppled to their death, often pushed aside by their comrades in their hunger to be the next in line. Kiva waited for the signal.

A whistle came from the officer behind, and the shield-wall closed up tight and dropped down, taking a momentary breather as the enemy thundered against the linen and wood of their shields. In response to the whistle, the rear two lines joined the second in jabbing with spears, thrusting over the top of the shield-wall, a forest of clacking and rattling wood and iron as they thrust and withdrew, thrust and withdrew. Kiva felt the strange, sickening exhilaration of battle flow through his veins, suffusing his entire being. To take a life was an abhorrent thing, yet something primal within him thrilled to the feel of the blade biting deep into flesh and then sliding through the easier matter within before pulling back for a release to the air in the knowledge that one more bastard who sought the downfall of the empire had gone to meet his gods while Kiva still drew breath.

And that was the mantra that became his killing song.

A nomad taken through the cheek, the spear smashing teeth and jaw and emerging through the other side covered in blood. Withdraw.

Another enemy of the empire gone and I still stand.

A straight thrust to the chest of a barbarian, deep between the ribs, severing the beating muscles of his heart. Withdraw as he topples from the wall.

Another enemy of the empire gone and I still stand.

A nomad again. This time a glancing blow to the upper arm that was naught but a flesh wound, but a twist with the spear and the screaming, injured clansman hurtled from the wall to certain death.

Another enemy of the empire gone and I still stand.

Suddenly, in the press, Kiva spotted an imperial captain's uniform. The grey tower insignia put him as one of the men of Aldegund's rebel westerners. Kiva, gritting his teeth, stepped forward, pressing into the mass of his soldiers to get at the traitor. He'd seen many men die today wearing an imperial uniform, and a number of them had been among the enemy, but this was the first time he had been able to strike the blow himself. Would that it were Aldegund himself. Kiva let all the fury of a man betrayed flow through his shoulders and into the great spear shaft. The soldier's eyes burst wide as the spear entered his throat mid-way between apple and chin, and erupted from the back of his neck in jets of blood. The soldier tried to shriek, but nothing came out barring a gobbet of blood.

Kiva was astounded at his own strength. He'd never been strong – not like Quintillian or Titus – but suddenly he seemed a Titan among men, his muscles rippling and straining as he lifted the spear, the thrashing soldier hanging from the end by his neck. There was an awful tearing sound as muscle and sinew in his throat ripped away, and the head came loose flopping to one side. The sudden release of pressure sent Kiva staggering back with his empty crimson spear, while the ruined, dead rebel plummeted from the wall top, his head finally separating completely during the descent.

Kiva stared at the spear in his hands. For a moment he was utterly lost in confusion, unsure whether to exult and launch into the fray anew with his weapons or to run and collapse behind a shelter as he stared in horror at his own hands.

A crash shook him out of it as the man at the end of the shield-wall fell from the roof into the courtyard below. Kiva frowned in confusion, but a moment later half a dozen arrows thudded into the other shields, then a dozen, then more. Men in the second, third and fourth line fell with screams, though the shield-wall, bristling like a hedgepig, continued to keep the enemy back from the roof.

'We cannot hold!' yelled a captain a heartbeat before an arrow took him in the eye, spun him around and to the floor, shrieking his brief way into the afterlife.

Kiva rose from where he now realized he was crouched in shock. This was it. The end.

'Sire!' a prefect shouted. He was pointing at the wall.

Kiva simply shook his head. During the last preparations to hold this roof, a rope had been slung from the parapet down to the palace harbour, some 150 feet below. It would be the last chance of escape, and he knew that they meant it for him. The last emperor, fleeing for his miserable life down a slimy rope to ignominy.

No. He wouldn't do it. He had determined he would stand here and he would fall here, and that was damn well what he would do. No one had the right to make him live on in a world he would despise.

He cast aside the spear and drew his sword again.

'Sire!' bellowed the prefect urgently.

'No! I shall *not* run!'

'No, sire… look!'

The emperor turned in confusion. The officer was not at the harbour wall. He was at the far wall. Below there was nothing but a seething mass of the enemy. He rose, weary, his legs still shaky from the fight, and began to cross the rooftop slowly, arrows clicking off the stones around him as he walked, heedless of the danger.

The prefect was pointing. Kiva squinted.

The light was failing, the sun now little more than a golden dome over the horizon.

The shapes were initially hard to make out. He felt a tiny flutter in his heart.

Ships. The *Khan* had no ships. *Aldegund*'s ships were docked uselessly on the far side of the city, maintaining his supplies. These ships had to be…

He lost count. His questing finger found dozens, then scores, then hundreds. Were there thousands? And now as his eyes adjusted properly, he realized the sea was covered with vessels. Countless ships – some great imperial galleys of five oar-banks, others faster coastal skippers with single rows. And among them, mixed and not separate, the black sails of the Pelasian fleet. Ashar's ships.

Kiva felt a slow smile cross his face.

It remained even as the arrow thudded into his back, the head bursting from his chest in a shower of broken chain links, gleaming a wet pink.

He frowned then for a moment. Why was there no pain? Perhaps the joy of the ships made him impervious?

He turned, feeling an odd tearing in his chest from the shaft as he did so, tottering back across the roof. Men were shouting now. Everyone. The officers were shouting in joy. The soldiers shouting in relief. The enemy were shouting in panic, for suddenly the besieging force had become the besieged, trapped in a ruined city even as the first ships began to hit the beaches to the south of Velutio and disgorge their armies.

Panic among the enemy. Joy among the imperial survivors.

Already the fight at the wall was breaking up as the enemy began to pull back in fear.

Apart from one man. Standing on the wall not far away, Kiva recognized the towering bulk of Ganbaatar, lowering his bow with a look of immense self-satisfaction.

No. Not to him! Kiva was prepared to die, but to fall to that monster!

And now the Khan's son was rallying a small force to accompany him, and they were doing it, for they were more afraid of the giant warrior than they were of the newly arrived army. There were not many of them in the scheme of things, but given the tiny number of remaining defenders, there was little hope that Ganbaatar could be held back from the roof.

Kiva sighed. Would he live long enough for the Khan's son to torture him anyway?

He staggered over to the harbour wall, his legs beginning to feel leaden, and peered down. Another ship had docked and the people down there, as yet unaware that they were saved, were pressing to get on board. His gaze rose to the island in the distance.

At least the people were safe. And the imperial line, too.

Goodbye, brother.

CHAPTER XXX

Of Vengeance and Endings

Quintillian blinked. The world was a blur of gold-orange and indigo fading to deep blue. Ah, yes. Sunset. But it wasn't sunset yet, surely? Why did his head hurt so much? His vision gradually cleared to reveal the shapes of three men leaning over him. They were speaking but all he could hear was the thumping of his own blood coursing around his body. Blood. There was something about blood. And the city. And Kiva.

A moment later he sat bolt upright, dragging in a hard breath, and the sounds of the world rushed in as though he'd been lying beneath water and had suddenly surfaced. The sound was immediately all-consuming, and Quintillian recognized the din of ongoing battle instantly.

'Brother!'

'Shit!' yelled one of the figures leaning over him, clutching his chest as the prince sat up. The other two were equally surprised.

'I thought you said he'd be out for hours yet.' Quintillian focused on the speaker. He was wearing the uniform of a prefect of the guard.

'I did. He must have the constitution of an ox,' replied a man in a white robe bearing the winged staves of the medical corps.

'Where is my brother?' Quintillian snapped.

'Fighting on the walls, sir,' the third man – a guardsman – said in a dark tone.

Quintillian looked about himself. He was lying on a makeshift pallet formed of two exploded hay bales and a military cloak. Other goods stood around in barrels and bales and crates and jars, and he could see a huge crowd of people surging around a ship on a dock. Widening his scan, he found the high walls of the palace and the archway of the long staircase to the grounds above.

'The harbour?'

'Sir,' acknowledged the guardsman. 'The emperor gave my commander specific instructions that you were to be ferried on the next ship to Isera, but the Prefect of the Port here would not permit it.'

The prefect standing above him saluted with a sly grin. 'I had a feeling I might pay a costly price if I shipped you out to safety, sir.'

Quintillian tried to nod but his head felt as though a horse had stood on it and he was immediately sick at the movement.

'Do I know you?'

The prefect nodded. 'I served under you in the eastern provinces for two years, sir.'

Quintillian squinted. 'Laetius. Received a silver crown for valour at Lappa, right? You were a captain then.'

'Time marches on, sir. But when this lad and his friends brought you down here, I took one look and stopped them. The marshal I served at Lappa wouldn't want to be shuffled out to safety, and I have a feeling the city needs you yet.'

Quintillian sat straight, slowly, gently feeling the back of his head. A smile crossed his face. 'You are absolutely correct, Laetius. Absolutely right. Congratulations. Have you drawn that sword yet today?'

'No, sir. Been on harbour duty all day.'

'A waste. Time to change that, then.' He turned to the concerned guardsman who'd brought him here. 'You take over here. Laetius, come with me.'

Carefully, he rose, but it seemed that now he'd been copiously sick on the hay pallet and the poor guardsman's cloak, he felt a lot better. As long as nothing touched the back of his head and he didn't twist around too suddenly, he'd be fine.

'There're too many men down here now,' he said to the guard. 'You only need half that number for the civilians left. Laetius, grab every other man and make for the steps.'

The prefect saluted with a satisfied look and hurried off to gather a new small force as Quintillian reached down and collected his weapons, which had been lying by the side of the pallet. A moment later he was scurrying up the steps into the archway. He could see from the absolute darkness ahead that the passage had been secured. Normally a small square of light would be visible at the top. And if the gate had been sealed that meant the enemy were in the palace grounds. That explained why Kiva was fighting on the roof. In theory, the harbour was secure from the palace with that door shut. And in theory, the roof was inaccessible from this position. But Quintillian had spent much of his youth exploring this great complex with his brother and Titus, the three of them fascinated by the ancient palace buildings.

Several of the torches that lit the staircase had burned out. With the sealing of the door the stairs would no longer be used and no one would consider replacing them. Quintillian hopped lightly up the steep, slightly damp steps seeking the marker, the whole place smelling of briny mould. It took three trips up and down the middle section of stairs to find the step with the broken corner. From there he counted four more steps up and crossed to the left wall. Behind him, he could hear the prefect and his new small force moving into the stairwell, and the light from below was partially blotted out. Good man. He was quick as well as bright.

The prince's questing fingers found the stone with the chipped corner and he pushed two fingers into it, feeling them tear cobwebs and dig deep into muck and dust. It was highly unlikely anyone had done this since the three of them were children.

Putting all his strength into it, he hauled on the brick. With a sound like a mountain tearing, which echoed up and down the stair tunnel, a small section of wall juddered outward. It was a difficult job, but then this door had never been intended to open from this side. It had been designed so that some ancient, nervous emperor might flee his sumptuous apartments in times of peril and reach the harbour and the safety of the imperial island all via hidden routes.

'Laetius,' he barked. 'Help me!'

A moment later, the prefect was next to him, a small group of guardsmen hovering expectantly on the steps behind. Without enquiring, seeing what the prince was about, Laetius leaned in next to him, grabbing what he could of the lip of the wall. 'Urso,' he said, 'give us a hand.'

There was a shuffling of men on the stairs and a figure the size of a small house pushed to the front. Taking a place behind the two officers with difficulty, the big man reached over and grasped the stonework, hauling on it. The combined strength of the three men was enough. The section of wall ground quickly open, revealing a pitch black corridor hung with decades of cobwebs.

'Torch,' he shouted, and a guardsman quickly passed one to him. 'Every fourth man grab a torch and follow me.'

With Laetius and Urso close behind him, the latter having to stoop to enter the tunnel, the small force pushed into the secret passage. Quintillian held the light source forward and used his free hand to sweep aside the worst of the cobwebs as they moved through the narrow confines, the flickering torch half-blinding him and filling the choking, musty space with unpleasant fumes. Five turns and they entered a narrow stairway that climbed steeply, doubling back on itself repeatedly as it rose through the palace. After what seemed an age, and enough steps to give each man shaky legs, they emerged into a narrow flat passage that led to a dead end. This wall was fitted with an ancient loop of half-decayed rope. Without bothering trying this time, Quintillian pushed himself against the side wall and gestured to the rope.

'Urso?'

The big man squeezed past him, gripped the rope and hauled, and the blocking wall slid easily inward with a stony grating noise. Every man in the corridor blinked at the sudden intrusion of light. The doorway opened onto a wide room with huge, bright, arched windows. The floor was one giant mosaic filled with the figures of gods and emperors, animals and monsters, hunts and battles. Pillars formed a central circle within the room – a focal point where Quintillian had eaten many social meals in his life. As the unit emerged from the passageway, Laetius looked back at the wall, noting how the section that had slid open was perfectly aligned with the geometric designs in the painting.

'Clever.'

The men fell silent for a moment at the sound of the fight outside, and then the prefect joined the prince as they rushed to the windows. Nomads, barbarians and rebel soldiers flooded the grounds below and were emerging from the roof of the palace in the next building.

'Looks like we're just in time to lose the fight,' Quintillian noted sourly.

'We can still buy time for another ship or two, sir,' the prefect said, and the prince nodded at the staunch tone of the man's voice.

'Come on, then.'

Without delay, Quintillian led the small force through the imperial apartments. A few of them probably knew some of the building from guard duty, but few if any would know the whole palace as well as the prince. Passing through a marble-floored lobby, he led them to the narrow, rarely-used roof access. The door at the top of the staircase led out onto the top of the palace, very likely where the last fight was now going on. Some enterprising defender had locked it and removed the key. Damn it, but that had been part of Quintillian's own defensive plan.

'Urso? Care to earn yourself a decoration?'

The big guardsman grinned and moved forward as the two officers stepped aside. Grasping the heavy handle of the door, he wrenched. There was a cracking noise from somewhere within the wall. A second tug and a third brought the same noise, and the fourth jerked the door inward, along with two large pieces of shattered brick around the lock. Quintillian smiled at the fact that the entire mechanism was still intact and attached to the door. Urso had simply broken the wall to free it.

The guardsman stepped back deferentially and the prince, with the prefect at his shoulder, emerged onto the rooftop in the last golden light of the day. It so happened that the exit from the stairway faced south and the view he was immediately greeted with was of the next block where the rebels were massed, as well as the palace walls behind it and, in the distance, the sea.

Quintillian's breath caught in his throat. He couldn't help but see the fleet. A thousand vessels of varying sizes, both black and brightly-painted, filled the wide expanse of the sea, forming myriad small dark blots among the golden reflection of the sun on the waves. The army had come, as well as Ashar's Pelasians.

And the enemy had seen them, too. Now that his gaze slid to the next building once again, he could see that the flow of men was going two ways. The majority were trying to leave the wall tops, fleeing in an effort to escape the palace before they found themselves cut off there, besieged by the imperial army and their Pelasian allies. A smaller number of men were still trying to get to the walls, but many of these were turning at the news from above.

They were going to win! At the very last moment, at the dying breath of the empire, they would be saved.

'Sir.' He felt Laetius's hand on his shoulder and turned.

His heart jumped into his throat and froze at the sight of Kiva staggering across the roof, an arrow jutting from his chest.

'No!'

A moment later he was running. The emperor fell against the parapet above the harbour and slid to the ground. An officer was rushing over towards him. Quintillian was vaguely aware of the prefect and the small unit behind him, but his eyes only slid from Kiva at a familiar voice calling a familiar word.

'Ba'atu!'

Something changed in that moment. His heart was still in his throat at what had happened, but suddenly what had threatened to become soul-crushing sadness found a new outlet. That voice galvanized it into hatred. Without looking round at Ganbaatar, knowing it was his arrow that stood proud of Kiva's chest, Quintillian walked across to his brother. Kiva's eyes were closed, but his wounded chest still rose and fell. The prince had seen more than one such chest wound in his time, and there was a possibility – not a *probability*, but a *possibility* – that the wound was not fatal.

'Watch him,' he said to the officer, then turned to Laetius, who stood nearby, respectfully silent, his men with him.

'The Khan's son,' he said simply, and the prefect nodded.

Already Ganbaatar and his small force of howling nomads had all-but broken the line of defenders at the wall's end. The brute had no renegade soldiers with him, Quintillian noted, nor any northerners of Aldegund's force. They would all be doing their level best to get away. If they could be far from Velutio before the relief force retook the whole place, they might never be known as rebels. Many would escape punishment. The nomads had no such luxury.

'Ba'atu! I will pluck out your bones and use them to skin the corpse of your brother!' howled the Khan's son.

'You've lost, Ganbaatar,' Quintillian shouted as he closed on the fight at a steady walk, sizing things up as he went. 'You'll never have the city now.'

'I don't *want* your city, Ba'atu. I never did. My *father* wanted your city. He has lived with a hole in his soul all his life and sought to fill it with your empire. But I am a clan rider, and I do not want to rule an empire. I want the wind in my hair and a horse beneath me. I want women bent to my will and the gold of my enemies in my bags. And I want your skulls for my drinking cups.'

Quintillian snorted as they approached the fight.

'You can't drink out of a skull, idiot. Too many holes.'

Roaring, Ganbaatar swept aside the last of the shield-wall defenders and he and his nomads burst forth onto the roof of the imperial apartments. Some poor soldier managed to score a line of red across the calf of the Khan's son even as he lay on the floor bleeding out his life. Ganbaatar barely seemed to feel it, lifting that leg to peer in interest at the blood before he stomped down on the head of his attacker, bursting the soldier's skull like an overripe watermelon.

The nomads spread out, trying to deal with the last imperial soldiers on the roof, buying room for the Khan's son to face the emperor's brother, and Laetius gave a few economical gestures to his men, who peeled off to take on those nomads. The prefect stayed close by Quintillian as the giant warrior approached him, but the prince shook his head. 'Find someone else to fight, Laetius. Ganbaatar is mine.'

The Khan's son had his sword out already, the blade slick with blood and filth. The prince remembered that blade well from the first time they met at Ual-Aahbor, a sword no normal man would be able to wield in a fight, so long and heavy was it. And now, watching the man raise it, he was aware of just how terrifying the weapon was. Quintillian bore two blades, though both were little more than knives compared with that thing. His sword was a traditional imperial infantry one, 2½ feet of steel with an almost straight, slightly tapering blade which came to a wicked point. His dagger was a standard issue one, tapering from the hilt and then widening to a leaf shape. He'd learned long ago that when not carrying a shield, a soldier could parry effectively with a knife and counter-attack with a sword, but that seemed a rather feeble assumption when facing a blade almost as long as he was tall.

Ganbaatar swung.

The first blow was slow, wide and ponderous, but it had not been intended as a true attack. It was simply testing the water. After all, Ganbaatar had never fought Quintillian but the nomad city had been rife with tales of the imperial prince's fight with Arse-hat in the woodland arena, and the Khan's son would have heard embellished accounts.

Quintillian settled on his plan of action quickly and started to edge to his left. Over there, Prefect Laetius was busy cutting a nomad to pieces, but there was a reasonable amount of space.

Ganbaatar's sword came swinging again, this time with force and unpredictability. The blade began at head height, then dipped as low as Quintillian's knee mid-swing before rising to chest height once more. And the sword was recovered quickly, coming back ready to parry. But Quintillian had no intention of launching an attack yet. Instead, he simply danced back as he moved to the side, staying out of the way of the heavy, swinging blade and wincing at the pain the jerky movements brought to the aching mass at the back of his head. The nomad champion's face twisted into a number of expressions in quick succession. A sneer of superior disdain for this man who merely stayed out of the way of the blade. Suspicion as to why and what was coming next. Joy at the knowledge that he had killed one of the brothers and would soon kill the other. And hunger. Naked, slavering, salivating, disgusting hunger. Ganbaatar wanted Quintillian dead more than anything else in the world. Possibly more even than life itself.

Now the prince was passing him, and the big nomad turned as he danced around the edge. 'There's no escape,' he snarled as he brought that monstrous sword around in another arc. This time, either Quintillian had misjudged the blade's reach or Ganbaatar had been quicker than he anticipated, for the tip of the blade scratched a red line across Quintillian's upper arm, cutting neatly through three of the leather strops that hung protectively from his shoulder armour. Like Kiva, Quintillian had foregone polished steel armour today and settled for a shirt of leather-backed mail that was much less glorious and imperial, but much more manoeuvrable in a fight. Sadly, as Kiva had found out to his cost, mail was poor defence against a well-placed arrow.

Mentally reminding himself not to underestimate Ganbaatar just because he was a primitive, Quintillian took another pace back. And then sideways again, but slowly now, as he was near where he wanted to be. He felt his foot sink into something that squelched.

The man with the burst head. He was here.

Ganbaatar leapt forward a pace, uncoiling as he did so. His huge sword had been pulled back behind him and now it swept out and around with the force and inevitability of history, swiping through the air unstoppably. Quintillian threw his dagger away and dropped to the floor, heedless of the unspeakable goo in which he was now rolling. His head pulsed with the unpleasant movement, and he fought a brief wave of nausea brought on by his earlier wound. His grasping hand found what he was looking for and he seized it even as the nomad's blade swished through the air just half a hand above him.

With little difficulty, he pulled the dead soldier's sword from his fingers and continued in his roll, springing to his feet a few paces further on just as the nomad champion readied himself once more. Quickly, the prince swapped the blades between his hands. The dead soldier had been wielding a cavalry sword, almost a foot longer and built more for sweeping with an edge than thrusting with a point. Now he had the longer and heavier weapon in his stronger hand. Handedness counted in a fight.

He took two slow, deep breaths, and steadied himself. Two swords was not an easy skill to master, and even Quintillian, who'd had the best teachers in the empire, could hardly call himself an expert. But when faced with something like Ganbaatar's sword, he had to seek any advantage.

The nomad pulled his sword back, and Quintillian prepared himself for the next swing. Instead, at the last moment, and in a move subtle and agile for a man his size, Ganbaatar masterfully twisted, turning the swing into a thrust that lanced out with almost the reach of a spear. Had Quintillian not only just reminded himself not to underestimate his opponent, he might have been caught out, but he was watching his enemy closely. And as he'd always been taught, he did not watch the blade. Blades could be tricky. Instead, he had been taught 'watch their feet and eyes before they move and their hands before they strike'.

And the Khan's son's grip on his huge sword hilt had shifted very slightly before the blow, so that the power of his arms would be driven with the tip rather than sideways into the slicing blade. The sword point that would have taken most opponents through the gut instead slid harmlessly past Quintillian, a hand's breadth from his ribs.

The prince didn't have much opportunity for a counter-strike, given the need to dodge out of the way at the last moment, but his sword caught the nomad's arm a glancing blow and he felt it bite through fur and into flesh. Ganbaatar simply grunted and stepped back, examining his arm in surprise.

'You are better than I thought, princeling.'

'And you are uglier than I believed possible, shithead.'

Ganbaatar roared and swung again. Quintillian back-stepped twice and ducked to the side, easily avoiding the swing. Pride. Pride was the key. It was like fighting barbarians. In the imperial army even officers were trained knowing that the key to all war from the grandest battle to the smallest punch-up was control. When you lost control you lost the ability to anticipate and to react. And Ganbaatar was proud of being the best, which made him easy to goad.

Good, because in a straight fight, and knowing that the nomad was good enough to be able to change his tactics even as he carried them out, Quintillian hadn't been sure how he could beat the man. But now it was just a matter of goading him into mistakes and then finding a way to deliver the fight-stopping blow.

Ganbaatar was glaring at him now with intense hatred, watching him carefully.

'Nice sword, yours,' Quintillian noted lightly. 'A little too large for comfort. You can't do much with it but lunge and chop and swing.'

'I can *kill* with it,' snarled Ganbaatar.

'But can you kill *me*?'

A risk now. A gamble, but he had to enrage the man. How had *he* been taught? Did he watch the blade, or the eyes, or the hand, or the feet? The feet, Quintillian decided. Nomads fought on horseback by nature, so when dismounted they would be less sure. They would automatically watch the feet.

Accordingly, Quintillian, his eyes still locked on those of his opponent, his swords held ready at each side, danced to the left, ready to swing and, as Ganbaatar's own gaze flicked momentarily down, catching the tell-tale movement, and he brought his sword out to the right to counter, Quintillian changed his own strike. Moving with the agility of a dancer, he twisted on his right foot, mid-lunge, and instead arced past the nomad's left side rather than the right.

Both swords lanced out as he passed and both drew blood. A moment later, Quintillian was still as Ganbaatar, furious, spun to face him, blood spraying from the two large gashes in his left arm. The nomad champion roared, his eyes burning with rage. Quintillian chuckled. He'd not be able to do that again. The nomad was bright enough to learn and adjust as he went. But he was also becoming angry to the point of idiocy. A few more nudges…

Shock rang through Quintillian as he felt a white-hot piercing pain in his left thigh. Momentarily, he glanced down to see his breeches beginning to saturate with blood. A tear several inches long identified the wound. A thrown spear had grazed him and come dangerously close to severing the hamstrings. The spear itself clattered off across the ground. His eyes rising once more as he tested his leg for strength and found it acceptable, Quintillian spotted a triumphant nomad a mere five paces away. Ganbaatar had also seen the man who had come to his aid. He took two long steps towards the grinning nomad and with a roar, swung that great sword of his, severing the victorious spear arm and biting deep into the man's body, lodging halfway through the ribcage.

Pride.

Ganbaatar would not now be able to gloat that he had killed Ba'atu single-handedly.

The dead nomad fell away, his eyes wide with shock as the champion pulled his long blade back out of the body and turned, stamping towards the prince once more. Quintillian chuckled.

'This amuses you?' the nomad snapped. 'Your skull will smile when I wipe my arse with it!'

The prince simply laughed. 'Then even from beyond the grave I would still irritate you and cause you pain.'

The nomad's eyes narrowed and he heaved in steadying breaths. Can't afford to let him regain his temper, Quintillian mused.

'Will this help? Make it a fairer fight for you?'

Almost casually, he tossed away the shorter of his two blades.

'I need no aid in besting a whelp.'

'Then explain how that poor bastard with the spear did me more damage in a heartbeat than you've managed so far. You have muscle and speed by the wagonload, Ganbaatar, but you lack discipline, and that makes you weak.'

The nomad champion let out a dreadful roar and thundered suddenly towards Quintillian, his sword flicking this way and that, rising and falling, sweeping and stroking, a blinding, flashing, brilliant gold web of reflections in the dying sunlight. Another gamble.

Quintillian stood firm and let it come.

Two blows, well aimed and executed, were all he needed, and for all the skill and unpredictability of the nomad's furious onslaught, any strike from such a web of swings would fail to carry the full strength that a single sweep would.

Quintillian took the blow that could kill him with stoic calm, hardly moving. He only began to gauge the seriousness of the strike as he turned and delivered his answer. As the raging Ganbaatar barrelled past with his own blow, Quintillian turned, lancing out with his sword. The slash as the big man passed was perfectly-placed and caught his enormous sword arm at the inner crook of the elbow. And as the huge beast stumbled on to a halt, a second swift blow caught the back of his knee.

As the big nomad staggered to a standstill, fuddled by what had just happened, Quintillian closed his eyes and flexed every muscle he could think of. Only when he leaned to his left did he learn where the champion's blow had landed. His gut, on the left-hand side. Finally, preparing himself for the worst, Quintillian opened his eyes and looked down. His mail shirt was shredded. The blow had entered somewhere below his ribs and as the man barrelled past, his blade had torn back out, leaving a huge, deep rent in both the shirt and the man beneath it.

He couldn't be sure. He felt as though everything was working, but a blow there could be fatal for many reasons, some of which would tear the life from him in mere heartbeats and some of which could take days to kill him. Or, just possibly, it had torn flesh and muscle, and nothing else.

But the blow could have been so much worse had Ganbaatar landed it with precision rather than raging past in a flurry of lesser strikes.

Quintillian, on the other hand, had taken care and done exactly what he intended.

He straightened and looked into the nomad's confused eyes as the great sword fell from his grasp.

'You are right-handed, I note,' Quintillian said as he lurched forward, gripping the wound at his side. 'You often use both hands, but never just your left. I conclude that your left arm is not strong enough to swing the blade alone. And I have severed the cords in your right elbow. You will never swing anything again with that arm, though the deficiency will not trouble you for long, I assure you.'

Ganbaatar simply continued to stare in horrified fascination as he toppled to one knee.

'And because you are so clearly right-handed, you are almost certainly right-footed. I also cut the strings on your right knee. You will never run again, or even walk without aid.'

Ganbaatar's mouth opened and closed in shock.

'And because you cannot walk and you cannot swing your sword, I would say that you have lost.'

Stepping close, despite the danger of the man still having strength in his other limbs, Quintillian slowly circled his downed opponent as he clutched at the angry wound in his side, ignoring the fiery pain emanating from it. The big warrior seemed disinclined to attempt rising, perhaps still suffering from shock. Just in case, Quintillian took careful aim and pulled back his cavalry sword. Swinging it down, he hit the nomad's bent left knee, smashing the kneecap into tiny shards and ruining the joint, all-but severing the leg altogether. The prince staggered back, gasping at the intense pain in his side the movement brought. Ganbaatar howled as he fell to the stone-flagged roof, floundering on his back, tears streaming down his bulging cheeks. Quintillian was not in a merciful mood, nor any longer willing to gamble. With little difficulty he stepped close and swung down, severing the champion's left arm above the elbow.

Not one working limb. The man was truly at his mercy now, and he had none.

'If I were you, I would now be finding my skinning knife and torturing you beyond the ken of a normal human for what you have done to my brother, my people, my city and my empire. Fortunately for you, while I have no mercy to give, I am an imperial soldier and therefore civilized. And a civilized man does not stoop to your depths.' He cast aside his borrowed cavalry blade and, bending, picked up the Khan's huge sword with some difficulty. The pain in his side was so intense.

Placing the tip of the huge blade over the big warrior's throat apple, he pushed down with all his strength and every bit of his weight. The blade tore into Ganbaatar's throat, pushing through skin, bone, gristle and soft matter, severing the spine and finally digging with a grating noise into the mortar between two paving slabs beneath. The nomad's eyes bulged and he gasped for a moment as pink froth bubbled up amid the torrent of blood. His skin began to grey even as Quintillian watched the eyes whiten and fade. Finally, as the man's ruined limbs stopped twitching, Quintillian collapsed.

'Laetius?' he bellowed.

A moment later half a dozen guards were there, helping him rise. Prefect Laetius was beside him.

'How's Kiva?'

'The emperor lives, sir. Beyond that I can say nothing for sure.'

Quintillian nodded, gritting his teeth against the pain. A quick scan of the roof told him they'd won. Only imperial soldiers and fur-and-leather-clad corpses remained. 'Any update on the siege?'

'They're all on the run, sir. The nomads are milling about in panic, but their camp is already under attack by the army who're landing more men every moment. They'll not escape in force. Aldegund, on the other hand, was far enough away that the fight against the nomads has kept him relatively free so far, so he's decamping and preparing to leave.'

Quintillian smiled at the look on the prefect's face. 'You want him, don't you?'

'A rebel lord and a traitor army? Shit, yes, sir.'

The prince laughed. Ripping the signet ring from his finger – a crown with a sword down through it – he passed it to Laetius. 'The empire is still short by two marshals, Laetius. I'm giving you a field promotion and making you Marshal of the West. The ring carries my full authority. Head down to the army assembling on the beach and gather all the forces you think you need, then chase that traitor bastard west and make him suffer.'

Laetius stared at the ring and then up into Quintillian's pained face. 'Sir?'

'Every moment you waste, Aldegund gets further away. Go, Marshal.'

With a savage grin, former Prefect Laetius saluted and ran off.

Quintillian listened as he was helped slowly across the roof. Every moment in a battle had a tone, and this was the discordant, melancholic timbre of a rout. The city was filled with troops fleeing from a trap into a fight for their lives. Velutio would survive. Buildings could be rebuilt and territory recaptured. But they had saved the people, and people were what mattered.

Kiva's still form sat propped by the wall, his chest rising and falling in shallow breaths. The soldiers hadn't laid him down due to the arrow protruding from both chest and back.

The emperor wouldn't die, either. Not if Quintillian had anything to say about it.

'Someone get down to the harbour and fetch the doctor.'

Wincing, he slid down the wall, blood slicking his leg, and slumped next to Kiva.

'The doctor is coming.' He leaned over and smiled weakly. 'We won, Kiva. We won.'

And he closed his eyes and let himself drift.

EPILOGUE

It did not escape Quintillian's notice that this was the very room where Kiva had found their father on the morning of his death. He gazed out of the window of Isera's Raven Palace, through the rows of fruit trees to where the graveyard lay, a series of mismatched grey teeth rising from the neatly tended green towards the broad blue canopy of the late spring sky.

It was not the peaceful view Quintillian had been used to as a boy due to the brutal activity off to the northern edge of the cemetery. If he squinted hard he could almost see their faces as they solemnly rested their neck on the block and waited for the heavy sword to fall. The Khan, captured in his own command tent and regally defiant to the last, had refused to accept any kind of terms. The prince was pleased, in truth. He'd not been keen on Kiva's offer to accept the Khan's fealty. This process of inviting barbarians into the empire had clearly failed. But the Khan had not accepted an overlord anyway, stating that he would rather die a thousand times than live one day under another man's rule. The Khan would receive the heaviest, sharpest sword and would die quickly and well. One blow. In accordance with his rank, regardless of any ills he had caused, he would be buried in the imperial cemetery, among the rulers of a nation he had coveted. A better end than Ganbaatar, whose corpse had been rolled from the palace parapet and left to rot on the rocks.

There was a ragged cheer in the distance, indicating that another head had fallen. Would that be the Khan? Perhaps. But Aldegund of Adrennas was in that queue also, fated for a blunter blade than the Khan. Traitors deserved more than one blow, after all. And his body would be cast into the sea among the rocks for the gulls to peck. The traitor lord, true to form, had left his army to die and fled northwest with his household and his personal bodyguard. The new marshal, Laetius, had caught the rebel on the plains of Danis. They were already referring to the result as the Battle of Danis, though from Laetius's description it hardly deserved the name. The rebel army had been overcome some halfway between here and there, putting up the meagerest of fights. Aldegund himself had been bound and handed over by his own guards, spitting fury and bile at his captors and the men who had turned traitor on the traitor.

Aldegund would die badly. But so too would each officer of the imperial army who had fought for the enemy at Velutio. Two prefects and nine captains would die by the blunt sword on that green sward to the west of the Raven Palace. The non-commissioned officers had had their sword hands struck from their wrists and been discharged. A life as a beggar was likely the best they had to look forward to for their treachery. The ordinary soldiers had simply been dishonourably discharged without pay or pension to seek a new life in another sector of society. After all, if the emperor punished *every* man, there would be weeks of constant funeral pyres at Velutio.

Another distant cheer.

It was over. Already the army's engineers were moving through the city, logging the damage and planning the rebuild. The sigma was being cleared and would be built anew, much stronger, though Quintillian had his own worries about that. That new tube weapon of the Khan's had been capable of destroying even the heaviest walls. They had the weapon, of course, but no one had any idea how to work it. The Khan had had his artillerists executed as soon as he realized he'd lost. Titus's engineers were poring over the thing trying to work it out, but no one could understand what the burn marks were made by and what propelled the stone. Quintillian continued to worry. The Khan came from the east, from the lands of the Jade Emperor, and he'd brought this monster from there, for this was clearly not the work of horse nomads. And that meant that the Jade Emperor had access to this technology. In the future, would even the strongest walls protect Velutio?

Still, for now they had won. They were secure. Ashar's Pelasians were encamped in the former enemy positions and were aiding the imperial military in the immense task of removing and burning the dead, clearing the rubble and so on.

Behind him, the connecting door opened and a man entered, bowing low with respect. That very doctor who had tended him at the palace harbour the evening of their victory. Wearing a newly-pressed, clean white robe emblazoned with the twin winged staves, and a circlet of copper in his hair, his expression was grave. Quintillian turned, wincing, from the window.

'What are you doing out of bed, sire?'

Quintillian sighed. 'I needed the air. You said air was good for me.'

'The same air wafts across the window as across the bed. I'll wager you've opened your wound again. I've stitched that side so often in the last four days that it looks like freckles now. And your leg will be suffering too.'

The prince sighed and grabbed his stick, limping back towards the door. He could feel the wetness as fresh blood began to blossom on his clothes, and he smiled wanly at the long-suffering look from the doctor. 'I will rest shortly. But first I need to see Kiva.'

Hurriedly, the doctor closed the connecting door behind him. In the next room, Jala, Titus and King Ashar of Pelasia were gathered around the emperor's bed.

'Sire, I am still concerned about your brother – confused even. He is a man on the cusp – death hovers by his shoulder waiting, and I cannot fathom why. The arrow was not a critical strike. The emperor was phenomenally lucky. The shaft passed through his body with such minimal damage the gods were clearly watching over him. His lung was cut but should heal fully if he rests, since he has stopped producing blood from his mouth. His heart muscle was grazed, but again it was a scratch and there is no pooling of blood to drain. He is in recovery. He is wounded but there is no life-threatening damage, and yet he continues to decline. He cannot take food and I can identify no medical reason for it. It is almost as though he is *fated* to die no matter what I do.'

Quintillian winced again, and the doctor pursed his lips. 'I need to tend to you, though, sire.'

The prince shook his head. 'See to me later when the visitors have gone. You said I was in no danger.'

'I said you were in no danger as long as you rested, sire, but you are up and out of that bed with astonishing regularity.'

'Later,' Quintillian said firmly, and tottered forward, using the stick for support. The doctor sighed and opened the connecting door once more. Flashing a calculatedly irritating grin at the medic, he entered the next room and closed the door behind him, shutting the man out.

He had not seen Kiva thus far this morning, and Quintillian's breath caught in his throat at the sight of his brother lying prone amid the white sheets, his skin colour not much darker than the linen. He looked dreadful, and thin as a rail.

Jala was seated by his head, fresh tear tracks glistening down her face. On the far side, Titus sat with an expression of forced levity, telling one of his most off-colour jokes. In happier days, Quintillian would have rushed over and shut him up before the punchline, given the presence of the empress, but it hardly seemed to matter today.

'…and so the merchant said, "But you should see the size of his scrotum now!"'

Across the bed Ashar, God-King of Pelasia winced at the joke as Titus chuckled to himself. Kiva smiled weakly and his chest rose and fell into a coughing fit from which it took him surprisingly long to recover.

'Eat something, you lazy sod,' Quintillian said lightly as he limped across the room.

'I… I cannot eat, Quint.'

'As Titus here would say, bull bollocks. You *can*. You just *don't*.'

'It makes me sick, Quint.'

'I've not seen you vomit, nor even take a bite. Eat some bread. Bread harms no one.'

'Can't, Quint.'

'Kiva, the doctor says you should be recovering. There's nothing truly life-threatening about your wounds. You and I, we were watched over by gods this past week. We fought like lions, both of us, and our enemies lie dead, yet we walk and we will live. The army are calling us god-born. You believe that? They call you Kiva the Golden. Laetius says it was because when you were fighting on the roof, your mail glowed gold in the sunset. I think there's more to it than that. You have to get better. You can't disappoint your people.'

'My people are in good hands, Quint,' the emperor said, weakly but meaningfully.

'Listen: your lung is recovering. No more blood in your spittle means the wound is healing. And your heart was grazed, but the doctor says you're not bleeding inside any more and there's nothing else left that's wrong. Your heart wasn't pierced, Kiva. It will recover like any other muscle.'

The emperor favoured him with a sad smile. 'I think not. Some maladies cannot be cured.'

'Kiva…'

'No, Quint. I am drawing my last breaths as we speak. I will not see sunset, which is good. The last sunset I shall truly remember as I go to the next world is the one in which we saved the empire, you and I, and Ashar and Titus… and Jala. Only one thing needs be done now.' He turned to Titus. 'You have the documents?'

The marshal nodded. 'I do, but I don't want to do this, Majesty.'

'For the love of gods, Titus, call me by my name at least in my final day. We have known each other all our lives. I introduced you to your first girl.'

Titus grinned for a moment, though it quickly slid into a sad melancholy again. 'I'm ready.'

'What do I need to do?' Kiva asked, then coughed badly again for a while.

'Just your signature, Kiva. The rest is already set down.' He handed the vellum sheet across to the emperor, who took it and then the proffered stylus. Briefly, he scanned down the text. He trusted Titus implicitly, of course, but some things had to be checked carefully.

'What is that?' asked Quintillian suspiciously.

'Confirmation of the succession. No one would argue, I am sure, but given what we've just been through, I want everything done legally and officially, so that there is no room for argument. You will be emperor tomorrow.'

'Kiva…'

'No. And I have the easier job. I just get to rest and pass away. You have hard years ahead of you, Quint. You have a city and an empire to heal and rebuild. You have the border policy with the barbarians to consider, the west to bring back under control, though I think your friend Laetius will be useful there. And then there's the problem of the horse clans. Now that they know what they can do banded together this will not be the last time they rise. There is so much to do you will not have time to mourn me.'

Quintillian gave him a sad, sour, grief-filled look, his eyes sliding momentarily to Jala. She was crying again. When his eyes slipped back to his brother, Kiva was giving him a knowing smile.

'You will be greater than I, Quint. You will be the best of emperors, I think. And after an appropriate period of mourning... well, you know.'

'Kiva.'

'No,' the emperor said weakly, quickly scrawling his mark on the document before handing it back to Titus. 'And now I need to rest so that I have the strength to meet my ancestors face to face. Titus, have that filed with the records office immediately, but keep it to hand. You will need it in the morning. Quint, you need to go back to bed. The doctor tells me you won't get better if you don't rest.'

'This from you!'

Kiva smiled a pale smile. 'And Ashar, if you would give me some time. I want to speak to Jala alone.'

With sad smiles of regret, the three visitors made their way back out into the other room, leaving Kiva and Jala alone. Titus and Ashar bade him farewell and then left the suite. After a few moments at the window, Quintillian crossed to the bed and slumped into it, feeling the tension in his wounds relaxing again.

Kiva was right about the tasks facing them, but already Quintillian was thinking and planning all the work to be done. The Library of Carius would be his grandest project. Rebuilt, possibly as the Library of Kiva the Golden, though to consider that was to accept that Kiva would die. But it would be greater than ever. And he would have to have that weapon investigated again. Perhaps it was time to send a deputation to the Jade Emperor. Perhaps they would learn something useful while they were there. One thing was certain: the world was expanding now. The empire was no longer the world itself, with scattered barbarians at the borders, but needed to be viewed more as a single patch in a quilt of such pieces.

At some point in his thought process, Quintillian, marshal and prince, drifted off to sleep and when he woke in the darkness of late evening to the muffled sound of Jala's tears in the next room, he was no longer that man. He was Quintillian the Great, Emperor of Velutio, and the world waited on him.

END

EMPEROR'S BANE

A NOVELLA BY S.J.A. TURNEY

(Being an account of the Khan prior to the events of Insurgency)

AUTUMN

Tenzhin Khanzada was seven cycles of age when his father died and he learned the first great lesson of his life. As the gods rolled their dice and men screamed, Tenzhin stared at the horror around him, silently contemplating how such a disaster had befallen them.

The nine tribes of the Khmar Badlands were warriors. It was considered a matter of extreme dishonour to die of nature's degradation, when a man could die with a blade in his gut and his enemy's spittle upon his face. Death in battle was the norm and the only acceptable way. The children of the tribes learned to use a curved knife, a straight sword and a long spear before they learned even the litany of their fathers and their father's fathers. Tenzhin himself had memories of being beaten by his father only two years ago for being unable to lift the great, heavy spear for long enough to strike a dummy – the corpse of a captured Lekhmi tribe warrior. Even the tribeswomen were trained in the arts of war so that in the event of a dire defeat they could protect their lands, and as often as not, the women would bloody their blades in the endless disputes between tribes.

The world might have trembled at the Khmar tribes' very name, except for one sad and eternal fact: for a thousand years the nine tribes had fought one another tooth and nail over territory, or successions, or insults, or theft or, if the urge took them, nothing at all. For the tribes would fight each and every war season, and unless they wished their families whittled down to nothing fighting among themselves, the answer was to fight one of the neighbouring tribes.

And in the months between the war seasons – known as the life seasons – the tribes would recover and take their cattle and goats to the high plains, gathering fodder for the rest of the year and watching the new life grow among their herds.

Then, three life seasons ago, everything had changed. The engineers of the Jin Empire to the south had extended their massive wall, the height of four men and dotted with heavy towers. The great fortification sealed in the sacred lake of Zhuona and cut off one of the widest of the watercourses, redirecting it into the empire's borders where it now irrigated farmland. The following three years were difficult enough with the droughts that had been gradually increasing each cycle, but with the lack of water from the lake and the river, the herds had begun to starve and die, and with them the tribes to which they were inextricably linked.

During the last cycle, for the first time in the history of the nine tribes, a moot had been called for a reason other than settling a dispute. The Bhakhan of each tribe, along with his advisors and the most influential warriors, met at the great Eagle Rock where the skulls of the ancients were kept, and what had always been a tribal tribunal became a council of war.

The tribes unanimously decided that the Jin Empire had to pay for its misdeeds. The Jade Emperor's wall must be breached, his lands plundered and his peoples enslaved for the benefit of the tribes. They would raid and return with enough booty to rebuild their lives independent of the great Jade Emperor.

But then Tenzhin's father had spoken. At just four cycles of age, Tenzhin should not have been in attendance, but his mother had died of a rotting wound that cycle and so he was to be kept close to his father, as was appropriate for a tribe's heir. Tenzhin had watched with impassive fascination as the Bhakhans of the tribes fought for the right to lead the war. After all, everyone knew that no group of men could lead as well as one man alone. Four Bhakhans died in that dreadful contest, and of the four other losers, two died of their wounds during the next cycle. Tenzhin's father lost an arm but won the right to lead. As he burned the stump with gritted teeth, he changed everything. He was no longer Bhakhan, but would be full Khan of all the tribes.

And as long as he would lead the collective, Tenzhin's father would not settle for raiding and theft. Had he not seen a new future? The tribes lived in badlands that barely allowed them to eke out a life, even in the best years. Rocks, deserts, salt-marshes; the only good grazing land on the high plateaus. Freezing in some seasons and searing in others. And across that high wall, still under construction, lay fertile land and cities of wood and paper that were filled with food and loot. Why should the tribes take only what they could carry and return to their own poor territories, when these lush lands to the south could be theirs forever?

Invasion.

A war of total control. After all, what people in the world could hope to face the Khmar tribes if they fought side by side? It was an infectious idea, one which raced through the hearts and minds of the tribes and seized their desire. The war began early. The tribes could gather with remarkable speed, and with this great roll of the dice there was no longer any need to remain tied to the war and life seasons. And so that life season, rather than taking their herds to the high places, anyone who could lift a spear rode or marched across the dusty ground to the section of the Jade Emperor's wall that was still covered in bamboo scaffolds and surrounded by work camps.

The Khmar, when united, were so numerous that they swarmed the imperial wall like ants across a country meal. There was no finesse to this attack. The new Khan had made it clear that it was a matter of prime importance to hit the wall hard and fast, and then to move on. The Jin Empire was a snake, and the Jade Emperor was its head. Take off that head, and the snake would die. And so there was no consecrating of the bodies to the ancestor spirits, no displaying of trophies or torture of survivors. They fought, they killed, they moved on.

The great wall's massive building party was dispatched in a morning, and the tribes moved on south. A regional fortress of the Jin army was next to fall. The Khan had been thorough. His riders had skirted around the fortress first to cut off the horsemen that would inevitably leave the fortress with news of the attack. No word of the battle left the region. The heavy stone installation fell quickly, its walls simply swamped by men and women and children – for no one would be denied the right to take part in this great war if they could bear a weapon. Tenzhin himself had hefted his spear and made to take part in that first glorious conquest. He had stepped forward, the hunger for battle gleaming in his eye, his muscles tensed, and his father had shaken his head.

'You are too small.'

Tenzhin was furious. He could fight better than some boys a cycle or more older. He felt no fear. *And* he was the son of the Khan of the tribes. It was his *duty* to fight. He had argued and his father, sneering, had held up his hand and taken ten steps back. 'Run at me and pierce my hand,' he had ordered. Tenzhin had stared. His father only had one hand since the moot, and the old man would risk it now? But the boy's blood was up, his honour riding upon it.

Tenzhin ran, with the spear held before him. And as though his father had known – he *had* known, obviously – the immense weight of the long spear shaft dragged his arms down, and he missed his father's hand by a clear forearm-length. The Khan had laughed and told Tenzhin to keep training, then gone back to his battle. The fortress was left ruined and burned in the tribes' wake, filled with the headless bodies of the emperor's womanish soldiers.

The same scenario played out across the northern reaches of the Jin Empire. The tribes moved with lightning speed, overrunning towns and forts, villages and temples, putting everyone they found to the sword, regardless of age, gender or occupation. If this weak Jade Emperor could not have his people ready to fight for their lands, then they *deserved* to die.

The small provincial town of Shuxiang was the first permanently occupied settlement to fall. The pile of heads reached as high as three men, and the crows would eat well for weeks. However, the small measure of discipline the Khan had instilled in the tribes – born purely of the knowledge that they must keep moving to achieve their goal – almost broke at Shuxiang, when the warriors began looting. Still, by midday they were moving south again. Farms burned, villages were levelled and all humanity was removed.

The first true challenge came at the city of Jiezhan, which was a provincial governorate. With a sizeable garrison and stout walls, the place could have been something of a threat. Certainly, for the first time in their campaign, the tribes lost a significant number of warriors. The walls were higher and better defended than any they had previously seen, and the tribes were unable to swamp them the same way. The battle was ultimately won when ten men of the Lekhmi tribe scaled the gate tower and opened the city to their compatriots. The revenge they took upon the city was the stuff of nightmare. Not for the tribes, of course – their nightmare was what Tenzhin was suffering, being forbidden to fight. The Khan even allowed an extra half-day at the city to allow his people to roast the survivors on griddles made of swords and spears.

As they moved south, the territory gradually changed. The huge swathes of cultivated land turned into smaller farms, more rigidly organized and packed into tighter, neater squares. There were irrigation channels crisscrossing the land regularly and neat, straight roads. Each region had its own symbols and signs, and everywhere were the marks of government. It seemed that the Jade Emperor lived his life by a system of taxing and monitoring every single individual in his empire. Paper and money ruled every aspect of life here, unlike in the free lands of the tribes to the north. The warriors found it funny. They laughed at this rigid adherence to paper. How could such people consider themselves human?

Ever greater challenges confronted the Khmar tribes on each stage of their journey into the heart of the empire, and yet they overcame each with the casual, enthusiastic brutality that every warrior lived with in their heart. In the garrison city of Zhenluo they acquired a new pride and joy. The soldiers there had something called a 'battering ram': a glorious thing formed of a huge tree's bole, carefully adzed and planed to smoothness, then fitted with a massive, heavy bronze head shaped like a horned dragon. Mere heartbeats of torture had revealed its use. It was for opening city gates.

They tried the ram, which the Khan had named *Lohnak* – the tribe's name for the dragon soul eater – on the next city, Qinhong. It had smashed the city gates into splinters in such a short time that the tribes had to rush to take the city, so unprepared had they been.

Qinhong was the first of three cities to fall to Lohnak. Regular interrogation of the beaten imperial subjects – before their heads were removed – had confirmed the tribes' intended route. The Hailun River, the empire's greatest waterway, would mark the end of their journey.

One rainy day, as the tribes traipsed across the sodden grass, the riders ahead had found the Hailun River. So wide a city could have been built in its depths, the river was filled with a seemingly endless succession of barges rushing this way and that, loaded with goods. The tribes' eyes had boggled at the sight. Boats in the Khmar Badlands had been one- or two-man reed affairs used to cross the minor waterways or sail out onto the sacred lake. None of them could believe the boats in front of them could possibly float. And the width of the river… how were they supposed to cross? It would take days, if not weeks, to ferry the entire army to the far side of the river, and they needed to cross it to reach the Jade Emperor's capital city of Jiong-Xhu.

A brief beating of a captured farmer revealed the existence of a bridge not far downstream, across which they could travel with ease. The sight of that great structure took Tenzhin's breath away. The bridge was of smooth grey stone and arced from bank to bank, rising high on a series of thirteen arches, the innermost of which was high and wide enough for even these great loaded barges to pass through cleanly. It was a thing of both grace and beauty, of strength and power. For the young Khan's son, it epitomized everything a warrior and a leader should aspire to.

That afternoon, the nine tribes of the Khmar crossed that wide bridge and bore down on Jiong-Xhu. This would be different, and Tenzhin knew it from the first glance. The great cities and fortresses they had overcome on their route were as gnats to this wolf of a city. Its walls were impossibly high and strong, surrounded by a water-filled channel. And the size of the place was unimaginable. How many people must live in that city? If the Khmar tribes concentrated on nothing but breeding for the next ten generations, they would still fill only one corner of that city, leaving room for another whole nation beside them.

His father was taken aback. The Khan did a good job of hiding it beneath his calm war face, but Tenzhin knew the signs. For the first time in this campaign, his father was uncertain.

Still, nothing was ever gained by delay, as the Khan was wont to say, so he deployed the tribes. The city was too big to even hope to surround, and with one side facing the delta of the river it would be impossible to attack there anyway. So the tribes deployed along one great wall – the north, facing their home – with its single gate of high, black timber, studded with bronze dragons.

Scouts went to look at the moat. It was too deep for a man to cross, even on a horse. Men gathered up Lohnak, the dragon ram, and charged at the city's great north gate. A cloud of arrows fell from the battlements and took out the entire attack before they could even approach the moat bridge. Three dozen hearty warriors lay dead around the fallen ram.

The tribes remained in position for some time. The sun rose, watery and pale, and failed even to burn off the moisture remaining in the grass. Finally, there was a small war moot, and a decision was made.

Tenzhin stood on a slight rise and watched the Khan's next plan play out. Hundreds of local peasants were rounded up and made to carry earth in baskets and barrows. They were directed to the moat and instructed to fill it to a level where a man could slosh across. Many of the peasants were killed by the archers above, and others refused to work until the tribes gave them permanent, bloody marks to remind them of their place in the world. Over the rest of the morning, a small section of moat was filled.

Once the leaders of the tribes deemed the causeway wide enough, the attack began. Several thousand warriors took the lead, carrying lengths of rope with grapples and the long ladders they had taken from various military compounds en route.

Tenzhin watched from his mound as that sizeable force crossed the moat, losing a dozen men with every heartbeat to the endless clouds of arrows. The ladders were raised, sinking deep into the muddy, hastily-built causeway and even Tenzhin, with his inexperience of war, knew at that moment that the attack was doomed. The ladders stopped well short of the battlements. Still, fuelled by their earlier victories, the tribesmen climbed the ladders, many plummeting to their deaths with feathered shafts jutting from them. Those few who reached the top tried to climb the remaining man-height of stonework, either falling through inability or being repulsed by the defenders. Not one man reached the parapet. Similar troubles struck the grapple throwers. Not one among them had the strength to hurl a grapple that would even approach the top of those walls.

The attacking force thinned out so fast, Tenzhin could almost see how long the rest would remain alive. He watched his father's thin lips and twitching jaw as the attack failed. He waited for the Khan to give the order to pull back, but instead the leader of the tribes called for a second wave. Tenzhin watched with dismay as his father threw more good warriors after the doomed force at the wall. He watched each man fall. The new ladders and new ropes were no more able to reach the parapet than their predecessors. The young boy watched them die.

An arrow in the throat, plummeting from a ladder.

An arrow in the eye, falling to the ground, tangled in his own rope.

A long spear thrust to the face, pushed from a ladder into space where he fell, flailing and spraying gore into the mass below.

And so it went on. Tenzhin watched the power of the tribes waning, wasted against those walls. On another desperate push, men went to retrieve the ram and have another go, hoping that the archers would be too busy at the wall assault. They were not. A hundred shafts rained from the gate top, peppering the men, each falling body sprouting at least four deadly missiles. The ram had moved less than a horse's length towards the city, at the cost of fifty men.

The boy looked across at his father. The Khan was almost twitching as he realised that he had utterly underestimated the city that was his goal. The old man must have known by then that there was simply no way he was ever going to cross those walls. Tenzhin's eyes slipped to the top of the wall, and he squinted into the damp grey light to see the enemy as best he could.

What little he could make out was not encouraging. The Jin army atop the wall looked relaxed. They were contemptuous of this pointless waste of life: just some northern barbarian throwing away his men. They were barely making an effort to repel the attack. They had no need. They shot a few flights of arrows every now and then, but otherwise the defenders spent most of their time watching the tribes' siege fail and die by arrow or error.

Now, Tenzhin was pleased that his father had kept him from the fighting. Not because he was afraid of battle or even of death – he was not – but he had no interest in being the object of scorn for the Jin defenders, throwing away his life in a futile attempt to scale a wall that was destined not to be crossed.

As the attack faltered and failed, less than a hundred men returned to the forces gathered about the city, the rest preferring to die there rather than suffer the indignity of living as a retreating failure. The nine tribes looked smaller than ever before, and even the Khan must have been certain that there was no longer any future in the campaign. Tenzhin fidgeted as he watched his father and the other tribes' Bhakhans in deep discussion about their next move. The war was over. He knew it. Had he been leading, the tribes would now be retreating and falling back on the original plan of taking what they could from Jin lands, to see them through the next few cycles. It was the only feasible choice.

And then the world taught Tenzhin that no matter how bleak things become, there is always room for them to get worse. Somewhere in the city a huge bell rang out, and that massive north gate began to grind open. The tribes dithered, unsure whether to rush the portal and try to effect entry into the city, or to wait and see what happened. But it seemed that the north gate was not the only entrance that had been opened. From his platform, Tenzhin Khanzada watched the might of the Jade Emperor emerge from Jiong-Xhu. Apparently tired of the Khmar tribes' display of ineffectual arrogance, some commander in the city had decided to swat the pest.

Each gate had given birth to an army. More men than Tenzhin had ever imagined could exist emerged from the city. So many thousands – he could not hope to count them – approached around the city's corner towers from other gates, even as thousands more poured from the north gate.

As the massive force began to fall into formation facing the tribes, there was a series of hissing noises from the walls. Something had been launched into the air, but they were not arrows. Whatever they were, they left a trail of fiery sparks across the dull grey, leaving bright spots in the back of Tenzhin's eyes. Half-blinded by the glare, he watched in astonishment as the missiles struck amid the gathered tribes.

The first explosion and the terrible inferno that followed claimed more than a hundred men. The column of smoke that rose from the crater stank of seared flesh and of burned intestines. Again and again the missiles struck, and the sixth was close enough to Tenzhin's viewpoint that he could see the charred flesh in the depression left by the blast, the bodies fused together in the extreme heat, blackened and cracked and agonized. Some – the truly unlucky ones – lived. It was enough to make the world itself shudder.

The Khan had little choice. They could flee, but there was little chance of the tribes making it back across that bridge half a day away, with the Jin army at their heels. Or they could stay and fight. To the death.

The signal was given and the nine tribes of the Khmar Badlands ran at the Jin army, crying their battle songs. It was like watching a small herd of ibex running at a huge pack of wolves. It was hardly the thing of song – no tale of heroic loss that might be sung around the skull monuments of Eagle Rock by future generations. Of course, it was now highly unlikely there would *be* any future generations.

The armies met in the dance of carnage. The warriors of the tribes – and the women were now with them – howled their ancient chants and songs as they flew into the fray, hoping to make their ancestors proud enough of their deaths that they would grant them access to the halls of the dead. The Jin army stood silent, apart from a rhythmic drumming from the rear of the huge blocks of black-and-red-clad soldiers. The men wore identical suits of laminated wooden armour, helmets of scale and plate, and the flags of their regiments rising from their shoulders.

It was total butchery.

Tenzhin watched as his people were flensed and filleted by the Jade Emperor's army. Heads rolled, limbs were severed, guts stabbed, chests ripped, arteries torn, faces mangled. And all without a single Jin soldier breaking formation. While every kill the Khmar warriors achieved – of which there were precious few –

was defiled and ruined in the joy of battle, the enemy did not waste time on such frivolities, dispatching warriors then moving on mechanically.

Tenzhin was impressed, even though he was watching the end of his people.

It took a little less than half an hour for the entire Khmar army to be pushed back to a narrow circle of older men, women and children. At this point, the Khan, having foreseen the end, gestured to two other warriors, who grabbed Tenzhin and dragged him over to join the crowd. If the tribes were to die, they would all die together.

The Jin army manoeuvred them gradually towards the walls and low fields before the high defences, and there it ended. Another bell rang, and a voice called out in the tribes' tongue.

'The Jade Emperor requests that your leader step out and identify himself.'

Nothing happened for a tense moment, then suddenly three arrows thudded into three of the silent, sullen tribes-folk. They fell, dead, with gore spilling from their faces.

'Where is your leader?' the man asked again.

Again, there was no movement, and again, three men toppled to the muddy, damp grass, their blood pouring out. Tenzhin waited with bated breath and expectant eyes on his father. The Khan could not allow this to continue. Those six men had died like cattle under the butcher. Their spirits would forever be bound to this place: due to the poor manner of their death, their ancestors would not allow them into the dead halls. The Khan could not condemn any more warriors to that fate.

Sure enough, he stepped forward.

'The children will now be separated,' the voice called. 'If you make any attempt to stop this, our archers will loose again. The Jade Emperor cares not if you are made extinct.'

Again, subdued, the tribes allowed all the young to be shuffled off to one side, Tenzhin among them. Many had to be disarmed, as they had been fighting among the adults.

'Now the women,' called the voice.

Soon, the plain held three groups of tribes-folk, the stony-faced Khan watching them from behind the threatening points of a dozen serrated spearheads.

Two soldiers, one apparently an officer, walked among the children, further separating them, so the ones dressed well and clearly of noble lines were pulled to the side. They knew what they were looking for, clearly, since Tenzhin found himself in a group of six, all of whom were sons of the tribes' leaders.

A gap opened up among the enemy lines and a hundred Jin soldiers casually carried the dragon-headed ram to an open space near the defeated tribes, then dropped it to the ground. Other soldiers pushed the Khan towards the great trunk and bent him over it, while another man sharpened the longest sword Tenzhin had ever seen. There was a pause. The only sounds came from the whetstone and the general moaning of the defeated tribes-folk, anticipating either a life of drudgery or a death that would condemn them and separate them from their ancestors. The tribes were not given to public displays of emotion other than battle-hunger, but this situation was unprecedented, and some were even crying, especially the younger boys near Tenzhin. Two soldiers pushed them roughly into a line facing the ram, and finally a new figure appeared through the Jin ranks. Preceded by a well-equipped honour guard, the Jade Emperor was impressive. He was tall and willowy, with a pinched, cadaverous face and a long white beard and moustache. He appeared to be wearing a dress like those the tribeswomen wore when courting a man, and some of the Khmar warriors laughed, albeit briefly.

'Fools,' the emperor said in the tribes' tongue, laced heavily with the thick Jin accent. 'Little more than wild animals, and you think to storm the greatest city in the world? Your leader has brought you nowhere but to death.'

He flicked a hand out and that great sword fell, slicing through the Khan's neck as though it were butter and digging deep into the timber beneath. The Khan's head rolled a body-length away and, as luck would have it, came to a halt only a couple of steps from Tenzhin. The boy stared down into his father's eyes. The old man's face looked oddly apologetic, for the first time in his life. The boys and girls were all wailing now. To dishonour a great leader and a noble warrior in such a manner was unheard of. And if the Khan's spirit was made into an unloved and left bound to this field, then there was no chance of his line behind him ever entering the halls of the dead.

'Did you think my wall was built to keep you out?' the Jade Emperor demanded as he strode along the lines of captives. 'Did you think I *cared*? The wall was built to control those *within* the empire. Until a messenger came from Qinhong, I had never even *heard* of the Khmar tribes! *That* is how unimportant you are. I had to ask my scholars and geographers who you were, and even *they* were contemptuous of you. Your language is a crude form of old Jin, not spoken for centuries.'

The emperor finished walking past the lines of women and gestured to an officer. 'Have the men killed and burned. Send the women to the whore pits.'

The wailing began again, all across the field, as the Jin army bent its methodical skill to executions. And now the emperor was stalking along the lines of crying, snivelling children. Tenzhin was not one of them. He was looking down into his father's eyes. The emperor was right: the Khan had been a fool. Too swept away with their early successes, he had not *planned*. He had simply *done*. And look where it had led them. In fact, Tenzhin was not panicked or tearful. He was *angry*.

Suddenly his father's head was gone. Tenzhin looked up into the face of the man who had casually kicked it away. The Jade Emperor, whose eyes were the same palest green as all the Jade Emperors before him, looked down at Tenzhin with interest.

'You do not cry, boy. Why?'

Tenzhin met the old emperor's gaze. 'What good would it do me?'

The emperor frowned for a moment, and then nodded, gesturing to his officer. 'Take this one. Skin the rest.'

WINTER

The province of Zhaotong was breathtaking, even for one born to the high places of the Badlands. Known as the province of the tiger-teeth mountains, it was aptly named. Great stacks of pale brown and russet rock covered with thick green vegetation rose from an area of lush, steamy jungle. Not just a single small cluster of mountains, the saw-tooth range stretched over the whole province, from the lofty white mountains of Zhou in the west to the Liang plains to the east, and the coves and isles of the sea to the south.

Tenzhin sat back on his cushion and looked over the high temple's lofty parapet at the staircase that led from the town below. His nerves twanged and his blood rushed when he contemplated the great height. The child of the Khmar disaster was now eleven years of age. He had long since abandoned his old interpretation of a year as a cycle of war and breeding and instead adopted the imperial year and its seasons. If the Jin Empire had taught him anything, it was that there was infinitely more to life than he had ever dreamed of during his time among the Khmar tribes.

He had been taken from the battlefield by the Jade Emperor's own men. Tenzhin was not the only survivor, but he was the only one *grateful* to have survived. The children's flaying had produced screams that still haunted his nightmares. Some had lived for three or even four days without their skin. And the women? Well, some of them were probably still alive, servicing sailors in the whore pits along the coast. But of the whole Khmar region, only one tribesman could truly say he had done well, and that was Tenzhin.

Four years he had spent in Jiong-Xhu after the failed invasion. At first it had been brutal. He had been washed, shorn, changed into Jin dress, and unceremoniously dumped upon the palace of the Jin princes. Here lived the dozens of children of the Jade Emperor by his wife and various concubines: Jin princes, both legitimate and not. In addition, there were others seemingly fostered by the imperial household: nobles of various subject peoples. There seemed to be little distinction between the true princes and the foreigners, though the latter were still clearly subjects of the empire from the shapes of their faces and the hue of their skin.

Tenzhin did not look like them. His face was flatter, his skin a little darker and with more of a saffron tint, his eyes narrower and more slanted, and his hair thicker and less neat. He was, moreover, a head taller than all others his age. It seemed that the lofty emperor was unusual, tall in a land of the short. Moreover, in the four years since his arrival, Tenzhin had never again seen green eyes like the ruler's.

He had enquired of his tutors about these numerous questions. It seemed that the jade colour of the emperor's eyes was not a trait he was born with. The tone was gifted the moment he took up his badges of office. Whoever became emperor acquired the colour. Consequently, any child in the Princes' Palace could become emperor. Even those not of his line. For when the emperors died, all the princes ready and willing to take on the role – and there were rarely less than a dozen – would fight to the death, with the winner seizing power. This was how it had been done for two thousand years, and it created only strong emperors. Ruthless ones, too, of course.

Tenzhin's first year in the palace had been unpleasant. He was very much an outsider. So much so, that even the princes of subject peoples sneered at him as a foreigner. There had been fights, and even one or two spirited attempts at assassination. He had learned much about his co-princes that year, but in return he had taught them that he was careful, a light sleeper, and a man who knew how to fight and wound. He had never quite killed anyone, though. There seemed to be no rule against it, but he could hardly imagine that a royal death at his hands would appeal to the emperor, and it would certainly forestall any chance of peace within the palace.

Over the course of the year, he gradually came to be accepted, and his eyes were opened to a vast and complex world. There was a way, for instance, to mark words on paper or stone. Those papers the Khmar had laughed at as they advanced south into imperial territory were, in fact, records and documents of value. Dusty old tutors taught Tenzhin how to write and read back those words – delicate brush strokes forming elegant characters that could convey meaning without the use of lips or tongue. The young man devoured this learning with an insatiable appetite. A *world* was gifted to him by those dry old teachers, and he absorbed it the way a sponge soaks up water.

He had learned, among other things, that the empire was made up not only of the Jin, who were the true people of the central flatlands, but of many other peoples of different race, culture, religion and colour, subjugated and assimilated over the centuries. Truly, no province in the Jin Empire fully shared the blood of their neighbours. And yet all seemed to live harmoniously in the perfectly ordered system, devoting their lives to bettering the Jade Emperor's world.

Tenzhin had learned his histories in that time: even, fascinatingly, the background of his own people. It seemed they were nowhere near as ancient as he had believed, and owed most of their culture to the interbreeding of the western horse clans, the northern mountain people descended from the Jin, and the bulky, warlike Aina of the Eastern Islands. He had learned the history of the Jin Empire itself, including each of its seven dynasties, and the prophecy that there would be eleven dynasties before the world-eating dragon came. He had learned about the Inda people to the southwest, who were strange and otherworldly, worshipping monster gods and painting themselves in rituals. He learned of the horse clans who were blood brothers to his own people and seemed to share their ridiculous inability to work in concert. And he learned that there was another empire somewhere far to the west, though it was considered decadent and feeble in comparison to the Jin. It had sent trade envoys every few years until recently, when it seemed that empire had undergone some kind of civil war and subsequent collapse.

He had learned mathematics and poetry. He had learned of ores and metals and wood and paper. He had learned the seven sacred ceremonies that marked him as a learned nobleman. He had learned the spells of ancestor worship – so unlike the crude skull piles and songs of his youth – and of the gods in their many forms, and how each would help him to achieve perfection if he followed the path and the trail of learning, with its 31 forms of purity.

Then, this summer, Tenzhin's education among the palace tutors of Jiong-Xhu had been pronounced complete. He knew then that older princes were taught how to fight with sword, staff and open hand, and was looking forward to the martial training: he had something of an advantage over his peers, since he had lifted his first sword as soon as he could walk. But it seemed weapons were not yet on offer. Fighting was kept for last, for clear and very logical reasons. If an emperor died, only the oldest would be trained enough to fight for the throne, the younger princes remaining out of the succession, eliminating one random element from the process.

Instead, he had been packed off in a small, bouncing carriage for the 800-mile journey to this temple in the clouds of Zhaotong Province. For having learned all the things of the mind, yet being too young to learn the matters of the body, he was to study all the aspects of the soul. Here, he would build upon those fragments of philosophy he had been shown by his first tutors. He would discover patience and understanding and would set himself upon the path to perfection. He would not leave the temple until he had more than a passing understanding of all 31 forms of purity, apparently. His father would have laughed himself sick. But then his father's short-sightedness had cost them their world.

His arrival had been odd. Tenzhin and his guards had been met at the gates of Caohai by a small force of the provincial garrison and escorted to his destination. This seemed exceedingly strange. Having travelled nearly a thousand miles through varied terrain, braving bandits and random attackers with only four guards, needing a detachment of 30 soldiers to take him the last three miles was most unexpected.

Caohai was a small city by Jin standards, though large enough for Tenzhin. It boasted a governor's palace, a barracks for the garrison, docks on a wide river, five low, rich temples and powerful walls. But Caohai was merely a stop en route. From the edge of the city rose a set of steps that ascended into the clouds above. The city was surrounded by those odd, sharp peaks so common in the province, and it was up one such stack that the stairs climbed, winding this way and that, sometimes carved from the rock, sometimes constructed of elegant stonework. Some sections were little more than a wooden walkway riveted to the side of a cliff, and one memorable stretch was a long, narrow rope bridge slung between two spurs, below which a thousand feet of mist separated him from the city in which he would be buried if he fell. The extra guards had left him at the bottom. Indeed, so had his original escort, leaving only the three slaves to carry his goods up behind him, and they would not be staying.

Finally he had arrived at the Temple of the Lauded Silver Moon high upon a mountain. It was so far up that he found he spent most of his day looking down nervously upon the clouds. That was a blessing, really, for when the clouds cleared, the view down to the city below was heart-stopping. In his first week at the temple he had gained a certain level of inner peace, but to acquire it he'd had to also accept the first nervous stages of a lifelong fear of high places. He had envied the slaves who, despite their enforced drudgery, at least returned to a sensible altitude once they had delivered his gear to his room.

*****

One of the first things he had asked the old priest assigned to him was how the empire had achieved such harmony. How had so many disparate peoples been goaded into working together? He had been surprised by the honesty and forthrightness of the answer.

'What makes you believe there is harmony?'

'What?' Tenzhin had asked, confused.

'I watched your face two days ago as you stepped into our temple. You were serene and placid. You wore a mask of harmony. But through that mask I could see eyes that danced with fear from the Stairs of Unwinding. Were you harmonious when you arrived, just because your face was calm, or were your innards churning and your blood racing beneath your mask?'

And Tenzhin had understood. It fitted with everything he had seen of the Jin Empire. The order of this world was a brittle thing based on a mix of respect, logic, common sense and fear – heavily weighted in favour of the latter, Tenzhin thought. Peace, in the Jin Empire, was a veneer that covered a seething sea of trouble.

His respect for the Jade Emperor and his power was to some extent enhanced by Tenzhin's realization that the cadaverous man held together a whole world simply by being who he was and playing the part perfectly. His reaction to the Khmar invasion from the north – from the plain contempt he and the defenders had shown, to his uniformly brutal treatment of the survivors – was a prime example of how the emperor could use examples to enhance his perceived strength.

It was the first of several revelations Tenzhin experienced during his time in Zhaotong Province.

Almost a year at the temple brought with it abilities and aspects of consciousness that Tenzhin would never have believed possible. He found a serenity that had previously evaded him, perhaps due to the violent Khmar blood that coursed through his veins, even now demanding that war be his priority. He learned how to control that tendency to aggression, to channel it and force the energy in other directions. He started to understand how his mind worked – or so he thought, though every time he believed he had grasped the true power of his consciousness, the priests at the temple introduced him to some new wonder.

Thus it was that Tenzhin became aware of the trouble in the province, which in turn brought the most important of his revelations.

One of the forms of purity required the student to enter a trance-like state and experience things outside the realm of his body. A master should be able to do so unaided and at will, apparently, though a student was allowed to drink a helpful brew made from certain leaves that grew in the crevices of the rock stacks and smelled like an old laundry house. This 'form' was one with which Tenzhin had a great deal of trouble. He had mastered six forms in his early days, but would not be permitted to progress until the Form of Far Understanding was his. For a while he had only pretended to drink the leaf tea, pouring it away when no one was looking. He did not like the idea of surrendering up his will to some controlling force, even if that force was nature herself.

Eventually, though, he had succumbed, for to never advance would mean spending the rest of his life in this quiet, lofty place. Even with the aid of the hallucinogen opening up his mind, all he seemed to achieve were minor headaches and a tendency to drool while awake.

It happened on a cold winter morning while he was sitting on a rug, his legs crossed beneath him, cupping the warm copper bowl of stagnant brew in his hands. For almost an hour he had attempted to clear his mind of all distractions and focus upon the inner darkness. And for almost an hour he had failed. Then, as he contemplated the mask-like nature of Jin society, suddenly he felt a blurring and his stomach churned as though after a bad meal.

Through a mental mist, he saw Caohai as though he walked its streets far below, his focus on the square before the squat golden pagoda. He blinked in surprise. He was there, yet he was also not there. It was as though his eyes had been plucked from his head and cast down to the city to look around for him.

There was war. Startled, he saw the provincial army in their red and black, with their regimental flags rising above ducking heads and jerking shoulders, running across the square with their long spears ready. He could also see a force of men in mismatched armour that looked somehow old-fashioned, preparing to meet the charge, their own spears levelled against the onslaught like a hedge of steel points. The defenders were locals. Tenzhin had been in the empire, and in Zhaotong Province specifically, long enough now to determine the subtle differences in face, deportment and shape between the Empire's peoples. And these were definitely local men. Somehow he had the impression that the armour and varied uniforms they wore belonged to local lords. These were retainers and private armies, facing the serried ranks of imperial might.

The defenders began to chant.

'*Zhaotong! Shan! Zishi!*'

Zhaotong. Mountains. Autonomy.

The idea of an outlying province seeking independence was nothing new, as far as the empire's history was concerned. It had happened more than once a century, from what Tenzhin had read. And yet it had never succeeded. Not once in the two millennia of the Jade Emperors' rule had a regional revolt lasted for more than a month.

A charging Jin soldier, who was the first to reach the defenders, paid the price for his devotion to duty, impaled on two different spears, one sliding through his side between the straps of his laminated armour, the other into his neck, where it missed the throat but tore through the muscle and the tendon that attached his head to his shoulder. The man screamed, but his death cry was lost amid the din of battle. One of the two spears that had glanced off his armour and skittered past him drove deep into another soldier's upper arm.

The two lines crashed together like the sea upon the rocks, and the spirit of death began to stalk the lines, selecting his victims. The spears did their initial work on both sides, thinning the ranks. Then the swords came out, and most discarded their spears, useless in such close fighting. A sword cleaved a shoulder, hot blood spraying out across the press of men. There was a scatter of tiny plates as a local warrior's armour was ruptured by a powerful blow. The screaming that rang out above everything changed pitch as more voices cried out in agony, now, than in anger. Sprays of blood filled the air, to the cacophonic symphony of metal scraping on metal.

A young man, not that much older than Tenzhin, opened his mouth to scream, but the only thing that emerged from his crimson maw was the barbed point of a spear.

Tenzhin tried to pull himself out of the scene, but somehow could not. It was not that battle horrified him. Far from it – he was Khmar, after all. But the sudden thrill and lust for violence that coursed through him was undeniable, and since he had spent so many weeks in the temple attempting to master those urges and put them to use, he had no wish to surrender to them now. Moreover, he had no idea how submitting to base urges might affect this strange trance he had entered. It seemed that after so many days trying to achieve this form, he had suddenly done so with such thoroughness that it would not let him go. He resolved, even then, never again to take that pungent tea.

A man – too old really to be facing such a charge – took a blow to the chest that managed to angle beneath his armour's overlapping laminated plates and scythe across his ribs, carving meat and clacking off bone. He screamed, but even his cry of agony sounded defiant. He fell and a young man with a wide, innocent face took his place, lancing out at the soldier, only to be rewarded with a blade to the head that took an eye and cleaved his nose, smashing his jaw on the withdrawal.

'No!'

Tenzhin was not sure whether he'd said it in the waking world, in the dreadful bloody world he was watching, or possibly just in his head. As if in response to his shout, the scene shifted with a sickening blur and he saw the dim interior of a building. Women and children waited nervously, an old man with a razor-tipped spear standing protectively before them, watching the door.

Surely not? Why would he wish to see this? Had he not witnessed enough torture and defilement of his *own* people at the hands of the Jin army? But the door did not open. Nor did it disgorge an army of provincial soldiers. Instead, he could hear scraping noises and the sound of wood thumping outside. What was happening?

Smoke. He smelled smoke.

He actually *smelled* the smoke! How was that possible? That was a new aspect.

'No!'

His previous cry had seemed somehow to trigger a change of scene, and it was worth a try, but this time nothing happened. Just the increasingly strong smell of smoke, the diminishing light from the cracks in the room's walls, and the beginning of an all-consuming, oppressive heat.

'No! No, no, no, no, no!'

The room began to burn. He could hear the soldiers talking outside. There was no joy to their voices, nor fear. Just the sound of mechanical discipline, threaded through with the satisfaction of a job well done. The women whimpered. The children shook. The timbers crackled and hissed as the fire took hold of the dry, brittle building. Tenzhin willed something to change. Were he truly there, in the building, he might be able to do something, but as a silent watcher he could not interfere in any way. Even his voice apparently went unheard. And yet he could smell the sweat and the smoke, feel the blistering heat building in the walls. Would he feel *everything*?

The old guardian, realising that his spear was now pointless, hurried over and tried the door, but not only was it shut fast, it was becoming too hot to touch. He recoiled, blowing on his sore fingers. Retreating across the room, he exchanged quiet words with some of the women, who nodded reluctantly. He produced a knife from his belt and passed it over.

Tenzhin watched with a dispassionate distaste as the mothers cut their children's throats to save them the agony of burning alive, then went about the business again on themselves as they cradled their silent, blood-soaked children.

He watched the last of them fall, then the old man killed himself, calmly and without a murmur.

The realisation hit him that without a physical body there was no way Tenzhin could save himself in the same manner. His heart began to race as the first burning timber fell from the roof. The heat was becoming intense. If he'd had skin it would have begun to blister. A gust of flame burst through the wall and engulfed several of the dead women and children, immediately igniting their clothes, adding to the growing, unstoppable inferno.

Tenzhin stood, helpless, as the building burned down around him, feeling every degree of pain and panic until he slid into blessed blackness.

When he awoke, he was lying in his cot. The old priest was seated cross-legged next to him, sipping some sweet-smelling brew. Tenzhin sat up sharply, checking his body for burns. There were none, of course. He had never truly been in that house. Was it even real, or just some figment of his imagination, brought out by the drug tea?

'You went too deep for one untrained,' the priest murmured calmly.

'I never... I didn't want...'

'You constantly fight the process rather than seeking to learn and master it. Normal progression does not apply to you.'

Tenzhin shuddered. 'It was so real.'

The old man frowned. 'What makes you believe it was *not* real?'

'People cannot do that. Go somewhere else in their mind, I mean.'

'The evidence, I would suggest, says otherwise. Wouldn't you agree, young one?'

Tenzhin sighed. 'Then what just happened?'

'What did you see?'

'A battle. The Jin army against some local force. They were shouting about ceding from the empire, I think. Something about the mountains.'

The old priest nodded. 'The revolt has been going on for three days now. Come.'

Helping the shaky young man from his cot, the old priest led him out of the dormitory and across the courtyard, to the arcade of delicate columns and arches atop the low wall above one of the most vertiginous drops at the temple. Tenzhin felt his heart rise into his throat as he approached the edge, but the priest led him forward anyway and, still shaky, he reached the low parapet and looked down. Perhaps fortuitously, perhaps not, this was one of those few times each day when the clouds did not obscure the land below. A narrow column of smoke rose from the northern commercial district of Caohai below. Tenzhin shuddered.

'Three days? This has been happening for three days, and we've been sitting up here quietly as though nothing was happening? Why did you not tell us?'

'What difference would it make?'

Tenzhin stared at the old priest, who gave a nonchalant shrug and a comforting smile. 'There is no illusion here. Well done, young one. You have achieved the Form of Far Understanding. You have yet to *master* it, but you have found your way to it, and now we can move on with your studies.'

'But what of the revolt?'

The priest's brow furrowed in incomprehension. 'What of it?'

'Surely we cannot continue to sit in this temple and ignore the troubles below. The province is in revolt. Whether the revolt fails or succeeds – and we all know it will fail – there will be a backlash. We are in the heart of the province and I am of the Princes' Palace – the very symbol of what they are rebelling against.'

'Nothing will happen to the temple. We are safe. We have no connection to what happens below.'

'I am unconvinced, master. You did not see how thoroughly and brutally the army are putting down the revolt. I think they will not stop until every living thing is cowering.'

'It is the way of the Jin,' was the old priest's dismissive answer.

'What is so important about this province?' Tenzhin asked suddenly.

'Mmm?'

'Zhaotong. It's nothing but thick forest and mountains. There's no great river, no important frontier, no large cities. Just mile after mile of pretty but inhospitable terrain until you reach the untroubled Inda border. Why is the empire so concerned that they would even burn women and children?' He knew the answer – or at least part of it: The emperor's harsh, powerful response would enhance his image of strength and would help deter other such risings elsewhere – for a while. The ruler of the Jin must always balance brutality and wisdom in order to remain on top.

'The locals believe that they can bargain with the capital if only they can throw out the provincial army,' the priest said in an offhand manner that suggested he couldn't care less about events in the wider world. 'Zhaotong Province is riddled with caves. The locals provide much of the nitre for the empire's flash powder.'

The young student opened his mouth to ask what flash powder was, but was suddenly assailed by a memory of his first day at Jiong-Xhu and the siege of the Khmar. The hissing death that had come from the walls and punched craters among the tribes, burning and fusing together bodies in their wake. *Flash powder*. The importance of Zhaotong Province was suddenly exceptionally clear.

Gazing down at the city far below, Tenzhin could almost hear the ongoing clash of arms, the death being dealt in brutal fashion to warrior and civilian alike for daring to oppose the established order.

Yes, the Jin Empire was a keg of that same flash powder, lurking beneath the veneer of order imposed by the Jade Emperor. It was a wonder that the emperor lived to such an age given the stresses that must assail him daily. Who in their right mind would want to rule such a place?

Tenzhin shivered, stepping away from the edge. There was much to be learned from the Jin Empire and its rulers. Every passing month swelled his knowledge, but the last scion of the Khmar peoples was beginning to suspect that there was just as much to be learned from this culture about what *not* to do.

SPRING

It was the Year of the Unwashed Dog and Tenzhin, now aged fourteen years, had been back in the capital for only a month since his sojourn in the south. Having at least nominally mastered the 31 forms of purity, he had been released and returned to Jiong-Xhu. After years of enforced serenity, he had hoped against hope to be presented to the battle trainers, though, in the event, he had just been dropped straight back into calligraphy, ceremonies, academia and drudgery.

Two weeks earlier, the oldest of the princes, Sang Zhuo, had been given his adult robe and left the palace to take his place in the world. He had ridden west, commanding a cavalry force, to join the Kaidu province's military on a campaign of 'chastisement'. It seemed that several of the western horse clans had crossed the imperial border in a region as yet unwalled and gone on to commit the most violent incursion in a thousand years. Towns had been burned and slaves taken. Tenzhin had been surprised that the empire bothered chasing the clans back across the border, given how inherently difficult it was to bring nomads to battle, and had questioned his tutors over the matter. It was through his subsequent lessons in imperial defence policy that he came to understand the difference between what was happening in the west and what had happened to his people seven years before.

Incursions and invasions were different. The horse clans were not invaders. They were far too fractious and disorganized to ever hope for conquest. All they wanted was to sack, loot, rape and take slaves, and after doing that they would return to their own lands. Usually their raids only extended a few miles across the borders. The Aina of the Eastern Islands, who raided the coast, behaved the same way. Such incursions were left to run their course and then the aggressors were chastised in retaliation. It served twin purposes: the military were exercised in enemy territory, which kept them alert and sharp; and it reinforced the value of imperial protection to the rest of the empire.

When the Khmar tribes had come south, though, they had clearly been executing an invasion, and their forces had been so numerous it would have been over-costly to try and stop them en route. And so the Jade Emperor had sacrificed the outlying northern cities to the invader in order to exhaust the Khmar, eventually allowing them to dash themselves to pieces against the capital's walls before he finished them off. Again, it served as a warning to other regions, but it also meant that the entire Khmar people could be easily exterminated in one place, saving the Jin army from spending long, costly years scouring the Badlands for them.

But this particular year, the horse clans went beyond their usual light raids, delving deep into the empire and sacking the city of Zhidoi, the hub of the western trade routes. Even so, they would probably have got away with a light swatting as usual, but for the fact that this time they burned the gubernatorial palace and butchered the entire staff, including the governor himself, who happened to be a cousin of the Jade Emperor.

The imperial response was swift and absolute. The three horse clans known to have taken part in the raids were targeted. As might have been expected, given their natural inability to combine their strength, it appeared that one clan had begun the incursion, and two others had independently jumped upon the chance to join in, making the most of the opportunity to take new slaves.

The clan which had led the incursions was exterminated – or at least that was the *official* line. From what Tenzhin understood of the horse clans, however, it was highly unlikely that the Jin commanders had succeeded in destroying them entirely. When it became clear that they had lost, the clan's remaining folk would have scattered for survival, and the army would never find them all. In that respect, the clans were far different from the Khmar, who would rather die in battle than run from it, but it *did* mean that that clan would go on, unlike the extinct Khmar tribes. Another lesson to be learned, Tenzhin thought: honour was important, especially in war, but not at the expense of survival.

The two clans which had merely capitalized on the raid were heavily beaten and sent back to the steppe country with their tails between their legs, though not before a number of prisoners were taken from both.

One spring morning, while Tenzhin sat beside a window contemplating the differences between late Yang Dynasty and early Shu Dynasty ceramics, the victorious Jin army arrived at Jiong-Xhu. The young student sat straight and peered through the window, tilting the screen to squint into the great Square of Green Dragons outside. Only the army's generals and honour guard had entered the square, but they had with them a wagon full of people.

Two other princes hurried into the room and ran across to the window. 'Did you see, Tenzhin?' one of them asked.

'What?'

'They brought prisoners from the clans. First time they've ever bothered with slaves. A few hundred peasants for the mines, and four of their barbarian *nobles*. I hope they are turned into house slaves for us. I think I could enjoy sitting back and resting my feet on a nomad chieftain while I eat my morning meal.' The prince – a generally inoffensive fellow named Qin – chuckled and peered into the square. 'See? In the cart.'

Tenzhin squinted. There were four figures in the cart, three boys and a girl, though the girl was so similarly attired to the boys it took long moments to pick her out as different.

'I think you might be disappointed,' Tenzhin muttered. The princes watched as the officers outside separated, the most senior reporting to the main palace to prostrate themselves before the Jade Emperor. The lesser officers pushed the nomads roughly out of the wagon. After making a brief enquiry with the steward, the three boys were marched towards the Princes' Palace, and the girl to the house of the princesses nearby.

'Surely not?' demanded the prince who had entered with Qin, a rather brutish older boy named Lau. 'They cannot be imposed upon us? It's taken us seven years to wash the barbarian horse shit off you, Tenzhin. And you're positively *civilized* next to this lot!'

Tenzhin ignored the idle jibe. He knew he would always be an outsider, no matter how much he learned, but even as an outsider he had become accepted. A curiosity, but a comfortable, harmless and familiar one. Long gone were the days when his peers sought to do him harm.

The three of them waited until the doors opened and the soldiers ushered the new arrivals into the room. The three nomad boys were faintly reminiscent of the Khmar peoples to whom Tenzhin had been born, though their faces were more pinched and their skin lighter. They were dirty and haggard, their faces lined and weathered like old men despite their obvious youth. And all three were scarred: some of the criss-crossing white lines were old, some more recent.

'Three new arrivals,' an officer said abruptly, earning a reproachful glance from the steward who accompanied them.

'You will temper your tone with respect, general. You may be a senior officer, but these are princes of the Jin Empire. The lowest and youngest among them outranks you, as a dragon outranks a worm. Now leave.'

Such was the nature of the Jin world, Tenzhin reflected. So rigid were the rules of etiquette and the system of seniority that a servant could talk down to a better without fear of reprisal, if he were defending someone even more senior. The general flashed a faintly apologetic look at the room, bowed formally and then left, with a withering glance at the steward. The other officers bowed and followed him out, closing the door.

The steward gave the three dusty, odorous new arrivals an appraising glance and clearly found them wanting. 'Do you speak a recognizable tongue?'

The three stared at him uncomprehendingly, silent and dour.

'Very well,' he went on. 'You wait here,' he said loudly, then repeated it, doing his best to mime waiting, pointing at the floor with each word. He glanced at Tenzhin and the other Jin princes. 'If you would just watch them momentarily, masters, I will send slaves to take them to the baths and have them appropriately attired.'

'Go,' Qin nodded, and the steward, clearly still rather thrown by the new arrivals, scurried off.

'What *are* you?' Lau sneered, gesturing at the three nomads.

'*Khau*?' barked one of the boys, and Tenzhin frowned. Add just a little Jin inflection, and *khau* would have been a passable copy of the Khmar word framing a question.

Lau walked towards the nomads. Qin went to hold him back, but was too slow. As the eldest of the three princes, and with a year of martial training under his belt, Lau was cocksure. He walked in a slow circle around the captives.

'You smell like dung. You look like you rolled in it, too. Why in the name of all the ancestors would they admit *you* to this place?'

'*Oan at khau*!'' snapped the largest of the new arrivals, without even looking at Lau. Tenzhin's mind ran over potential translations – based on his native tongue with a strange, non-Jin twang – and realized that the boy was asking who this idiot was. He smiled to himself. 'I think you need to be careful, Lau. I don't think they're afraid of you.'

'Who asked you, you flat-nosed barbarian?' snapped Lau.

Narrowing his eyes, Tenzhin turned to the three nomads and cleared his throat. After seven years of disuse, he had to rake his memory thoroughly to pick out the words he needed from his native language, and try to apply the western accent to it.

'*Ogtun bainu uach Lau-a ikh oghmun.*'

The three foreigners turned sharply to face him. He hoped he'd used the correct tone, and clearly they had understood. *This goat's penis is called Lau.*

The older of the three burst out laughing, and Lau stopped dead, levelling a suspicious look at Tenzhin. 'Somehow it doesn't surprise me that you can speak their barbaric language.'

'I'm warning you, Lau, don't push them. They're not afraid.'

'Then they fucking *should* be,' Lau snapped, jabbing out with the flat of his hand, pushing the smallest of the three – the bully's eternal habit of picking on the weakest.

The prince's eyes widened in shock and then pain as the diminutive nomad, no more than seven or eight years old, moved with lightning speed and grabbed his arm, twisting it and yanking it downwards. Lau's elbow snapped, his arm coming loose and dangling sickeningly. He didn't have much time to do anything but stare in horror as the small nomad pivoted and lashed out with a pair of fingers pressed together, punching them into the prince's throat. Lau's voicebox and windpipe were crushed instantly, and he fell to the ground, his right arm flopping uselessly while his left clawed at his fatally ruined throat. All that escaped his mouth were wheezing noises, as his face went slowly purple and then grey. He thrashed about wildly, then shook for a while before he was hit by three spasms that finally robbed him of his life and left him lying silent.

Qin stared in horror as the new arrivals simply returned to waiting, calm and unperturbed.

'I have to get the guard,' he said nervously.

'I would strongly advise that you stay exactly where you are, Qin,' Tenzhin said quietly. 'They do not know who to trust yet, so they see everyone as a potential enemy.'

Qin was shaking his head, but Tenzhin noted that rather than walk across the middle of the room, the younger prince sidled around the edge then slipped through the door, leaving the four of them alone in the chamber.

'How do you speak my language?' asked the older nomad in his own tongue. Tenzhin was surprised at how quickly he was becoming accustomed to it. It was almost like slipping on an old, comfortable pair of boots.

'I was of the Khmar tribes to the north. We are almost cousins, you and I.'

The third, slightly younger nomads sneered at the idea, but the older one simply nodded slowly. 'I had heard your people were no more. Killed by the Jin.'

'I am a living monument to their death, taken by the Jin seven years past as you are now.'

'I will not become their puppet like you,' snarled the middle boy, earning a nod from the smallest.

'Then you will die,' Tenzhin said in a matter-of-fact voice. 'It matters not how strong or how fast you are. The Jin are better, and their resources are almost endless. If you had seen what I have seen…'

'We are of the Kino clan,' snapped the small, apparently violent, nomad. 'We will never submit.'

'*You* are of the Kino,' the oldest noted. Your clan is small and backward. It would be a boon for the clans in general if you two died. Two less Kino to hold us back.'

The small one rounded upon the oldest, and Tenzhin could see him readying for a fight.

'And what of the Orkhon clan?' he snapped. 'Who turned like frightened foxes and ran for the hills when the Jin appeared?'

'And therefore survive in strength,' retorted the older one. 'Count how many of the slaves brought here are Kino and how many Orkhon. You will soon see your folly.'

Tenzhin rolled his eyes. It was almost like stepping back ten years and watching the Khmar chiefs at the moot, arguing over the meanest things.

'The three of you have two choices,' he said quietly, and they turned to him in surprise. 'You can bicker,' he went on, 'like you are now. You will probably kill each other, and then no one wins but the Jin. Or by fighting you will weaken each other, and then the true Jin princes in this palace will pull apart the remains, and again you will not win. Or you can band together and decide that you will not be beaten by the empire. Learn from their strengths and learn from their mistakes, as I have. The Khmar tribes are gone for *two* reasons. Firstly, they were unable to see the advantage in working together, and their fractious nature prevented them from understanding their folly until it was too late. Secondly, they rushed into war without carefully contemplating every angle and every outcome. That inevitably cost them their lives. Decide now whether you wish to fall and disappear like the Khmar or to remain and grow strong.'

No answer was forthcoming, though, for at that moment the doors slammed open and in walked half a dozen of the palace's myriad slaves, accompanied by four soldiers and a gaggle of fascinated younger children. The soldiers immediately rushed over to the body, lying grey and lifeless. Lau was a senior prince from Druzha Province, not one of the emperor's own brood, but still important in his way. As the slaves clustered around the three nomads uncertainly, one of the soldiers gestured at them. 'Who did this?'

The three new arrivals needed no translation and the short one, his head defiantly high, stepped forward. 'Hold him,' barked one of the soldiers and the other three grabbed the small nomad. He struggled and succeeded in stamping hard on one soldier's foot but, no matter how fast and strong the boy was, the soldiers were veterans, big and strong, and their grip was unbreakable. The boy snarled in defiance as they forced his arm out straight. The fourth of their number drew his sharp, gently curved blade, raised it, and then brought it down hard, severing the arm below the elbow. The nomad hissed at the pain, his eyes watering, but he did not cry out.

The half-arm thumped to the floor, where the fingers twitched for a moment as blood cascaded from the severed end and pooled around the limb. A steady stream of crimson was running from the stump, and at a gesture from the soldier, a slave ran over with linen and began to bind the wound.

'Learn your place, barbarian,' said the soldier, cleaning and sheathing his sword. 'The matter will be brought before the emperor. He will decide whether the arm suffices, or whether we need to take your head as well.'

The soldiers let go of the nomad, bending to collect the arm and the discoloured form of Lau. At a signal from the officer, the slaves began to beckon to the boys. The three foreigners frowned uncomprehendingly, the smallest one pale from loss of blood but otherwise oddly unruffled by such a violent episode.

'They want you to go with them,' Tenzhin said quietly to the three nomads. 'They want you to bathe and dress like them. I know you will hate this, but unless you wish to fight the entire palace to the death – yours, for certain – then sooner or later you will end up doing as they ask. I suggest you acquiesce now without argument, for it will save a great deal of trouble and time. Do not do anything to make things worse right now. You are lucky Lau was a provincial prince and not one of the emperor's get. You might still avoid the death penalty.'

There was some discussion among them as to the necessity of a bath, and when one of the slaves reached out to touch the young nomad he had his hand broken for his trouble. Eventually, though, the three nodded and were led off. The older one paused and turned to Tenzhin. 'They took my sister. Where will she be?'

Tenzhin smiled reassuringly. 'There is a palace for the girls like this one. She will be well looked after.'

'She will break arms, I fear,' the nomad replied with a grin and was gone.

Once the party had left and Tenzhin was alone with the gaggle of other princes, he noticed that Qin was among them, his face still registering shock.

'They are rough,' the younger prince said quietly.

'Rougher even than you were, Tenzhin,' added an older boy from the crowd. 'They will never fit in.'

'You said that about me.' Tenzhin smiled.

'And you still don't fit in!' called a wag from the back.

*****

The morning passed in urbane, dull civility, and once the noon meal had come and gone, Tenzhin strolled through the Garden of the Seven Blossoms. He was wondering how the new arrivals were doing with the Jin cleaning rituals and the fine clothes the slaves would be attempting to put them in, when a door opened ahead and two old female slaves appeared, escorting the nomad princess.

She had been bathed and clothed in a delicate silk dress patterned with lilac and white blossom. Her hair had been untangled, but otherwise left alone. Where the princesses and noblewomen of the Jin world always wore their hair piled high in intricate designs that required pins and fans and rods to hold in place, the nomad girl's lustrous black hair hung straight and gleaming, framing her fascinating face. She was attractive. Not pretty. Far from pretty. There were Jin girls in the palace that would easily outshine her. But there was something about her that drew Tenzhin's eye.

He was walking towards her, wondering how best to begin a conversation, when a warning bell rang out from the Princes' Palace. With a dreadful sense of foreboding, he threw an oddly apologetic glance at the girl, who seemed unconcerned, and rushed out of the garden and over to the courtyard. He swallowed his tension as he skidded to a halt on the gravel. On the far side of the square, the smallest of the nomads was being dragged, bleeding and bruised, from the doorway of the palace. He had been subdued with some force. His half-arm, though tightly bound in clean white linen, was spotted with fresh blood from the beating. Tenzhin's sense of foreboding increased tenfold as two more soldiers appeared behind the captive carrying a figure on a wooden bier. He recognized Qin's form immediately, and almost as quickly registered that he was dead.

The body had been opened up from breastbone to nethers – an angry wound, torn rather than cut. It must have taken a great deal of force and anger to achieve such a thing. Even as Tenzhin watched, the young nomad bit one of the soldiers, taking a sizeable chunk from his arm. The soldier howled and another slapped the lad hard around the face, but the nomad just laughed and spat out the piece of arm, grinning through pink-stained teeth.

In the doorway behind the procession appeared the other two nomads. Despite their clan alliances and enmities, both of them were looking at their young companion with expressions of extreme disappointment.

Tenzhin sidled round the edge of the courtyard until he met up with them.

'What happened?'

'He took a dislike to your friend. That and nothing more.'

'He's going to die for it, you know?'

They shrugged. 'He doesn't care.'

'If you two want to stay alive, you need to think more than that. Killing members of the Jin ruling dynasty is a strict no. Judgement is still pending for the death of Lau, but he was not of the emperor's blood. He was a subject prince, but Qin? Qin was one of the emperor's own sons. One of the better ones, too. Your friend will be tortured to death for it. He'll be begging for the end long before they get as far as peeling off his skin.'

The other two merely shrugged again.

'You'll probably both be beaten as well, just to set an example. I strongly advise you to take it without comment.'

Again, silence.

'Listen,' Tenzhin said, grabbing them and pulling them aside, away from the activity and other prying ears, 'time is growing short in the palace.'

They turned uncomprehending eyes on him.

'The emperor is old. Very old. He is not yet ill, but general opinion is that he has not many years left on the jade throne. And when he dies, those senior princes in the palace will fight for the succession, and those few who are out in the world like Sang Zhuo will race back to butcher their peers. In theory, their struggle will not affect the younger, untrained princes, but from what I understand, such dynastic struggles are rarely limited to the elders. The fight for the throne will grant them all the opportunity they need to remove anyone from the palace they have taken a dislike to, or consider a threat – either present or future. Some will even die through random accident. This place will become a bloodbath. And it is understood that when the time comes, each prince is out for himself alone. So I propose that we watch for one another. We become allies in this place. There are none among the Jin children who will side with you, and even after seven years, none would side with me. But together the three of us might just ride out a dynastic war.'

'What if I might want to fight?' the younger of the two remaining nomads asked quietly. 'Perhaps I might wish to be the next Jade Emperor?'

Tenzhin rolled his eyes. 'Even if you kill every other living thing in the palace, the army would stage a coup before allowing a horse nomad to rule. And besides, I have been studying the empire for seven years. Only a complete fool would desire to rule this place. Their emperors are bound by necessity to adopt a mask. They lose who they were and become the Jade Emperor, like their predecessors. And when one of them fails to live up to the role, which has happened occasionally, it always ends up in civil war, beheadings, and a new dynasty on the throne. No. Only a fool would wish to sit atop that throne. But I am beginning to think on a grander scale than the Jin Empire. I am beginning to contemplate a future without the emperor's interference.'

He reached out and grasped the two nomads, marching them away across the courtyard. Behind them, the young prisoner shrieked as his eyes were taken out, beginning the slow, torturous execution.

'What can you tell me of the west?' Tenzhin asked his new allies.

SUMMER

Rumour had been circulating in the palace for some time. The emperor was dying. Well, depending which rumour one listened to, anyway. According to some, the spirit of death was hovering over the emperor's bed, ready to claim him. Others claimed it was only a bad illness. Some said he had been poisoned, others that he had eaten bad fish. Asking ten different people about the cause, nature and severity of the trouble would result in ten different answers, but the one common thread was this: the emperor was ailing. And inevitably that turned the palace into a hive of activity. Every prince who could wield a blade was preparing to fight for his life in the war that would create a new emperor.

Tenzhin had celebrated his seventeenth name day only the previous week – albeit it had been a rather vague affair, since in truth he had absolutely no idea upon which day he had been born. His father had told him once that it had been in the war season, which was unusual, but that was it. So the palace officials had supplied him with an arbitrary date, and each year he had been given a gift. It had always been a book – more to learn. There was *always* more to learn. Until last week, when he had been given a sword.

He had been training now with the martial tutors for almost a year. It had surprised them how quickly he learned their skills, though they constantly complained that they had to break him of bad habits he had developed in his youth. Still, in less than a year Tenzhin had levelled the field, and was sparring as though born to it against highly trained princes two years older than he.

Today, as the instructor yelled at him yet again – telling Tenzhin to hold his arm straight and extend with his whole upper body from the hip, not bend like some river reed – his gaze slipped from his sparring partner, who stood with a rather smug smirk at this latest reprimand. There, off to the side of the Courtyard of Steel Dragons, were his two constant companions, the former horse nomads Uldin and Edeco. They stood beneath an arbour of delicate blossoms, watching their friend train. The three of them, including the girl Erekan, had become not only close allies but firm friends following that most gruesome death of their diminutive companion.

Their studies kept them apart much of the day, but during the nights and at the various free or social times they were rarely apart. Of course, the nomads' clear idiosyncrasies made them all but outcasts to most of the palace, which also had made Tenzhin unacceptable. By extension, he was once more classified as a barbarian. It mattered not a bit to the four of them, but what did matter was the fact that while none of the older Jin princes would band together at this critical time, each seeking the throne for himself, it was clear that they all considered this group of foreigners a threat. Consequently, the moment the old emperor breathed his last, the palace would be full of flashing knives, most meant immediately for the throat of Tenzhin and his friends.

The nomads were, of course, far behind Tenzhin in their studies. They had no idea how old they were, but calculated estimates put their ages between eight and thirteen. They had almost finished their studies in the capital now, each able to speak the Jin tongue with barely a trace of their old accents, and aware of the history, geography and science of the empire. They were already being prepared for their sojourn to discover their soul. Each would be sent to a different region, and it seemed highly likely that the boys would be far from Jiong-Xhu when the emperor died, which would make them safe for now, but leave Tenzhin in dreadful danger.

As a woman, Erekan followed a different path of study. Soon she would be offered for marriage to some noble or official, though it seemed unlikely she would be taken willingly.

Things were very much on the brink of disaster. No path through the coming days looked good.

In one scenario, the emperor died and they were all still in the palace. They would find themselves fighting for their lives, discovering scorpions in their beds, poison in their meals, and so on.

In another, the emperor lasted until the nomad princes were sent off to their spiritual learning. Tenzhin would then face the danger alone. Most likely, the others would also die mysteriously during their temple retreats.

A final unpleasant scenario involved the very real possibility that one or more of the older princes might attempt to secure a head start in the game by removing a few obstacles even while the emperor lived.

None of these were attractive propositions. After everything the four outcasts had endured over the years, it was beginning to look as though they might become footnotes in the record of a succession war. Tenzhin had considered the possibility that he might have been more secure had he not sided with the nomads. But then, while that would make him safer for now, it negated the potential future gain the others represented, and Tenzhin was not willing to risk his long-term plans for the sake of immediate danger. Failing to think ahead had been his father's failing. It would not be his. One big risk remained – one great gamble – and then everything would fall into place.

Uldin and Edeco nodded at him. Tenzhin nodded back and turned. At the far side and one storey higher, three princesses sat on a balcony, paper screens shading them from the hot sun. The two Jin girls performed their elegant tea ritual while Erekan sat and watched the sword training in the courtyard, her straight hair gleaming in the light, still resisting anyone's attempts to pile it atop her head. Just as in the Princes' Palace, Erekan was ostracized by the other girls, and even though she shared a balcony with them, it was clear from their body language that they were not together.

Good. That made things easier.

Erekan nodded.

Master Shang Chao barked his disgruntlement at Tenzhin, grasping his wrist and yanking it forward, steadying it and angling the sword where he clearly expected it to be. Out of the corner of his eye, the student saw his two nomad friends turn and walk slowly along the arbour, towards the triple Gate of Three Justices.

The two other pairs of students were busy with their own teachers, grunting and calling out the forms of attack and defence they were attempting to perfect. Tenzhin glanced at them momentarily.

'No!' shouted his teacher, slapping him hard across the cheek with the back of his hand, drawing blood from the student's mouth. Tenzhin levelled a look of utter hatred at the man and the teacher recoiled slightly at the ferocity of his expression.

'I teach you the moves well, but *you* do not *learn* them well, Tenzhin-prince.'

'Because your forms are too rigid and inflexible, Master Shang. You may be a master at the art of the sword, but what you teach and what you know is just a dance with a weapon. It is not fighting.'

'You are insolent, Tenzhin-prince. This is part of the reason you do not learn fast.'

Tenzhin knew, though, that the man was wrong about that. He *had* learned fast. Extremely fast. He wondered for a moment whether the teacher was actually a little afraid of him. If he wasn't already, he soon would be.

The two boys reached the entrance and stood within the arch, watching the weapons practice from behind the grille of the gate itself.

Tenzhin made a quick calculation and nodded to himself. A feral smile crossed his face.

'You think this is amusing?' asked the teacher sharply, reaching out with an arm to deliver another slap.

Tenzhin reacted in a flash. His own arm lanced out and he caught the teacher's swinging hand by the wrist. With a sharp jerk, he snapped the wrist at right angles. The teacher stared in shock, but had no time to react further as Tenzhin's sword came up from below, entering his head under the chin, driving up through the mouth and into the brain. In a single fluid move, the prince let go of the teacher's wrist, dropped back into a crouch, ripping the sword from its meaty scabbard, and spun.

The blade – the beautiful sword he had received for his naming day the previous week – sheared through his sparring partner's legs above the ankles, severing both. Sparring blades were not meant to be so sharp, but Tenzhin had been at work with the whetstone every night this week. The other prince let out a muffled squawk as he fell from his severed feet.

The courtyard fell into a shocked silence, and as Tenzhin rose from his crouch and took two steps across to the next sparring pair, his eyes darted to the balcony for just a moment.

Erekan was there, as expected, her teeth gritted and the knuckles of her hands whitening as she used a silk sash to throttle the life out of the prim princess beside her. The other girl already lay draped over the balcony parapet, blood sheeting from her neck and spattering down to the courtyard below. Damn it, but she was quick and fearless.

Uldin and Edeco were now opening the gate to the training courtyard, a place forbidden to those not yet old enough for weapon training.

As Tenzhin advanced on the next sparring pair, the two princes realised that they were in mortal danger. Raising their arms in a sign of capitulation, though keeping their swords in defensive positions, they retreated to the corners of the courtyard. Their sword master glared his hatred at the rogue student and levelled his weapon.

As Tenzhin came to a halt, the man began to move against him. He used the various sword forms perfectly. And perfectly predictably, too. *Stork one* and then *four*, *Dancing dragon*, *Rearing bear two*, *Crane one*, and then *Hunter four*. It was a sequence Tenzhin had been made to practice a hundred times in his first two months alone. And long before he was truly bored of the sequence, he had spotted the numerous flaws in it.

It was not fighting. Just a dance with a sword. The teacher's blade was perfectly positioned to ward off almost any blow, his stance ready to dance to either side.

Tenzhin raised his free hand and cast the fistful of grit he had scooped up in his crouch. The dust enveloped the sword master's head, blinding him as he cried out in surprise, waving his sword like a novice in the hope of striking this dreadful student.

Tenzhin shouted 'Dipping crane!' as he lunged forward, the blade slamming into the teacher's chest and driving between the ribs, directly into the heart. As the blinded teacher gasped and coughed, Tenzhin sneered. 'Note how I extend from the hip with my whole upper body and do not bend like some river reed.' The teacher gasped again, blood spouting from his mouth and chest, where Tenzhin now twisted his sword through ninety degrees and ripped it back out.

'Note, also, how I hold my arm straight in the process,' he snarled at the teacher, who toppled gently backward and collapsed to the flags, coughing.

The remaining pair of students followed the example of their peers and backed away to the corners of the square. The third teacher was armed with a glaive – a blade as long and sharp as a sword jutting from the end of a long staff, something like a cross between sword and spear. He levelled the weapon at Tenzhin, a look of superior satisfaction crossing his face. The teacher was comfortable with his chances. He knew he had the reach and Tenzhin would be unlikely to get close enough to deal him any real damage.

His face changed from contented arrogance to agonized shock as Erekan drove the knife deep into his back, wrenched it out and repeated the process twice more. Tenzhin had noticed her dropping from the balcony as he approached, but had deliberately not looked at her, so as not to tip off the teacher as to her presence. Again, the teacher was just a dancer. Fighting involved planning and the ability to work outside rigid forms. Combat was fluid and ever-changing.

The teacher was suddenly wracked with spasms as Erekan cut through organ, muscle and nerve. In the end she gave the man a gentle shove and he toppled over onto his face.

'Come on,' Tenzhin murmured, turning and making for the gate. Erekan followed, covered with the blood of her victim, pausing only long enough to rip the glaive from the teacher's grip. Tenzhin crouched as he passed and gathered up the swords from the two other dead teachers, tossing one to Uldin and the other to Edeco. The four students still in the courtyard remained at the edges, watching nervously.

'Any who follows us dies,' Tenzhin said in his flattest tone, and with the three nomads strode from the courtyard.

'You were at your lessons this morning?' he enquired of the other two boys.

‘Of course.’

‘And everything is as planned?’

Edeco grinned, and as they passed out into the arbour, he dipped and swept up a leather case. ‘All here. What do we do when the alarm goes up?’

Tenzhin shrugged. ‘I am relying on the slow wits, nervous dispositions and sense of self-preservation among our peers in the yard. It will be some time before any of them dares to venture out from the courtyard. By then we should be in. The only one among them with any real guts was Chou, and I killed him.’

A moment later they rounded a corner and crossed the Square of Green Dragons, making for the Four Dynasty Gate. As always, there were two guards on the gate, and though they shared a confused glance at the approach of three armed students and a princess, they made no immediate move to intercept them. As they approached the gate, Tenzhin and his friends separated, and the guards’ eyes widened as Erekan stepped out from her position half-obscured behind the boys, her delicate silk robe sluiced with blood. Both guards opened their mouths to shout, but the man on the left merely hissed as Tenzhin’s blade cut across his throat deep enough to bite into his spine. The guard on the right let out an agonized gasp as the glaive slammed into his face, smashing the upper jaw and grinding through bone, tongue, teeth and eye as it entered the skull. Uldin flashed an irritated look at his sister, who had beaten him to the kill by half a heartbeat due to the superior reach of her new weapon. With a contemptuous snort, the nomad princess twisted the blade in his head a full rotation, mincing his brain, and then pulled it out with a dreadful sucking sound.

Both guards dropped, thrashing, to the steps.

The Jin empire’s love of organisation and visual order was working against it and in favour of the rebels, as Tenzhin had expected. Across both palace and city, everything happened at precisely the same times every day. And as the session of weapon training in the courtyard took place just before the noon meal, so the slaves and countless administrators in the palace were busy either preparing meals or readying to eat them. And while these two guards had died only 500 paces from their nearest comrades at the Silver Bough Gate, they were on the far side and unable to see what had happened. Such was the need for perfect harmony in the palace's visual aspects. Pockets of guards would leave the place looking untidy, so they were placed in fixed positions, mostly out of sight, where they could not spoil the ordered view from the palace windows.

Without a pause, Tenzhin pushed open the door within the huge gate and entered, the others slipping in behind him.

There had been one further advantage to the time they had chosen: the location of the emperor.

The old man was as much a creature of habit as his subjects, and it was his custom to take the air before the noon meal. He would still attend to administrative affairs, but would do so in the Garden of Ancient Wonders rather than the stifling confines of the palace. The only element of true chance for which Tenzhin had not been able to account was whether the old man's frailty had forced him to change his routine. That, and the toss of the coin upon which their futures rode anyway.

Ignoring the painted screens with their panoramas of rural terrain, wildlife, small stone bridges and courting couples, the interlopers moved swiftly across the hall and through the next door. They were just in time, as it happened. As the rebels slipped through the door, a small troupe of slaves emerged into the hall from another entrance and passed beyond the screens, carrying the emperor's meal.

Tenzhin had managed to engineer a visit to the garden once, earlier in the year, when it had been cold and the flowers and trees dead and bare. He knew largely what to expect, but had no idea what the situation of guards would be like with the emperor in residence.

Fortunately, all four of them were prepared. The two guards standing just inside the doors were as easily dispatched as the two out the front. Quite simply, such a bold attack could never have been expected by the Jin mind, constrained by rigid thought as it was.

The emperor sat at a low desk at the centre of the garden. Two more guards stood close by at full attention, and there were pairs by the other three doorways leading back into the palace. Hearing the gurgling death cry of one of the men the rebels had just put down, all the soldiers in the garden shouted and converged on the emperor at its centre.

Reports of the old man's decline had clearly been exaggerated, at the very least. He looked the same as ever to Tenzhin's eye, though perhaps a little more rounded in the back. The emperor was hunched over his calligraphy, a bottle of squid ink on the table and a long bamboo pen in his hand. The paper upon which he wrote – unheard of outside the empire, but manufactured here in vast mill complexes – was strewn across the table in what looked to be a haphazard manner. Tenzhin was certain that if he could examine them there would be a perfect order to their positioning. Nothing the Jade Emperor ever did was disordered.

This was the critical moment. The great gamble of Tenzhin's life. During their discussions of this day, the others had pressed him many times as to how they would overcome the guards in the emperor's presence. They all knew there would be too many to simply overwhelm, and they would be the best of their kind, too. The soldiers that had fallen so far had been taken by surprise. That would not work on the eight strong, well-armoured veterans closing in now to protect their master.

Edeco and Uldin flashed Tenzhin a nervous look, but he just smiled reassuringly at them and led the way along the perfect orchid-lined path to the central paved area where the emperor and his guards waited. The soldiers all had their weapons drawn now and were bristling, protecting the old man. The emperor merely finished his writing as though this were just another day and a meeting of administrators.

'I cannot help but be intrigued as to how you intend to achieve my death,' he said, under creased brows.

Tenzhin simply walked closer, slowing as he neared, staying safely out of the soldiers' range.

'Given the rumours that I hear circulating,' the emperor went on, 'I am rather surprised to find that it is you and not one of my own sons who seeks to be first to the throne. On the other hand, this is perhaps symptomatic of your barbaric backgrounds – that you rush to the conclusion and end up facing insurmountable odds. My own children would have either waited for my demise or found a more subtle way to come at me – say, in my bath, where the guards would be easier to pass. In my own day, I forced my father into the imperial menagerie and thrust him into the bear cage. He died in a particularly messy fashion.'

Tenzhin stopped and bowed respectfully.

'That, Imperial Majesty, is because your own sons seek to occupy your throne, and if necessary, to remove you from it first.'

A look of genuine amazement crossed the emperor's face. The guards took a menacing step forward, and the interlopers could hear the sounds of more soldiers emerging through the door behind them. They were clearly trapped now, and hopelessly outnumbered. Tenzhin could feel his friends' nervous eyes on him, but the emperor waved a hand, holding the guards back.

'You have me intrigued.'

'I do not *want* your throne, Imperial Majesty,' Tenzhin said in the most offhand manner he could conjure.

'Why not?' the old man asked, genuinely fascinated by this turn of events.

'Because your empire is like a bad egg. It is maintained by a thin shell that keeps it looking smooth and perfect, unblemished and pure. But inside, beneath that beautiful shell, is the rot. A miasma of foulness, and it is only a matter of time until you can no longer patch the egg and the rot starts to leak out. In the name of all the gods and all the forms of purity, why would I wish to sit upon that eggshell, waiting to be plunged into the stink when I could no longer maintain the veneer? No, the Jin Empire is not for me. And *that* is why I have not come like a murderer in the night to kill you in your bath, like your own children will.'

The emperor sat back in shock. 'You insult a hundred generations of emperors with your ill-chosen words.'

'The truth is not always pretty to hear. I come to strike a very simple deal with you, Emperor of the Jin.'

Once more, the soldiers took a step forward, swords ready. Once again, the old man motioned them back, his face still a mask of surprise.

'A deal? How intriguing. Given that I took everything your people had and burned the evidence, and that these nomads with you are as impoverished as your tribes were, I am fascinated to hear what you believe you can offer me.'

Tenzhin wiped his sword on his sash and sheathed it. They would never fight their way out, anyway. That had never been his plan, whatever the others expected. It would have been suicide, no matter how they attempted it. Instead, he folded his arms and rocked on the balls of his feet.

'The reason we came now, here, in the face of all your guards, Great Majesty, is because you are at your administration, with your pen and your seal. I propose that you write out a document granting my friends and me free passage at any guard post across the empire, the pick of horses at any courier way-station and free room and board at any official lodging.'

The emperor chuckled. 'And why would I do that?'

'Because, in return, I am prepared to take my companions and leave your lands altogether. We shall return to the realm of the horse clans, and once we pass your border, I give you my word that we shall not return, and that the horse clans will no longer raid the western Jin provinces.'

'An impressive promise, but it is hollow and meaningless. No one can control the horse clans. No one can offer such a guarantee.'

Tenzhin simply smiled. 'Look into my eyes, Jade Emperor. I am a man of destiny, and a determined one. If I were to set my sights on your throne, nothing short of the Black Dragon of Fate could stop me. If you are any judge of people, you will recognize that I speak the absolute truth. If you deny me now, be assured that somehow we will leave your lands, regardless, but that I shall return with an army the likes of which you have never seen. Will you test me, Majesty, or will you recognize sense when it stands before you, and issue that document?'

There was a long pause, and finally the Jade Emperor began to laugh. 'If my own sons had balls the size of yours, young Tenzhin-Khan, they would be bow-legged. Very well. I shall write out your letter and you shall leave my domain. And when you are gone, I shall finish my wall. The Jin shall remain on one side and your barbarians on the other. Pray I have no need to cross it.'

Tenzhin bowed and motioned for the others to sheath their blades. They did so with some reluctance, Erekan leaning on her glaive rather casually. The two boys were watching Tenzhin with a look composed largely of disbelief and nervousness. But still, they had replaced their weapons. They would never fight their way out of this place. He had known that all along.

Half an hour later, four scions of foreign tribes, erstwhile princes and princesses of the Jin Empire, emerged from the palace's main gate. They were leading a horse each, with an extra beast carrying their packs. Tenzhin was smiling. The map Edeco had taken from their morning geography lesson had been a particularly fine one, and marked not only the rough territory of the horse clans and their moot circle at Ual-Aahbor, but also those distant far-flung lands beyond them, as well as the Inda – a world tantalisingly civilized, yet baser and more malleable than the rigid domain of the Jade Emperor.

Armed with the warrior blood of the Khmar, the knowledge of the Jin, and the possibility of doing with the horse clans what his father had tried with the nine tribes of the Badlands, Tenzhin had become a Khan himself. He had not realized it until the emperor had named him as such. A Khan needed an army and an empire. The former was awaiting him in the lands beyond the wall; and the latter? Well, now he had a map that told him all he needed to know of that far-off western world. Just as the Jin had Jiong-Xhu, that far empire had Velutio, a city that was its heart and its brain, and, unlike his father, Tenzhin-Khan would take his time and plan this campaign down to the last detail.

Velutio would be his, and the empire with it.

If you enjoyed Insurgency why not also try:

The Thief's Tale

(First book of the Ottoman Cycle)

by S.J.A. Turney

Istanbul, 1481. The once great city of Constantine that now forms the heart of the Ottoman empire is a strange mix of Christian, Turk and Jew. Despite the benevolent reign of the Sultan Bayezid II, the conquest is still a recent memory, and emotions run high among the inhabitants, with danger never far beneath the surface.

Skiouros and Lykaion, the sons of a Greek country farmer, are conscripted into the ranks of the famous Janissary guards and taken to Istanbul where they will play a pivotal, if unsung, role in the history of the new regime. As Skiouros escapes into the Greek quarter and vanishes among its streets to survive on his wits alone, Lykaion remains with the slave chain to fulfill his destiny and become an Islamic convert and a guard of the Imperial palace. Brothers they remain, though standing to either side of an unimaginable divide.

On a fateful day in late autumn 1490, Skiouros picks the wrong pocket and begins to unravel a plot that reaches to the very highest peaks of Imperial power. He and his brother are about to be left with the most difficult decision faced by a conquered Greek: whether the rule of the Ottoman Sultan is worth saving.

Marius' Mules: The Invasion of Gaul

(First book of the Marius' Mules Series)

by S.J.A. Turney

It is 58 BC and the mighty Tenth Legion, camped in Northern Italy, prepare for the arrival of the most notorious general in Roman history: Julius Caesar.

Marcus Falerius Fronto, commander of the Tenth is a career soldier and long-time companion of Caesar's. Despite his desire for the simplicity of the military life, he cannot help but be drawn into intrigue and politics as Caesar engineers a motive to invade the lands of Gaul.

Fronto is about to discover that politics can be as dangerous as battle, that old enemies can be trusted more than new friends, and that standing close to such a shining figure as Caesar, even the most ethical of men risk being burned.

Praetorian: The Great Game

(First book of the Praetorian Series)

by S.J.A. Turney

Promoted to the elite Praetorian Guard in the thick of battle, a young legionary is thrust into a seedy world of imperial politics and corruption. Tasked with uncovering a plot against the newly-crowned emperor Commodus, his mission takes him from the cold Danubian border all the way to the heart of Rome, the villa of the emperor's scheming sister, and the great Colosseum.

What seems a straightforward, if terrifying, assignment soon descends into Machiavellian treachery and peril as everything in which young Rufinus trusts and believes is called into question and he faces warring commanders, Sarmatian cannibals, vicious dogs, mercenary killers and even a clandestine Imperial agent. In a race against time to save the Emperor, Rufinus will be introduced, willing or not, to the great game.

"Entertaining, exciting and beautifully researched" - Douglas Jackson

"From the Legion to the Guard, from battles to the deep intrigue of court, Praetorian: The Great Game is packed with great characters, wonderfully researched locations and a powerful plot." - Robin Carter

61661325R00251

Made in the USA
Lexington, KY
16 March 2017